0

BEING ALEXANDER

I was nice. Alex was nice. That's the first word
people used to describe me. But did that get me
anywhere? Did it get me ahead in life? Was it good
for my personal life? Was it good for my career?
What do you think? Of course not. I existed. I
breathed. I was a pushover who got trampled ever
deeper into the slurping sucking pit of mud at the
bottom of the hill. While others pushed and shoved
me aside in their struggles to emerge as king of the
mountain. I smiled and shrugged and good-naturedly
stepped further to the side to let them pass. But no
more. N   re.

NANCY SPARLING

Being Alexander

FLAME
Hodder & Stoughton

copyright © 2002 by Nancy Sparling Symonds

First published in Great Britain in 2002 by Hodder and Stoughton
A division of Hodder Headline

The right of Nancy Sparling Symonds to be identified as the
Author of the Work has been asserted by her in accordance with
the Copyright, Designs and Patents Act 1988.

A Flame paperback

2 4 6 8 10 9 7 5 3 1

A CIP catalogue record for this title is
available from the British Library

ISBN 0340 81947 2

Typeset in Sabon by Hewer Text Ltd

Printed and bound in Great Britain by
Clays Ltd, St Ives plc

Hodder and Stoughton
A division of Hodder Headline
338 Euston Road
London NW1 3BH

To John, for always believing in me

ACKNOWLEDGEMENTS

Special thanks to Eugenie Furniss, Wayne Brookes, Tracy Fisher, Alicia Gordon, Lucinda Prain, and to all those at Hodder and William Morris who have shown such support and enthusiasm for this book. Thanks to my parents and my sisters for their encouragement. And to Angela Fisher for the years of laughter.

Life is not about love. It's not about friendship. It's certainly not about honour or virtue or living up to some imaginary morality. It's not about kindness or caring or giving. Or even sex. It's about success. And, above all, it's about money.

'Ah, fame and fortune,' you say, but you don't understand, that's not it, that's not it at all. A splash of good old fame is fine, but it's not enough; fame comes and goes and the public is notoriously fickle, loving one moment, destructive the next. It's fortune that matters, solid material wealth. Enough of it to withstand whatever life throws your way. Success and power to survive the attacks by the enemies you've undoubtedly made on your way up.

And I want it. I want it all.

My name is Alexander Fairfax and I'm twenty-nine years old.

Yesterday I was Alex, but today I am Alexander. I have been born anew. Today is the first day of my life. Not of the rest of my life. Of my life.

ALL THE YESTERDAYS
(BEFORE THE HAZE WAS LIFTED)

I would have been content to carry on as I'd carried on before, and the days and weeks would have turned into months and years and I would have turned into a drone. Get on the train, go to work, spend money, buy a flat, buy a house, get into debt, buy designer clothes, eat at fancy restaurants, go on expensive holidays, work harder, work harder, earn that bonus, spend that money, owe money, owe money, owe money.

THEN

At the instant of death, the defining moments in life are supposed to flash through your mind like a series of golden holiday snaps with you, the victorious, all-conquering hero, at the centre. Yet what would I, the old I, the Alex of yesterday, have seen?

A grey-hued, gut-wrenchingly bland life. A glorious waste of my allotted three score and ten years.

Sedate, calm, a good sport, a good winner, a good loser, an all-round likeable bloke. I was kind to strangers and considerate: I always gave up my seat on the tube to the elderly, the pregnant, the infirm. I was nice. But what, exactly, is 'nice'? It's a boring word to describe boring people who have no memorable qualities. Interesting people can be kind and considerate, but I bet you fifty pounds you'd think of at least half a dozen other adjectives to describe someone you find intriguing before you got round to calling them 'nice'.

I was nice. Alex was nice. That's the first word people used to describe me. But did that get me anywhere? Did it get me ahead in life? Was it good for my personal life? Was it good for my career? What do you think? Of course not. I existed. I breathed. I was a pushover who got trampled ever deeper into the slurping, sucking pit of mud at the bottom of the hill. While others pushed and shoved me aside in their struggles to emerge as King of the Mountain, I smiled and shrugged and good-naturedly stepped further to the side to let them pass.

But no more. No more.

Fuck the rest of the world. They've already fucked me over. Now it's my turn. And I won't just sit here silently hoping that curses, murder and mayhem will follow those who've wronged me. Oh, no, Alexander's a proactive chap now. I have work to do. Lots of work to do.

Maybe, instead, I should thank them for opening my eyes. It's because of them, after all, that I'm in control now. My id, my self, me. Me. Me. Me. Me. Me.

I matter. Fuck the arseholes.

And fuck forgiveness. Let's see how they like the new me.

A week ago everything was normal. I was normal. I was happy. I thought my life was pretty good. Maybe I wasn't a movie star or a millionaire, but I was doing okay for myself. Attractive if not actually handsome, I'd hit the highest tax bracket at twenty-four. I had enough cash for designer labels, even if I hardly bought any. I'd spent my money on my car. I had a great car. I was content. I was happy being a nobody, a loser. I was nice, placid, blissfully ignorant Alex. But looking back now I can see that it was all a lie. My life was a fucking disaster. It was, I tell you, it was.

The transformation was tough. Painful. It was agony, but being Alexander is so much better than merely being Alex. I acknowledge that with honesty, but it doesn't change things. Not for them. My life, Alex's life, might have been pathetic, but it was mine. And I'll never forget my revenge.

Everything that could go wrong has gone wrong in the last seven days. I could order the incidents from best to worst or most humiliating or most surprising or even most funny for onlookers, but that would spoil it. Chronological order is the only way. Event building upon event building upon event.

Monday morning, and I'm talking early Monday, in the wee hours of the morning you still think of as Sunday, I only say Monday because you have to get the date right for the insurance people, I was woken by a car alarm. Or, rather, by an elbow in the ribs and a voice in my ear. 'Alex, are you awake?'

Spluttering, I came to, snapped away from an all-too-vivid dream in which I was growing smaller and smaller, shrinking in size until I was slightly larger than a penny. I don't know what would have happened if it had continued. Would I have shrunk to nothing and died not only in my dream state but also in reality? Should I have performed some sort of post-Freudian, post-Jungian psychological interpretation of this dream? Was my subconscious trying to tell me that I was nothing? Or that I was in danger of becoming nothing? Was it an early-warning sign that my complacent, comfortable, content waking self would never have recognised?

'Alex. Alex, wake up.' Sarah's voice, so gentle and lilting in the day, seemed harsh and screeching, unkind even, as if her lack of sleep was all my fault. As if she were blaming me.

'What?'

'Wake up.'

'I am awake.'

'Then do something,' she said.

5

The car alarm, lost to me in the confusion of my pull from deep sleep, suddenly seemed to grow in volume. The more I listened to it, the louder and more strident it became.

'Damn things,' I said, pulling my pillow over my head to dampen the noise. 'Bloody nuisance. Don't know why people bother.'

Sarah snatched away the pillow. Slowly, as if she were explaining the concept of crayons to a dull-witted five-year-old, she said, 'It's your car alarm.'

'Shit.'

I leapt from the bed and raced to the window, snatching the curtains aside. Out on the road, three floors down, I could see a group of four teenagers. Male, of course. Probably no more than fourteen, with that particular aura about them so you just *knew* they were going to be spotty and greasy, and stringy, squeaky and unpleasant in a way that girls never are, no matter how big their glasses, how shiny their metal braces, how riddled with acne their faces. For a second I felt sorry for them, for their ages, for what they were suffering, for what they were going to suffer in the next few years, then I saw what they were doing. Surrounding my car. Kicking my car. Breaking my windscreen. Slashing my tyres.

'Hey,' I shouted. Idiot. Of course they couldn't hear me. I grabbed a pair of jeans from the floor and tried to pull them on as I ran to the door. Why is it that when you're in a hurry something always goes wrong? I should have been sensible and logical and known that I couldn't run and put on jeans at the same time. Instead, I tried to do both and wasn't very successful at either. So, hobbling with one leg hampered by the jeans I couldn't pull up, I flung open the door and ran out into the hall. Thud. The door slammed shut behind me and I quickly became aware of a few things all at once. The door was locked and I didn't have any keys. I'd only managed to pull my jeans up to my thighs. Mrs Roberts, the sixty-something insomniac from next door who'd taken to roaming the stairs at all hours of the night, was staring, goggle-eyed, at the first testicles she'd seen since her husband had run off with an air stewardess the year before. And I wasn't wearing any shoes.

Okay, okay, I admit it. They weren't necessarily all of the same importance, but that's what happened. I'd like to say that I shrugged it off, zipped up my jeans and ran outside to kick the shit out of those four little punks, but this is Alex we're talking about, not Alexander.

I blushed beet red as Mrs Roberts (I don't know her Christian name) continued to stare, and to make matters worse, as if it were aware of the scrutiny, as if it wanted to give a poor lonely old woman something to remember, my own flesh betrayed me.

'Hello, Alex,' said Mrs Roberts, as she stared, a smile hovering around her lips.

I yanked up my jeans, nodded and ran down the stairs as I tried to do up the zip. I felt as if I'd betrayed Sarah. And with a woman older than my own mother. I decided not to think about it, to leave the incident unanalysed, fearful of what conclusions I might draw.

So, bare-chested, bare-footed, I raced down the stairs, sick at heart, sick to my stomach, certain only that I was angry. I flung open the foyer doors and went out into the street.

They were gone. I didn't even have the satisfaction of shouting at them or chasing them down the street. I didn't even have the chance to get into a fight. They were gone and all that was left was my poor, battered car.

It was defaced. It was wounded. Sacrilege. Tyres slashed and deflated, front and back windscreens smashed, all but one side window gone. The clear outline of a boot print on the driver's door. Indentations up and down the bonnet. Key scratches ruining the paintwork. The stereo – one of those where you take off the front panel so thieves can see it's not worth breaking in to steal it – smashed in and useless. The leather seats – soft, welcoming and so inviting – slashed and hacked into pieces. Even the car alarm was broken. Ruined. Vandalised.

A Jaguar XKR Supercharged Coupé is a work of art. Its contours are smooth and rounded, the paint shiny and fresh, the tyres a perfect fit, the lights sexy and sleek. I'm one of those men who love cars the way women love clothes and shopping, the way other men are mad about football. If it were up to me, the Tate Modern would be filled with sports cars, luxury cars, seductive, shiny points of worship. Who needs the cross-section of a sheep or a pig's foetus in formaldehyde when you can have a Porsche? A Jaguar? A Lamborghini? That's real modern art.

Okay, okay, our flat's in Finsbury Park, I should have known better. It used to be safe when I lived in Clapham and had my own garage (a wide one so I didn't have to worry about scraping my car), but Sarah wanted us to move in together, I wanted it too, and we ended up in her flat. (She insisted on living north of the river as she comes from Luton.) I know I shouldn't have parked it on the street, but the waiting list for a garage that's reasonably close and wide enough inside to open the driver's door is over two years. I wasn't going to give up my car. I couldn't wait that long. Anything can happen in two years. I could be dead in two years. I decided not to store it in my old garage all the way across town, as it was impractical and inconvenient. I'd thought it was worth the risk. I'd decided – maturely, logically – that I could cope if it was stolen. It was beautiful. There's no other word to describe it. It never crossed my mind that it would be subject to this sort of mindless violence. Only a man without a soul would wantonly cause such destruction to a Jaguar XKR. Or a handful of spotty youths. Philistines.

They didn't even try to take it on a joyride.

THINGS COULD ONLY GET BETTER, RIGHT? WRONG

Although it had happened in the middle of the night, by the time I'd sorted out the insurance, the police report, and been to A&E to have my feet cleaned and stitched – they had been cut by splinters from my shattered windows (I told you it was a bad week) – it was eleven a.m. before I made it in to work. I'd phoned at seven and left a message with the receptionist (why on earth do they insist Reception is covered at that time in the morning if they're not going to bother doing anything with the messages the receptionist receives?) to say I'd be late.

My feet swaddled in huge white bandages – you'd think that alone would have caused some decent human reaction – I hobbled into work. A little bit of sympathy wouldn't have gone amiss. I was annoyed at the time, but I understand it now. It's all about self-promotion and success. Never mind that it was Alex. Never mind that I'd done them countless favours over the years. Never mind that they were supposedly my mates. I hadn't been there to fight my own corner so that was too bad for me.

'Sorry.' That was the first word he said to me. At the time I thought he'd received my message, heard about my car and was sympathising. But he wasn't looking at my feet, didn't even seem to notice the bandages.

That should have been my first clue that something was wrong. Maybe it was guilt. Maybe the guilt was eating him up so badly that he had to talk, to spew it out before it festered any longer.

Jed. Jedidiah Wright. My boss. For such a big, butch,

American-sounding lumberjack name he's really just a weedy, self-satisfied, middle-class twit. Or that's what I think now. I rather liked him once.

'I tried to reach you,' Jed said, as I collapsed with relief into my chair.

'I—'

He cut me off. 'I phoned and phoned, but all I got was a message saying your mobile's unavailable.'

'Is it?' I pulled it out and switched it on. 'It's working now,' I said. And it was. My phone was on; it was only my career that was dead.

'Kenneth,' Jed was saying, ignoring my comments as if I hadn't spoken, 'called a last-minute meeting about the Guinness campaign. I tried to reach you.'

Kenneth – that's Kenneth Wilmington-Wilkes to you and me – is our managing director. He's legendary for holding impromptu meetings, hoping to surprise unwary teams and skewer under-performing employees. He calls it 'culling bad management from the firm'. We call it being a heartless bastard.

I suppose I should have been thankful. I hadn't lost my job. In fact, I hadn't come to Kenneth's notice at all. You see, he was rather taken with 'our' latest campaign. 'Our' meaning me, Thomas and William led by the invincible Jed.

Thomas and William have now been 'moved' (promoted, I know the pecking order around here, next step is for them to move into supervisory positions with the resulting salaries that entails) on to the latest Cadbury's ad (one of our bread-and-butter clients). No doubt Jed has been given a hefty bonus (not that he told me: our contracts specifically forbid discussing salaries and other such mundane issues; for fear that we lowly hard-working employees would rebel when we discovered the huge pay discrepancies in the company).

Neither Jed nor Thomas nor William had thought to mention me to Kenneth. Now that I'm no longer self-effacing or modest, I can spit it out point blank that I made that campaign what it was. Those were my ideas that had so impressed Kenneth Wilmington-Wilkes. If there's any justice in this world Thomas and William will fall flat on their faces and be seen as the talentless hacks they are without me. But they won't. There is no divine figure of justice wandering the city and controlling the scales. It's up to me to see that they get their just deserts.

Their excuse – and I think they expected me to fall for this – was that they hadn't dared mention me to Kenneth as they didn't know where I was.

These were Jed's words: 'We couldn't tell him, Alex. You were over an hour late and you know how Kenneth feels about shirkers. You would've been sacked.' He claimed not to have received the message I left with the receptionist.

That was it. That was his excuse. That was his reason for not giving me the recognition and credit I deserved.

I rose to my feet, stared into his beady little eyes and punched him on the nose.

I did no such thing. I was still Alex.

I gave him a sickly smile, pointed to my feet, explained about the car and shrugged.

It was pathetic. I was pathetic. I was a wimp. I deserved everything I got.

It was five p.m. on the Monday from hell. I'd spent the afternoon tidying up my files before handing them over to Jed. With a smile. I handed over the files I'd busted my guts over for six months with a smile. Spineless moron. That's what I was. That was my work, those were my ideas, and I just handed them over with a nod and a flash of teeth. Jed would sort out the last few issues, it was no longer my responsibility. It was sort of an insurance policy, I think, in case Kenneth had any further enquiries. Jed couldn't risk Kenneth finding out about me, not now.

'Here you go, Jed,' I said, passing my work, my sweat, my late nights into Jed's hands, 'here's the last of those files.'

'Thanks.' He smiled at me. A slow, predatory smile that told me even then that I was no better than the dirt on the soles of his shoes. I recognised it for a split second before telling myself I was imagining things.

I smiled, nodded and half turned to go.

'Oh, Alex,' he said, stopping me in my tracks, 'I have a favour to ask.'

A favour? He wanted to ask a favour of me? Rot in hell, slimeball.

'Yes? What is it?' My body was frozen, not daring to move. My head performed half a dozen *Exorcist* spins to face him. Or maybe I only glanced over my shoulder.

'Do you know Richard Morris?'

'Yes.'

A gleam of satisfaction in his eyes. I could see it. I knew what he was thinking. If I knew Richard Morris I was bound to like

Richard Morris (I was that sort of person, I liked everybody, more fool me) and even if I was reluctant to do a favour for Jed I wouldn't be able to say no to a favour for Richard Morris.

Jed smiled broadly for a second, his expression saying, 'Gotcha.' Then his smile disappeared and his face grew solemn. I hate him. I really hate him now. How could I not have seen what he was like back then? How could I have let his let's-be-pals attitude fool me?

'I'm afraid,' said Jed, all serious empathy now, 'there's been an accident. Nothing serious. Don't worry, Richard is fine. But he's fractured his leg in three places and he'll be off work for six weeks.'

'What happened?' That was genuine concern on my part, my bottled-up frustration with my career forgotten. You see, I told you I used to be nice.

'He went cycling during his lunch break and was hit by a car that ran a red light.'

'He's lucky to have escaped with just a broken leg.'

'He certainly is, and that's why I've come to you, Alex. I know you wouldn't want Richard's position here to be compromised.'

'But surely he's on sick leave,' I said, not understanding.

'Of course he is, and his job will be waiting for him. But, you see, Richard's been working on the Shire Horse Centre campaign and his proposal is due at the end of the week. I'm afraid he's not really come up with anything original and I know he was planning on working late all week so he'd be ready when the clients turn up on Friday. Now that he's in hospital he won't have time to finish. I wouldn't want Kenneth to discover he's been lagging.'

Now let me tell you something here. I work on national campaigns, with television advertising, with magazine spreads, with radio jingles, with entire newspaper pages filled with my products. What I do not do is graduate-quality work on small animal sanctuaries that can't even afford local newspaper ads.

I've worked here for six years, and outgrew such campaigns after four months. For five years and eight months I've been given responsibilities. As part of a team, yes, but I've worked on a number of multi-million-pound campaigns. If you're alive, if you're not a hermit, you've seen my work.

'You mentioned a favour,' I said, feeling the quicksand slowly sucking me in. There was no way out. I couldn't refuse without looking churlish. I couldn't refuse even if I didn't mind looking churlish. I was Alex, I was nice.

Jed was suddenly all smiles again. 'I knew you'd want to help.' He grabbed a slim file from his desk and passed it to me. From the weight of it I knew there couldn't have been more than half a dozen sheets inside. 'What I'd like you to do is take over Richard's campaign. It's only a week, Alex, and I know you're free now that your work on Guinness is over.'

'But we've got dozens of new graduates. Couldn't one of them handle this?'

'They're all busy, Alex. You're the only one who can do it. And I know the Shire Horse Centre will be so impressed with your work that they'll come back to us year after year.'

No, they won't. Small animal sanctuaries don't come back time and again. They get a good poster, they come up with a good slogan and they stick to it. Most of these local places don't have the budget for anything else. The only reason we bother to deal with them is that our esteemed managing director's wife has a soft spot for animal sanctuaries and wildlife parks. They certainly wouldn't be able to afford us otherwise. That's what it is. Charity. *Pro bono* work. (Who says I've seen too many American law films?) I was going to be stuck on one of these free cases and then another and another and another. I could see my future stretching out before me. And it was grim.

'Will you do this, Alex? For me? For Richard? It's only for a week.'

No, I will not, you gormless bastard. How dare you stab me

14

in the back and then expect me to roll over and let you kick me some more?

But did I say that?

'Of course,' I said. 'Glad to be of help.'

'Great.' He beamed at me. It wasn't just a smile. It was his lips, his teeth, his cheeks, his eyes, even his eyebrows coming together in one great smirk, as he thought, Ha, you sucker. 'I'd like to see your initial presentation at nine tomorrow morning.'

'Tomorrow?' I said, flipping through the folder. I'd been right. There weren't more than six pages. There were only five. 'But there's nothing here. You said I had until the end of the week.'

'No, I said the clients are coming in at the end of the week. I need your initial ideas tomorrow so we can go over them with the team.'

'I promised Sarah I'd be home tonight.'

'Sorry, Alex.'

So that was that. My beloved Jaguar had been trashed, I'd cut both feet and had stitches for the first time in my life, I'd been betrayed by my colleagues, and now I was stuck on a project any live, breathing body in the whole firm could do.

And I still had to phone Sarah.

Sarah is one of those women everybody likes. She's cute and sexy in a subdued way, but not so beautiful that other women instinctively dislike her. She adds a little bit of glamour to a group of ordinary people and a little bit of normality to a group of the ultra-successful. She's fun to be around, she makes you feel special. That's her best quality, I think. She stares at you with those pretty hazel eyes and really seems to look at you. She sees you, she listens, she doesn't spend every conversational gap waiting to throw in a little comment about herself. People genuinely like her. She's nice, but you could think of a dozen other adjectives to describe her. (I could think of a few more to describe her now, but that would be cheating. That's now and this is then.)

What about me, you say. If I was such a loser, why would she choose me? All I can say for myself is that I'm not ugly. I'm not Mel Gibson either, but people don't look at my face and run away in fear. Women seem to like me. Might be the niceness factor, but they do seem to like me. I'm tall, not too thin, not too fat, attractive in an average that way, whatever that means, though Sarah always says with the right haircut and the right clothes I could look really good. That I could look right. That I could be trendy. (I've never been popular and trendy, I'm Average Joe.) I'm a professional but also creative. I'm good at my job. I'm well paid and seemed to be progressing at work until Jed and the others betrayed me.

I loved her. I liked her. We were friends as well as lovers.

And yet I dreaded telling her that I was going to have to work late. Again.

As expected she didn't take the news very well. 'Oh, Alex, you've got to stand up for yourself. You have a right to expect a personal life.'

I could just picture her, striding down Oxford Street, dodging tourists, bag in one hand, phone in the other. I know she looked cool and poised and successful. No one overhearing her conversation would imagine she was talking to her boyfriend. No one that together could have a partner so spineless.

I explained as best I could. Disappointment. Anger. Acceptance.

'Call me,' she said, 'and let me know how it's going.'

By nine I could see that it was going to take me most of the night to come up with a reasonable portfolio. You may think that a horse centre doesn't need much advertising, but you'd be surprised. They need posters and slogans that will attract visitors and donations, that will present their cause, their centre, in a better light than the dozens of other equally valuable causes in the area. I decided to surprise Sarah and go home. If I was going to be up all night working I might as well do it from the comfort of my own sofa.

I caught a cab back to our flat, refused the cabbie's generous offer of assistance up the stairs (*he* noticed my bandaged feet), and opened the door. The lights were dimmed and I heard soft music coming from the living room. Sarah had a weakness for Lionel Richie love songs from the eighties. She knew they weren't my favourites so mostly she played them when I wasn't home. Many nights when I'd worked late I'd rung and heard his husky tunes throbbing in the background.

The living room was empty. As softly as my hobbling gait would allow, I headed towards the bedroom. Poor darling. She must be catching up on the sleep she missed last night.

There was a soft moan and I hesitated. Sarah didn't usually make noises in her sleep.

I eased open the bedroom door. And stopped.

'Sarah?'

I was in shock. I couldn't believe what I was seeing. There was my Sarah, my bonny, pretty, loyal Sarah. Naked. In bed with another man. Straddling a naked man.

Both faces turned towards the door. Sarah started to pull away from him, but he grabbed her waist and held her in place and right there, in front of me, he thrust into her again and came.

It was only then, while he was having his orgasm, with his nasty, dirty little prick still inside my darling Sarah, that I realised it was Jed.

Jed had screwed my Sarah.

Sarah had fucked my boss.

They were having an affair.

Oh, God.

I strode to the bed, pulled Sarah off (as gently as I could, I didn't blame her, not then), grabbed Jed by the neck, dragged him from the bed and slammed his head against the floor. Again and again and again. His blood splattered the walls, his blood splattered Sarah as she struggled in vain to stop me, his blood splattered me, but I didn't care. Slam, slam, slam. He stopped fighting me. Even his legs stopped twitching. Slam, slam, slam. He got what he deserved.

No, of course I didn't do that. In reality I puked. I stood in the doorway and puked all over the floor and my own feet. Flecks of vomit covered my previously pristine bandages. On top of my big toe was a recognisable pea. It was green and round and perfect, not discoloured, not misshapen. Perfect. I marvelled. I stared. A pea. It must have come from the vegetable samosa I'd had for my afternoon snack. For that one second I stared at the pea everything seemed right with the world. Until I looked up. Until I saw them.

Sarah scrambled up from the bed and grabbed her robe, pulling it tight, shielding her nakedness, when it didn't matter, not now. We both knew what she looked like naked. I knew. And Jed knew.

Jed stayed in bed. Jed stayed in *my* bed and just looked at me. He was naked, slim and thin and all together too skinny, naked in my bed.

'Alex,' said Sarah, 'you didn't call, you didn't say you were coming home.'

I just looked at her for a long moment. Then I said, 'Surprise.' The acrid taste of my vomit made me want to puke again, but I didn't. I stood there in a pile of my own sick and tried to look proud and wounded and strong all at once. I failed miserably, of course.

Sarah turned to Jed and made a face at him I couldn't quite see. 'I think you'd better leave,' she told him.

'I'll stay if you want,' he said. He was still in my bed and made no move to rise.

'No, leave. I'll call you,' said Sarah.

Jed shrugged, climbed off the bed and stood, his penis half erect. He slid off the condom (oh, good, safe sex, that was considerate of them), tied the end into a knot and tossed it into my bin. Jed tossed a condom filled with his spunk into the bin beside my bed. And then he gave me a little smirk.

He pulled on his boxer shorts and trousers (more sensible than me, he didn't try to run at the same time), slid on his socks, his shoes, his shirt. He picked up his briefcase (the bastard had obviously come here straight from work, knowing I'd be stuck at the office) and made to kiss Sarah on the cheek, but she stepped away. He shrugged.

'See you, Sarah,' Jed said. 'See you tomorrow, Alex. I hope your presentation will be ready.'

Honest, that's what he said.

He walked past me, disdainfully eyeing my vomit-soaked feet, his nostrils flaring slightly at the smell, and then, finally, he was out of my bedroom. His footsteps receded down the hall, the front door opened and closed and he was gone.

I remained silent, not knowing what to say, waiting hopefully for some sort of apology, for an explanation that made sense.

Sarah had the grace to look uncomfortable.

'I think you should move out,' she said.

'What?' I gaped at her. My mouth fell open into a perfect O and I just stared. What? Just like that?

'I don't want to live with you. I don't want to be with you.'

'Jed's moving in here?' Into my flat? Into my life?

She shrugged, probably aware of what a heartless bitch she was being but not really caring. She was able to make a clean break. My walking in had freed her from this double life. 'Maybe.'

Maybe meant yes. She was ditching me for my boss. The same boss who'd killed my immediate chances for promotion and stuck me on to a dead-end project. No, it wasn't enough that he'd maliciously tried to destroy my career, he'd had to wreck the rest of my life as well.

'Can't we talk about this? Work it out?'

'I'm sorry, Alex, I really am, but I don't love you any more. I don't want to be with you.'

I nodded. Take it on the chin. Take it like a man. 'I see.'

'I'm sorry,' she said. 'I hope we can still be friends.'

Take it like a man. Take it like a man. Take it like a man.

Slobbering, pleading, 'Give me a chance. I can change. I'll do anything. Come on, we're so good together.'

'Used to be. The magic's not there any longer. It's gone. It's been gone for a long time. I want to get married and have children, and I don't think you're the man I should marry.'

'And Jed is?'

'I honestly don't know, but I don't think we're cut out for the long haul, Alex.'

What she was saying was that I wasn't successful enough. That I'd never be successful enough. Not for her. It'd been fun while it lasted, but now that she was almost thirty it was time to settle down with a man who could provide for her and her ovaries.

'When do you want me to leave?' I asked.

BACK AT THE HOSPITAL

I sat in the waiting room at my local A&E for five hours. It wasn't really an emergency, but I had nowhere else to go. I was shell-shocked. I couldn't face any of my friends. I couldn't face anyone. Not that night. And I did need my bandages changed. Under the circumstances I could hardly ask Sarah.

Sitting there while chaos reigned supreme around me (you'd expect Monday nights to be quiet, but I'm telling you, we had car accidents, a man who'd lopped off two of his fingers doing some late-night DIY, heart-attacks, strokes, screaming babies with high fevers, people with all sorts of unpleasant lumps and bumps and rashes) I had plenty of time to think.

According to Sarah, she and Jed had been sleeping together for two months. For eight weeks my Sarah had allowed Jed to worm his slimy little hands down her pants. During these same two months Sarah and I had discussed plans for holidays abroad, redecorating the flat, buying a flat of our own. It was only five months ago that Sarah and I officially moved in together, even if we'd been practically living together for a year before that. Surely things couldn't have changed so drastically between us overnight. It must have been gradual. But if she'd been having niggling doubts, why had she suggested the flat in the first place?

There hadn't been any signs or clues. Our sexual patterns hadn't changed, she hadn't suddenly turned into a love bunny frenzied with guilt, neither had she shut me out. We talked, we laughed, we made plans, we made love, we were a couple. When had all that changed for her?

In my mind I replayed scenes from the past few months over

and over and over again. I must have missed something. What had I done wrong?

Finally there was a lull and someone took pity on me. Pity being the operative word. Who'd puke on their own feet? Thankfully my stitches didn't need to be taken out and resewn; the vomit hadn't soaked through and there was no risk of infection. After a little cleaning and a reapplication of bandages, I was free to go.

Free to go. But where?

As I shuffled out of the hospital, haggard, drawn, my soul in agony, Sarah's last words echoed in my head.

'When do you want me to leave?' I'd asked, like the coward I was. I just gave up. I didn't fight, I didn't argue, I simply accepted. It was done. A *fait accompli*. I was out.

'As soon as possible,' she'd said. ASAP. ASAP. ASAP.

'As soon as possible.'

Nine the next morning found me in the meeting room with Jed and four of Jed's graduate groupies I can't be bothered to name. They were young, they were keen, they were in Jed's pocket. Jed the Almighty. Jed the Invincible. Jed the God of Advertising. I'd believed it once. Now it was up to the next generation to carry the torch to his glory.

For someone who'd had no sleep the night before (after the hospital I'd wandered around the streets of London, the dirtier, the darker the better, I'd almost wanted someone to mug me: if I was severely beaten, if I was killed, Sarah would be sorry) and little sleep the night before that, I was looking remarkably well put together (showered, change of clothes, hair brushed, eyes no longer wild and staring).

I'd finally succumbed and returned to the flat around seven. She was gone. I'd spent the night in agony, not wanting to face her, not wanting to go back to the scene of the crime, and she wasn't even there. I mean, did she really think I wanted to live there? That I wanted to be reminded of Jed's smirking face in my bed?

I can't lie to you. I wanted her to love me. I wanted her to take me back. I wanted to forgive her, to love her, for everything to go back to the way it had been. I was a poor, pathetic little bastard. I cringe when I remember my thoughts. I still had hope. Even after I'd seen what I'd seen, even after she'd told me to leave, I still had hope. (Once she changed her mind surely she'd agree to get a new mattress? I'd like to burn the current mattress, but we didn't have to. We could give it away, donate it to charity and buy a new one. She'd agree to that when she took me back. Wouldn't she? That's what I was thinking. That's what I was like. Fool.)

'This really isn't up to your usual standard, Alex,' said Jed, bringing me back to the meeting with a jolt. He had my half-completed file spread across the table. 'Even if they're not paying very much, they are paying for our services. We can't offer them this.'

The graduate groupies were embarrassed for me.

Bastard. Jed stood there lecturing me with a knowing half-grin on his face, thinking, *I've screwed your girlfriend in your own bed and you can't do anything about it*. He knew I wouldn't say anything. He knew me. Bastard. He knew I was a coward. He knew I wouldn't make any waves.

'Well,' said Jed, with a grand sweep of his arms, 'I'll give you another day. We all know how upset you are over the loss of your car.'

Loss? It's not lost. It'll be repaired. It'll be just like new. Or as new as a three-year-old used car can be. (I've only had it for eleven months.)

'And don't let me down, Alex. The owners of the Shire Horse Centre are personal friends of Elizabeth,' he said, rubbing it in that he was on Christian-name terms with Mrs Wilmington-Wilkes. 'This is an important account.'

NEW FLAT, NEW LIFE, SAME OLD ME

You don't need to hear the boring details of how I spent the next two days searching for somewhere else to live. I worked late on Tuesday (good old Alex, slogging away at work, earning more money for the firm) and returned to the flat – my flat, our flat – to find a note from Sarah. She was going to spend the next couple of nights away, to give me time to find a new flat. She didn't say where she was staying, but I knew she was staying with that rutting bastard. Sarah wouldn't even face me. No doubt she didn't want to be mean to 'nice' Alex.

Wednesday night I moved into my new room. Room, I say (a flat of my own would have taken too long to find and organise and, besides, I was still hoping she'd take me back, that this was only temporary). I now live in a room. I no longer have my own bathroom. I no longer have my own kitchen. I don't even have my own TV. I am sharing a flat in Islington with four strangers. Well, three complete strangers and one friend of a friend of a friend of a friend of a work colleague.

I moved into my room with one bag of clothes, a few CDs, a couple of bags of food (freshly purchased, wouldn't want to take anything from Sarah's place in case she missed it, would I?) and a head full of sorrow. I've left most of my stuff at the flat. At Sarah's.

I live in a room whose last occupant was named Daisy. She wasn't very artistic, but that didn't stop her painting dozens of her namesake flower above the bed, on the ceiling, so that when you lie in bed you look up and see a sky filled with daisies.

'Do you like it?' asked Amber, one of my new flatmates, when she'd shown me the room.

It sucks.

'It's lovely,' I'd said.

'Great.' She'd smiled, this open, honest-looking woman-girl wearing a snug Greenpeace T-shirt. With her big grey eyes, her tiny nose and her slender but very curvy figure, she might have been the model for one of the more busty Disney cartoon heroines. Sarah would be jealous, Sarah's always wanted to be slim and voluptuous at the same time, but Sarah's only slim. And Amber is also a pleasant person to be around. 'You can move in as soon as you like,' said Amber. Translation: they needed help paying the rent.

'Super,' I'd said. 'Tonight?'

'Great,' she'd said, beaming. They must really need help paying that rent.

I lay under a sky of daisies. The night passed in fits and starts so I suppose I must have slept at some point, but I don't recall any dreams. And in the morning when I stared up at the yellow-centred daisies I suddenly grew calm and then I realised that I was ravenous.

Twenty minutes later I sat down in front of my masterpiece, my ham-filled, pepper-filled, mushroom-filled, cheese-filled omelette and took my first bite. Mmmm. It was delicious. If there's one thing I can cook it's omelettes. Crack the eggs, whisk the eggs, chop the vegetables, meat and cheese, cook the eggs, fill the eggs, turn the eggs. Eat the eggs. That's the most important part. I closed my eyes and took another bite, savouring the taste.

'Don't you know that free-range chickens aren't actually free?'

'Huh?' I opened my eyes and blinked.

Noreen, whom I'd met vaguely the night before as I'd been shown round the flat, stood with her hands on her hips and her lips compressed in fury.

'Free range,' said Noreen. 'You do know what that's sup-posed to mean? Chickens running around wild and free. But free range doesn't actually mean free, it's just a con, they're not actually free, they're hardly any better off than battery hens even if technically they're not battery hens.'

She paused and I looked down at my cooling omelette. 'Oh,' I said.

'You shouldn't eat eggs at all,' she said. 'It's not fair on the chickens. Or if you insist on eating eggs, you should try those cholesterol-free, healthy-eating fake eggs they've brought out. They're really tasty. And they're good for you too.'

I just bet they are. All those chemicals and additives.

'I'll try them sometime,' I said, attempting a smile. I sneaked a glance down at my plate. Would it be too rude to take a bite?

'And just how many eggs do you have in that omelette?'

I was beginning to see why it had been Amber who'd shown me round the flat. Noreen had been a smile, a wave and a jumble of curly black hair, and then we'd moved on to the next room.

'Eight.' I was sheepish, but I'd been hungry. I hadn't eaten properly since I'd found Sarah and Jed in my bed. But Noreen didn't need to know my reasons. I'd paid for the food, I'd bought the eggs, they were mine to eat whenever I wanted to eat them.

'Eight?' She was horrified. 'That's revolting. Eight eggs could feed a family of four in Africa. And what have you got in it? I bet you don't even use organic vegetables.'

No, I don't. I don't eat vegetables. They're for sissy nancy-boys. I'm a carnivore. So what do you think of that? That's a lie, of course, I've already said I had peppers and mushrooms in my omelette, but that's what I wanted to say. How dare she attack me at six in the morning? I didn't even know this woman.

'Of course they are,' I said. That was the truth. I was a nice bloke. I was concerned with the environment. I was concerned with my own health. I could afford it. I didn't need to eat all those pesticides.

'Oh, good.' Noreen was mollified, but only for a moment. She sniffed. 'Is that meat?'

'Ham,' I said. Always like to be of help.

'How can you pollute your body like that? And what about the poor pigs? A tour of an abattoir would turn you into a vegetarian. All those horrible squeals. The pigs know they're about to be slaughtered. They can smell death. And all that blood. Blood everywhere.'

I don't want to be a vegetarian. I don't care if she wants to be a vegetable-lover, but I like meat. So there. It tastes great. It smells great. Juicy chicken on a grill, thick, rich steak juices dripping down on to the coals of a barbecue. That is my idea of a little piece of heaven. (And, no, even as Alexander I don't want the animals to suffer unduly. I'm sure we could come up with ways to kill them less cruelly. As Alexander I can still be kind to animals. It's people who should suffer.)

'You shouldn't be eating such food,' she said.

I touched the edge of my omelette. It was cold.

I'd thought I was quick, but she'd seen me.

'Fine, eat it,' she said. 'See if I care.'

Did she want me to waste it? To just throw it away? What about all those poor starving kids in Africa?

Noreen thrust her nose into the air and stormed out of the kitchen.

Well done, Alex, you'd made a new friend. And without even trying.

I tucked into my omelette. Even the cheese was cold.

See? That's what I was like. A pathetic jellyfish with no backbone, no courage. I could have cut her dead with my witty repartee (there's always hope), but I just sat there like a lump of coal. That's what I was. A lump of stone. Totally inert.

I'd lost my car (I was lying before, it'll never be the same, I'll always know), my girlfriend, my flat, my promotion at work, and now I was stuck living in a room advertised as cosy (i.e. small) with a psychotic flat-mate.

Yet I was still Alex. I was still Mr Nice Guy.

Makes you want to puke, doesn't it? Just watch out for those shoes.

Push, shove, stomp, bite, elbow. Let me on. Just let me get on. Let me squeeze in. Push, shove, squeeze, squeeze, squeeze. Surely there's room for one more. Push, shove, squeeze. Me, me. It's my turn. Me. Me. Let me on. Push, shove, squeeze.

Stay orderly. Stay orderly. We're British.

On at last.

Sweat and stink. Armpits in the noses of the petite. (The real reason London women wear high heels.)

Push, shove, squeeze. Let me off. Let me off.

Please let the passengers off first.

Push, shove, squeeze.

I'm off. I'm off.

Follow the swarms to the escalators.

Twice a day we put up with that.

We've survived the Blitz, we can put up with anything.

Quiet. Stiff upper lip. No complaints.

Push, shove, squeeze.

WHY THE SANDWICH MAKER
HAS A BETTER LIFE THAN I-DO

Think about it. I buy a sandwich from my corner sandwich shop five days a week. Plus various cakes, snacks, and drinks. A sandwich costs two or three pounds. I spend ten to fifteen pounds per week on a few slices of bread and some cheese. That's around five hundred pounds per year on sandwiches alone, plus another three hundred or so on drinks and snacks. And the queue is always three or four deep.

Get an education, they said. Enter a profession. Slog your guts out. Die of a stress-related heart-attack before you're fifty. Make something of yourself.

And never forget that money shows success.

Last week I saw the sandwich maker pull up to work in a brand new S-Class Mercedes.

(I've been had.)

If money is proof of success then he's winning.

Thursday. Sarah rang me up at work. She *apologised* for ringing me at work as if it was no longer her right to do so. As if she'd surrendered all those girl-boy privileges when she'd dumped me. Despite that I felt hope bloom in my chest. She just felt awkward, that was all. Everything would be back to normal soon.

'Would you come round to the flat tonight?'

Hope. Rainbows of joy. *The* flat. Not her flat. She wanted to see me.

'If you're sure.' Fool. That was too nice.

'I want you to collect the rest of your stuff.' Translation: she needed to make room for Jed's things.

Oh. I didn't know what to say to that.

'I'm sorry, Alex.'

I'm sorry, Alex. I'm sorry, Alex. I'm sorry, Alex.

For the rest of the afternoon I hatched wild, mad plans to make Sarah fall back in love with me. I'd take her flowers. I'd send balloons. Too boring. Too predictable. I'd book a helicopter flight to Paris and whisk her away for a long weekend. I'd reserve a hot-air balloon for just the two of us. She'd be amazed at my spontaneity, she'd be amazed at all the extra money I had to spend on frivolities. She'd see me as a potential provider. I could do it. I would do it.

Heart in my fragile, outstretched hand, I knocked on the door of the flat. Our flat. My flat. Her flat. I still had the key but felt awkward about using it. Officially I'd moved out, officially we were over. But I knew I could change that. If she'd just listen to me, if she'd let me touch her, let me kiss her, she'd be mine. I knew it.

The door opened.

Buckets of cold water in my face.

Jed stood there, staring at me for a second, his face open and honest in its viciousness and victory. Then he sort of shifted back into his let's-be-mates expression.

'Alex,' he said, like I was the person he most wanted to see in the world (I probably was, the bastard, he couldn't get enough of this rubbing it in). He stepped to the side and held the door open. 'Come in. Sarah's just popped out for a moment.'

I dutifully stepped inside. I allowed Jed to welcome me into my own home. If I'd been shocked by Jed opening the door, seeing what had happened to the flat was like having my head plunged into the middle of an iceberg when I'd been merrily surfing along in Hawaii. It looked like someone was moving out. CDs and books were stacked in precarious piles. Even the photographs I'd hung above the sofa (the ones with artistic merit I'd taken on various holidays and insisted upon hanging) were gone, now leaning against the armchair, leaving only the empty nails sticking out of the walls like forlorn flagpoles abandoned at the end of a long and drawn-out war. Signs of the end of the occupation. That's what it was. I was the new enemy and now my occupation was at an end. Over. Finished. I was through.

'Sarah popped out to pick up some more boxes and black bin liners. Didn't know you had so much stuff. That's a fabulous CD collection you've built up. It's a shame Sarah's so honest, she could do with keeping a few of yours.' He lowered his voice, confiding in me, his pal from work, knowing that I, better than anyone else, would understand. 'She's got to get rid of her love-song collection. If I hear Chicago, Celine Dion or Lionel Richie one more time—'

Jed stopped abruptly at the sound of a key in the lock.

The door opened and Sarah entered, arms full of boxes. I

couldn't speak; I just stared at her. Sarah. Sarah. She was beautiful. It struck me then that I loved her, really, truly loved her, despite what she'd done to me, despite what she was doing to me now.

Jed kissed her cheek and relieved her of the boxes all at once. I should have thought of that, but I couldn't move. I was frozen.

'Hello, Alex.'

'Hi.' It was a croak, but I'd done it, I'd managed to speak.

'I've been packing up your things. I thought it'd be easier that way.' She strode into the room, all smiles and forced joyfulness. 'You do have room in your new place?'

'Of course,' I lied. 'Plenty of room. It's a great place.' If you're a New Age vegan with a fetish for daisies.

'Will this be enough boxes?' asked Jed. He had to insert something into the conversation, couldn't let us forget about his presence, now could he?

'There're a few more in the car. Would you get them for me, please?'

Bless Sarah. What an angel. She did want to see me alone. I knew she would. Jed must have insisted he be here during the Great Handover. That was it, he didn't trust me, he was scared I'd woo Sarah back with my smooth love talk, that she'd be so impressed with my manly handling of the situation that she'd realise she'd made a mistake.

Sarah handed Jed her keys. 'Will you give him a hand, Alex?'

What? Had I heard her correctly? Did she know what she was doing? She was ruining everything. She was destroying our chance of a short time alone together. Jed smiled at me, as if to say, 'Ha, so there, I knew I didn't have to worry.' But I wanted to speak to her. Oh, sure, I wanted to kiss her, I wanted to jump her bones and give in to carnal frustration, but I would have been happy with words. I deserved a few words with her. We'd been together for nearly two years. Surely she owed me that much?

'Glad to help,' I said. Glad to help? Of course I wasn't bloody well glad to help. I wanted to shout, scream, demand some time alone with her, but did I speak out? Did I look imploringly at her? No and no. I followed Jed meekly to the car – her car, the car I knew so well – and allowed him to unlock the doors (he made a big show of it, as if saying to me, 'It's my right now, worm') and fill my arms with the empty boxes Sarah had brought home to remove my things from her life.

I wanted to hit Jed on the back of the head, to knock him out and stuff his body into the boot. I wanted to push him in front of a car, throw him into a busy street, shove him on to a train track. It wasn't fair. It just wasn't fair.

What did he have that I didn't?

Jed and I carried the empty boxes upstairs and helped Sarah pack my things. He put his slimy hands all over my possessions, my stuff, examining each and every item and making disparaging comments about my favourite socks, my lucky Pearl Jam T-shirt, the rare comics I'd saved from my teens (laugh all you want, Jed, those babies are worth a couple of grand each).

It was only after everything was packed (thanks for the tea and biscuits, Sarah) that I realised I had no way of getting all these boxes (how on earth had I acquired so much stuff?) to my new flat. My car was still in the garage, was going to be in the garage for weeks. (But that's another story.)

Sarah, bless her, she was so thoughtful, really she was, realised this at about the same time as I did. She was so kind. She offered her services as chauffeur for my boxes.

She kept the television, video, and stereo after ascertaining that I was in a shared dwelling, deciding I already had access to such electronic equipment. 'But when you move into your own place,' she said, 'we'll sort something out.' Sort something out. The stereo and television are both mine and we bought the video together after my old one wore out. I would really have liked a stereo and television in my new room, but I didn't put up a fight (I didn't even protest – at least I'd be able to see her again). And I knew there wouldn't be space for anything in my room with all these boxes (they were going to be stacked from floor to ceiling as it was).

We loaded up the car and then Sarah and Jed drove my things, all my belongings, to my new flat. There wasn't room for me in the back seat – I had a lot of boxes – so I took a cab. (I was so mature and adult and understanding as they pulled away with Jed in the passenger seat rather than me.) Unfortunately, it took me longer than I would have liked to hail a cab so by the time I pulled up outside my new building, Jed, Sarah, Amber and Noreen were already unloading the car.

I'd planned on dumping the boxes in the hallway and only taking them to my room after Sarah and Jed had left, but when Jed had knocked on the door and explained they were friends of mine helping me move, Amber had let them in and led them straight to my room. (The only, *only* good thing about that was that Amber is young, nubile and cute, and I could see that Sarah noticed. I could see that Sarah noticed Jed noticing. But I didn't want her to be jealous over Jed, I just wanted her to be jealous over me. I certainly didn't want Jed noticing Amber: she's too innocent for the likes of Jed. Why is it that Jed has to fancy the same women as I do? Does he do it on purpose? Is his sole aim in life to destroy mine?)

As we piled the last bag of clothes on to my bed, I could see Sarah take a look around the room and there was pity in her eyes when they caught mine. Once I'd organised the boxes I'd have room to walk from the door to the bed and from the bed to the door. Jed smiled broadly, winking at me as he caught Sarah's hand. He was ecstatic, I could see him all energised and excited and, no doubt, so sexually aroused that he was going to take my Sarah home to my flat and shag her brains out. On our mattress. It was so easy to be victorious over me.

They didn't stay long, not even for tea or coffee (told you Jed was hot for it). After they'd gone Amber and Noreen commented on how nice it had been to meet some of my friends and what a lovely couple Sarah and Jed had seemed.

And Amber said they appeared so in love and asked how long they'd been together.

'Since Monday,' I said, 'when Sarah dumped me after I walked in on them having sex in my bed.'

That shut them up. And Noreen looked at me with the light of admiration in her eyes. She now thinks I'm amazing, so laid back and cool that I can still be friends with them not hampered by jealousy. She thinks I've outgrown my animalistic urges and that I've moved on to the next higher plane of evolution. I think she's even forgiven me for eating eight eggs for breakfast.

They invited me to go out drinking with them and our other two flatmates the following night. Whoopee. Perhaps Noreen wanted to discuss the inconsistencies of my behaviour: meat-eating Neanderthal on the one hand, compassionate, understanding New Man on the other. Then she'd want to tell me all about how celery screams when we cut it. Doesn't it sound fun?

I LIKE DOGS
(IT'S THEIR OWNERS WHO SHOULD BE SHOT)

Dogs shit. Dogs pee. And then they shit some more. Dogs urinate. Dogs defecate. They like to leave little droppings to declare their presence. *I peed here. Smell me, I was here.* (It's a dual-purpose function, biological and behavioural.)

Dogs leave their pee and poo *on purpose*.

People should know better. (Especially city dwellers.)

(For all of you dog owners who do clean up after your pets, this does not apply to you. You should be hailed as paragons of virtue and rewarded with medals and trophies for civic duty.)

Dog owners who do not pick up their dog's dung (there are many novel implements in pet stores designed for this purpose if the owner is too squeamish for mere carrier-bags) should be taken to Tower Hill and shot. Oh, all right, then, if shooting's too extreme, prison sentences and ten-thousand-pound fines should be imposed. And maybe branding on the forehead so we all know and can throw stones and spit at them whenever they appear in public.

I am sick, *sick* of people being so inconsiderate.

Doesn't anyone think of anyone else but himself? Or herself? (Let's be fair, men and women are both at fault.)

No, of course they don't. Well, Alex used to, but I, the new Alexander, have to learn to become just like the rest of them. The rest of you. Sod society and sod the world. If I want a dog and I don't feel like cleaning up after his first, second, and third bouts of morning diarrhoea in the park, then too bad for all those schmucks out there who do mind. Who cares if it's in the middle of the path, right? No one else would pick it up. Why should I?

You'd think I'd have learnt my lesson. You'd think I'd have found some way to disassociate myself from Jed. There were other managers in the company who admired my work, and I'm sure I could have persuaded someone to let me transfer to their group. But, no, I held my tongue and slaved away on my horse-poster slogan. I knew that Jed couldn't keep me on such campaigns for ever, that it would start to look suspicious if someone of my experience and salary kept being assigned grunt work. But what I didn't suspect, what I couldn't have known, was that Jed was willing to sacrifice just a little bit of company prestige to take care of me once and for all.

Oh, he was so clever, he'd obviously thought it through, and when the first opportunity had arisen he'd struck. He couldn't have known I was going to walk in on him bonking Sarah that very same day and that Sarah would immediately thereafter dump me. But I don't think he'd have cared, I don't think it would have mattered: he wanted me out of the way with no chance of a comeback. And what a godsend it must have been when Richard Morris broke his leg. A minor, inconsequential project was perfect for Jed's plans for me. (No lasting harm to the great firm that way.)

Friday morning Elizabeth – Mrs Wilmington-Wilkes – duly arrived with her friends from the Shire Horse Centre in tow. She'd decided to sit in on the meeting, no doubt so she could feel generous, kind and philanthropic all at once, as well as gloating to her friends that her husband owned such a fine company.

I had on my best suit, a crisply ironed shirt, a tie that declared my competence and my friendliest smile. I was calm and in control. I wasn't nervous, even in Elizabeth's presence. This was easy. I'd given dozens of presentations and I knew these clients would be satisfied. I'd come up with a brilliant poster that was far better than any of the graduates could have done.

As soon as I'd finished and asked if there were any questions I could see that the clients looked uneasy, that Elizabeth was concerned. And Jed appeared embarrassed.

'That's a very fine poster, Alex. I'm sure the Shire Horse Centre will be able to use it,' Jed said, 'but that's not really why they're here. Why don't you present the radio ad now?'

Radio ad? What radio ad? Jed had mentioned nothing about a radio ad. I'd have known if he'd told me to do one. Small charities like this one don't normally do radio ads. It's practically unheard-of.

I smiled uncomfortably and glanced around the table. 'Radio ad?'

Jed, stern now: 'You do have a radio ad?'

Mutely, I shook my head. I'm glad I wasn't a girl or I would have been tempted to cry. And while tears might cause pity if they're coming from a woman, believe me when I tell you a crying man at work is not a figure for sympathy unless a very close family member has died. Then the women will think the man is sensitive and the other men will just be embarrassed by all that emotion, even if the momentary lapse in carrying on the tradition of the stiff upper lip is forgivable. I'd never really been in trouble before (not at school, not at university and certainly not at work, I'd been a good boy all my life) and I knew, *knew* that this was sabotage. Deliberate, malicious sabotage.

Elizabeth's face paled. At that precise moment I could clearly see the future. Mrs Wilmington-Wilkes had been humiliated by a mere employee and therefore that employee would pay. Kenneth would be all too happy to oblige. There was nothing he liked better than sacking an incompetent, turning another human being into a quivering wreck with his temper and threats of litigation.

Jed apologised to the clients for their wasted trip and assured them that we'd be working on the campaign throughout the weekend and that we'd have something by Monday morning. Elizabeth insisted the clients – her friends – remain in London at company expense rather than make another journey. I tried to apologise and explain, but Jed cut me off and then they were gone. Jed told me to wait in the meeting room.

I knew then, although I had no proof, that it had been a deliberate ploy by Jed. We'd been alone in his office when he'd asked me to take on the work and at the graduate groupie meeting he'd only said that my work was incomplete. He'd never told me about the radio ad. Never. But I had no proof.

A few minutes later Kenneth – Mr Wilmington-Wilkes, yes, sir – burst into the room. In his wake came Jed (one of Kenneth's sycophantic favourites), his expression respectful, mournful and regretful all at once, but I knew that the shine in Jed's eyes was one of victory.

Jed said, 'No, really, Kenneth, I take full responsibility. I know I should have checked his work. But Alex has never disappointed me before.'

'He's a grade five, isn't he?' Kenneth's crisp upper-class accent was sharp enough to cut glass.

'Yes, he is.'

'Then you shouldn't need to check his work. Young man,' Kenneth said to me, 'do you have an explanation?'

I felt like standing to attention and saluting, but I didn't dare. 'I didn't know about—'

'Didn't know? Didn't know?' Kenneth's voice thundered and I half expected his roar to start an avalanche. All I can say is that it was a good thing we weren't in the Alps in winter or a few more ski chalets would have been buried in the snow. 'Didn't listen is what you mean.'

'I'm so sorry, Kenneth,' said Jed, smoothly cutting me off. 'He said last night that everything was finished. I asked him if he wanted me to double-check anything, to look things over for him and he said no. It was an error of judgement on my part. I never should have trusted him. He obviously wasn't ready for the responsibility.'

This was excruciating. Kenneth was buying his bullshit. Even if I had been to blame it would have been Jed's fault as much as mine. He was the manager. It was his job to make certain everything was in order for the client.

Kenneth paused and stared at me for a full minute.

The silence was terrible. I wanted to scream, I wanted to shout, I wanted to point an accusing finger at Jed, I wanted to confess, anything, anything to end this torture.

'You, young man,' said Kenneth, pointing at me. He turned to Jed. 'What's his name?'

'It's Alex,' said Jed. 'Alex Fairfax.'

'Well, Alex Fairfax, as of this moment consider yourself dismissed for incompetence.'

'But—' I said.

'No buts,' said Kenneth. 'And don't expect just to sail out of here. All the client expenses for the weekend will be deducted from your last pay packet. Hotel, food, entertainment, everything. You're a fool if you expect the company to pay for your negligence.' He turned back to Jed, mentally dismissing me. 'Have him escorted from the building. Immediately.'

Back ramrod straight, no doubt proud of himself for his masculinity, Kenneth strode from the room. He was probably going to see his wife, and if he was anything like Jed, he'd want to give it to her while he was feeling all big and full of testosterone. I hoped the clients were still in his office. I hoped Elizabeth would feel obliged to spend the day with them. I hoped they all went out to dinner and to the opera and came back to the Wilmington-Wilkes house for late-night coffee. I hoped he wasn't alone with his wife for days (even if I was going to be paying for all that entertainment, even if it took all of my last month's salary).

Jed summoned two security guards (*two*, as if I would have put up a struggle) to escort me to my desk. Jed led the way, stopping at his own office to retrieve an empty Ariel box. He handed it to me and I stared at it for a moment. I wondered if it had been one of the spare boxes Sarah had collected yesterday from Tesco. I'd bet my entire savings account that it was. Jed had probably set it aside last night, knowing what was coming, knowing that his third strike would soon bear fruition.

My feet were still a little sore, but I wasn't really hobbling now, even if I felt like a goblin the way everyone in the office was staring at me. No one would meet my eyes. They were all embarrassed for me. There was pity too. But most of all there was relief that it wasn't them.

Jed stood behind the guards, smirking as I packed up my belongings: my favourite pen, a Dilbert desk diary, a South Park coffee mug given to me by Sarah, yesterday's *Times*, a Twix for my mid-morning snack.

Then Jed and the two guards walked me to the front door. Jed took my key card and my company ID, and then I was out on the street.

I'd been sacked.

Jed stood on the other side of the windows – on the inside – and watched me clutch my little box and walk away. I looked back before I turned the corner and he was still there. He was standing there with a grin on his face, watching until I was out of sight.

I was unemployed. I was soon to be on the dole. Can you even claim dole after you've been sacked? After they say it's your fault? (But I'm innocent, honest. How many times have they heard that one down at the dole office?) And what if you have savings? Can you still claim dole?

So there I was. No car. No girlfriend. No flat. No job. And probably no dole. Only a room.

And a cardboard box. I mustn't forget my cardboard box. It's not large enough to sleep in, though.

THEY SET A MAN ON FIRE

They poured oil over him, struck a match and deliberately set him alight.

(It's happened a number of times in different parts of the country.)

They called it a racist attack and it probably was. But how can anyone hate a stranger enough to set him or her on fire? Think about the true horror of the attack. It's not like a gun. It's not like pulling a trigger. It's immediate and personal. The kicks and struggle and screams are *right there*. In your face. You'd be able to feel the heat, smell the burning flesh.

Now if it was something personal, then maybe I can understand, if it's some individual who has done you great wrong, if it's a vendetta. (Don't worry, Jed, you're safe, you're going to be humiliated, your reputation annihilated, pain and suffering aren't enough for you, even death isn't punishment enough, it'd be too easy and it would be over too soon, no, Jed, I wish you a long life, a very, very long life.)

Oh, it's just a bunch of young men who've had too much to drink. Yeah, right. I've been pretty drunk and while I've succumbed to the urge to piss in the street, the thought of deliberately burning someone to death and watching them die has never occurred to me.

It must be mob mentality, then, and fear and anguish and feelings of inferiority and desperate longing to belong to something. The situation escalates from chasing to punching and beating, but then on to *setting someone alight*? That's a pretty extreme reaction, if you ask me.

And once a person's been burnt, all their skin burnt off, don't we all look pretty much the same?

Is that the answer, then? Do we all need to burn off all the skin and all the hair so we can be these identical creatures of blood and bone and muscle? Would we then attack people for being different sizes? For being too short or too tall? Too fat or too small? For having blue eyes? Or green? Would we have to tear our eyes out next?

Everyone should have a moment of catharsis, just like me. Now that I'm Alexander I can see everything with perfect clarity. Skin colour doesn't matter. I don't care if they're black, brown, white, yellow, red, pink, purple or green; there's only them and me. There's me on the one hand. And everyone else on the other. And I know which hand I'm going to be looking out for.

I walked around London all morning carrying my little cardboard box. I think I must have looked desperate. Even in my fine suit (do you know how much I paid for this suit? Sarah insisted I buy a designer label so she could tell her friends) people kept shying away from me. I guess my shuffling walk (my feet are killing me, I could feel the blisters forming on top of my stitches and at my heels and at the tips of my toes) and my shiny suit shoes just didn't sync. They all knew that I was an impostor. That I no longer belonged in the world of honest, employed and employable people.

My cardboard box must have told them I'd been sacked.

I spent the afternoon in my room, staring at the sky of daisies above my bed. They were really quite comforting. I didn't think, I didn't plan, I didn't worry about the future, I just studied the daisies, petal after petal. There are one thousand five hundred and sixty-six daisy petals painted on my ceiling.

At seven there was a knock at the door and Amber poked her head into the room. (My room. I've got a room.) The physical evidence of my sacking, the pathetically empty cardboard box, was lost among all the other boxes. She didn't know. She couldn't know.

'Alex, you're in.' She looked delighted to see me. How could anyone be so cheerful all the time? 'We thought we were going to have to leave you a note.'

'I got home early.' I didn't lie, but I didn't want to spoil her good mood. I didn't want to depress my new flatmates with my tales of woe. They already felt sorry for me over my split with Sarah, and I didn't need them to think there was something wrong with me. (There was something wrong with me, I was too nice.) And I didn't want them to have to worry about me paying the rent and my share of the bills. They didn't know me yet, they didn't like me, so they weren't about to cut me any slack. I doubt they suffered from the too-nice bug. Except maybe Amber, but she'd be outvoted.

'Come on,' said Amber. 'We're all going to the pub.'

We. Was I part of a we again? Amber and Noreen. Clarence and Diana. And me. I was there, almost there, hovering on the edge, teetering on the border between inclusion and exclusion.

So we went to the pub in one big, happy group.

Clarence, towering over us all but so thin he looked like a strong gust of wind could blow him over, was placid and calm, and an easy grin hovered on his lips. The smell of cannabis surrounding him was so strong that as I inhaled deeply I felt just a little bit calmer. I could do it. I could get through this night. I could pretend that everything was right with the world, that I was still me, that I still had my life, that it was nice and ordered and settled, just as I liked it.

Diana, on the other hand, is short and sturdy, not fat, just chunky, thick-limbed and solid. She's like some sort of earth goddess from prehistoric times, only the slimmed-down modern version without the massive belly. I almost wished she was a goddess, then I could get down on my knees and pray to her to make everything all right. It would have been a whole lot easier than trying to fix it myself. How would I get another job with no reference to show? I had been sacked, so I couldn't claim anyone as a referee.

The evening was going along really well. I was chatty and even cheerful (after the first two hours it wasn't forced). I had cash in my wallet and didn't worry about the price when my first round included three expensive cocktails for the ladies. Tomorrow was soon enough to worry about the future. There was an alcohol buzz in my blood, a smile on my lips, and I was beginning to relax. Maybe I should start to appreciate the single life again. I could sit here in the pub and get stinking drunk if I wanted, stay past closing time (at least until they kicked me out) and then go to a party down the road, and I didn't have to worry about Sarah, I didn't have to worry about anyone. I could do anything I damn well pleased. I was my own man. I was in control.

It was half an hour to closing time and I was winding my way back to the table with the first half of a fresh round of drinks when a male roar boomed above the sounds of laughter, chatting and clinking glasses: 'Oi, those're my wife's tits you're staring at.'

Was this for real? Could a man like that have a wife?

The pub quieted and all eyes turned to the drama now unfolding. The crowds stopped moving and I was stuck where I was, holding two pints and a wineglass.

A thick-necked, bull-backed man of about thirty-five was glaring at a man ten years his junior and probably half his weight. Two women sat at what was obviously the older man's table, both busty, both blonde, both wearing skin-tight cloth-ing with plenty of cleavage on display.

The younger man looked at the older one, then turned and began to walk away, towards the bar, towards me.

'Don't you bloody ignore me, mate,' said the married man.

The smaller man kept on walking and the crowds parted to let him pass.

'Oi, you.' When the younger man didn't react, the older one grabbed an empty pint glass, smashed it down along the table edge so that the end broke off and threw it, jagged edge forward, at the man who had offended him.

The bullish man must have been very drunk or he was just lousy at sport because the glass went sailing past the head of its intended target and hit me, smashing into my left temple and the side of my head. The force of the blow made me stagger and drop my drinks. The glasses shattered and the alcohol spattered my shoes and trousers. Blood spurted everywhere, flowing down my face and neck, staining my shirt, dripping on to the floor. Gingerly I felt the top of my ear, fearing the worst, but it seemed to be in one piece and it was definitely still attached. The upward trajectory of the glass had saved me from deformity. Scars I could live with, but I didn't want to lose my ear. Sarah would never think I was trendy then.

I'd thought Monday was busy at A&E, but it had been nothing compared to Friday night. There was blood and gore everywhere, not to mention drunks who'd collapsed and others who were staggering around demanding to be seen. Even though my injury was worse than Monday night's (it had been only vomit on my bandaged feet then), I still spent six hours there.

Oh, sure, they put me in a little bed and saw me every now and then to pick out more glass, but they couldn't give me their undivided attention. I didn't blame them and I didn't care. It was much more entertaining listening to the sounds of efficient doctors and nurses dealing with crisis after crisis than it would have been counting daisies in my room. The little curtain around my bed didn't keep out the moans and groans of the lesser wounded, like me, but I was thankful that I was up at the far end and couldn't really tell if the man with the heart-attack had lived or died.

Amber and Noreen, bless them, accompanied me in the ambulance to the hospital. (They lied and said they were my sisters so that they could come with me, but I don't know if that was necessary or not.) And Amber held my hand the whole way to the hospital, squeezing every so often, letting me know she was there, that I wasn't alone.

The staff at the pub had been kind too, giving me clean towels to press against my head to try to staunch the flow of blood. They were cautious, though, not to touch me, not to get too near. As I noticed their reactions it suddenly struck me that maybe I wasn't as safe from AIDS and other STDs as I'd been assuming. For two years I'd only slept with Sarah, but she, of course, had been screwing my boss and who knows if he was the only one?

According to Amber and Noreen, for I was too preoccupied with the pain and the sight of all that blood – my blood – dripping to the floor, the glass thrower fled the pub, dragging both of his busty blondes along with him as he ran. We don't know whether he eluded the police.

I'd never been in an ambulance before.

After two hours I received a message from one of the junior nurses that Amber and Noreen had gone home (who could blame them?), but that I was supposed to ring them when I was finished and they would come and collect me. I was no longer in any life-threatening danger (and according to the doctor I never had been, but she wasn't there, she didn't see how much blood I'd lost) so it was safe for my flatmates to leave and, let's be honest, they hardly knew me. It was good of them to stay as long as they had.

Once all the glass had been removed, the stitching began. Between the stitches on my feet and those on my head I felt like a piece of human embroidery.

My head was thickly bandaged and I looked like a war victim as I was discharged. I was only missing the smeared blood and dirt on the bandages to look really authentic.

I thought about calling my flatmates and asking for a lift but decided against it. I felt like walking. And besides, it was almost dawn, the streets would be empty. There was no sense in waking up Amber and Noreen when a little bit of fresh air (okay, outside air, then, it wasn't particularly fresh) would help clear my head. It was only a mile or two home.

So there I was, ten minutes from the hospital, my head aching, my feet aching (I'd forgotten about the blisters from my long walk home from work), when I was mugged.

'Stand and deliver,' they said.

No, they didn't.

It was more like 'Give us yer wallet.' Two male thugs backed up by knives. Knives longer than the legal limit.

By this point I'd had enough. I stood on one foot in *Karate Kid* preying-mantis style and let them have it. I was victorious. I was amazing.

No, I admit, that's not quite how it went.

I tried to ignore them and keep walking, but they surrounded me. 'Give us yer money and yer watch.'

Did they think I was wearing a Rolex? Did they think I was staggering around the streets of London at this insane hour of the morning with a thickly bandaged head and that I was loaded? They could have my watch. Sarah had given it to me for my birthday last month. Good riddance. I didn't need the memories of that night, the way she'd snuggled close and told me she'd love me for ever even though she'd been screwing Jed for weeks.

'Have the watch,' I said. I unclasped it and tossed it to the ground, hoping that would distract them, but it failed. One picked it up and snorted in disgust, but he still pocketed it.

'That's not enough of a toll,' he said. 'Give us yer money.'

'Look, I'm unemployed,' I said. 'I don't have any money.'

'Sob, sob.' The other one brandished his knife. 'Give us yer money.' And he stepped closer, pressing his knife into my throat. I could feel a sharp pain and then a trickle of blood. That answered *that* question then. They were serious.

I withdrew my wallet, intending to hand them the cash, but the bastards snatched it and ran away, disappearing down a side-street. They had stolen not only my money but my credit cards, my bank card, even my library card.

I stood there staring after them, helpless with fury. I knew I couldn't catch them. My feet hurt too much. My head hurt.

At that moment a cab drove past, its for-hire sign lit. But I couldn't take a cab, I didn't have any money.

I fingered the wound on my neck. Yep, definitely bleeding.

I decided then that I was a coward.

The pub injury had been mostly just bad luck, though if I'd been more agile, quicker, better co-ordinated, I'm sure I could have dodged it. But the mugging had been my own fault for not even trying to fight back. Sure, I might have lost, I might have been stabbed, severely beaten or even killed, but at least I would have known that I'd stood my ground. It was the principle of the thing.

I'd acquired another adjective to describe myself. No longer was I just nice. I was a nice coward. Not a sometimes coward as I used to be, like when I was dealing with Jed at work, but a full-time coward. I had irrefutable proof.

The others were all asleep when I arrived back at the flat. Amber had made me a get-well card (drawn by her own fair hand) and left it on the table. (Had she expected me to return by cab after all?)

I decided not to tell them about the mugging. I didn't want them to know how pitiful I was, didn't want them to wonder if I'd been cursed or if my misfortune would rub off on them. I didn't want to be a pariah. I didn't want Amber to regret holding my hand or to think I was a loser. I didn't want her to know the truth. I was a loser.

I spent an hour on the phone, quietly reporting the theft of my credit cards and bank card. I'd neglected to report my change of address (hoping that Sarah would come to her senses) so American Express and Visa said they'd only send my replacement cards to Sarah's. (Was it Sarah and Jed's now?)

I didn't know what to feel at the prospect of seeing Sarah

again. I couldn't decide if it was good or bad. She'd know about my sacking. Jed would have told her the story with glee while trying to seem sad about it. She'd feel sorry for me. If there was one thing from Sarah that I didn't want, it was her pity.

But all wasn't doom and gloom.

Just before bed I discovered twelve pounds and twenty pence in my pocket – change from that last round that I hadn't bothered to put into my wallet.

(I'd forgotten or I'd probably have squandered half of it on the cab.)

I'm not totally broke.

My curse was spreading to other members of my family. My mother rang (waking me, but a good son doesn't care about such things) early on Saturday to tell me that her rhododendron was missing. Someone had come along in the middle of the night and dug it up from her front garden, leaving a big black hole in the ground.

Aren't people grand?

From this moment, I've decided to cease giving money to any people charities. You can't designate your money for the decent folk and I bet the selfish push their way to the front of the queues and take all the medicines and other goodies before the polite and considerate have a chance to see what's on offer, so it's pointless. No sense letting the nasty profit even more from my sweat.

I'll only be making donations to animal or environmental organisations. The earth and its animals deserve to be saved.

REPLACEMENT CARD

I know librarians are traditionally portrayed as fierce dragons who wander constantly around the hallowed rows of books shushing people, but I always expect them to be kind, friendly and understanding, as if our shared love of the written word ties us together in some deep bond of humanity.

I forget that librarians are just like the rest of us. Some are kind. Some are nice. And some are not.

As of this moment I am still without a library card. Did you know that at my library they charge five pounds for a replacement?

I explained that I'd been mugged, I explained that it wasn't my fault, but Ms (you could tell she wasn't married even without the evidence of no ring) Head Librarian would hear none of my excuses. I had a great big bandage covering most of my head – I mean, I *looked* injured – but she didn't care. Five pounds was the rule, so five pounds it was.

I had twelve pounds in my pocket. (I could have taken my chequebook to the bank and withdrawn some cash from the counter but after my mother's call I went back to sleep and then it was too late, they'd closed.) Twelve pounds to last me until Monday. I was sad, desperate and depressed, I needed to keep busy, I needed my twelve pounds, I might want to spend it on something else, on something fun, on entertainment.

I'm unemployed, I've been traumatised by a head injury, mugged, and now my library won't give me a replacement card until I give them five pounds. You'd think they'd be kind to an unemployed person who wants to read. That's the whole point of libraries, isn't it? They're supposed to be free.

And, Ms Head Librarian, I *did* look after my library card. It was the men with the knives who weren't so careful.

(How much is a stolen library card worth on the black market? I bet it's not five pounds.)

I love action films. The ideal action film has no slow moments. No poignant moments. No moralising. Just action after action after action. Constant movement and constant excitement. When I go to see an action film I don't want an hour of characterisation, I don't want time to think about the dirty laundry waiting at home. And I certainly don't want a lull during which the audience can grow restless and talkative.

I pay my money to escape from everyday life. I want to see what it's like to be a suave spy or a kick-ass army man or a swashbuckling hero. I want the characters to be dashing and strong if they're male, and sexy and alluring if they're female. That's all. I don't ask for much. I'm easily entertained. If I want drama, if I want Oscar-winning acting, I'll go to another film. I want an action film to *be* an action film. It's pure escapism. Bad guys get what they deserve. Good guys win. (Or cool, likeable, anti-hero bad guys win against uncool other bad guys.)

If you've paid good money to sit in a cinema and see a film, you really shouldn't be planning to use the time to phone up one of your mates to discuss the day's football match, play by play by excruciating play.

I wanted to be on my own. I just wanted to sit somewhere and be entertained without having to make small-talk and pretend to be happy and content with life, so I went to the cinema. To see an action movie.

I ended up buying a ticket for a film I'd already seen the week before (with my brother, not with Sarah who always complains about the plots or lack thereof), but it was the only pure action film out there. I didn't want action-comedy, action-drama, action-mystery, I just wanted action. Bombs, guns, explosions, natural disasters, a bit of sex was okay, but no real relationship-forming stuff. I certainly wasn't in the mood for that. As I'd seen it the week before, I knew what was going to happen, but then again, you always do: it's the visual and audio effects combined with the fighting and stunts that make it what it is. I'd loved it the week before and I was thoroughly prepared to love it again. I knew that it could make me forget what a mess I, the sorry wimp, had made of my life. It was worth spending half of my cash on a post-matinée, Saturday-evening show. I knew it would give me a buzz and a feeling of invincibility that would stay with me for a few hours at least.

During the first half-hour the action came thick and fast. The opening scene was stunning: I don't think I've ever seen so many bombs go off, so many cars, trees, houses and office blocks disintegrate. But then – I could hardly believe it – I came back to myself with a jolt. No longer was I lost in the adventures on the big screen, no: once more I was only poor unemployed Alex Fairfax and I was annoyed. People were talking. And being loud about it too. There was laughter, giggling and chatting from only a few rows behind me. Okay, okay, there weren't any bombs going off now, but it was still exciting: the hero was crawling through a mine-infested jungle and the enemy were all around him, the music had that eerie quality so you just knew something was going to jump out at him at any moment. And people were talking. Why had they bothered paying to sit inside this cinema if they only wanted to chat?

After a few minutes of this I shushed them. They laughed louder. And then other members of the audience (I'd started a trend) tried shushing them too. More giggles and talking. I turned and glared at them and shushed very loudly. There were six of them, three couples, all in their early twenties, old enough to know better. One of the girls stuck out her tongue at me – she actually stuck out her tongue – and they all broke into hysterical laughter.

Livid, flushing, I turned back to the film. I'd been right: the hero had been cornered and now he was busy busting noses and breaking necks, all the while protecting the token woman (sexy, of course, and her clothes had been half torn off in a previous battle scene) he was now duty-bound to protect.

More laughter and talking from behind me. I squirmed in my seat. This wasn't right. I forced myself to try to shut it out. I always found the volume in cinemas too loud, but right then I was thankful for the noise and I kept hoping that the big gun battle I knew was coming would begin. Surely the sounds of all that gunfire would block out the noises from behind.

Then, suddenly, I heard, 'Hiya, mate. Did ya see the game?' I turned once more to glare and one of the men, his arm around his girlfriend, was on the phone. I could see its glow next to his ear. He started talking about the day's match.

'Shut up,' I said, loudly.

He gave me the finger and continued talking. 'No, but did you see that second attempt? It was brilliant.'

(Keep in mind that my head was practically entombed in a thick, white bandage that showed up quite visibly in the cinema lighting. I might have been dying. I might have been recovering from brain surgery.)

That was it. I'd had it. I was so sick of these people who thought they ruled the world and could do anything they damn well pleased. Well, no more. I wasn't going to let them.

I rose to my feet, clutching my nearly full Pepsi in one hand, and faced them. 'Shut the fuck up,' I said.

'And who's gonna make me?' asked the bloke on the phone.

That was it. I'd had it.

I stormed up the aisle and into the row in front of them. By some quirk of fate it was empty, waiting for me to enact my destiny. This was how it was meant to be. I'd suffered enough and the Fates had decided it was time to even the score. There had to be balance and redress and it was my turn to be the man on top. I was now the action hero of my very own movie.

I stopped in front of them. The girls were laughing. And I threw my Pepsi right into the face of that bastard on the phone. They stopped smiling then.

There were cheers from the audience and I knew I was centre stage now.

Spluttering, Wet Face dropped his phone and rose to his feet, cocking his fist.

And I drew back my own arm and socked him straight on the nose.

There was an eruption of blood and the sound of crunching bone and cartilage. I'd hit the bull's-eye.

That shut them up. Let's see them try that again. The girls were frozen in their seats, screaming at all the blood, too scared to flee, for I was still standing there. Waiting for their next move.

The other two blokes stood up, trying to look threatening, but I just stared at them and they sat down again.

Blood was dripping everywhere. (Noses bleed a lot when you hit them.) I rubbed my knuckles and I couldn't stop smiling.

I laughed. 'Thank you for being quiet,' I said. 'Have a nice day.'

And I turned and walked, tall and proud, from the cinema.

There was no cheering and clapping this time. I knew that my fans were shocked. I exited the cinema to the sounds of machine-gun fire coming from every corner of the room. Sure did like that Dolby-surround sound.

I went to the men's toilet and washed my hands, careful to turn the taps with pieces of toilet paper as I didn't want to leave my fingerprints anywhere in case the police were called in. (I'd always known those cop shows and films and books I'd read as a teenager would be good for something one day.) I was really lucky: there wasn't another soul in sight. No members of the audience, no employees. Just me, the madly grinning lunatic in the mirror.

And then, I like to think this was really clever, I unwound the bandages from my head, wrapped them and the bloodied tissues in toilet paper and stuffed it all into my pockets to be disposed of later.

As I left the toilet, crowds streamed out of the cinema across the hall and I knew I was home, free. I joined the swarm and headed towards the exit. In the lobby I could see the manager and a few employees clustered around the hunched and bloodied figure of the man I'd punched. (I'd punched someone, I'd punched someone. For the first time in my life I'd punched someone and it felt good. He'd deserved to be punched. He'd been asking for it. He was lucky I was in control or I'd have beaten him to a pulp. And he would have deserved that too.) The man's posse (his five friends) stood nearby scanning the crowd, looking out for me, a crazy man in white bandages. You don't wind up a crazy man in white bandages. It's like telling the man behind you in a darkened cinema in Times Square, New York, to shut up if you suspect he's dealing drugs. You just don't do it.

Like everyone else in the crowd, I peered interestedly at the wounded man, but I didn't smile, I didn't gloat, I didn't catch anyone's eye and then I was outside. I was free. I'd made it.

I knew there was no way they'd trace me. I was pretty average-looking and nondescript without my bandages, this wasn't my normal cinema, and I'd paid in cold hard cash. No one had been killed. It would go down in police records as an unsolved crime. They had more important matters to attend to. (Like looking for my wallet.)

I have to say it's a good thing I didn't have a gun or I would have shot that little prick where he sat. I would have shot him through the heart. And it wouldn't have been done in cold blood, no, my blood had been hot at the time. I'm glad I hadn't had a gun because then he would have been dead and everyone would have blamed me (I'm not a fool: I know if I'd shot him the police would have spent the time and resources necessary to track me down). And I hadn't wanted him dead, I'd wanted him to suffer. No longer would he be so arrogant and inconsiderate. No longer would his friends look up to him and think him invincible. Oh, no, his little girlfriend, his little buddies, they'd all seen him moan and whimper with pain. He wasn't such a man any more.

And I was an action hero.

I knew that the audience, when they'd gone home, when they'd had time to digest what had happened, would realise that too. I'd stood up for them, I'd stood up for us all. I, alone, had defeated the enemy. I'd punished the wrongdoer. I'd made everything right for us all.

I'd never been a hero before and now I was an action hero. Pow. Jab. Smack. Punch. I was invincible.

In just one punch I'd moved from being a loser to a hero. Suddenly I had 'It', whatever it is. I could feel the blood coursing through my veins as I wandered the streets of London. It got later and later and the crowds thinned and I began trawling the streets near where I'd been mugged the night before, longing to bump into the thugs who'd stolen my wallet.

I never saw them, but I did see other unsavoury characters waiting for drug deals or prostitutes or whatever other mischief they were up to, looking menacing and hard, and I just didn't care. In me they recognised a similar hardness and I was left alone. It was a shame for I would have welcomed a fight (said I'd leave the film with a buzz).

I'd finally grabbed my life by the balls. I was in control.

After my moment of infamy in the annals of north London cinema history, I knew suddenly that my misfortunes of the past week had been no one's fault but my own. That's right. I was the one to blame.

Sure, Jed, Sarah, Kenneth and the others might have been the instruments of evil, but I had been at fault for letting them take advantage of me. It doesn't mean I'll forgive them – I never will – but they have opened my eyes to the wider world. Humanity, like the rest of the animal kingdom, however enlightened we pretend to be, can be divided into two categories: predators and prey.

My whole life I'd been prey. Now I was a predator.

But I was a new, self-aware kind of predator. I decided to become the so-called king of the jungle. My prey was going to consist solely of other predators. Oh, yes, they'd had their field day, they'd had their easy run, but now it was my turn. I was going to stand up and fight back for all those saps out there who were still too nice to do anything for themselves. I was going to be Superman and Batman all in one. But I was going to be his evil, darker twin. I was the Vigilante.

I was a predator. And to predators, the ends most definitely justify the means.

In the early hours of Sunday morning, I reached epiphany.

I was Alex Fairfax no longer.

My name is Alexander Fairfax and I'm twenty-nine years old.

Yesterday I was Alex, but today, from this moment on, I am Alexander. I have been born anew. Through blood and suffering, I have been forged into a better man.

I am Alexander. Hear me roar.

THE FIRST DAY OF MY LIFE

If I'm going to get my revenge – and I'm going to get my revenge – I need a plan. I need lots of plans.

Revenge, revenge, revenge. Sounds good, doesn't it?

What better way to start a new life than clearing up the rubbish from the last life?

THE LIST

If I'm going to get the revenge I deserve, does that make me the revenger and them the revengees? Is that my super-hero title? The Revenger? The Great Revenger? (I can't be the Avenger, too many associations, though the most recent one, of Uma Thurman in black leather, isn't bad.) Or maybe I'll be the Great Taker of Vengeance. For my cause is mightier than mere revenge, the greedy fools deserve to be punished for their betrayals, their cupidity and, most of all, for their hubris. It's vengeance I'm after.

Vengeance.

They will be punished.

My list of those who deserve to suffer (in chronological order):

1. Spotty kids who trashed my car.
2. Jed, Thomas and William for betraying me at Monday's meeting with Kenneth.
3. Jed for assigning me the Shire Horse work.
4. Sarah and Jed.
5. (I've forgiven Noreen for her breakfast tirade. She's not a morning person. Hurrah for Noreen. No vengeance required.)
6. Sarah and Jed.
7. Jed's even greater work betrayal on Friday.
8. Kenneth Wilmington-Wilkes for believing Jed and sacking me.
9. Sarah and Jed.
10. Glass-throwing brute at pub.

11. Two muggers.
12. Five-pound Ms Head Librarian. (I've included her just in case, though I haven't decided whether or not she deserves punishment, as she's only petty and annoying, not actually evil. I'll have to think about this one.)
13. People who talk in cinemas. Full stop.
14. Anyone else I deem worthy of vengeance.
15. Any other bastards out there taking advantage of the innocent (a.k.a. the prey).

A pretty comprehensive list you might think, but I have another way of ordering it.

My list of those who deserve to suffer (from most to least):

1. Jed.
2. Everybody else.

STEP ONE

I have a plan. I have a great plan. I have a great, secret plan.

This is what I chant to myself in the silly voice of a superhero villain – internally, I'm not crazy – as I head towards home. Suddenly I stop, I freeze in mid-motion the way they always do in cartoons, and I smile. I smile this great, beatific smile as it hits me. I'm free and single. I'm young, free and single. And now I'm one of the élite: I'm a predator. Sarah was for the old Alex, the nice me. The new in-control me can do better.

I know instantly what I'm going to do. Standing there, legs spread in the middle of a pace, I have a moment of perfect clarity. Everything will work out exactly as I want it to because I will make it do so. I will be a great puppeteer to the thousands of lesser mortals out there. I've worked in advertising, coming up with catchy slogans and clever ways to get the public to part with their cash: I've become an expert at manipulation without even realising it. And now it's time for the games to begin.

Pah, I don't care about fame. I'm not going to be some actor baring his arse on a thirty-foot screen. What I'm going to be is filthy, dirty, stinking rich. I'm going to set up my own advertising firm. I'm going to become the new Saatchi & Saatchi. I'm going to disembowel the firm of Wilmington-Wilkes as I draw away their clients one by one. I'm going to become a king.

Sarah is going to wish she'd never given me up. She'll rue the day she lost my love, the day she lost her chance to be at the centre of it all.

And if magazines and newspaper columns want to devote their space to me, well, so be it. I didn't say I wouldn't take fame, but for me it's just a side effect. The power and money of success is what I want.

I start moving again, walking, and then I begin to run, legs flying, arms pumping, eating up the pavement. In ten minutes I am home. The sky is lightening and it will soon be dawn, but I don't need any sleep. I shower and change and then I start to work.

I spend the day flying the wave of my euphoria, working on brilliant new advertising campaigns for my three chosen targets from my bed. (I find the daisies oddly comforting and inspiring at the same time. They're so bright and cheery and bold, simple and confident all at once with their fifteen hundred and sixty-six petals.) My chosen targets are three big, but not the biggest, clients of Wilmington-Wilkes. Three companies in which I have contacts, three companies I've worked with previously under the Wilmington-Wilkes banner, three companies I know will soon start thinking about new advertisements, three companies that need some fresh ideas.

That evening I stop, satisfied. I'm like John Travolta in *Phenomenon*: my brain is working so fast that in the space of fourteen hours I have completed three separate campaigns. And my concepts are brilliant, not so revolutionary as to shock the poor public but so original and breathtaking that I know, just know, that I, Alexander Fairfax, am going to have my first three clients by the end of the week. In the space of a single, albeit very long, day I have done the work it would normally take a four-man team two or three months to complete. I am free of the rules and restrictions, the protocol and politics of a big company, and my mind has no boundaries. It's so easy to think when you're free.

And I don't need fancy graphs, I don't need models in bikinis holding client products to grab their attention, I just need me. Me and my ideas.

Tomorrow I will enter the arena. The Jeds and Kenneths of this world won't know what's hit them. I won't give them time to step aside: my stampede will crush them underfoot. But it's not just about survival: it's about survival with style.

I don't fool myself. Alex would have come up with the same ideas. He is, after all, me, and I am him, but Alex would never have had the balls to do what I am about to do.

For a second I feel a flicker of unease. What if no one likes my concepts? What if they're not good enough? What if *I*'m not good enough? Then I look up at the daisies and I smile. Of course I'm going to succeed. I am Alexander now. I'm no longer a loser. I'm not Alex. I will never be Alex again. I will never be that coward. I am Alexander. I. Am. Alexander.

ONLY FOR IDIOTS OR THE UNWARY
(SORRY, MUM, I KNOW THIS INCLUDES YOU)

I know that salesmen are supposed to be persuasive, that a good salesman is supposed to be able to sell anything, that I'm a sort of salesman myself, but I could strangle those who come door to door. The latest policy seems to include knocking on one's door with a clipboard and a wet, crumpled-looking badge or ID card and nothing else. No literature. No terms and conditions. Nothing.

They start their spiel – about electricity or gas, burglar alarms or double-glazed windows – and tell you that you have to decide then and there, while you're getting cold in your shirt-sleeves holding open the front door. We've got a fantastic, unbeatable offer on an alarm system, they'll tell you, it's only thirty-two pence a day compared to the forty-one pence you'd be paying if you went with the competitor down the road. But you can't think about it, you can't look into it on your own, they're forbidden to return to the same house twice. They have a sheet of paper you can sign saying you want to sign up, but that's it. No price lists, no descriptive brochures, no real proof that they're even valid companies.

And if you ask for documentation, well, you might as well ask to fly to the moon for free.

No time to consider. No time for comparison-shopping. No time to work out the figures for yourself. Decisions must be instantaneous or you'll miss out on their unbelievable offer.

My mother – kind, thoughtful and meticulously polite to all – has fallen for a number of these schemes. And schemes they've turned out to be.

I'm not saying they're all criminal, I'm sure most of the offers are totally upright and valid, but if they are real companies and if it's such a great deal why can't I have it in writing?

I appreciate the fact that fewer people respond to a direct postal drop (I actually read the flyers before I throw them away, but then, I am in the business), but I want to feel safe, peaceful and secure in the comfort of my own home, I don't want hassle, I don't want *Angst*. I don't want salespeople knocking on my door, disrupting my nap, disturbing me when I'm in the middle of painting the spare room.

And how do decent companies expect you to trust them when they employ the same tactics as shady ones?

Just give me something in writing. That's what I want.

Oh, and stay away from my bloody door.

STRONG MIND AND STRONG MUSCLES
(TIME TO CLAIM BACK MY LIFE)

I could have gone to bed early – hell, my body deserves to go to bed early after what it's been through in the past few days – but I'm wired, I'm floating on a sea of elation and I know I won't be able to sleep so I go to the gym. Before Sarah I used to work out on a regular basis, three or four times a week. But once she'd sunk her claws into me that changed. Oh, sure, it was slow and gradual: she didn't sit me down and forbid me to go, but she always wanted us to 'do' things together, even if it was just sitting at home watching TV. Gradually my days for the gym dropped to two or three a week, then two, then finally I was lucky if I could manage one. It's funny, really, because I still think of myself as quite fit and I've kept my gym membership going, but it's been three weeks since I've passed through these doors. Three weeks.

I've never really thought about it before, about how I let Sarah control my life, but she did. I was such a weakling. My will was impotent. I was useless, weak, a fool. At the time I thought I was making decisions, but I wasn't, not really. Oh, sure, Sarah let me choose my own food from the Chinese take-away, but it was always her decision whether we ate Indian or Chinese or had fish and chips. I thought we were having discussions, that we were both compromising, that I was being kind and a gentlemen in letting her have her way (she used to get so upset and claim her stomach just couldn't face a curry the first few times I expressed an interest in anything other than pizza or sweet and sour chicken or whatever it was she particularly fancied that night), but I was a wimp. If we'd stayed together I would have become one of those hen-pecked men who aren't trusted to collect the correct newspaper from the corner newsagent.

All that's about to change. It's time to claim back the real me. Or the new and improved me.

I decide to have a real session, none of this hurried namby-pamby business of having to get back to Sarah. I could really start hating her, but I'm honest enough to accept my share of the blame. I let her control my life. I let her stomp all over my heart and my self-esteem and look at where that got me. No one (bar one's own mother and perhaps one's father but definitely not including siblings or spouses or probably even one's children) will ever love and look after a person as much as that person needs or wants. Everyone is looking out for number one and it's up to me, as my own man, to ensure that I am happy and satisfied. Sarah wanted to be in charge, that made her happy. She sure as hell wasn't concerned with my happiness.

They're playing the theme tune from *Rocky* in the changing room. I cock my head and listen for a moment, wondering if this is one of the songs Sarah played while she was screwing Jed. (I know she likes to make love to music and match her thrusts to the tempo when it's not a slow song.)

And what about poor Lionel Richie? For ever more I'll associate his music with the smell of vomit and the sight of Jed's face as he came into my Sarah. And no one, certainly not a singer who entertains millions, deserves such an association. That's another black mark against Jed and Sarah, making me involve a man who's innocent of wrongdoing and whose voice just happened to be in the wrong place at the wrong time. An acrid taste forms in my mouth as I hear Lionel Richie's voice in my head and I take a deep breath and force my thoughts away. I am Alexander. That is my mantra, and I repeat it internally. I am Alexander. I am Alexander. I am Alexander. And suddenly I feel better.

A surge of excitement shoots up my spine as I enter the exercise room. Previously I'd always been plain old Alex intent on my weights and repetitions, clocking heart-rate and muscle mass and all that, but now, whoa, hold on world, I am Alexander. A man in charge of his own life.

I'm not a fool, I know that outwardly I still look the same (except for the stitches on my head), but it must be because I'm more aware, or the confident way in which I carry myself, for I'd swear that people notice me when I enter the room. I'm not conceited. I know I'm not a gorgeous hunk and I know that not every man, woman and child in the world will instantly love and fancy me, but I know I've got something going. I'm special and sexy and I'm oh-so-ready for action. I'm strong and confident and I know where I'm headed.

I've always thought all that talk about gyms being pick-up places for singles was just so much garbage, but that was because Alex wasn't looking, because Alex wasn't invited to participate in such an activity. But as Alexander it's obvious I've entered a whole new world.

I could get used to this.

No, I'm used to it already. This is how it should be.

After I've jogged two miles on the treadmill I head for the rowing machines. A buxom blonde sits at the one next to mine as I begin to row. (Sarah would insist on telling me the woman's a fake blonde, but if I listened to Sarah I'd have to believe there wasn't a single natural blonde in all London, that they were confined by quarantine laws to Scandinavian countries.) The blonde – fake, natural, who cares?, she looks good – is wearing makeup and her nails, painted blood red, are so long that last week I would have called them talons (and then not kindly). The overall look is rather cheap and tacky, sort of like a housewife striving to look more like a prostitute to win attention from her straying husband, but I'm instantly turned on.

Yesterday afternoon, before my moment of catharsis, before

I became Alexander, it would have been a real turn-off: I would have thought she was trying way too hard for the gym, but today I think she's fantastic. Women should look after themselves, and I bet she keeps her bikini line and pedicure in tip-top condition all winter long.

'Hi,' she says, and smiles at me as I'm wondering if I'll get a chance to see for myself if she's a natural blonde.

'Hi,' I say, turning to look her in the eye. And in that split second I see lust flash between us. She wants me. Sure, she might be a psycho or desperate or even diseased, but I don't care, I can handle myself and, besides, it's probable she's just like me, feeling horny with a need for some pleasant relief of that ache.

I think all this press about women never thinking about sex is a con. I bet they think about it as much as, or more than, we do. They've simply got more control than men. You can't tell me that women never go out shopping or to a bar or even to a gym and don't wish they could take a particular man home with them and screw his brains out. Maybe a woman is less likely to act on her impulses than a man (I blame this on society), but I'm as certain as I'm certain about anything that women feel the same as we do. We're all animals, not bodiless minds in perfect control. Our bodies scream out for sex. It's an instinct thing.

'I'm Kate,' says the blonde. She starts to row and I slow so that we're pulling in sync.

'Hi, Kate. I'm Alexander.'

Even as this is happening I know it's pretty inane as conversations go, but I know – somehow – that in half an hour or an hour Kate and I are going to be shagging. I smile at her, then see her eyes widen and her pupils dilate slightly. Oh, yes, I'm in. Alexander is going to get lucky. Women who look like her don't play hard to get. And what's the point in waiting, in denying yourself pleasure when the sex is inevitable?

'What happened to your head? Were you in an accident?' she asks.

Shut up and let's fuck. I think this, but I don't say it, I'm not stupid, I know we have to pretend, for formality's sake, to be interested in one another as people, when in fact it's just the body we want. I'm not interested in her for her conversational skills, but I can pretend. I'm a male, I'm a good actor when it comes to such things. As Alex I was actually interested in women, I enjoyed talking to them and look where that got me. Better not to have a heart and to expect nothing but the moment and then you won't get hurt.

'No, I was mugged a couple of nights ago,' I say. As it comes out it doesn't sound pathetic, it makes me sound dashing and exciting, like I live life to the full. A bar fight would sound too pedestrian and would make me seem a thug and the reality, that it wasn't a bar fight, that it wasn't a brawl, that it was a one-sided attack and that I was just an unfortunate bystander, would make me sound pitiful.

'Oh.' She looks impressed so I decide to tell her the truth. Alexander's truth.

'I was walking home alone after a night out and these two hooligans jumped out and demanded my money.' True, true, all true, if not the whole truth.

'Did you give it to them?' she asks.

'No way. "Not even over my dead body," I told them.' This is the truth, or would have been the truth if I'd been Alexander on the night I was mugged.

'Really? You stood up to them? What happened then? Did they hit you?'

I shrug modestly. I've seen what I'd wanted to happen in my mind enough times so I don't have trouble describing what would have happened had I been Alexander that night and not cowardly Alex. 'They had a knife,' I say.

'A knife?'

'Uh-huh. They both attacked me, but I managed to punch one on the nose.' I had punched someone on the nose, just not the mugger. I know what it's like to feel crunching bone and cartilage with my knuckles, to see the blood erupt like a geyser. 'The bloke I hit went down, but the other managed to get me on the side of the head.' I indicate my stitches. 'I thought I was a goner, but I shook him loose and then I kicked the knife out of his hand. As soon as that knife skittered away on the pavement it's like their courage disappeared, just like that, and they ran off.'

'Wow. I'm impressed.' Her voice is huskier.

Does the talk of violence excite her? Does she see me as a powerful man? Does she think I'm strong and assertive and flowing with enough testosterone to satisfy her?

I spot a dimple on one of her cheeks and I grin. Oh, yes, I'm going to enjoy this. For two years I've slept with no one but Sarah, for two years I was faithful to that trollop while she was screwing around, and now it's my turn for some fun.

I know I promised myself a long workout, but let's just say I'm not disappointed when Kate invites me back to her place for a drink. Sex is, after all, very good exercise if you're doing it right.

MAKEOVER DAY, OR THE
PHYSICAL EXORCISM OF ALEX

Monday morning I wake up feeling refreshed as if my four hours of sleep had been twelve. All this adrenaline, all this excitement, all this hope for the future, all this new attitude is keeping me going. I know it won't last, that at some point I'll have to go back to my seven or eight hours of sleep a night, but while I don't seem to need it I'm not going to complain. It leaves me so many more hours a day to implement my plans.

I smile as I slide from bed. My bed. In my room. After four hours of hot, steamy sex with Kate (I said it would be a good workout), I kissed her goodbye, left my mobile number and walked home. I don't think she was disappointed that I didn't stay. She didn't seem disappointed.

But did she really want me to stay? Did she want to sleep in my arms? I snort to myself. Why the hell should I care? I'm not Alex. Alex would care, Alex would have stayed the night, Alex would have cuddled with her in the morning, but I am not that man. I will never be that man again. (And Kate didn't seem upset when I said goodbye. She didn't act let down. It's simply likely that she doesn't sleep very well with a stranger in her bed.)

I may see Kate again, I'd like to see her again, but it'll be for the sex. The last thing I want or need at the moment is a woman who thinks she has the right to tell me what to do. And even though she lives in a shared flat with one of her girlfriends there wasn't a single book in sight. Not one. Just some glossy women's magazines. I can't take anyone seriously who doesn't own at least two or three books. Airport thrillers, romance novels, anything will do, I'm not fussy. But no books at all? That's like trying to talk to someone whose musical taste never progressed beyond Michael Jackson's *Thriller*. Sure I liked it when I was a child, it was an amazing album for its time, but life goes on. Tastes change. There's always something new to try.

I slip into the bathroom just as I hear Noreen's alarm clock go off in the next room. 'Excellent,' I say, in a Bill and Ted voice, mimicking Keanu Reeves. I feel like I'm leading a blessed life, that since my rebirth as Alexander luck and fortune have been on my side and will continue to be so for the rest of my days. If I was still Alex, I would have left my room just as Noreen slammed the door of the bathroom and I would have been forced to wait half an hour for her to finish washing all that hair as I hopped up and down, growing more and more desperate for the toilet.

When I get my own house I want at least three toilets. Five people for one toilet is just stupid. It's ludicrous. Who designed this flat conversion anyway? Five bedrooms and only one toilet that's locked away in the bathroom, unavailable whenever anyone has a shower or a bath, is verging on a the inhumane. It's a fact of life that people need toilets, no use glossing over it or pretending that that side of life doesn't exist. And it's not like we can go outside and duck behind a tree: we'd be arrested if we tried that in London.

But at least today it's Noreen who has to wait. I'm glad I'm no longer nice or I'd have to offer her the use of the toilet and then she'd probably say yes and ask if I'd mind if she had a shower as she was in there. What a drag being considerate is. No wonder most people are selfish – it's more comfortable. I'm certainly finding it so. And my bladder thinks so too.

After I shower and dress I grab my chequebook, stop by the bank and withdraw a thousand quid. It's makeover time. Let's see if Sarah was right and a new haircut and clothes can make a difference. I don't feel that I need them, but I want them. I'm the new me and I deserve to look my best. I want to look suave and sophisticated. I want all traces of the loser eradicated. Alex has to be annihilated, both physically and mentally. It's like an exorcism. I can feel him inside my head at times clamouring to get out, but I won't let him. He wants to be soft, he wants to moderate my actions, he wants me to offer Noreen the bathroom first tomorrow. But I won't let him contaminate me. Alexander is stronger than Alex is. Alexander is a winner. And I am Alexander.

Now I just need the clothes and the haircut that will show it to the world at a glance. For the first rule of success is to look successful.

It's snip, snip, snip at the hairdresser's, one of those expensive salons that charges you two hundred pounds for a simple wash and style, but I have to say it's worth it. I look different. I normally have a short back and sides, and this new style is as easy to maintain, but I look good. Better. I could be a playboy, the son of a media tycoon, a man who lives off the interest of his trust fund. What I do not look like is a loser who was just sacked from his last job. I don't look like Alex any longer. Alexander is here to stay.

(It's not only the haircut you're paying for, you're paying for the experience, for the secret little thrill of having an attractive brunette running her fingers through your hair and giving your shoulders a little massage before the shampoo, spending your time hoping she'll brush her breasts against your back just one more time. I say it's value for money.)

I give Bond Street a miss until my replacement credit cards arrive, but I do head to Savile Row and order two bespoke suits, buy a ready-made one from Austin Reed, plus new shoes, shirts, ties, a briefcase and some casual clothes. (I have to pop back to the bank three times for more cash.) Nothing ill-fitting or cheap for me. It's not a complete new wardrobe, but it'll do. The rest can come later.

I catch a cab back to the flat. Everyone's out working but me, thank God, and I can make the necessary phone calls in peace and quiet.

I've never really played chess, but now I'm beginning to wonder if I should take it up as a hobby, for I, Alexander Fairfax, am a master tactician. Even Napoleon would be proud of my thrusts, jabs and initial forays into warfare. For this is warfare. Life is warfare. Me versus everyone else, and I'm determined to come out the victor. Starting with Wilmington-Wilkes.

'Hey, Steve,' I say, to Steve Kasinski at Cornwallis Investment once the obligatory minute of small-talk is out of the way, 'I've got a new campaign you're just going to love, but I can't sit on it long. Can we set up a meeting for tomorrow?'

'Tomorrow?' I can hear the hesitation, but Steve owes me big-time. He'd hired a bunch of amateurs (cheap and cheerful, compared to the considerable amounts charged by Wilmington-Wilkes) for Cornwallis Investment's last ad campaign, and when it all fell through at the last minute, he came scurrying to me with his tail between his legs, desperate to save his job and his reputation. In three short days I'd pulled it all together and salvaged what might have been his very short career. 'I was planning to ring Wilmington-Wilkes in a few weeks to start work on our winter campaign.'

'I've gone freelance, Steve,' I say. 'I'm no longer with Wilmington-Wilkes. I think the ideas I've come up with would be perfect for you, but if you're not interested I have someone else in mind. I just thought I'd give you first stab at it.'

'Well . . .' He still hesitates.

I wonder briefly if I should try to blackmail him over the cover-up of his near failure if he refuses, but I decide that's probably not a good approach to the man I want to be my first client.

Instead I try to be persuasive. 'We could meet for lunch tomorrow,' I say.

'Sure thing, Alex.' He gives in. He knows he owes me. 'Tell you what, you come in at half twelve and I can give you an hour. I'll get some sandwiches in and listen to your presentation.'

I say my farewells and hang up before he can think up any reasons to postpone our appointment. There's no way he can reach me to cancel, I didn't leave a number, and he'd never be rude enough to let me travel all the way to his office without seeing me.

My next two contacts are harder to persuade than Steve, but I've chosen my first targets carefully. I've always had an excellent working relationship with all my clients, but these three are special. They were my favourites and I made sure there was always plenty of money in the entertainment budget for me to take them out for expensive dinners. They know me as a person. Or they knew Alex and that's close enough for my purposes. I've gone the extra mile for them all and they've seen me at work, they've seen me come up with ideas on my feet so they know that I'm good and that I'm not just a body on a Wilmington-Wilkes team.

Half an hour later I have my first three meetings arranged. Tuesday with Cornwallis Investment, Wednesday with Quest Technologies, Thursday with Marriott Hotels.

I'll blow them out of the water.

I think I'll blow them out of the water.

I will blow them out of the water. My ideas are good, I know they are, even Alex would know they are. I will succeed. I can't not succeed. I am Alexander.

Next comes the necessary but more tedious aspect of setting up business on my own. At Wilmington-Wilkes they offer a complete advertising service: they come up with the ads, they produce them, they buy the space and decide where and when to place them. I can't photograph, film, or draw the campaigns myself, but fortunately not all of the Wilmington-Wilkes work is done in-house. I've always been a hard-working boy (bless me, no, bless Alex, I used to be so good and upstanding) and diligently recorded all of the names and numbers of the people I used on my campaigns in my personal address book just in case I needed to chase them up in the evenings or weekends. The old me was good for something after all.

An hour later I have it all arranged.

Not only am I a lean, mean fighting machine, I'm a suave, smooth-talking master of persuasion. I am hot. And soon all the world will know it.

'I rang you at Wilmington-Wilkes,' says my mother, the second I answer the phone, her tone hurt and chiding all at once, 'but they told me you no longer work there.'

Uh-oh. Here it comes. I can hear the storm brewing. But she won't yell at me, she won't raise her voice, she'll just sound wounded, sorrowful, disappointed in me, her eldest child.

'Were you planning on telling me?' she asks. 'I know I'm only your mother, but can you imagine how I felt, being told by a stranger that my son had left his job and I didn't know?'

'I'm sorry, Mum,' I say quickly.

'When did this happen?'

'Friday.'

'But we spoke on Saturday morning,' she says. 'I rang and told you all about the theft of my rhododendron. You could have told me then. Or at least sometime over the weekend.'

She's right. I could have done. I should have done. But I was too busy feeling sorry for myself on Saturday, I was too busy sticking my head in the sand like an ostrich, hoping my troubles would just go away if I didn't acknowledge them. And, to be honest, after the cinema fight it didn't even occur to me to phone her and give her the news. I was too full of myself. I wasn't in the mood to share.

'Why did you leave?' she asks. 'You were doing so well. And I thought you liked it there. This doesn't have anything to do with Sarah, does it?'

'It was the redundancy money,' I blurt out. I don't want her to know the truth. I don't want her to know that I was sacked. I don't want her to be ashamed. I want her to be proud of me.

But I'm lying to my own mother.

'Redundancy? I didn't know Wilmington-Wilkes was downsizing,' she says.

I feel a sweat break out across my forehead, over my whole body. She'll know. She always knows. She'll know I'm lying.

But I'm not a child now, I'm an adult, I'm a man, I'm Alexander. She won't know. She can't see my face. She won't see the lie written across my face.

'Well, no,' I say, somehow stopping myself babbling, 'they're not downsizing, not exactly. They just decided to get rid of a few of us and I leapt at the chance. I was ready for a change.'

'Oh, Alex, I know splitting up with Sarah hit you hard, but you didn't have to do this. Changing the rest of your life won't help matters. You need stability. Sarah really is wonderful. Maybe you should apologise and tell her you're sorry for whatever you did. She's such a nice girl. You should try to get back together. I'm sure she'll forgive you if you keep trying and show her that you mean it.'

And just like that it hits me. Even after what Sarah did to me I was protecting her. I was protecting her reputation. I didn't stand up for myself and tell my own mother that Sarah was the one at fault. I let my mother blame me. I was worse than pathetic, I was the lowest of the low. Well, no more. No more. I'm not prepared to shoulder blame I don't deserve, I'm not prepared to be pitiful now. Not in my new life. I'm different now. I'm strong and I'm the one in control.

'Sarah was having an affair,' I say. 'It's over between us. I don't want to take her back.' My mother doesn't need to know that Sarah never offered to come back.

'Oh.'

Have I shocked her? Poor Mum. I think that's the shortest sentence I've ever heard her utter. She's not usually at a loss for words. And then I smile. It'll be easy to reassure her. Life is good. Life is grand. My mother will see that soon, she'll be happy for me, she'll see how well I'm doing, she'll be so proud of me. I decide to set the record straight.

'Leaving Wilmington-Wilkes had nothing to do with Sarah.' Another lie but it's for a good cause. And then I tell her my plans for my own company. I don't mention clients or revenge on Wilmington-Wilkes or any of that, I just tell her how I've always wanted to be my own boss and test the strength of my own ideas. And as I say it I know it's true, it's merely that I never realised it when I was only Alex. It's easy to convince her that everything is going to be fine, that everything is going to be better than fine. For it will be. I know that it will be.

So you want to set up your own business? What do you call it? I could call mine Alexander Fairfax Associates or Fairfax Enterprises or Fairfax and Stone (in tribute to my sex goddess of all time, Sharon Stone, but I can't really explain that one to the clients, not with a straight face) or even Alexander Advertising, but I decide against such names. I have no need of the limited immortality such a name would give me. Fame is not the be-all and end-all of life. Money and success covers that ground. I do not require the mass public to recognise my greatness so long as those who are powerful and successful do. And my name in the company would give the game away. Kenneth is bound to hear he's lost some clients sooner or later and I don't want him (or more probably his subordinates like Jed) recognising my name. I only want Wilmington-Wilkes to discover my identity when I'm ready to reveal myself as a player. A major player.

I'll go for something more original.

I rather fancy something animal-orientated like Jack Rabbit. I could even have a logo with a cute little rabbit with long ears for listening and long legs for jumping high into the sky and leaping to success, but whenever I think Jack Rabbit I think Jack Rabbit Stew (not that I've ever eaten such a thing, nor do I even know if it's edible) and I'd rather avoid connotations of death and stewpots. Couldn't really show a picture of a dead bunny in a bowl on my stationery and business cards.

I could go for Phoenix. After all, I have been burned and risen from the ashes young and fresh and that name would reflect my rebirth, but it's not quite what I'm looking for. It's good, it would be good enough for Alex, but Alexander deserves more.

I'll stick with animals. I know. Duck-billed platypus. Platypus. Platypus Advertising. No, not quite. Platypus something. Platypus what? Platypus-fox. Unique. Different. I like it. My logo can be a furry little fox curled round a duck-billed platypus. Platypus-fox I shall be.

Next stop is to set up Platypus-fox as a limited company and start the associated bank account (that'll be easy as I want no loan). Afterwards I'll need to alter some old Wilmington-Wilkes contracts (copies of which I found tucked into my Filo-fax when I was searching out the telephone numbers of my contacts). I'll get my brother to set up my website (he's a computer person).

Platypus-fox, here we come.

SARAH, SARAH, SARAH

I listen to Sarah's voice as she answers her mobile and I could laugh as it strikes me. This is the woman I thought I was in love with only a few days ago and now she makes me feel nothing. Well, that's not strictly true: nothing but a desire for revenge.

'Hello?' she says.

'Hi, Sarah. It's Alexander.'

She hesitates and I wonder if she's even noticed I said Alexander. 'Oh. Hi, Alex. What can I do for you?'

'I just wanted to let you know that I lost my wallet.'

'Yes?' I can tell she's wondering if I'm about to break down and plead for another chance.

I'm not about to tell her that I was mugged, not even the new and improved story. Jed would probably ridicule it. And Sarah would never believe I'd punched an assailant then kicked away his comrade's knife. For the old Alex wouldn't have done those things. The old me couldn't have done those things. And I didn't do those things, now, did I? I, the old me, was pricked with a knife like a roast pig and then my money and watch were stolen. I put up no more resistance than a child losing his lollipop to the school bully.

I decide it's better not to lie directly so I don't bother making up some convoluted tale of loss, I stick to the point. 'I didn't get round to changing my address for the credit cards and bank card so they're sending them to your flat.'

'Oh, I see,' she says.

I know she's still wondering if this is some kind of elaborate ruse and suddenly I'm happy that I have an excuse to see her – and Jed, I know he'll be there – again. It'll fit in so well with my plans.

'They're supposed to arrive tomorrow,' I say, 'so is it okay if I stop by in the evening after work?'

'After work?' she asks.

A hot flush sweeps across my face and suddenly I feel inadequate. I experience again the shame, horror and outrage of my sacking. It's all come back. The impotence. The inaction. The lack of protest.

Then I feel anger as I think of that bastard Jed relating the tale to Sarah. I know he made the story sordid and ignoble, and cast me in the light of villain. And Sarah, naked and still straddling his hips in their post-lovemaking frenzy, would have felt a stab of pity and wondered how she could have spent two years with someone as pathetic as me.

As pathetic as Alex.

But I am Alex no longer. I am Alexander. (Alexander, Alexander, Alexander.)

And, Jed, old buddy, old boy, you ain't seen an ignoble dismissal yet. But you will. You will. That I promise you.

I smile, and I can tell that it's more like the flashing of my teeth and a silent snarl, but I'm feeling better and my flush recedes.

There's been an awkward pause while I collected myself, but I don't care, I'm in control now and it can only work in my favour if Sarah is, later on, totally shocked by my transformation. There's no need to give her any clues. She doesn't deserve warning. I'm not about to set off the air-raid sirens and let Sarah and Jed prepare for the storm I'm about to unleash on them. Oh, no, let them be surprised, let me take them by stealth and cunning.

I clear my throat, trying to make it sound as awkward as I can. 'Shall I come over at about seven?' I let my voice drop, let her think I'm humiliated that she knows about the sacking. (I am humiliated, I was humiliated, I will continue to be humiliated until that smug lecher pays for what he did to me.) 'Don't worry, I won't stay long.'

'Okay.' She's reluctant but she can hardly refuse when I'm being so civil.

We hang up and I smile, happy again. This is going to be such fun.

CHILDREN SHOULD BE
SEEN AND NOT HEARD

I think the Victorians had it right. Children should act like miniature adults. The world would be a pleasanter place if they did. I know that adults are still the same selfish bastards they were as children, but at least the full-grown human animal has the decency not to wail and whine and throw temper tantrums in the middle of the frozen-foods aisle at Tesco.

It's only in the past couple of hundred years that what we pukingly refer to as carefree childhood (like it was some sort of idyllic time, I was there, thank you very much, and I wouldn't want to go through all that again, even if it meant I could forget about any responsibility beyond feeding my pet fish) has been allowed to develop. Before that the little blighters were put to work and had to earn their keep just like the rest of us.

Children should not be allowed to talk incessantly during films, plays or any other sort of show. Parents should make some effort to control them. And children who do not behave should not be allowed out in public.

I don't care how non-politically correct this is. If children cannot behave they should be left at home. I'm sorry, but the rest of us don't think your snot-nosed little brat is cute. We much prefer the shy, quiet little girl who blushes when we ask her name.

And if parents won't even attempt to stop their children screeching and screaming then they shouldn't glare at us when we shush them. Those are my eardrums your little Billy is trying to break.

I don't see anyone until the evening when I venture into the kitchen. Amber and Noreen are both cooking. Noreen is a strict vegan and her food seems to consist of noxious mixes of lentils, lettuce and onions so it's not surprising that she's always cooking for one. Amber, on the other hand, is crafting a divine-smelling vegetarian lasagne and the scent of all that garlic sets me salivating.

'Hi, girls,' I say, by way of greeting, as I stride into the kitchen.

Both of them look up and smile. I imagine I see their eyes widening in appreciation of my new look, but as I'm on the lookout for any signs that they notice the changes in my appearance I have to admit that it's probably my mind playing tricks on me.

'Hey, nice haircut,' says Noreen. Trust her to be ruthlessly efficient and pinpoint the difference before Amber has a chance to wonder why I suddenly seem more attractive.

And I am more attractive. They – whoever *they* are – always say that true beauty is on the inside and I can feel my internal beauty, my strength, my confidence, seeping outwards through my pores. But the haircut and clothes help too. It's not only women who can benefit from a little fashion advice.

I'm wearing some of my new clothes and I wonder if Noreen will guess how much I've paid for them, but I'm already prepared for a counter-offensive. I'm planning on donating my old garb to Oxfam. That should halt some of her grumbling.

I'll be the first to admit that my new flatmates aren't people with whom I'm planning on decorating my new life, but I want them to like me. I tell myself that it doesn't matter if people like me or not, that that's negative thinking, that Alex would be concerned with such matters, that Alex would want everyone to like him, but I can't help it. I am Alexander now, not Alex, I know that, but I can still want to be popular, can't I?

And Amber and Noreen are pretty harmless. They'd be considered prey by anyone's standards so I don't have to get all ruthless and aggressive with them, I can relax a little. I can't drop my guard (a successful man never drops his guard), but there's no need to reveal the extent of my merciless ambition. I can be kind. I can seem kind. If I seem nice, if I act nice when I'm with them, they won't guess that I'm not nice. They won't guess that there's any difference between Alex and Alexander.

I grab a piece of pepper from Amber's cutting board before she can add it to the frying-pan. 'Thanks,' I say, taking a bite. 'That smells great.'

'There's plenty,' says Amber, 'if you want to share.'

I'd like to think she's coming on to me, that she finds me irresistible, but I don't kid myself. She's cooking enough for three. She's just being generous in offering me a meal.

An hour later we're all munching away (well, Amber and I are eating real food and Noreen's chewing and chewing and chewing the soggy-looking brown and grey mush on her plate) and I'm amusing them with the Kate-version of my mugging.

'I kicked the knife away,' I say, a smile on my face and my arms dramatising my retelling, 'and as it skittered along the pavement they turned and fled.'

Amber and Noreen are rapt and Amber even gives a little clap as I finish. 'I can't believe you stood up to them,' says Amber. 'I can't believe you're so positive about everything after last week. I know you were cool about Sarah and Jed, but after being sacked as well, you're amazing.'

Sacked. I knew the gossip wouldn't take long to reach her. After all, Amber is the friend of a friend of a friend of a friend of a work colleague, but still, it's only Monday and I left Wilmington-Wilkes on Friday morning. The gossip mill is obviously well developed in London. I glance at Noreen and can tell she's not surprised. They've clearly discussed it.

I decide to be vague. It wouldn't do for me to lie exactly but there's truth and then there's truth.

'Oh, that,' I say, waving my hand negligently. 'I've been wanting to leave Wilmington-Wilkes for a long time and the severance package they offered was generous so I jumped at the offer.' Let them think I was talking about redundancy. If they thought I didn't care they wouldn't worry; they might simply assume that the rumour Amber had heard had been wrong.

Noreen leans forward, treating me to a glimpse of her cleavage. 'What will you do now?' I'm suddenly happy that I've removed her from my vengeance list. She's annoying, too sincere and rather obvious, but she's really quite adorable in her own warped sort of way. Like a gremlin before the change.

'You're looking at the new managing director of Platypus-fox.'

'You're going to set up your own business?' asks Amber.

'I already have,' I say. 'In another week or so I'll need to find some offices and think about hiring staff.' And as I say it I know it's true. If I can sign up my first three clients, and I will, I know I will, I'll not only be able to afford a few assistants, I'll need them to manage my day-to-day affairs while I chase new clients.

Noreen frowns and suddenly looks disapproving. 'You're staying in advertising?'

'Yes,' I say. 'It's what I do, Noreen. I'm not going to give it all up and become a professional protestor like you.' I don't want to spend the next six months camped out in the branches of some tree to prevent its destruction, even if I don't want it to be chopped down. It's just not me. I wouldn't be comfortable. I'd rather donate money. Not time. Time is too precious to waste on such endeavours when they'll only chop down another woodland while you're distracted by the first.

'But you could do so much more with your life,' says Noreen.

Don't be ludicrous. It's all about success.

Amber meets my gaze and I see her lips twitch. I have to look away or I'll start grinning inanely.

'I'm off to Cambridge for a presentation on Wednesday,' I say, wanting to change the subject.

'Really?' says Amber. 'I grew up near Cambridge. It's a fantastic city.'

Noreen sniffs. 'I suppose the architecture is pretty.'

Does she have to keep inserting herself into this conversation? Can't she see that I'm trying to talk to Amber? That I want to talk to Amber?

'Why don't you come along?' I say to Amber. The words spill out of my mouth before I can stop myself. What the hell am I doing? What was I thinking? I don't have time for holding hands. I don't have the time to spend a day with Amber. I have work to do, I have to get Platypus-fox off the ground, I have to get my revenge, I need to make myself into a success. Alex would want to spend a day with Amber, but I've got so many things to do. (Alex wouldn't have had the balls even to ask her, the sorry loser.)

'On Wednesday?' says Amber. She looks a little surprised, but she's smiling and then she nods. 'Okay, I can take the day off. I'll come.'

Amber works at Christie's, as some kind of trainee valuer in the art department. I guess the paintings can wait another day for her contribution to their assessment.

'I'm busy on Wednesday,' says Noreen.

You weren't invited, Noreen. I certainly don't have time to spend a day with you, even if half of it will be taken up with my meeting.

Amber turns to Noreen. Amber has to know that it was her I was inviting, doesn't she? Of course she does, Alexander, she's a clever girl and you were really obvious. Like a schoolboy with a crush.

'Oh, what are you doing on Wednesday?' asks Amber.

Noreen doesn't have a proper job, as far as I can tell. I think she performs odd jobs, but mostly she lives off the dole and dedicates her life – 'dedicates,' her word, not mine – to saving the world.

'We've discovered a greenhouse full of GM crops that we're going to destroy.'

What a cunning plan, Noreen. You're going to destroy the greenhouse? Or do you mean the crops?

Protest all you want, Noreen, draw some attention to it if you think it's a good idea, but why don't you use your head and mull it over? There might be unforeseen consequences with GM plants that we need to worry about, but sabotaging the greenhouse and potentially releasing spores and God knows what else into the environment is hardly going to help. We all need to worry about unforeseen consequences. And we need a lot more than just gut reaction.

'We'll be leaving early,' I say to Amber, not wanting to get into a long discussion with Noreen in front of Amber. 'My meeting's in the morning.'

'That sounds fine. Maybe we can go punting in the afternoon.'

'I'd like that,' I say. And it's true. I would like to spend the day with Amber, I want to go punting on the Cam with her. But you're not Alex, Alexander, so don't get carried away. You can have a good day, you can play the nice man, but that's as far as it goes.

Remember that it's all about success and revenge.

As the evening wears on, and neither Amber nor Noreen shows any sign of wanting to leave the kitchen, I wonder if I'd be able to sweet-talk Amber into sleeping with me. The idea has its merits, then I catch myself and dismiss it. Amber is adorable, but I must remember that my prey is to be other predators. I must remain true to my motto. The nice do not deserve to suffer. They can't look out for themselves so it's up to me.

No, I tell myself, it's hands off. Damn.

But, oh, I think as I lean forward to take another slice of garlic bread, my thigh brushing Amber's, there's no law against a little harmless flirtation, is there?

After the first five minutes of our lunchtime meeting, Steve Kasinski forgets all about food and for the rest of the afternoon his forlorn-looking, half-eaten sandwich lies drying out on a plate in the middle of the table. The other sandwiches and the pastries (I don't bother to eat, I'm too busy talking) die the same death of neglect and I feel a rush of adrenaline and pride whenever I happen to glance at the abandoned food for it proves that my ideas are more distracting than a few mere hunger pains.

After ten minutes Steve halts the meeting and calls in his assistant. After ten more minutes Steve sends his assistant to scour the building for the rest of his team, and within half an hour the ten men and two women who work for Steve are arrayed around the table, all wide-eyed and astonished at my ideas. And before I can wonder if they'll invite me back for another presentation, Steve whisks me into the office of his boss and it's a done deal. We shake on it and I have my first client. Not wanting to appear too eager I tell Steve I'll send over the contract tomorrow and Steve assures me he'll sign it straight away and return it with the first half of the payment as agreed.

Wilmington-Wilkes would have demanded double the fee and probably received it, but for me, working on my own and needing clients more than money, it's money enough. And it's not bad for a third of a long day's work. Not bad at all. Of course I don't tell Steve that.

Instead of saying goodbye and sending me on my way like the unimportant backroom worker I was last week, Steve escorts me to the front door. As he shakes my hand I can't help wondering how long it will be before Wilmington-Wilkes contacts Steve and discovers they've lost a client. Two, maybe three weeks. Plenty of time for my new offensive. Plenty of time before they're even aware that I've poached a number of their clients. (But not all of them, I don't want them all. A lot of Kenneth's clients are bloody annoying, too demanding and interfering for me to want to take on that kind of hassle. No, I'll leave the awkward clients to Wilmington-Wilkes.)

To keep suspicion away – and for the health of my company – I know I need to draw in new clients, too. I need to be so big and so successful that by the time Kenneth and his cronies realise what I've done it'll be too late. Thank God they never got round to insisting we all sign the new contracts. Pity for them I never agreed to the non-competition clauses. But I can be magnanimous. I'll be glad to take on many of my old colleagues. I will, after all, need a large staff. And it'll be easy for me to sort the wheat from the chaff. I think I'll be very good at culling the bad from the good. In fact, I'm rather looking forward to it.

LET'S PLAY BALL

I arrive at Sarah's at seven, late enough so that Jed has a chance to be there, early enough that he'd have to leave work promptly to make it. I knock on the door and once again it's Jed who opens it. This habit of his is really beginning to annoy me. Does he think Sarah incapable of opening a door? Does he imagine that his puny little body would stand in my way if I truly wanted to go after Sarah? Is that how he sees himself? As her protector? No. I can see he only answers the door to gloat.

His smile fades as he gets his first good look at me. It's not what he expected. I don't look cowed and I'm certainly not defeated.

'Alex, you're wearing a suit,' he says, holding the door open like an idiot and blocking my view of the inside.

'No. Really?' I ask.

You can tell from the way his jaw muscles clench that he regrets his stupid remark.

'Are you going to invite me in?' I ask, before Jed has a chance to do so.

He flushes, and I smile inwardly. Score two for Alexander. This is so easy. I sincerely hope the bastard will show a little more backbone in the ensuing battles to come, but I'm confident he will once he gets over his initial surprise. I wouldn't want my victory to be too easy. It's going to be total and absolute, and I want to think I've earned it. I want to take more pleasure in my triumph over him than Jed took from his over me. I was a pushover and easy to defeat. Let's hope he puts up more of a struggle. I picture him like a great big fish wiggling his way deeper on to my barbed hook. It's an image I want to savour.

Jed opens the door wider and steps aside. 'Come in,' he says.

I stride past him and into the sitting room to find Sarah curled up on the sofa flicking through a magazine. As if she weren't waiting for me.

I nearly set down my briefcase on the coffee table like I used to when I was planning to work at home, but I resist. I'm not that Alex any longer. I am not Alex. I'm not. I am Alexander. I am Alexander.

'Hi, Alex,' she says, as she looks up, and I see her freeze. Her eyes widen and her gaze takes in all of me, from the top of my new haircut to the tips of my new shoes. 'You look—'

'Like you've been working,' says Jed, as he follows me into the room. He gives me a nasty little smile. 'Or was it out interviewing?'

I'm so happy I want to laugh. Jed's getting back his nerve and his efforts are so obvious that I want to jump into the air and kick my heels together with glee.

'I was sorry to hear about your job, Alex,' says Sarah.

I see the look of pity in her eyes. I'll accept pity from no one. Especially her. I loved her once and the only thing I want her to feel when she thinks of me is regret. Huge, serious, kick-yourself-for-the-rest-of-your-life regret.

I smile. A genuine smile, as I imagine her down on her knees keening for the loss of my love. I'll make her regret what she did to me, I'll make her suffer as I have suffered, I'll make her realise the ugliness of her true self, I'll cut away her excuses and leave her betrayals bare and stripped of euphemisms. She will feel shame for the rest of her life. 'It was the best thing that could have happened,' I say. 'The work environment was stagnating at Wilmington-Wilkes. I needed to make a fresh start.'

'Talk about sour grapes.' Jed's words are muttered but they're loud enough for us both to hear.

Sarah flashes Jed a look of disapproval, her eyes and eyebrows telling him to behave. I merely smile.

'Really,' I say. 'I should thank you, Jed, for organising such a little scenario. It would probably have taken me another year to get round to leaving.' It would have taken the old Alex a lot longer than that. I had been into comfort and stability in those days, I had had a place in the world and I had been happy to fill it. I would never have left. Not to set off on my own. Alex would have been content to plod on with the years passing by and every day the same.

'But I had nothing to do with it,' says Jed.

I tut and shake my head, then turn to Sarah. 'Really, he's so modest. He engineered the whole thing, you know, and I have to say I'm impressed. He saw a weakness and he went for the jugular.' Sarah looks confused. I turn back to Jed. 'But we won't go into ancient history, will we, Jed? That's last week and this is now, and I would so hate to spoil the happy couple's illusions.'

'Just what exactly are you implying, Alex?' asks Jed.

'Please, call me Alexander.'

'A new name for a new haircut?' Jed's tone is snide, but I retain my civility.

'No, a new image for a new me,' I say, the epitome of calm.

'So why exactly are you wearing a suit, Alex? Out to impress them at the dole office?'

Sarah frowns and even Jed can tell he's gone too far in front of her. He flashes her a little smile and shrugs as if to say he's sorry.

'I had business,' I say. Let them wonder. Jed will find out when I want him to find out and not before. Dismissing him, I turn to Sarah. 'Have my credit cards come?'

'I think so.' She picks up four letters from the coffee table and holds them out to me. 'These are for you.'

'Thanks,' I say, as I take them, feeling the plastic cards inside the envelopes.

'How did you lose your wallet, Alex?' asks Jed. 'Oh, sorry, I mean, Alexander. How did you lose your wallet, Alexander? Were you being careless of your property again, Alexander?'

I shrug as if it's no big deal. 'It was stolen. There are so many thieves in the world, don't you think?'

Sarah's had enough and she stands up. 'Boys, behave. We're all adults here.'

I grin. 'If you say so.' I glance around the room. Jed's obviously moved in or at least moved most of his stuff over. Sarah's CD collection has quadrupled over the weekend and a couple of abstract paintings hang on the walls where my photographs once were. 'The old place looks homey again. You've done well to fill it up.'

I can see Sarah glance at Jed, as if they've discussed this and are expecting me to throw a big fit, but I must say I'm happy to disappoint them.

'How's your room?' asks Jed.

'Fine. Fine. It'll tide me over until I find a place to buy,' I say.

'You want to buy?' asks Sarah. 'But I thought you were out of work.'

I laugh. 'Oh, ho, is that what you told her, Jed?' I shake my head. 'I was sacked, that much is true, but out of work? Hardly. I've never been busier.'

'And what exactly are you doing, *Alexander*?' asks Jed. Alexander he says. Emphasising the word. Trying to ridicule my new name.

'Oh, a bit of this and a bit of that. You know. I like to keep myself busy.'

'You've got a new job?' asks Sarah. 'Already?'

'I'd be happy to give you a reference, old boy,' says Jed. 'I know it was just bad luck last week, you really are a good worker. Normally. I never had any complaints before Friday.' What a creep. It's obvious he's just trying to make sure Sarah doesn't find out what he's really like.

I want to take a knife and cut off your fingers one by one, mate, and then your toes and after that your nose, and then how much will Sarah love you? And maybe I'll stab your testicles or cut them off completely so that no poor children will

106

be brought into this world cursed with your genes. What do you think of that, eh, Jed?

'Thanks, that's very generous,' I say aloud, 'but I don't need any references.'

I can see they're dying with curiosity, but I don't say any more. Let them wonder. Let them stew. You can't have everything you want out of life, can you?

'So,' says Sarah after a moment, trying to fill the gap, uncomfortable as always with silences, whether polite, or like now, not so polite, 'where are you thinking of buying?'

'I don't know. Kensington or Chelsea, Mayfair or Belgravia, somewhere like that,' I say.

Jed snorts. 'Looking for a studio flat, are you?'

'No, no,' I say, 'a proper home. I'm getting fed up with all this moving around. I'll look for somewhere with at least three or four bedrooms. Maybe a flat. Maybe a house. I'll see what I can find.'

'But how will you get a mortgage?' asks Sarah.

'A mortgage? I don't need a mortgage.' And that's the truth. By next week I won't need a mortgage. I'll be able to buy myself a nice little three or four-bedroom place for cash once I sign up a few more clients.

They look confused and I can see more questions forming on their lips so I decide to leave. Conversations with the enemy are so tedious when you're all trying to be civil.

I take another look around the sitting room, my eyes halting on the stereo. 'Once I move into my new place I'll come round and collect my TV and hi-fi.'

Sarah glances at Jed. Jed opens his mouth to protest.

I smile at them both. 'But you can keep the video. Consider my half a moving-in present to Jed.'

Being single and being Alexander is better than anything Alex ever dreamed about. I absolutely love being Alexander. It's like the rest of my life was some bizarre dream, perhaps a play where I was forced to act out a part that was nearly me but not quite. I feel more myself than I've ever felt before.

I leave Sarah and Jed's on a high. I'm so pumped up for action I want an excuse, any excuse, to pummel some sorry loser into the ground. I need action.

Not wanting to punch any old someone walking down the street – I'm not a complete animal, I have my principles – I go to the gym. As soon as I enter the fitness room I see Kate and then I smile this wolfish smile of victory. A shag will do just as well as a fight to alleviate my restlessness. Kate blushes, she actually blushes, when she sees me, like she's embarrassed, like she's never done anything like that before when I know all too well that she has.

'Hi, Kate,' I say, as I climb on to the bike beside her and begin pedalling.

'Hi.' She smiles at me and then looks away, her flush deepening.

I'm really quite amazed that she can blush. She must have had dozens of one-night stands over the years. Surely she's beyond such maidenly responses. And then I remember that she is a natural blonde (ha, so there, Sarah) and that her skin is really quite thin and translucent despite the layers of makeup, so her blushes would be more obvious than most other people's.

'You didn't call,' I say. As if I've had time to notice. I figure I might as well go on the offensive before she has time to get all coy and cold and blame me for not phoning her.

'No.' She shakes her head. 'I was hoping to bump into you here.'

'Did you come yesterday?'

She blushes again and I laugh. She did, she came to the gym on Monday, hoping to see me. Poor dear, she must have been so disappointed when I didn't show up.

'Do you fancy a coffee?' I ask.

'Now?' She looks startled. I have, after all, just arrived.

'Why not?'

Her surprise turns to pleasure, that I would give up my workout to be with her, but I plan that she will be my workout.

And, of course, that's what happens. I never realised how valuable my gym membership was before. I may have missed out on the rowing machine and weights, but I get plenty of exercise of the horizontal kind.

Another five hours of sex with Kate and I'm really beginning to like her. Not enough to make firm arrangements for a date, but enough that I don't mind confirming for her that I will see her again. I don't know when, I quote late nights at work as an excuse, but I'm willing to allow her to be a member of my harem.

I feel a flicker of that old possession feeling – Alex again, trying to break free – as I leave Kate in the middle of the night. She looks sad this time and even I, the Alexander I, can tell that she wants me to stay. But I don't. I can't. That is something Alex would have done. He, me, I, as I was then, would have stayed whether I wanted to or not. But I'm Alexander now. I do only the things I want to do. I am not nice. I will not be a nice man. I will not condemn myself to that road again. I will not be a drone and a drudge to niceness. I will not. I. Am. Alexander.

Punting isn't as easy as it looks. And it doesn't look easy.

When you go to Cambridge and walk along the river you see all these students, or people of the right age pretending to be students, nimbly standing on the stern of their punts (if a punt has such a thing as a stern), holding a long pole, lifting it, letting it slide through their hands and hit the bottom then pushing. These silly little flat-bottomed boats are propelled by this single pole pushing against the river bottom. They're certainly not as fast as a good rowboat, or is that just me?

The boats – other people's punts – glide up and down the river Cam, weaving in and out, avoiding swans and ducks and everything in their path. But, alas, the same cannot be said for me.

I'm standing on the end of the boat (not in a suit, I'm not a moron, I brought a change of clothes), a small, flat area that's wet and slippery, trying desperately to steer around an overhanging tree rather than straight through it. I'm having limited success and at least Amber doesn't have to duck.

She giggles as I dodge a particularly stout branch at the last moment, narrowly saving myself from being hurled into the river. The sound is joyful. And contagious.

Soon I'm laughing too, we're both laughing and I realise I'm having fun. This is the best day I've had in ages.

My meeting went well, I now have two clients. Everything's working out just as I planned.

I stick the pole into the river, give it a little tug, but it's stuck. I have a moment's panic. What do I do? I can't lose my pole. I need my pole to steer, I need the punt to go forward.

Amber holds her stomach she's laughing so hard. 'Let go,' she puffs, trying to speak over her giggles, 'let go.'

If I was Alex I'd freeze, I wouldn't be able to let go, my fingers would refuse to unclench and I'd be left there swinging from the pole as the boat carried on. I'd be hanging on desperately, trying to balance so I wouldn't fall into the river, but I'd be sliding down, down, down. Fortunately I'm Alexander and I have Alexander's luck if not Alexander's style at the moment, for if I'd been paying attention, if I'd kept myself alert, I wouldn't have lost control of it in the first place.

I let go of the pole and I stand there and the punt glides miraculously forward and slows and ever so gently bumps against the shore and we are saved. I jump out and pull the punt up on to the bank. I help Amber out and then we stand side by side and contemplate the sight of our lone pole sticking up out of the water.

It looks sad somehow, abandoned, and then I start to laugh. And Amber's laughing and we're choking and chortling and snorting it's just so funny. It's one of those private jokes that you have to be there for that Amber and I will be able to crack up over for weeks to come. We're not going much further by river today.

If I'd been Alex I would have ended up in the water. If I'd been Alex I'd be sopping wet. If I'd been Alex I would probably have tumbled into the river and the pole would have come unstuck and hit me on the head and I would have been knocked unconscious and I would have drowned, or Amber would have had to leap in and save me.

But I'm not Alex.

My laughter dies away.

I'm not Alex. I'm Alexander and I shouldn't be indulging in this silliness. I should be working for the future. None of this is going to help me. I don't need to know how to punt to make it in the boardroom.

And then Amber turns to me and looks up at me with her

wide grey eyes and she smiles a smile of such tenderness, she's
so pretty and so attractive, that I think it doesn't matter. None
of that matters at this moment. I can take this one afternoon
off: Amber doesn't know I shouldn't be acting this way, Amber
won't tell anyone, she won't give me away.

I nearly kiss her, my lips are ready, her lips are ready, but I
don't. I can't. I won't do this to Amber. Amber isn't the kind of
woman I need.

Thursday's meeting is a repeat of Tuesday's and Wednesday's. Well, strictly speaking, that's not true. The client and the ideas are different, it's only the speed of the success that is the same. Wilmington-Wilkes has become so stale and predictable that it's easy to impress others with my fresh campaigns. At the end of my first three presentations I have my first three clients.

Maybe Jed does deserve my thanks. If it weren't for him I would never have had the balls to go freelance. Maybe just before I disembowel him with the final thrust of my vengeance I'll show him my genuine gratitude for his help in turning me into Alexander. I am, after all, a stickler for fairness.

Now that my career is on its way to becoming a runaway success, it's time for some justifiable vengeance. With all the fun I'm having, both professionally and socially, I must never forget my prime objective of revenge. The new me has made a first brush against Sarah and Jed's supposed togetherness, and Wilmington-Wilkes will feel my bite before too long, but if I'm to do this properly I need some practice.

It's Thursday evening now and I've got special plans for the night that have nothing to do with being single, free and wealthy.

After a mild flirtation with Amber over dinner I retire to my room for a well-deserved nap. I'm tempted to invite her to join me in bed, but I don't want to hurt her and I can't afford for tiredness to slow me down tonight.

At ten minutes to midnight I wake up before my alarm and climb out of bed smiling. If I thought I was an action hero at the cinema when I broke that bloke's nose (I must have broken it, there was that satisfying crunch and all that blood), then tonight I will become a true superhero. Not anything corny like Batman or Spiderman (I mean, come on), I will be Justice and Judgement rolled into one. Prosecutor, jury, judge and executioner all at once.

I slide on a pair of faded black jeans and a black T-shirt. I almost take my black jacket, but it's too confining – I need freedom of movement – so I grab a dark jumper instead.

I slip out of my room. The flat is silent but for the sound of a radio in Clarence's room so I'm careful as I make my way to the front door. A moment later and I'm free, I'm outside and the night is mine. I walk down the street, strolling, casual and confident on the outside while inside my blood is boiling. I am so ready.

My run of bad luck (though part of me acknowledges that maybe it was good luck in disguise) all started with those spotty teenagers who trashed my car. I don't delude myself that I'll be able to find the exact culprits, I know I wouldn't recognise them if they passed me in the street, but this one at least is a mutable form of revenge. Any gang of spotty youths will do. I see them attacking a car, I see them breaking a window, hell, I see them breaking a milk bottle and they're mine.

The only thing I need to avoid is the police. And areas where there are CCTV cameras (see, good people of London, those cameras do work, at least against a good boy like me). I'm not overly concerned about getting black eyes or a bloody nose. If someone mars my pretty face (it would be a shame for my sex life, which I'm hoping to expand, but at least I've already got Kate), I can explain it away as a minor car accident or something like that. It certainly won't halt my revenge.

I pass a few couples and a handful of lone men wending their way home after a night out at the pub, but I know it won't be long before they're all tucked up in bed. Thank God for eleven o'clock closing time. In the past I'd always resented being kicked out so early, but now I'm thankful that all those hardworking men and women will be safely behind locked doors. Wouldn't want them to witness what I'm planning, poor dears might get rather alarmed and upset. Give it another hour and all honest folk'll be in bed.

I wander the streets, heading nowhere in particular, just walking. Just walking and waiting.

A bit after one a.m. I hear the sound of breaking glass. I sprint towards the noise and as I round the corner I see two young boys of nine or ten crouching between two cars, waiting to see if anyone has noticed the noise. The passenger window of a BMW across the street is broken and I see the young hooligans smiling and nudging one another. Now, I'm not as big a fan of BMW as I used to be, not after what they did to Rover (and after all their promises too), but they make some damn fine cars and I'm not about to stand by and let any vehicle be desecrated. There's a special bond between a man and his car and it's a form of emasculation to deliberately damage all that metal and glass. I'm sincere when I say it's sacrilege.

I step between the cars and out into the street. It's quiet but for the distant hum of traffic, but in this London suburb the houses are in darkness and parked cars are lining both sides of the road. Not a creature is stirring outside our little drama.

I hear another giggle and then they see me. The boys drop their rocks and they turn and run away. They run from me.

No. This is too easy. This isn't what I wanted. I nearly shout for them to stop, but I don't want anyone to hear me. It wouldn't look right for a grown man to be seen chasing such small children. People seem to think youngsters are incapable of real mischief, but I know it's not the age that matters, it's the soul. I was always an angel, I never did anything wrong, I was not a bad child, but I bet Jed was always plotting and conniving and getting others into trouble, acting innocent and passing any blame to his unfortunate co-conspirators.

I give chase, my long strides eating up their head start until I'm nearly on them. The little fools stick together and it's easy for me to reach out and grab them both by the collars.

'Just where do you think you're going?' I ask, lifting them from the ground.

'It wasn't me, it was him,' says the blond one, pointing a finger at his chubby friend.

At this revelation the chubby one stops fighting me and starts trying to kick the smaller blond boy. 'Shut up,' he says. 'I didn't do it, you did. It's my word against yours. So there.'

The blond boy splutters. 'But—'

'Boys, boys,' I say, shaking them ever so gently. Or maybe it isn't that gently. 'You're both to blame and I'm sure the police will be happy to accept my eyewitness account.'

The chubby one turns his baleful, piggy eyes on me. 'Oh, yeah? Well, you didn't see a thing. It was a group of bigger boys, we were just watchin'.'

'Oh, really? Now, tell me, who is the police going to believe? You? Or me?' I look fierce as I glare at the two criminals. And suddenly it hits me that they're very young. Why are they out on the streets at this time of night? Did they sneak out? Or don't their parents care? I almost relent and release them, but then I picture my Jaguar defaced and wounded. It's boys like these who grow up to destroy things of beauty like my car. They're old enough to know better. They're old enough to learn.

I lift the boys higher – this is better than weightlifting at the gym – and they renew their little kicks, aiming both at one another and at me.

'Maybe we don't need to involve the police,' I say. I never intended to involve the police, I'm a vigilante, I don't have time for all that nonsensical paperwork and due process.

'Really?' The blond one looks hopeful.

And then it hits me like a sledgehammer in the gut. If I'm not going to the police there's nothing I can do. I can't punch them, I can't beat them up, they're way too young. It'd be child abuse.

'We'll never do it again, we promise,' mutters the chubby one, but even the old Alex could have told he's insincere.

I have no choice. I have to let them go. There's nothing I can do.

'I'll let you off this time,' I say, knowing I'm being ineffectual, 'but don't do it again.'

And I'm forced to lower them to the ground and release them. They flee. The chubby one stops after ten yards and sticks his tongue out at me. 'Nah nah na-nah nah,' he says, in a singsong voice.

Horrible child. I bet that's exactly what Jed was like when he was that age.

I watch them run away.

So I can't solve all of London's crime problems. I never thought I could.

I start walking, heading in the opposite direction Chubby and his friend took and, after a few minutes, I hear a faint sound. Is that the sound of someone kicking a car? Could I be so lucky again?

My pulse speeds up and I'm smiling as I run and run. The sounds are getting louder and I know I'm right: someone's definitely trashing a car. I know I shouldn't smile, for someone's pride and joy is being dented and damaged, but I'm so anxious to confront them that I can't hold in my delight. I turn left on to a smaller street and then I see them.

Five boys in their teens, two of them nearly as big as I am. I run towards them and as I get nearer I call out, 'Hey, stop that.'

Like deer caught in the headlights of a big truck, they whip their heads in my direction and freeze.

I continue running towards them and as I plough into the stunned group I let swing with my right fist and punch the nearest in the stomach. No need to break their noses, I think, They're young, I wouldn't want to scar their faces.

I snarl. Those are Alex thoughts. The little thugs deserve to have bent and crooked noses for what they've done.

I feint and jab and use a right hook to hit a different boy on the nose and a great fountain of blood sprays out. He doubles over, clutching his nose. Is it broken? Is it broken? Is it broken?

Like a pack of hyenas the boys circle me, wary, but soon they'll rush in as a group and attack. One flicks open a knife. A switchblade. The boy – he looks thirteen – is threatening me with a knife.

The bloodlust roars in my ears and I'm readying myself for their attack when a wailing noise approaches. Sirens. The police.

I take off running, we all take off running, tearing away in the same direction. For now I am part of the pack. Our rivalries are forgotten as, together, we run to elude the police. Over a low wall, down an allotment path and behind a row of garages we all run together. At the garages we stop and I realise that this is their hideout, their den, the place they feel safest and strongest.

Suddenly they seem to remember that I'm the enemy and they gather in a group, waiting to see what I do. I can feel the Alex in me cringing in fear, not wanting confrontation, but I do not flinch. I am Alexander.

'Touch those fucking cars again,' I say, 'and I'll fucking kill you all.'

Sad I know, verging on the pathetic, I mean talk about an empty threat, but I can't think of anything better.

I turn away, presenting them with my back, showing my contempt, half expecting someone to attack me from behind, half wanting them to attack so I'll have an excuse to fight.

They do nothing. I walk away into the night, no longer concerned about the police. They didn't see me before and if they see me now they'll see a lone man walking along the street at night. They're looking for a group of teenagers. And I am not a teenager.

Tomorrow I'll ring the police anonymously and report the hideout. Maybe the police will keep an eye on the boys in the future. I certainly won't have time.

As I walk towards home it begins to rain. I turn my face towards the sky and the raindrops fall on to my face like a benediction, approval for what I have done, for what I am doing.

People suck, I decide. And there's nothing I can do to change that.

We're selfish and destructive and rather horrible when it comes down to it. Think about how long it takes to build a house compared with how long it takes to destroy it. Weeks and months to build. Only mere hours to destroy with a sledgehammer.

Civilisation is like this. It's taken us hundreds, no, thousands of years, to get this far, and give us a motivational speech from someone like Hitler or even just the hysteria that overtakes an angry mob and it's all gone in seconds. Where are our fine principles then?

In the wee hours of Friday morning I let myself back into the flat and collapse on to my bed for a few hours of sleep. I don't, by any means, think I've obtained justice and revenge against those yobbos out there who destroyed my car, but I like to think I've taken one small step for mankind in my quest.

Friday is a busy day, taking care of endless business details, looking into hiring an assistant, getting the rest of my stitches removed, working on new ideas and organising things for my existing clients.

Three. I, Alexander Fairfax, have three clients of my very own. They're mine. Earned by my hand, with my ideas, persuaded by my tongue.

It's fair to say that I can rate the first week of Platypus-fox as a success.

For one insane moment I nearly pull an Alex and invite my flatmates out clubbing. What horror. As fond as I've grown of Amber and Noreen in the privacy of our kitchen (I've hardly seen Clarence and Diana, the one too stoned to leave his room, the other at her boyfriend's most of the time), I don't kid myself. They're not the kind of people I can afford to associate with in public, not here in London. It's not my fault. It's a cruel world and I'm determined not simply to live in it but to thrive.

I retire to my room before my mouth can do any damage. (I like Amber, I'd enjoy her company and I know that's bad. Alex would enjoy her company, Alex would want to spend the night dancing with her and buying her drinks, but I'm Alexander, I'm Alexander, and I've got other plans.) I change into my clubbing clothes. Nothing too trendy or too dull: my new trousers and shirt reek sophistication. And money. Understated money. Let's never forget that success breeds success. I'm determined to have fun tonight, but I'm also on an agenda. If I'm going to be an ultra-successful business tycoon – which I will be – I need new friends. I don't kid myself, my old friends (well, most of them) go back a long way and I genuinely like them, but they're not the sort of people who get featured in the pages of *Hello!* magazine, are they?

(And I don't even want to see any of my old friends until I can wow them with my great successes and feats of derring-do, until I no longer need to fear the Alex in me rising up and fighting for control of my conscious self. I can't take the risk that Alex would gain strength in their presence. And I can't be seen in public with them either. I have an image to maintain. Standards.)

I say farewell to Amber and Noreen before I leave and I can see from their expressions that they're impressed, that they're dying to ask where I'm going, but they don't. I decide to leave them in suspense and then I'm out of the door. I walk down our little street and out on to the main road, and what do you know? Within seconds I catch a cab. Not ever in his long twenty-nine years did Alex catch a cab so quickly.

I tell the cabbie to head to Pyramid X.

He doesn't need an address. I'd never heard of Pyramid X until a couple of hours ago when I saw the listings in the newspapers, but the cabbie says he's been taking people there for months.

The cabbie knows where the in-crowd goes, but I had to look it up in a newspaper.

I blame Alex. He should have had more of a life. But I won't be a social reject like Alex. I won't.

Traffic is heavy and we're forced to crawl towards the door, but I don't get out, I want to be delivered to the entrance. We creep forward and I watch the people in the queue, all dolled up and ready, hoping that tonight of all nights will be the night when they're finally spotted by a model agency or a film director and told they have something special and that they can make it. The crowd snakes around the corner and I experience a twinge of discomfort in my stomach. What if they won't let me in? What if they expect me to queue like the rest of them? What if the bouncers refuse me entry?

I take a deep breath and think of daisy petals. Of course they won't refuse me. I am Alexander.

The car in front stops at the club and a slim, lanky woman – I swear I've seen her face before, not a model, not an actress, but one of those society girls continually cropping up in magazine events' photos – is assisted out of the back seat by her chauffeur and she saunters to the front door. The bouncers (two hulking testimonies to the power of weightlifting) smile, greet her and let her pass. She calls them Paul and Bobby (I hear her through my open window) and flashes them a winsome grin.

I'm only in a cab. Should I have come in a car?

Ignoring the crowds, knowing they're staring at me, I hand the cabbie his money, climb out and slam the door. Coolly, so coolly, I approach the entrance. The queue, full of ordinary Joes and wannabe Tracys, watches me, half in anger, half in awe, as I nod casually to the bouncers and greet both of them, 'Paul, Bobby,' without stopping, without slowing my pace. I don't smile, for that wouldn't do, that might give me away. They look at me, they wonder if they know me – they don't, not yet, but they will – and they step aside. I look right. I am right. I fit in. I've passed the first test. Sit back, world, and take notice.

Inside the music rolls over me like a wave crashing against the crumbling sand of a beach. It is loud, very loud, and for a second I wonder how the hell I'm supposed to converse with anyone in here and then I let my worries disappear. I remember it's all about hedonism and I smile. Thank God the music's loud: it'll drown out all that unnecessary small-talk. And if I do want to talk, I'll have to lean in close and shout into her ear like it was the faintest whisper. Oh, yes, I suddenly have a new-found respect for these club owners. They know how to ensure a good time. At least for winners like me.

I scan the crowd, getting a feel for the people and the scene. It's one of those ultra-trendy places that was probably a hidden pearl until word got out to the masses. At some point, perhaps tomorrow, perhaps today, please, God, not yesterday, the glamorous will turn their backs on this club and flee to somewhere else, the latest hip place that only those in the know would think to attend. I vow to myself that by the time that happens I'll be one of those people.

Pyramid X is crowded, but not too crowded, and from the look of things only a handful of punters are allowed in at a time.

I head to the bar and a path seems to clear for me, I don't even have to push my way forward, it's like magic. And the bartender flashes me a little smile and serves me right away, ignoring those poor bastards who're clutching their money, waiting to be noticed, and I know he's flirting with me. I'm momentarily surprised and then I'm flattered. I'm not interested, but I'm a tolerant fellow and it gives me a pleasant buzz to be considered lustworthy.

I order a vodka. Straight and simple. Alex would have ordered a martini, trying to be sophisticated. Or a beer. But Alex would never have come to a place like this, not while it was still *the* place to be. And Alex would never, ever have been served so quickly. I would have stood there, thirsty and tired and hot, clutching my money for ten minutes, waiting patiently to be served while others pushed their way ahead of me. Finally my date would have come to search for me and she'd find me just as the bartender turned his attention to me so it looked like he was only reacting to the presence of a female.

Thank God I am Alexander. Life is good.

I smile to myself, take a sip of vodka and catch the eye of a beautiful (beautiful, really beautiful) woman. She's wearing a scarlet dress and for an instant the lyrics to Chris de Burgh's 'Lady in Red' (my mother's favourite song and one she works into any familial celebration, be it Christmas, Easter or even Father's Day) flash though my mind until I suppress them.

She – I already think of her as my woman – is sitting at a table with two other women, both equally beautiful, but both wearing all black so that my woman stands out, looking so alive and hot enough to eat. She doesn't smile, neither do I, but she's as aware of me as I am of her and if I was any animal but man I'd be able to smell the sexual pheromones we're both secreting.

I stare into her eyes and she stares into mine, and it's like some corny film where our eyes meet across a crowded room. I hold her eyes and approach her table. Vaguely, out of the corner of my eye, I note that there are waitresses (short black leather skirts and lots of cleavage, proof enough that this club is owned by a man) serving the tables, American-style, so that the fashionable folk can avoid the jostling at the bar. I pass to the table next to hers where there is a free chair and take it with a brief smile and a nod for the couple seated so close together and so intent upon one another that they barely notice the chair's absence. I swing the chair and place it down with a little swirl right beside my woman, sliding into the seat and signalling the nearest waitress all at once.

'What will you have, ladies?' I ask. The music is loud and I have to raise my voice, but there must be some special acoustic design that makes this seating area slightly quieter than the rest of the room, and it's easier to hear than I expected.

I include them all but it's obvious where my interest lies.

They don't react to my presence, so used to such attention from members of the opposite sex that my appearance is nothing unusual.

One of the women in black, she looks about twenty-five – they all look in their mid-twenties – flicks her short blonde bob, shifts infinitesimally in her chair so that I'm afforded a quick glimpse of bosom before it's hidden away again. 'Cranberry and vodka,' says she, in a voice so posh I know instantly that I've chosen the right table.

The other woman in black, her perfectly straight brown hair stopping at her shoulder blades, tilts her head to one side, takes a sip from her wineglass and then says, 'I feel like champagne.'

Of course. They're testing me, seeing how deep my pocket is. Part of me wants to stand and leave right then and I think, Bitches, they're only after my money, they're not interested in me, and then I recall that I want something too. And it's not really sex, though that would be good: I want their social connections. I need women of a certain standard, a certain level. And money will be my password. Money and attitude. They'll have to be. They're all I have.

Finally I turn to my woman. The woman in scarlet. Her hair, it's difficult to describe, is a rich, deep brown, but I can see flashes of auburn caught in the lights of the club, and it's thick and shiny and luxurious, hanging half-way down her back, and I have to resist the urge to reach out and stroke it. Her eyes are bright blue, the colour of the perfect tropical sea that adorns postcards from around the world. Her height – it's difficult to tell, she looks small, slim, but not too petite. And her legs, her legs look nothing like the legs of a short person.

'Champagne,' she says, her voice slightly throaty in a way that screams sex. She flashes an unreadable look at her brown-haired friend. Perhaps this is a test they use to see if the male at their table will flinch at such a request, but I only smile.

The waitress arrives, looking bright-eyed and all too eager. Maybe she knows these girls, maybe she knows how much they spend and guesses how much she'll receive as a tip.

I order a magnum of their best champagne and a glass of cranberry and vodka. I know it's going to cost me a few hundred pounds but I decide it's an investment I need to make. And if the blonde ignores her vodka in favour of the champagne I won't complain. I won't say a word. I won't even deem it worthy of my thoughts.

If I want to join the high life – and I do – I have to prove that I can afford the lifestyle. No sense in them making a new friend who can't afford to eat out in the restaurants they like, who can't drop everything and fly off to St. Tropez for the weekend.

'I'm Alexander,' I say, and smile at each woman in turn before my gaze returns to the woman in red.

'Camilla,' she says, and holds out her hand. We shake and I feel an electric vibe pass between us. Camilla's beautiful blue eyes widen and I know she feels it too.

The blonde smiles briefly. 'I'm Della.' Her eyes turn to scan the room, casually, so casually, but you know she's on radar lookout for her own man for the night.

'Isabel,' says the third. She gives Camilla a little smile before leaning back in her chair, prepared to watch my progress with a shrewd eye, and I get the feeling that she's the hardest, most calculating of the group.

'I haven't seen you here before,' says Camilla, speaking into my ear so she won't have to shout.

That remark, if nothing else, confirms the signals she's been sending me. She thinks I'm memorable enough for her to have recognised me. I smile, somewhat ruefully. 'I've been busy.'

'Work?' she asks. I see her left eyebrow quirk and I think, You darling girl, and I want to take her into my arms and kiss her. But I don't. It's too soon. And this is too public. I'm not an untried teenager: I like to think I have a smidgen of control over my hormones. I know she's quizzing me, that's she's making certain I'm of the right quality and material wealth before she allows things to proceed any further, but I don't care. I'll have my questions for her too. I think my instincts were correct, but I need to make sure she's attached to the right crowd if this is to last the night.

I nod. 'I've been busy expanding my company.' True, all true, she doesn't need to know it's only been going for a week.

'Oh,' she says. I see her digest this. 'You're self-employed?' She doesn't know what to make of this. It might be good. Or really bad.

'I guess you could say that.' I laugh. 'I'm the managing director.'

She nods and smiles. Managing director, that sounds good. It could be good. 'And what do you direct?'

I lean closer, wanting to smell her perfume. 'I run an advertising company.'

'Really?' She's excited now. 'I work in PR, for KKJ.'

And then I'm the one who's excited. KKJ is a big firm. One of the best. Judging by her appearance and her accent I'd guess she's only working until she finds her Mr Right, living off her trust fund or Daddy's money (and not her salary – no doubt that barely covers her weekly wine bill) until she's safely married and ensconced in her country manor in the Home Counties and her townhouse in west London. I can tell then that she's my soul-mate. At least for the next few weeks. I'll be good to her. And she'll be very, very good for me. If she's any good at her job, and even if she's not, if she's just the sort of social butterfly she looks to be, she'll know everyone and all the latest gossip. She'll be a godsend. With her help I'll snatch clients from all the biggest firms, with Wilmington-Wilkes at the top of my hit list.

She lays a hand on my knee and I swear I feel a little tingle shoot up my leg. 'Why don't we go to the lounge upstairs? It's quieter and we'll be able to talk better,' she says.

I smile and nod and slide back my chair, helping Camilla to rise. Just at that moment our champagne arrives and I wonder for an instant whether this is another test or if this is mere coincidence, but it doesn't matter.

I can tell she's mercenary, but so am I. She wants me to be wealthy, I want her to have connections. Seems a fair swap. She'll use me and I'll use her and we'll both be happy.

I hand the waitress my credit card and order another bottle, tell her to bring it upstairs and leave the first here.

Alex would be disgusted by this extravagance. He'd see it as a waste. I was never a poser and I was never flash but for my car. But now I am Alexander and I can see that I must spend money to accomplish my goals. I must spend money so that I can acquire even more money.

I don't need to be frugal and thrifty. I am not Alex. I am Alexander and I have a beautiful woman tugging on my hand, eager to lead me upstairs. I resist her tugs only for a moment to bid farewell to her friends. I know, I knew as soon as I saw them, that they're all predators and not prey, but I have a front to maintain, we all do, and it never hurts to be polite.

Camilla is small, shorter than I would have imagined with those legs, but I find that I like it, that she makes me feel manly and strong, that I could take her into my arms and swing through the trees like Tarzan.

She leads me not to the main staircase behind the dance floor where I can see men leering down at the dancers (mostly female) below, but to a discreet staircase located in a corner behind the DJ. I don't fail to note the little wave the DJ gives her as we pass. She's known. The DJ, billed as the hippest, coolest man on the club scene, knows Camilla.

It's quieter upstairs but not deserted. Everything is white, white walls, puffy white sofas and chairs, all white. I wonder how they get the inevitable red-wine stains out of the fabric. But my thoughts are coherent only for an instant, for then Camilla is pulling me down on to an empty sofa in the corner and she's kissing me.

She's kissing me.

She's kissing me. For a moment I'm shocked. Women like that don't fall for me. I'm the nice boy, I'm never the winner. And then I snap back to myself and start returning her kiss. I'm not nice. That was Alex, but I am Alexander. Women like Camilla are going to be my future.

She's kissing me and I'm kissing her.

And I think, Thank God Amber and Noreen didn't tag along.

An hour later, maybe two, we emerge from our cocoon of passion to find Della and Isabel grinning down at us. Our champagne is gone, the waitress found us a long time ago and somehow we came up for enough air and kept our lips apart long enough to drink the bottle between the two of us. Camilla giggles and I realise she's a bit tipsy, but I feel it too, and it's certainly not the alcohol. Not for me.

'We're bored,' says Della.

Translation: she's found no man of her own.

'There's a party at Sebastian's that we want to go to,' says Isabel. Her eyes drop to my groin and I feel a momentary guilt, knowing that she can see how turned on I am, but then I don't care. It would be an insult to Camilla were I not aroused.

Camilla hesitates, torn. Clearly she'd like to go to Sebastian's, whoever Sebastian is, but she doesn't want our night to end, not yet. 'Would you like to come with us?' she asks me.

'Sure, sounds fun,' I say. Oh, yes, this is exactly what I wanted. I am in. I'm on my way.

Camilla smiles a brilliant smile and I stand and help her to her feet. She sways a little and I tuck her arm into mine.

Della and Isabel lead the way and half an hour later we're in the thick of the party. Sebastian turns out to be Sebastian Sinclair-Stevens, ranked Britain's number one most eligible bachelor. (I know this because Sarah is an avid reader of such lists and articles and I recognise him from the photo she left on our coffee table for a week last month.) Sebastian's not exactly good-looking (or so I judge, in an impartial way that doesn't take into account his bank balance), and he's certainly not what you'd call handsome. None the less, his house is crawling with nubile young women whose cleavages strain against their too-tight tops.

I spot a handful of television presenters. And then I see Madonna. I, Alexander Fairfax, am attending the same party as Madonna.

I'm flattered that Camilla sticks to my side, rubbing against me in all the right places. Della and Isabel soon swan off, lost in their own circles of friends and admirers, but Camilla, it's obvious she's been here before, leads me to a quiet corner on the third floor.

An hour later I'm so aroused I can't stand it and I ask Camilla if she wants to leave. She nods and I take her hand and lead her back downstairs so she can say her farewells to Della and Isabel.

Camilla introduces me to Sebastian (he was mobbed with admirers when we arrived so we didn't get round to it), and we shake hands, Camilla kisses his cheek and then we're off. It turns out she only lives a three-minute walk away, and I know then that she's definitely working for the joy of working, of saying she has a career until she marries and gives up work for ever.

If I were a woman I think I'd do the same. It'd be fantastic not to work all day (especially if you had an endless supply of money to spend). But I'm not a woman, I'm a man, and I can hardly resent a woman being sensible and opting for the best solution.

We go to her two-bedroom apartment (i.e. luxury flat) where she lives alone. She tells me her parents gave it to her as a present when she completed her English degree and that her father hadn't wanted her to go to university at all, but that her mother had managed to persuade her father that it would be a Good Thing.

After a brief (very brief) tour we end up in her bedroom and then I am unzipping her dress and pulling it off in one smooth move. I feel happy that Camilla likes me and I think that Camilla should be flattered that I wanted to leave without even speaking to Madonna.

(But the truth is I didn't want to speak to Madonna. What if I'd frozen? What if the old Alex had chosen that moment to fight me for possession of my voice? What if he'd succeeded and blurted out how much he'd fancied her as a teenager, how many times he used to watch her videos and dance to her songs? It would have spelled doom and gloom for my chances. I'd like to speak to Madonna. One day when I'm firmly ensconced in the inner sanctum. I mean, what would I have said to her? Anything I'd said would have sounded lame.

Maybe I should start feeling sorry for celebrities: maybe no one actually talks to them as we're all too afraid of sounding crass. But if I'm going to be the man I think I can be, I'll have to be prepared. I know that now, but I can't speak like a reject, I can't act like a member of the public and gush all over celebrities. That isn't the done thing. Not here in London. Oh, inwardly we may all salivate in their presence but, for God's sake, we don't act that way.)

And then Camilla is pulling off my shirt and I have the best sex of my life. I don't know whether it was the club or the buzz from the party or that Camilla's body might have been sculpted from a Greek statue, but we come and come and come again and I know that Camilla isn't faking it, she can't be faking it, not like that.

We sleep for an hour or so and then I wake her up and we have sex again. I kiss her, long and hard, and then gently and tell her I have to go, that I have work to do (it's not a lie). She looks sad, but I take her phone number and I can tell she's thinking, Well, that's the end of that, then, so I invite her out to dinner on Sunday.

'Sunday?' she asks, brightening.

'I'm busy tonight,' I say.

We agree that I'll pick her up at seven. (I'm hoping to eat early so there'll be plenty of time for dessert.)

I leave Camilla with the number of my mobile, telling her that I'm never home, so she may as well just have the one number. I can hardly give her the number of my flat, for she'd ring and Noreen, Amber or stoned Clarence would answer, and the last thing she needs to think is that I'm a managing director who has to share a flat. (And I won't for much longer, it is only temporary after all.) She looks slightly suspicious, as if she expects me to be married or something, but I kiss her again and she doesn't say anything.

I leave then, before she tempts my resolve not to stay, and as I walk down the road I consider sending her flowers. No, too desperate. I'm a high-powered business executive, I'm a very busy man. I'll bring her a nice present tomorrow and leave her wondering today.

I don't want her to take me for granted.

Alex was taken for granted and look what happened to me then.

My little brother, one year younger and one inch shorter – that one inch has given me no end of satisfaction over the years – is a computer whiz. I've never thought of him as a geek or a nerd, and in school he was too good at sport to be classified as such even if he did hang with that crowd, but he is a hacker. And to be a hacker – a good hacker – Paul's had to spend some incredibly long hours in front of those blue screens of his. He's been married for a year to a lovely woman who's a doctor. I don't know whether it's because she's always busy or because he's managed to convert his passion for binary code, bits and bytes into a proper job as a well-paid consultant but he convinced his wife that he needed the largest of the three spare bedrooms for his office. It is filled, from floor to ceiling like a library, with computing equipment. The room looks like something you'd expect to see in a movie or television show.

I catch the Tube to Waterloo then the train down to Kingston-upon-Thames where Paul lives in wedded bliss in part of a converted Victorian mansion overlooking the Thames. I don't bother ringing in advance, for I know his Emma will be on duty. It's late enough for Paul to have finished his early-morning run (he runs five miles a day to offset the hours he spends glued to his chair) and be tapping on his keyboard.

When I arrive I ring the bell. Wait. Ring the bell again. Eventually a wet-haired, freshly showered Paul opens the door. 'I guess it's true, then,' he says.

'What's true?' I ask, following him inside.

I try to stop the flush, but I can't. What has he heard? I don't want him to know everything, I don't want him to think I'm a loser. I don't want him to know what a loser I was.

'Mum said you and Sarah split up. She dump you?'

I look at him closely, searching for any hint of smugness, but no, this is my brother: we might have fought like demons as children, but we're friends now. We stand together against the world. 'I walked in on her bonking my boss,' I say.

I can tell he's taken aback for his eyes widen, but he merely nods. 'I see.' He doesn't know what to say. And what could he say? Sorry? It's not his fault. I can blame Sarah and Jed and even myself, but certainly not Paul.

'I need your help,' I say, taking pity on him and breaking the silence.

'My help? What can I do, Alex?'

I nearly ask him to call me Alexander, but I don't. Something stops me. It would sound silly asking my brother to call me something as formal-sounding as Alexander when I've been Alex all my life.

I decide to make an exception. I'll allow my family to call me Alex. I doubt they'd remember to call me anything else anyway.

'You can start,' I say, 'with a drink.'

And while Paul fixes us coffee I swear him to secrecy. Once he's promised eternal silence, vowing not to tell even his wife and certainly not our parents, I recount the whole story of the past two weeks.

Well, a highly edited and shortened version.

I tell him all about Sarah and Jed and how Jed betrayed me at work, but I don't bother with the rest of my disasters; nor do I reveal my failure as a man in speaking up for myself in front of Kenneth. This is my little brother. He's meant to look up to me. He can't ever know the extent of my humiliations. I want him to be proud of me, to come to me for help, to think I can tackle any problem and solve it. Not to look at me and think of my failures.

Talking to Paul it's almost like old times and I tell myself I have to be on my guard. I can't be complacent and let the old Alex slip in. I have to keep my mind on my purpose. I mustn't forget my reason for coming here today.

'I need your help,' I say. I correct myself. 'I'd *like* your help, but you can say no. It's probably illegal although not immoral and I don't want to get you into trouble.'

He stares at me for one long second that feels like it lasts an hour. 'I'll do it,' he says. 'What do you want me to do?'

Two hours later and it's done.

Paul hacked his way into the Wilmington-Wilkes personnel files. The actual hacking only took my brother about ten minutes, but he spent a long time camouflaging his entry, making it virtually impossible to trace. We e-mailed the salary details of every member of the Wilmington-Wilkes firm, from Kenneth Wilmington-Wilkes to their most recent graduate, to every single employee.

By Monday morning – maybe it won't take that long if some sorry bastards are working this weekend, and there's bound to be one or two – everyone will know what I now know: that there are huge, huge salary discrepancies within Wilmington-Wilkes. And sometimes bosses are earning less than star players on their teams.

Kenneth most certainly has his favourites.

And Jed knows that it pays to be a sycophantic bastard. I've seen the figures. No doubt Sarah feels secure and provided for, with her man earning such a handsome sum.

I'm tempted to ask Paul to make a few minor alterations – namely to the salaries of Thomas and William, my erstwhile back-stabbing partners of old – but I resist. That's not what I have in mind for them, and it would be too specific. They might begin to suspect me.

I wonder if good old Kenneth will call in the police, but as nothing exactly malicious has been done and nothing has been destroyed, I don't imagine the police will spend much time on it.

And if they do contact the police, they'll never think of me. Or they'll think of me briefly when they list all the latest sackings, but they'll dismiss me soon enough from the suspect list. Oh, no, not Alex Fairfax. He's too nice. He'd never do anything like that. It'll be unanimous. Oh, no. Not Alex.

Fools. Why not Alex?

Am I really so unlikely a suspect? Will they think me incapable of such a grand gesture in thumbing my nose at the boss man?

But, no, they won't think I'm incapable, they'll think that Alex wouldn't do such thing. And Alex wouldn't have dared. He would have been afraid, he would have thought it was mean, he would have been too busy polishing his CV and dwelling over what he'd done wrong to make Sarah go off him.

For that's the sort of man I was.

But no longer.

Screw them all, I say.

I'm Alexander now and it's my turn.

SALARIES
(FOR SHAME, KENNETH)

I have a printout of the salaries of all 229 employees of Wilmington-Wilkes (including dear old Kenneth who's on a million a year, plus a minimum fifty per cent bonus and various benefits). I'll destroy it in an hour or so, I just wanted the joy of holding it in my hands, of trying to commit the relevant numbers to mind without making Paul download anything on to his computer or maintain the link for too long. I'll destroy the list. I'll tear it up into little pieces and divide it into piles that I'll discard in various public bins around London (you can't be too careful).

Jed, my manager at two rungs above me in the so-called career ladder at Wilmington-Wilkes, was earning three times as much as I was. Scanning the list I can see that he was overpaid, earning more, even, than his supposed boss.

And I was underpaid. (The files list all salaries, present and past, and the dates of change, so I can see that I was underpaid from day one.)

But I do have some good news. Thomas and William, joining as graduates within a month of one another, aren't on the same wages. Yes, they're both on more than I was on, Thomas a third as much again, but William's on nearly double.

Thomas and William, William and Thomas, they've been working together for years, they're good mates, they go to the pub together, they play squash together, they've always been promoted at the same time. But they're not earning the same.

They're not so equal, after all.

Poor Thomas. Will he be jealous? Will Thomas and William be such bosom pals after this little revelation?

It's not enough revenge against them, I want it to be more direct, but it's enough for now. It's a start. Things won't be so rosy for them. They'll suffer just a little of the rage and humiliation I suffered. Not enough, but it'll do. For now.

Will dissension grow in the ranks of Wilmington-Wilkes? I wonder if there'll be riots.

Who am I kidding? The underpaid are mostly the nice, the quiet, the unassuming, those able to slog away and not worry too much about individual recognition as long as the team gets credit. They'll fume in silence and perhaps even mutter in secret among themselves, but they'll cause no fireworks. No, they'll just drain away over the coming months, looking for firms that are more fair and just.

Maybe I'll consider giving all the underpaid jobs at Platypus-fox. The nice ones, that is. I may be the man in charge, but they'll trust me, even the new me, for I won't take advantage of them. I refuse to take advantage of their kind.

Oh, there'll be some commotion. But most of those who would cause trouble are already earning more than their fair share. Only a handful will protest. A handful that will include Thomas. But even if he gets his raise, even if he gets his back pay to bring him equal to William, he'll be left with a bitter taste in his mouth. And to make things even worse for him (and better for me), everyone will know.

Noses will be bent out of shape. And Kenneth will be furious that his empire has been threatened, but I don't kid myself: he'll pull through.

But still, I smile, it's round one to Alexander.

I'd intended working on my next few ad campaigns while Paul was working on my favour, but I couldn't tear my eyes away from his flying fingers as he typed and surfed and cajoled and forced his way past the Wilmington-Wilkes security barriers. Hacking is a form of magic. It's all mumbo-jumbo to me, but with the right words, the right gestures, bingo, you're in.

Once the vast e-mail is sent (Paul thought we should send it from Kenneth's own e-mail account so we did, or Paul did, I just watched – let Kenneth sweat and wonder if he'd pressed a few wrong buttons by mistake), Paul and I spend the rest of the afternoon talking. Just talking and talking. Not about Jed or Sarah or even my revenge, just talking about everything and anything that crosses our minds. And I feel better when I leave, my mind is more at ease.

I walk north from Waterloo station, crossing Hungerford Bridge and thinking, as I always do, about that man who was thrown to his death a few years ago for the two pounds in his pocket. That's how little a single human life is valued.

I walk for a mile or so, dodging tourists, using the main roads, sifting small bits of torn paper – the remains of the salary printout – from my pockets into half a dozen trash receptacles. Then I catch a cab home.

And I work and work. And work.

At about seven there's a knock on my door.

Can't they just leave me alone? I've shut the door: that means I want a little privacy. That's not too much to ask, is it?

'Come in,' I call. It'd better not be Noreen coming to tell me off for polluting the fridge with more of my free-range eggs.

'Hi,' says Amber, poking her head into my room, 'sorry to disturb you.' She's dressed in tight black trousers and a sleeveless top and I could have died and gone to heaven she's such a sight of loveliness.

I feel instant guilt. Amber hadn't known I didn't want to be disturbed.

I set down my pen and smile at her. 'That's okay,' I say. 'I'm only working.'

'I was just coming to ask if, well,' she hesitates, 'if you wanted to come out with us tonight. With Noreen and me. We're going clubbing.'

Sorry, my sweet, I did that last night. And Noreen wouldn't be allowed into the sort of places I go to.

'Sorry,' I say, 'I can't.'

Her face falls and she flushes, and I realise that she's actually asking me out, that she worked up the courage to come here, knock on my door and ask me out and all I can say is no.

'I have to work,' I explain. 'I have so much to do. But how about lunch tomorrow?'

Hello, Alexander, knock knock, are you in there? What are you doing? You're not supposed to be nice, you shouldn't be giving her false hope.

But there's no reason we can't be friends. Surely Amber and I can be friends. What's the harm in that?

'Lunch sounds good,' says Amber.

Oh dear, is she expecting a date?

'I'm afraid I have to work tomorrow as well,' I say, 'so it'll only be a lunch break here at home. Is that okay?'

She's still smiling. 'That's fine. I'll even cook so it won't interrupt you too much. See you tomorrow. Good luck with your work.'

And Amber leaves. I worry for a moment, knowing I should just have said no and ended it all right there, but I couldn't bear the look of disappointment in her eyes, I didn't want her to feel embarrassed to bump into me in the kitchen, I didn't want her to think I'm not attracted to her, for I am. I just have to keep everything above board, on the straight and narrow. It'll be okay. I'm Alexander, I'm in control.

I get back to work, and work and work and work.

I go to bed at three a.m. (Amber and Noreen aren't back yet. Where are they?)

After my obligatory four hours I'm wide-awake and I return to my slogans and posters, my magazine spreads, radio jingles and television spots.

By noon I have enough material to present to four more clients. I've tailor-made two of the campaigns for clients of Wilmington-Wilkes, but I'm leaving the other two up in the air. It's time for me to try some cold selling.

After all my work, all my successful hours, I'm feeling happy and energetic and I want to do something to expend my energy. I have to do something to expend my energy.

I spare an hour for lunch with Amber. (Noreen's out protesting against the destruction of the green belt surrounding London and there's no sign of Clarence or Diana so we have the kitchen to ourselves.) She's obviously been cooking most of the morning and she's crafted a cheese quiche that melts in your mouth, along with homemade bread, salad, and my favourite, hot apple pie with ice cream and custard.

We're chatting the whole time, there are no awkward moments, and I have to force myself to tell her that I have more to do on my presentations. I help Amber wash up and then everything's put away and clean and I can't drag it out any longer.

'That was delicious,' I say.

'Thanks.'

She looks up at me and blushes. She's standing next to me holding a dishcloth and I know I shouldn't, but I just can't help myself, I lean forward and kiss her cheek. 'Thank you,' I say. 'Next time I'll take you out to dinner.'

Next time? What the hell am I talking about? There can't be a next time.

'I'd like that,' says Amber.

I force myself to meet her smile, I act like nothing's changed but inside I'm screaming. You bloody fool, Alexander. What the hell are you doing? You have to stop this right now.

I say goodbye and go to my room.

I have to get out of the house. I can't stay here. I'm weak. I like Amber. I want Amber, but I mustn't have Amber. She's off limits. She's off limits, Alexander.

I know what it is. I know what it must be. I'm feeling withdrawal symptoms. It's been over twenty-four hours since my last shag and I've been working so hard that my body is demanding a reward. I deserve some relief and I can't use Amber like that. I like Amber.

I nearly go for a run to clear my head, but I decide it's better to phone Kate.

She's home and I can tell she's thrilled to hear from me. I ask if she's free and when she says she is I ask if I can come round. She hesitates for just one second and I wonder if she's disappointed, I wonder if she wanted to go out, like on a proper date, a couple-y thing of holding hands and walking around Hyde Park. Kate? No, that's not Kate. Is it? We make arrangements for me to go to her place in an hour. (I wonder if she has to shower and shave her legs.)

And after I hang up I feel bad for a second. Am I using Kate? Does she expect more from this than I'm offering?

Alex would feel guilty, but I don't feel guilty. I can't feel guilty. I'm Alexander.

I relax. I'm using her exactly as she's using me. For sex. She's not a bad person but neither am I. None the less, as I make a detour to Oxford Street to buy Camilla a bottle of Givenchy's Indecence, which I hope is her favourite perfume, I buy Kate a bottle as well. (Okay, okay, I admit it, I did a bit of snooping when I was at Camilla's place. She had a bottle of Indecence in her bathroom and I sniffed it and it was definitely what she was wearing.) I don't know if Kate'll like it, but it sure smelt dynamite on Camilla. I'm tempted to buy Amber something too, not this perfume, something different, but I don't. I mustn't. I resist the impulse.

When I reach Kate's, I hand her the present at once and her face lights up and I can see instantly that she's delighted that I thought enough of her to buy her something. She opens the box and sprays on some perfume. She sniffs it and then throws her arms around me, giving me a hug and not a kiss. And the hug feels strange, more intimate somehow than the sex, as if she's saying, I know you and you know me and we're both people together in this world and we're more than just bodies. I feel uneasy for a second. Surely she's not expecting more from this than there is?

No, how could she possibly? We've never been on a date, we don't go out in public together, we're not seeing one another, we're hardly more than acquaintances even if I feel pretty acquainted with her body.

After the hug things go back to normal and Kate thanks me. Again and again.

I could grow used to such gratitude in a woman.

And the sex, well, for all her looking like she's had plenty of experience, Kate isn't as polished as Camilla. The little electric tingles aren't there, but it's still good. And there's something about knowing that I'm going to be screwing Camilla in a few hours while I'm pumping into Kate that really turns me on. (Alex never even slept with two different women in the same week but Alexander gets two women on the same day.) My orgasms are nearly as good as those I had with Camilla.

Afterwards I look at my watch and I see that it's time to go. I can tell that Kate wants to have dinner, but I can't be late for Camilla. I apologise and promise we'll go out soon.

Her face drops and I want to set a date, so she'll be happy, but I can't. I've got my future to think of. And Camilla, or women like Camilla, are my future. If I'm to be a success – which I'm going to be – I need the appropriate female accessory on my arm.

'I've got to get back to work,' I tell her. And it's the truth, or so close to the truth that it doesn't matter. Going out with Camilla is work. In a way. It's working towards my future.

'On Sunday night?'

Have we reached the nagging stage already? Is she trying to be my girlfriend? I won't be sticking around if that's the way she's playing it.

'I've been working all weekend,' I say. And I have. Revenge, making social connections, coming up with advertising ideas, it's all work towards making Alexander as successful as possible. I can't just sit back and relax because it's Sunday.

I'm slightly cold and distant as I tell her that I have a number of business trips coming up, that I'll be travelling most of the next month so I don't know when I'll be able to see her, but I know, looking at her moist eyes, that I'll squeeze her in somehow.

I take my leave and she puts me off a little, the way she clings to me at the door when we're saying goodbye, and I come back to my senses. We don't have a relationship, we don't talk, we really don't know anything about one another, why should I feel guilty?

As I walk down the stairs I feel a great weight lift from my shoulders. And then I am free.

I feel no guilt. I am Alexander. Alex would have behaved differently, but Alex would never have gone to bed with her in the first place, he would never have moved so quickly, he would never have been interested in a woman so enamoured of makeup. And I am not Alex. I feel no guilt. I am Alexander.

After I leave Kate's I go home to shower and change. I'm ready with my excuse. I'm planning to tell Amber that I'd left to go to my brother's but that I'd forgotten something. I'm planning to tell her I'm spending the day and probably the night at my brother's so that I can use his computer. (Wilmington-Wilkes kept my laptop when they sacked Alex, so this sounds like a reasonable explanation.) I don't want to hurt Amber. I don't want her wondering where I am. I don't want her guessing the truth.

Fortunately no one's at home so I don't have to lie. I get ready quickly and then I leave again, deciding that while perfume might have made Kate nearly swoon with delight, Camilla is more demanding. I contemplate flowers briefly. No, too predictable and she might have hay-fever. Chocolates? No. I've learnt over the years never to give a woman chocolate (unless you've been together over a year and you know her really, really well): either she won't eat it because she thinks they'll make her fat, or she devours the box in one day, feels sick and then blames you for making her fat. Or (this has happened) she might think you're hinting that she's too thin and needs to gain some weight, or on the other hand that she doesn't watch what she eats and therefore it doesn't matter if she guzzles the whole box. No, however much she may adore chocolate it's a definite mistake.

Clothing? I don't know her well enough. Lingerie? Certainly not. Regardless of how many times you've shagged, you should have known someone for over a month before you purchase such intimate apparel. Silly, really, but it's true. Purchasing lingerie for someone then giving it to her is a step beyond going to bed with her. I'd never give lingerie to someone I hadn't been to bed with, but equally, I can't give Camilla lingerie just because I've been to bed with her.

That's what it's like in today's world. You can know what a woman looks like naked. You can feel her all over, you can know exactly how she likes her clitoris stroked before you know what kind of music she listens to or what her favourite films are. Bizarre, but I like it.

I leave the house and glance at my watch. I have an hour to find another gift and get to Camilla's. I don't want to be too punctual, but I don't want to be more than a few minutes late. There's a fine line between being fashionable and annoying the woman who's waiting for you to turn up. If you're too early she'll be annoyed that she's not ready. And if you're too late, well, you're not eager enough and she'll probably give you the cold shoulder all night. (Unless you have a really good excuse, something like a car accident or a death in the family that makes her feel guilty for cursing you before your arrival. And I'm afraid traffic or Underground delays – God forbid mentioning you rely on anything like public transport to see your beloved, unless she's a committed environmentalist like Noreen – won't do. You're expected to allow for any such potential disasters.)

I need a gift that's original. Something that shows I appreciate Camilla for more than just her beauty and her body. (Not to mention her social connections.) I don't really know her tastes. I know she makes this funny little face – like a baby lion trying to roar, but without the sound – when she reaches orgasm, but that doesn't help me here. I can hardly buy her a vibrator. Jewellery? No. Too much too soon. I may be wealthy and successful, but I'm certainly not desperate.

I walk down the road and try to visualise her apartment, searching for a clue. Suddenly it clicks. Her spare bedroom is a mini-library filled with books. I can buy her a book. She lives alone, so those must be her books. A woman with a brain. A beautiful, sexy, wealthy, intelligent woman. Thank God we'll have more to discuss over dinner than the latest colours of nail polish.

A book, yes, that's what I'll buy her. But which one? I decide to get her a copy of John Irving's *A Prayer for Owen Meany*. He's one of my favourite authors and that's one of my favourite books, so at least if she's one of those people who has to analyse every last page it won't be too much of a chore for me.

As I climb the stairs to her flat, I suddenly have doubts. Is a book enough for her? Will she like it?

She should be flattered that I see her as more than a body built for great sex.

And there's also the perfume. I don't just come bearing a gift, I come bearing gifts.

I ring the bell at five past seven, perhaps a little too early, but I don't really know her tastes.

Don't think like Alex, Alexander. You don't care what her tastes are.

That's right. I show up when I'm ready to show up. Whether it's early, late, or dead on time it's what I want. (Alex was very punctual.)

Camilla opens the door and I forget to breathe for a moment. She is, simply, the most stunning woman I have ever seen in real life. And I know, right then, that she is exactly what I need. And what I want. Whatever doubts I might have been nursing that she wasn't as beautiful as I remembered have fled. And then, I think, I've slept with her. I, Alexander Fairfax, have tasted her luscious lips, have felt her bare legs wrap around me, pulling me deeper inside her. I'm the kind of man beautiful women sleep with. I'm a stud.

I give her a broad smile and kiss her cheek as she invites me in. She closes the door and gives me a longer kiss, on the lips.

'These are for you,' I say, and hand her first the perfume (wrapped, of course) and then the book (it's only in a bag but I don't think she'll mind).

'For me?' She gives me a slow smile and I know she's used to this, that men always bring her presents, and then I'm doubly glad that I didn't stop with the perfume. 'Which one shall I open first?'

'The wrapped one,' I say, wanting to save the book for last, partly to postpone the moment in case she doesn't like it, partly not to distract from it if she does.

She opens the perfume and laughs. 'You've done your homework.'

'So I have.' I step closer, take her in my arms and give her a big sniff.

She laughs. 'Yes, yes, it's my favourite. But I warn you, my favourites change. I get bored easily.' She says this with a smile, but I wonder if it's some kind of warning. Does she go through lots of men? I bet she does. They're probably queuing up, waiting for her to ditch her latest fling.

Well, thanks for the warning, Camilla. You just look after yourself and leave my life to me. I'm a big boy. I won't get burned. My heart and soul are never going to be yours and my body, it would miss you, but it could cope with the loss.

I release her and step back, wanting to watch her face. I know she can feel it's a book, but I can't tell what she thinks of that. She opens the bag and pulls out the novel. 'Thanks,' she says, and tosses it on to a table in the hall. Camilla doesn't smile.

She doesn't like it. She doesn't like it and I'm disappointed. I wanted her to like it.

'He's a really good author,' I say.

Camilla picks up her handbag. 'I know. I've tried him. I like his style.'

Then what's the problem?

I stare at her, annoyed. Alex would shrug it off and pretend this wasn't happening, but I'm not Alex. I won't tolerate this sort of behaviour. Amber certainly wouldn't act like this.

'What's the problem?' I ask her.

She shrugs. 'I was expecting something else.'

And then it clicks. I know where she's coming from.

Books are too inexpensive to give as presents. I'll have to see how long I want to keep her around.

'Where are we going for dinner?' she asks.

'Mirabelle.'

Camilla kisses me lightly on the mouth, all smiles again. The restaurant obviously wins her approval. 'In that case, I'm very hungry.'

I make a little bet with myself that she'll order the priciest items on the menu. And then she'll claim she's too full, she's eaten too much, how could she possibly manage it all?

INTRODUCING ALEXANDER

When we arrive at the restaurant Camilla is happy and flushed: she seems a different person from the petulant, spoiled brat I'd glimpsed at her apartment.

It takes ten minutes to reach our table, not from the neglect or slowness of the staff – on the contrary, they're very attentive and they all appear to know Camilla and greet her as they pass: our progress is slow because Camilla seems to know half of the diners and insists on treating our entrance as some sort of grand procession, stopping, however briefly, at all the tables along our route that contain her friends and acquaintances.

I forgive her for her earlier tantrum. I'm not with Camilla because I like her, I must remember that, I'm with her because of times like these.

'Darling,' she says, again and again, and leans down and kisses a few dozen people on the cheek (or the air near their cheek) as we make our way across the room. Others she merely smiles at. I wonder if we're causing a commotion, but then I think not. This is one of those places in which people like to be seen.

To give her credit, Camilla is meticulous about introducing me to all of the people she stops to greet. I meet City bankers, a marquess, the wife of the latest British Airways boss, a director of the English National Ballet, a crusty old High Court judge (a friend of Camilla's father, I'm told), various young women of about Camilla's age, most with double-barrelled surnames that have centuries of wealth and breeding behind them, and a handful of women friendly with her mother from numerous charities and art committees.

I smile and make polite conversation, but mostly I watch Camilla. She is gracious and charming. But clearest of all I can see that she fits in. She's one of the élite.

It must be obvious to her that I don't come from the same background. I have no regional accent, although I grew up in Surrey, and my voice is crisp and precise, but not as posh as Camilla's. Not that that's necessarily a sign these days when the younger generation of toffs assume common accents, and brothers and sisters often sound as if they come from different social classes. But more telling is that I don't know a single soul in this restaurant except Camilla.

I worry for a moment. Will she care? Will she think I'm a failure? That I have no prospects? Will she be like Sarah and think other men offer more security?

My stomach heaves and I have to clench my jaw so that no one will notice. I'm a nobody. One of the masses. Camilla matters. But me? The world wouldn't notice if I sank into the ground and was swallowed up in a pool of sludge and quicksand. Only if my disappearance was witnessed and judged to be unusual would the world take notice. But if something happened to Camilla, well, there'd be a fuss. Those in authority would miss her, she'd be discussed, she'd be a topic of conversation up and down the drawing rooms of the land.

I take a deep breath, my smile frozen in place as Camilla greets more people. I am not a loser. Alex was a loser. It's Alex's fault that I don't know any of these people. I am not a loser. I am Alexander. Yes, I am. I am Alexander. My smile relaxes. I am Alexander. And soon they'll all know it.

Camilla takes my hand and squeezes it. See? I knew it. She wants to be here with me. She's proud of me, she's showing me off.

And on our progress through the restaurant we're invited out afterwards for drinks. Each time Camilla looks at me, a question in her eyes. Part of me wants no more than to eat, go back to her place and fuck until dawn (she's that good), but another part of me knows I can't refuse, I need to make contacts. We'll go out for a few hours, meet and mingle, and then we'll go back to hers.

And each time we're asked out, I nod and smile and say, 'We'll try to make it.' Like I'm some sort of gracious prince. Another two or three weeks and I will be. I'll be a powerful man. I'll be sitting in restaurants such as these and the people-in-the-know will hope I remember them when they stop by to say hello.

Alex was a pathetic worm, crawling around in the dirt and the dung of the earth. He would have smiled and been friendly and liked everyone, and they would have eaten him for breakfast. Alex wouldn't have survived more than a day with this crowd. He would have been booted out. Alex wasn't one of the élite, but Alexander is joining it.

Eventually Camilla and I reach our table. I was expecting a romantic tête-à-tête. I hadn't thought tonight would be any more useful than in helping me to charm Camilla so that next time, or the time after, I could make use of her social contacts. But what a bonus. My plan is surging forward. I've set it in motion and now all I have to do is sit back and let events take their course, with a friendly nudge here and there, of course.

Camilla smiles at me, a dazzling smile that lights up her face, and for a moment I'm confused.

Did I misread her earlier? Were our signals getting crossed?

And how can a woman like her like me?

Stop it, you're not Alex any more, I tell myself. I am not that man. I am Alexander.

Amber might be nice and sweet and mighty fine, Amber would have done for Alex, but Amber is not for me. Amber is not for Alexander. Amber can never give me what Camilla is giving me now, here tonight, what Camilla will give me the next time I take her out and the next and the next and the next.

I deserve women like Camilla. They'll be crawling all over me soon. Camilla's beautiful and great in bed and she certainly seems to have the right connections, but let's not get confused here, she's no angel. She's probably fucked more men in one year of her life than I have women in the whole of mine. She's what nice girls would call fast and easy, a loose woman.

And thank you, kind Fates, or whoever's looking out for me. She's just what I need.

Camilla will do nicely for now.

Dinner is fantastic. The food is fabulous, the wine like ambrosia, Camilla's company convivial, the atmosphere electric. I feel like a goldfish in a bowl, wondering if they're all watching me, watching me watching them watching me, wondering who the man with Camilla is.

But I don't fool myself. It's not like that at all. Men must constantly be taking Camilla out to dinner. She's that sort of girl. People probably don't have time to sit back and wonder whom she's dating. Is she here with a different man every week?

After the best apple tart concoction I've ever had, we head to the flat of Harriet (her family's London flat, not their real home), one of Camilla's friends we bumped into at the restaurant.

I feel an ache in my groin and force myself to ignore it. I need Camilla's connections. Sure, the sex is good, the sex is great, but it's not the be-all and end-all. I can have sex with anyone, but not everyone can offer me the kind of life Camilla can. I need her support, her patronage, her introductions and then I'll be off. I can handle it from there, I just need to meet people – meet them properly and make certain that I'll see them again and that they'll remember me. I'm one of the big boys now.

We ring the bell and Harriet opens the door. She's a big, horsy-looking woman, obviously not a townie, and though she wasn't wearing tweeds and wellingtons at the restaurant, she looked like she ought to have been. She seems rather tipsy and throws her arms around Camilla with a cry of joy.

I take advantage of the moment and my eyes scan the room. There were eight of them at dinner, but the flat is crowded. It's obviously turned into a small party.

After a moment Harriet and Camilla pull apart and Harriet turns to me. Her face is flushed and I think, cruelly, that it does nothing for her complexion, but I push those thoughts away and smile at her. 'Hi, Alexander,' says Harriet, pumping my hand up and down enthusiastically. (She remembers my name. She remembers my name.) 'Glad you could make it.'

An older woman, thinner than Harriet but with the same strong jaw and wide-eyed stare, sees us and approaches. 'Darling,' she says to Camilla, as she kisses her cheek, 'it's so good to see you. And you look well. Your mother will be thrilled when I tell her you came to visit.'

Camilla laughs. 'It's all his fault,' she says, meaning me. 'He insists on being respectable.'

The woman, obviously Harriet's mother, raises an eyebrow and looks at me.

Camilla introduces us. 'Grace, I'd like you to meet Alexander. Alexander Fairfax. Alexander, this is Grace St John, Harriet's mother.'

'How do you do?' says Grace, and shakes my hand. She's frowning and staring at me, obviously trying to place me.

Well, tough luck, lady. You won't know me. You won't have heard of me. Alex had control of my life way too long for any of that. Deal with it. Enjoy meeting one of the people.

'The pleasure is mine,' I say, and give her what I hope is a charming smile.

'Have you known Camilla long?' asks Grace. She's wondering who I am, trying to discover if I'm worthy of Camilla, if I'm grand enough to be welcomed into her home with open arms.

Shove it up your rectum. You've no right to question me. No right to look down your snooty nose and judge me your inferior. The tables are turning, Grace, the tables are bloody well flipping over in their rush to do my bidding. You'd better be pleasant before I decide to step on you and crush your face into the ground. I make a bad enemy, Gracie, a fucking bad enemy. And I never forgive a slight. However polite the terms in which it's issued.

'Not as long as I would like,' I say aloud, and the answer seems to please her, for she smiles a little and relaxes.

'Charles,' she calls, not really raising her voice, but a big, florid gentleman, looking like a nineteenth-century country squire, hears her from across the room and approaches.

'Charles, look who's here,' says Grace, when he reaches our little group.

Charles looks at me and raises his brows, then sees Camilla chatting animatedly to Harriet. 'Milla,' he says, and gives her a big hug.

Harriet and Grace roll their eyes at one another and then Harriet grins at me, including me in their minor despair.

Camilla laughs. 'No one's called me that since I came to London.'

'Nonsense,' says Charles. 'You've been Milla since you were three weeks old and my Harriet couldn't manage all three syllables. You'll always be Milla to me. And how are you, Milla? Is London treating you well? You look good so I would have to say it is, but I was rather hoping you wouldn't like it. Poor Harriet has been distraught – she has no one to giggle with now that you're gone.'

Camilla glances at me, trying to make me feel included. 'Our families are neighbours in Gloucestershire,' she explains.

This seems to interrupt his train of thought, for Charles turns back to me with a frown. 'Do I know you?' he asks. He says it in such a way that makes it obvious he knows he doesn't, that he's never heard of my family, that he's sceptical of my prospects.

My stomach does a little jump, it's like I'm free-falling from the top of a roller-coaster that's lumbering out of control. He's not polite, he goes for the jugular. Alex would die of embarrassment.

'Charles, don't be rude,' says Grace. 'This is Alexander Fairfax.'

He shakes my hand. 'Alexander Fairfax. Alexander Fairfax.'

He thinks a moment. 'Any relation to the Oxfordshire Fair-faxes?'

'Not that I know of,' I say.

'Alexander is in advertising,' says Camilla.

She inserts this quickly. Is she on my side? Does she want me to win their approval or doesn't she care?

'Is that so?' asks Charles. He's obviously uncertain about this. Advertising is a big field. And not everyone involved is successful.

Camilla smiles and takes my arm. 'He has his own company.'

'Ah,' says Charles. That's obviously better. 'Anything we'd know?'

Grace sighs. 'You'll have to forgive my husband,' she says to me. 'He had a bump on the head in the night and has forgotten all his manners.'

'I'd be surprised if you've heard of me already,' I say, smiling at Grace to show her I heard, smiling at them all. 'I've only been in business for a week.'

I can feel Camilla's surprise. And her unease. I know she's thinking, Only a week? She drops my arm like it's a hot piece of charcoal that jumped out of a barbecue pit, trying to fit in where it doesn't belong. Does she want to dump me back into my dank little hole? Is that where she thinks I've come from?

She hasn't stepped away, but she's tense, her eyes aren't so warm, she's ready to disassociate herself from me in an instant if I don't measure up.

That's right, Alexander, you're being judged. Remember that. You're not the only one calling the shots. There are plenty of others out there who want to be king of the jungle, who think of themselves as king of the jungle, and they don't take kindly to young pretenders.

'A week?' Charles glances at Camilla. He doesn't know whether or not to disapprove. 'Do you have any clients?'

'Yes. Marriott Hotels, to name just one.'

'Your only client?' asks Charles.

'I have three, I'm expecting four more to sign on this week.'

He looks impressed, despite himself. It's not bad for a week. 'And before that?'

'If I didn't know better, I'd think you were Camilla's father,' I say.

There's a momentary silence. I wonder suddenly if I've inadvertently stumbled on to some dark truth, but then Charles bursts out laughing and claps me on the back. I can feel the tension draining away from the women and they're relaxed now. The worst is clearly over.

Camilla takes my hand and smiles at me. I'm acceptable now, am I?

'I like you, boy,' says Charles. 'I like you.' He winks at Camilla. 'Think of me as an old family friend. I am an old family friend. And Camilla's godfather. Who did you work for before last week?'

I smile. 'Wilmington-Wilkes.' I know this will impress him. It's a good firm. Except for the rotten boss at the top.

'Ah.' He nods. 'Never did like that old bastard. I can see why you'd want to leave.'

'Charles,' says Grace, her face heavy with disapproval.

I feel a burst of warmth towards Charles. I like him now. I can forgive him for his earlier aggression. He's obviously a good judge of character.

'Kenneth and I didn't exactly see eye to eye,' I say.

Charles claps me on the back again, a firm believer in the old-school heartiness-of-men theory. 'I'm sure you didn't.' He turns to his wife. 'Where's one of my cards?' he asks her.

Grace, long used to his ways, reaches into his breast pocket, withdraws a card and hands it to him.

He glances at it in satisfaction. 'Never could keep track of the damn things. Here,' he says, handing it to me, 'give me a call tomorrow and we'll set something up. I want to hear some of your ideas.'

I glance at his card. Sir Charles St John. And a telephone number. Not a company card. A personal card. I wonder what he does. Does he not work? 'Thank you,' I say.

'Call me,' he says, turning to greet some new arrivals.

Grace smiles at me. 'It was lovely to meet you, Alexander. I hope we see you again.'

Harriet studies me carefully as her mother walks away to mingle with other guests. 'I don't know if we can allow you to stay,' says Harriet.

'What?'

What's this? Have they seen through me? But I'm not Alex, not now. I haven't been him for days. I am Alexander. I fit in. I'm one of them. I am.

Harriet laughs. 'My father seems to like you.' She shares a smile with Camilla. 'My father doesn't approve of young men under forty. No one's good enough for me. And no one's good enough for Camilla.'

Camilla smiles. 'Enough. No more Spanish Inquisition.' She's on my side now, pressing against me, making it obvious to one and all that we're a couple. Clearly I've passed some sort of test.

Was that the real reason Camilla wanted to come along tonight?

We stay an hour, during which Camilla tells me that Charles is on the board of several well-known charities: Save the Children, WWF, Oxfam, and dozens of smaller organisations. She tells me he's very influential, that he can make recommendations for advertising and promotional campaigns. I smile. Now that I have been accepted Camilla is already helping to promote my career. She's deliberately helping to promote my career. She must like me. She must want to keep me around.

Mustn't she?

We go back to Camilla's.

I spend the night. Eventually we sleep. Need I say more?

I DON'T EXPECT LIFE TO BE
TOTALLY FAIR, BUT I WANT PEOPLE
TO MAKE A STAB AT IT

In our desperate desire not to offend anyone, we've gone mad. It's PC-this, PC-that, we're not allowed so much as to sneeze without getting prior approval and worrying that it's going to offend some group or the other. I've had enough of political correctness.

Take my gym, for example.

Every Wednesday night is ladies' night. From eight until closing I am forbidden to use the facilities in my gym, to go beyond the front desk. What do they get up to in there? Wild orgies? Parties of male bashing?

Yes, I can understand that women don't want to be leered at, but things aren't that bad. And, besides, a woman can wear a baggy T-shirt and baggy shorts or even tracksuit bottoms if she wants to hide herself away and I can guarantee you that most of us men will respect a pretty blatant signal like that. The Alex of old never stared at women at the gym, he was too busy exercising. That is, after all, what people go there to do.

And what if I don't want to feel like a piece of meat with women ogling my muscles? Where's my men-only night? Hmm? Tell me that.

I'm a male, yes, that's true. But it's not my fault. I've done nothing wrong simply because I don't have two X-chromosomes. It's not a crime being a male. It's not fair that we're punished, that we're treated worse than everyone else, that we're told we have all the advantages, and it's only fair that every bloody fucking other person in the world gets a leg up except us.

Women get their own time alone in the gym. Hell, even beginners get their own night on Saturdays where for three hours the gym is reserved for new members. I'm normally busy on Saturday nights or too lazy to work out, but it's not fair. I've paid my money, I've got as much right as the next person to use the equipment.

What about my rights? What about me?

Monday morning I wake up in Camilla's bed with Camilla sprawled half on top of me and half on her pillow. With her face relaxed in sleep and her mouth hanging open slightly, she looks different. Innocent. Not how she appears when she's awake.

My body starts to wake up and I become aware that she's naked, that we're both naked, and that I can feel the weight of her breasts resting on my left arm. I shift slightly, trying to ease myself out from under her so that both hands are free. She mumbles and snuggles closer. I haven't the heart to wake her yet so I make do with one hand. As if of its own volition, it glides across her curves, gently, ever so gently caressing. Her nipples harden and she makes a little moan, half awake, but not yet sure that this isn't a dream. My head lowers and my mouth moves to her breast as I fumble in her top drawer for a condom. My fingers find what they're looking for and then I'm tearing open the packet and putting it on. As I slide inside Camilla her eyes open, her mind now as ready for me as her body is. She smiles and kisses me and her breath is sweet, none of that odious morning-after halitosis that afflicts some people.

An hour later I can't say I'm sated, but the desperation of my desire has been temporarily subdued. As tempted as I am to bunk off – and I know Camilla would skip work in an instant if I asked her to – too much is at stake. I'm not a playboy. I'm a man of power. I have things to do.

As I'm finishing the coffee Camilla made for me, I can sense that she wants to ask me something. Probably something along the lines of when-will-I-see-you-again. I don't make it easy for her. She has to want me. She has to work hard to get me, for the harder she has to work, the more she'll appreciate me. I'm never going to be taken for granted again. Never. Not ever again.

'Alexander?'

The word is music to my ears. She never knew me when I was Alex. She has no preconceived notion of Alex's failures and foibles. She doesn't expect me to be nice.

'Yes?'

'You will phone Charles St John, won't you?'

'Sure,' I say, draining my coffee.

'Please. Phone him today. I know you're busy, but phone today. He could do a lot for your career. For your company.' This isn't what I expected her to say, but I take it as a good sign. Of course I was already planning on phoning him, I'm not a fool, but let her think she's convinced me.

'If you think I should,' I say, slowly, deliberately, as if I'm considering the situation.

She sets her coffee cup down and then slides on to my lap. 'Please?' she says, eyes wide. 'For me?'

'For you.' I smile and kiss her, and when she eventually pulls back, smiling, I ask, 'Why?'

She blushes. She actually blushes. 'I just want you to do well.' She can't quite meet my eyes. 'I want Daddy to like you.' Daddy. That's what she said. Honest. When grown women call their father Daddy I get rather concerned. Those are the sort of fathers you expect to show up at the door with a shotgun and a vicar to protect their darling daughter's honour.

I freeze for the briefest instant but she notices. She picks herself up off my lap and begins to clear up the coffee mugs, but I can tell she's embarrassed. We've only known one another a few days. I bet she hadn't planned on mentioning her parents yet. Is she having matrimonial fantasies already? I decide to be flattered rather than scared. I don't kid myself, she had been ready to dump me last night if Charles had found me wanting, but now that I've passed their little test she wants to keep me around.

If, at this exact moment, someone stuck a gun to my head and said I had to choose someone to marry, it'd definitely be Camilla. (I don't really know anything about her, but the sex is great and she knows people. And, let's be pragmatic here, there's always divorce.)

'I look forward to meeting both your parents,' I say.

And it's true. I do. They could do a lot for me.

She turns and I watch her face carefully. Her eyes light up and she grins at me, really grins at me.

My heart does a little flip in my chest – she's so gorgeous, physically she's like the ideal woman – and I suddenly wonder whether this is what she's always like in new relationships, if she's always desperately hoping that they're special, that they're The One. Inwardly I pull back. Don't be a fool, I tell myself, Alex would be susceptible to tender emotions, but I am not. It's not my heart that's at stake, only my loins and I've plenty of other opportunities for wild sex. It's just that Camilla is useful to me. She is. That's all it is. That's definitely all it is and I won't let the sex and her beauty fool me into thinking otherwise.

She kisses my nose. 'When will I see you again?'

I knew that one was coming. 'When do you want to see me again?'

'Tonight?' she asks.

'Why not?' I say.

'Really? You're not tired of me?'

Oh, Milla, Milla, you're the best shag I've ever had. How could I be tired of you? 'Tired of you?' I say, and laugh as I pull her back on to my lap, nibbling her ear. 'How could I be tired of you?'

She wiggles and squirms and I can tell it's going to be some time before I'm ready to leave. I glance at my watch. I can spare another hour.

Once I finally make it home it's nearly lunchtime. It's good to be your own boss, but it's risky, I mustn't let myself be distracted by pleasure. Not too often.

(Enticing as it is.)

I have work to do, lots of work to do, and if I want to get where I'm planning on going I have to buckle down.

But I can do it. I know I can. I will succeed.

It's tempting to work on ideas, to come up with more campaigns, but it's not a day for creativity. It's a day for details. Details and phone calls.

First I ring my four targets of the week and manage to cajole, flatter and persuade them all to meet with me. It's short notice, but I am in the zone and I convince them that my concepts are hot (they are). I schedule two of the meetings for tomorrow, one each for Wednesday and Thursday, and that leaves me with a free day on Friday.

No more lazy mornings with Camilla. Not this week. I don't have time.

I'm not going to allow sex to rule my world. It's only hormones. Ephemeral. Power is the constant I desire.

I ring a temping agency and arrange for a PA/receptionist to start work for me on Friday. I'm keen to start looking around empty office suites so I nearly put off ringing Charles St John until later in the afternoon, but then I change my mind, Camilla's words ringing in my ears. Clients. I need clients. Clients and exposure. The rest can wait until another day.

To my surprise I'm put straight through.

'Alexander,' says Charles, in his booming voice of authority. 'Good to hear from you.'

'You asked me to phone today,' I say, not wanting to bother with the small-talk I hate and guess he hates as much as I do.

'Yes, I want you to do something for me. I'm involved with the launch of a new charity to promote ethics in genetic engineering.'

'What's the name?' I ask.

'That's just it,' says Charles. 'We don't have a name, not a real name, nor a slogan, just an idea. One of the members of the board has asked Kenneth Wilmington-Wilkes to tackle the matter.'

I clutch the phone. Why is Charles telling me this?

'You've hired Kenneth?' I ask.

'No, Kenneth is making some proposals. Nothing is concrete. There's been no contract.'

I'm thinking quickly. I can do this, I know I can do this. 'And you want me to submit my own proposals?'

He wants me to give Kenneth some competition. If I do this it'll be showdown time, high noon at the OK Corral, and I've already got a loaded gun.

Look out, Kenneth, your time is coming. Your time has come. Enjoy your last few days at the top.

'Exactly,' says Charles, his voice booming approval. 'We're having a little dinner at my country estate on Saturday. I'd like you to come. And Camilla, of course. Her father will thank me for dragging her out of town.'

'May I ask you a question?' This is important. I'm sensing an ally here, but I need to know why.

'Certainly.'

'Why don't you like Kenneth? What has he done to you?'

There's a long pause.

'Let's just say we're old rivals and leave it at that,' says Charles.

I know there's more to it, that this is something personal, but

I'm not about to push. And I don't really care. Kenneth is an easy man to hate. I smile. By the weekend I'll be ready for Wilmington-Wilkes to learn about the new me. I almost laugh aloud as I picture Kenneth's face when he sees me. My smile falls. Assuming he recognises me.

Will he even remember my name? Alex Fairfax wasn't very memorable. Oh, sure, Kenneth will remember the sacking, but he probably won't recall me. I was a faceless, nameless employee, one more piece of driftwood to throw out to sea.

I feel sick as I remember that day.

Stop it. Stop it. I shove the thoughts away. I am no longer that man. I am not he. I am me. Me. I am Alexander.

I think Elizabeth Wilmington-Wilkes will know me instantly. She's the one I humiliated in front of her friends. She'll recognise me. I hope she has nightmares, doomed to experience the exact moment of the bursting of her pride bubble again and again and again.

I smile to myself. I did that. I brought her down a peg or two.

It was Jed's plan, but I was the instrument of her humiliation and just for a second I can admire Jed's cunning. Until I recall the consequences, until I remember that I was the one Jed was setting up, that Elizabeth was just an unfortunate side effect.

Revenge is going to be, oh, so sweet. Against Elizabeth. Against Kenneth. Against Jed.

'Well, Charles,' I say, 'I can't blame you if you don't like the man. I'm not too fond of Kenneth myself. Now tell me more about this charity of yours.'

IT'S NOT SOUR GRAPES
(I REALLY DON'T LOVE HER NOW)

Once I've quizzed Charles about the goals and prospects of his latest philanthropic venture I ring Sarah. Not at home. Not on her work number. On her mobile. Knowing that she carries this phone everywhere, knowing Jed's seen it, touched it, probably used it, I get a little thrill as she answers. I'm the one making the illicit phone calls now. A couple of weeks ago it would have been Jed ringing her on her mobile, not wanting the people in her office to know how often he called. Now it's my turn.

'Hello?' says Sarah.

'Hi, Sarah.'

'Oh, hi, Alex.' She recognises my voice instantly. I can picture her sitting forward across her desk, tensing up, still expecting Alex to break down on her. But doesn't she know? I'm not that Alex any more.

'How are you?' I ask, wanting to prolong the moment. She won't be rude to me. It would be so unsporting to be rude to such an understanding ex-boyfriend.

'Good,' she says. 'You know. Good. And you?'

'Great. Great.'

There's a pause. I won't make this easy for her, she deserves to suffer. She deserves to suffer more than this. Much, much more.

'So,' she says, after a moment or two, 'anything I can do for you?'

Well, I think, you can hack off Jed's penis with a carving knife while he's sleeping but apart from that, nope. Nothing.

'Actually,' I say, 'I'd like to meet up. Just you and me. No Jed.'

'But why?' I can tell she's wary.

'I wanted to have one last chat about everything. Tie up some loose ends. Come on, Sarah, we used to be friends, you know I won't bite.'

I hear her sigh, giving in, knowing she owes me that much, that so far she's got off lightly. 'Okay. Let's meet.'

'Lunch on Wednesday?'

'Sure.' Her answer is unnaturally bright and I know she'll dread the rendezvous as much as I'm looking forward to it.

'I have a meeting in the morning,' I tell her, 'so I'll give you a ring when I'm finished. If it gets too late go ahead and eat and we can pop out for a snack or something later in the afternoon.'

'What sort of meeting?' she asks.

I smile to myself. I've got her curious now. But I'm not about to give the game away. She's Jed's girl now and I'll never forget it. Never.

As soon as I end my call with Sarah my phone rings and I half expect it to be Sarah herself, cancelling our date.

But it's Charles St John.

'Good news, Alexander,' he says. 'I've found you an office.' His voice booms out, loud and authoritative, and I wish for one instant that my voice was like his. He speaks like a high-ranking member of the old East India Company. He sounds right, established, his accent is perfect, indicating to one and all that he's got it made.

He has got it made.

Why is he being so helpful?

I'm not a fool, I'm not Alex, I know it's not because he's taken a shine to me. It's not because of me. It's for one of two reasons: Camilla or Kenneth. And I'd put my money on Kenneth. Men come and go in Camilla's life and he's got no reason to single me out and try to promote my cause, it's nothing to him.

But as for Kenneth, well, Charles wants me to help him make Kenneth suffer. It's as simple as that. But I don't mind letting Charles think he's using me when all along I'm the one who's using him.

I'm the one who wants revenge. I deserve revenge, but I don't mind letting Charles St John in on the action.

During my earlier conversation with Charles, I'd mentioned, in passing, that I was looking for an office.

I don't know about this. I'm my own man. I don't need anyone else doing favours for me. I don't want anyone else trying to do things for me. I will be beholden to no man.

But wait a minute, one of the keys to success is to accept aid where it's offered. I won't owe Charles St John for this or for anything else. I'll use him as he's no doubt trying to use me. I won't be under any obligation to him. I feel no need to pay him back for assistance he's giving me of his own free will. I'm not Alex, I don't keep track of favours. Not unless they're owed to me.

'It's in Golden Square,' says Charles. 'You know it?'

'Yes. Just behind Piccadilly Circus.' The rents must be astronomical. I want an office and I must have an office in a good location, but can I afford it? Of course I can. My clients are rolling in.

'I've managed to get you the bargain of the century. One of my friends, Hugo Tarpington-Jones, owns the building. This office – it's on the third floor – has been vacant only a day, a surprise and abrupt end of a tenancy, I'm told. It's not been advertised yet, but I've called in a favour and Hugo says you can have it for half of the usual rate. Half, my boy. You won't find anything like this again.'

'I could view it this evening.' I don't want to be pushed into anything, but I'm not stupid. If it's as good an offer as it sounds (I can't trust him that the rent is cheap, I'll have to do my own checking), I'll take it.

'This evening? I don't know if Hugo's boys will be around after seven.'

'Then make it quarter to seven.'

He hesitates. 'Done. And if Hugo's management company can't make it I'll get the keys myself. Or give them to Camilla.'

Camilla. Not exactly the person I'd want to take scouting for offices, she might get the wrong idea, but then again, maybe she's exactly who I need. She'll be just the person to judge whether or not they're good enough. No sense getting an office she and her kind won't approve of.

'I'll give Camilla a ring myself,' I say. 'We have plans to see one another tonight, so maybe she'd like to come along.'

'When Wilmington-Wilkes hears of your new address, he'll be furious that you're doing so well for yourself. He hates it when ex-employees succeed without him.' Charles chuckles, unable to contain his delight at the thought, confirming my assumption that he's out for Kenneth's blood.

We discuss the rent and the building in further detail.

There's more to this than meets the eye. But, hey, what do I care? Charles can have his secret agenda against Kenneth. It doesn't bother me. And an office at cheap rent? Who am I to say no?

Now I have some phone calls to make. Letting agents, letting agents, what are your prices?

IT'S NOT NAGGING,
IT'S ANOTHER FRIENDLY REMINDER
(THE TENTH, TO BE PRECISE)

When my mother rings me in the afternoon I'm so happy, so excited about everything that I have to force myself not to blurt out all that's been happening. For I'm not stupid, I don't want my mother to know about the darker side of my new and improved personality. She doesn't need to know about my steps towards revenge. Let her just be proud of my success. That's all she needs to know about.

She quizzes me about my weekend and I only tell her that I went clubbing and worked. I'm tempted to tell her about seeing Madonna at the party, but I know it would come out wrong if I try to explain how I'm finally moving in the right circles. And, anyway, I'm Mr Cool these days, I'll be hanging out with lots of stars soon. It's unbecoming to make a big deal of it and I have no desire to namedrop. It's expected that I'll hang out at those sorts of places with those sorts of people. Mum might not know it yet, but I do.

Once the initial chit-chat is out of the way and we've had some quality conversing time together, she gives away the ulterior motive behind this call. 'I hope you haven't forgotten your father's birthday,' she says.

'Don't worry, I haven't.' How could I forget? She's been reminding me weekly for over two months. If there's one constant in my life, it's got to be her: she has her ways and she sticks to them.

'And you'll be here for his birthday dinner?'

'Yes, Mother. Next Monday. I'll be there.'

'Oh dear. It just occurred to me that Sarah won't be coming. Unless you two have made up?'

'No, Mother, Sarah will not be coming. We split up. Remember?'

'I'm not senile, Alex. I was only hoping you'd come to your senses and forgiven her. Maybe you should give her another chance. She's a really nice girl. We all make mistakes.'

'Sarah is not a really nice girl. She was having an affair with my boss. I don't want to forgive her.'

'But maybe she's learnt her lesson. Maybe—'

'Sarah is a slut. You really don't want a woman like that for a daughter-in-law.' I don't think she's ever heard me use such a nasty tone of voice before. But what does she expect, harping on about Sarah like that? And I'm only speaking about Sarah the Whore. Sarah lost her right to my respect days ago.

There's an awkward pause while she's waiting for me to say something more, but I don't oblige her, I don't want to talk about things. This isn't an AA meeting.

'Is there something you're not telling me, Alex? Is something bothering you? Has something happened? You sound strange.'

'Do I?' Is it so obvious that I'm more confident and no longer the self-effacing, placating wimp I used to be?

'Is anything wrong?'

'No, everything's great.' And it is. Life is wonderful. 'Look,' I say, 'I'll see you next week. I'm really busy today.'

I don't hang up on her exactly – she is my mother – but I don't give her time to start pestering me for more information. I say goodbye before I put the phone down. I really can't be dealing with this right now.

And yes, Mother, something has happened. I've changed. But I can hardly come right out and say, 'I've changed, Mum. I'm Alexander now.' That would sound lame. And lame utterances no longer become me.

I take a few minutes to calm myself. Breathe in, breathe out, breathe in, breathe out. I picture Sarah abandoned and alone,

Jed unemployed and poor, both friendless, both outcasts, both destroyed by me. And suddenly, as the images run through my mind, as I picture Jed huddled in a doorway somewhere, clutching a threadbare blanket and an empty beer bottle, I start to smile. I've regained my equilibrium. I'm back in the zone. I'm happy again. I shouldn't let my mother upset me. She means well. She always has.

MY NEW OFFICE

A sharp-eyed estate-agent type in his mid-thirties is waiting for Camilla and me as we stroll up to the building at a couple of minutes to seven. (Camilla had insisted on stopping to reapply her lipstick, making us a few minutes late when I had wanted to be on time.) He launches into a clearly rehearsed spiel about the benefits of this area and the office itself.

(I checked, the rate they're offering is fantastic. I won't find anything better. Not around here.)

The building is well maintained. It's old and stately in appearance and the interior is all polished wood and marble, yet the office available to me is surprisingly light and airy, a pleasant mix between the modern and the traditional. There's a large reception area, a kitchen, three good-sized offices and a fourth that I decide to use as a meeting room. (No furniture, of course, I'll have to provide that myself.) And there's even a balcony. The view isn't great, it looks over the back of another building, but if you lean precariously over the side you can just make out a small segment of the London Eye.

I could be happy here. I could work here.

'I'll take it,' I say, interrupting our guide in mid-flow.

Camilla frowns. 'You didn't ask if I like it,' she says to me. 'I thought that's why you wanted me along. Because you value my opinion.'

Spoiled bitch.

I stare at her for a second without speaking. She's not so cute when she's awake. Beautiful but not cute. You have to be cuddly and soft to be cute.

'And do you like it?' I ask, in an even tone, my face blank.

'Yes.' She smiles, instantly happy. 'I think you should take it.'

Well, I'm glad that's settled, then.

'Is that a yes?' asks the estate-agent type.

I turn to him, glad for the distraction. 'I'd like a one-year lease.' I'm not stupid, I'm going to have a proper contract. It's all got to be signed and legal. Who knows how things will turn out with Camilla? And I have a feeling, just a feeling, that Camilla turns nasty when she's let down, when she's cross or when she just decides she's had enough of you. I don't want to have to worry about what will happen if all doesn't go well between Camilla and me.

It's not that I want it to go wrong. She's exactly what I'm looking for, but you can't count on these things. You have to make allowances for extenuating circumstances.

He hesitates. 'We'd prefer a term of six months. And then we'd be willing to renew it under new terms.'

I shrug. 'One year. I don't want to waste my energy moving in only to have to move again.'

'Oh, we wouldn't force you to move, Mr Fairfax.'

No, you'd just raise the rents and try to charge me above market value to make up for the losses you'll experience under this first lease.

And in a year I expect I'll need bigger offices and I'll need to move anyway.

'One year,' I say.

He hesitates, his face slightly pale. He takes a deep breath, then he smiles, all business again. 'Done.'

He doesn't like this. It's obviously going to lose them a lot of money. That must be some favour Charles St John has called in. I shrug. It's nothing to me. Not really. Not once the papers are signed.

We shake on it and I'm happy. This is it, then. My offices. Platypus-fox is truly in business now. These rooms will comfortably hold between fifteen or twenty employees. That should do for a year. (I was exaggerating when I said I'd take on all of the underpaid Wilmington-Wilkes staff. Some but not all. I wouldn't want everyone anyway.)

'I'd like the paperwork ready for tomorrow,' I say.

'Certainly, Mr Fairfax.'

'And I'd like the lease to start on Wednesday. I'll need a day to sort out insurance.'

'Of course. If you could just pop round to my office tomorrow afternoon and sign the papers I can give you the keys first thing on Wednesday morning.'

Camilla turns the full force of her beauty on the estate agent and smiles a brilliant smile. 'Perhaps you could just leave the keys with us now?'

She's not even looking at me and I feel a little jolt pass through my body as I catch a glimpse of her smile. She's so gorgeous. And sexy. I want her. I want her right now.

He blinks. 'Tonight?' Clearly he's not used to beautiful women paying attention to him.

'Yes,' says Camilla. 'I'd like to help Alexander with his interior-design ideas. We need to get working if he wants the best furniture. We don't want to wait four weeks for his desk to arrive.'

'Well—'

'Great,' she says, stepping close to him and holding out her hand. 'I knew you'd agree with me.'

Dazed, he hesitates, then drops the keys into her hand.

'Don't worry,' says Camilla, 'we don't expect you to stay. You go on home. We'll lock up.'

And just like that he leaves.

When he's gone I grab Camilla and kiss her and she's kissing me and right there in the reception area we sink to the floor. We're like wild animals, tearing at one another's clothes, pushing them out of the way. We don't bother removing anything, just slide things up and down and then I'm inside her and then she's coming and I'm coming and I'm happy. The office has been christened.

I let my breathing slow, relaxing for a moment, wanting to do it again, but Camilla stands and pulls down her skirt.

What's she doing? I'm not finished. I'm not ready to leave.

'You'll drive this weekend, won't you? I detest driving in traffic.'

'Hmm?' I'm still wondering why she's not in my arms. Didn't she enjoy it? She did enjoy it, didn't she? She certainly seemed wild. But could I really tell the difference? Alex always thought Sarah was satisfied and look what happened there: she ran off with another man, a weedy, smug, skinny little bastard at that. Camilla's not like that. Is she?

But then she's speaking again and I force myself to concentrate. Of course she enjoyed it, she instigated it, didn't she?

'What kind of car do you have?'

'Car? Why? Does it matter?'

She smiles a hard little smile. 'Don't be silly. Of course it matters. I can't be seen in any old car. What would people say?'

I sit up and run my fingers through my hair. The sex is clearly over for the moment.

'I have a Jag.' I don't tell her it's in the garage being mended. (They've promised it'll be ready by Friday.)

'Oh, that's okay, then.' She suddenly sits on my lap, winding her legs around me. 'I like Jags.'

She starts to unbutton her shirt. I watch her fingers slowly parting the fabric. She's teasing me, but I can't tear my eyes away.

'Do you want to spend the weekend at my parents' house?' she asks. 'If we're going all the way out there for Charles's meeting we might as well make a mini-break of it. We're very close neighbours. It'd be convenient.'

'Okay,' I say, catching a glimpse of her lacy white bra.

I know she's trying to manipulate me, but I don't care. I want to meet her parents, I want to get more involved in her life. I need someone like her. She doesn't have to use her body for sex to get what she wants, but I'm awfully glad she does.

TWO MORE CLIENTS

By five p.m. on Tuesday I feel higher than the time I drank the jug of orange juice and vodka my father had placed in the fridge before a party when I was ten. I was thirsty, I'd just come in from playing football and I drank all of it. For the first hour I was floating around. I was funny. I was hilarious. And then I was very, very sick. My father was angry with me. My mother was angry with my father. But I saw the humour in it all. Or I did two days later when I felt better. It's a good experience for any pre-teen, I'd recommend it: it put me off alcohol for years.

My morning meeting went well, they signed me up straight away, but the afternoon appointment was more trying. For a second I could feel Alex-doubts and thought they were going to turn me down, but I carried on. I persevered, I talked and talked and persuaded them in the end.

Ching. Ching. Ching. (The sounds of an old-fashioned till.)

I now have five clients under my belt. Five. When I get to ten I'll be content. At least for a week or two.

I had a bit of spare time between meetings so I signed my lease and set up the insurance. I'm all ready to move in tomorrow. As fond as I've grown of my daisies, having an office will beat working in a room full of boxes.

I can't be selfish and have sex with Camilla on Tuesday. The world needs me. I have to remember my position as the protector and defender of the weak and meek. It's time for a little revenge.

Camilla is upset when I speak to her on Tuesday and tell her I'm busy, but I feel it's good for her. And I do relent and make arrangements to see her on Wednesday night. She needs a night to pine for me. I mustn't be too easy or she'll lose interest. Remember, Alexander, nice guys never win.

I go over my list of revenge. My plans are on schedule for Jed and Wilmington-Wilkes. I feel I've got Sarah in hand. Spotty youths who smash cars? Besides punching them on the nose I can't see how I'm going to make much difference. (And I can hardly go around beating up nine-year-olds.) Maybe I should donate a bunch of money for CCTV cameras. That's an idea. I'll consider it. The men who mugged me? No, I'll save that one up. Thomas and William at Wilmington-Wilkes? Not yet. Not yet. All in good time. The snooty librarian? Perhaps. I haven't decided whether or not her actions merit a measure of vengeance.

That leaves the Neanderthal at the pub who threw a glass into my face.

'*Oi, those're my wife's tits you're staring at.*'

Yes, yes, this one I want to do. I'm in the mood.

Now what would be the appropriate piece of poetic justice?

Violence? No. He'd understand that. It wouldn't be anything new. He needs to be taught a lesson.

That leaves a good old-fashioned dose of humiliation.

VENGEANCE ON THE OI MAN

The Oi Man. I call him that because it's the first word I heard him say and I imagine it's his favourite word. Oi this. Oi that. Oi, you.

I haven't quite decided what I want to do to him. I realise that the glass wasn't aimed at me personally, but anyone who could break a glass and throw it across a crowded pub is a moron and a thug. He needs to be punished. And not just for the pain and *Angst* he put me through, or for the scar along my temple that will probably fade over time but will never quite go away. No, he needs to be punished for humanity's sake, maybe even taught a lesson, but I try at all times to be honest with myself and I seriously doubt I'll have the patience to teach him anything lasting.

Wait a minute. What am I saying? It's not up to me to punish him for all of humanity. It's a selfish world. I'm Alexander, not Alex the Loser. I'm punishing the Oi Man solely for the wrong he did to me. Nothing else. An eye for an eye, a tooth for a tooth and all that. Though I won't enact literal vengeance. I doubt I'd enjoy smashing a glass in his face, and enjoyment is something I demand from my revenge. Vengeance is no fun if it's a chore. No. I have to be clever. Very clever.

Still pondering what form my revenge should take, I head to the pub where it all happened. I doubt they'll recognise me. I was only Alex then and, besides, if they remember anything at all it'll be all that blood. The tea towel I'd pressed to my head was like a sponge soaking up red dye. If it hadn't been happening to me, it would have been fascinating to watch and I wouldn't have cared who the poor bleeding bugger was, no, siree, not me.

I approach the pub, walking the same route I had taken on that fateful night (there's nothing deliberate or spooky about that, it's the quickest way from the flat to the pub). My heart-rate accelerates and it seems like I'm more aware, that I can hear things happening two streets away, that my eyesight is so sharp I can see the mole on a woman's collarbone across the street. I am aware, I am ready. Is this what a spy feels like at the start of a mission? Is this the euphoria an SAS man experiences immediately before parachuting into enemy territory?

With all the civility and professionalism of the past couple of days, I'm ready for something different. To Camilla, to the world, I cannot show this side of myself. No, no, the predator has to remain hidden behind a veneer of affability. But I know, all successful men know, that to be a success takes more than just politeness: a degree of ruthlessness is required and this ruthlessness can't be switched off, it can only be disguised. I am a man, and a mass of my testosterone is desperate for release. The Oi Man should never have messed with me.

The pub is not quite like I remember it. It's not so crowded (it's Tuesday now instead of Friday night) and it's not the seedy place I'd built it into in my mind. Inside it's just a pub like any other pub across the country. It's not the sort of place Alexander would frequent, but Alex would have liked it well enough. Actually, I did like it, Alex liked it. While I was here and chatting to Amber and the others I'd been able to stop thinking about the ruination of my career and the sad mess of my life. Until, that is, the glass smashed into my face and brought me back to reality with a jolt, forcing me to acknowledge what a sad bastard I was.

I scan the room, not really expecting to see the Oi Man, but stranger things have happened. He's not here and suddenly I'm relieved. I don't have a plan, not a real plan, and I don't want to confront him until I decide what to do.

Go away, Alex, I scream inside. I, Alexander, want to confront the Oi Man. I need to see him, to get inspiration on how to bring him down a peg or two. How will he be punished if I don't know where to find him?

Is this the Oi Man's local? It could be, but has he been back since the night of the fight? (If you can call it a fight.) The pub is half filled with a combination of builders (tanned, muscular, slightly rumpled) and office workers (pale, some thin, some flabby, all neat, with a desperate, slightly staring look in their eyes like they can't believe their good fortunes in having a few hour's respite away from the glare of their computer screens).

I'm just about to head to the bar and order a pint when I see her.

One of the busty blondes from the Oi Man's table. (Yep, Sarah, I'd agree with you here, she's definitely a fake blonde.)

She's dressed in skimpy, skin-tight clothing and wearing too much blue eye shadow. It's definitely her.

But is she the wife? Or merely a friend?

I decide it doesn't matter. Wife or not, she knows the Oi Man. She'll lead me to him.

(I wonder if the police caught the Oi Man after he hit me with the glass and if he's locked away in prison. No. Couldn't have happened. The police would have brought me in to identify him. Good. I'm glad. I want him free and on the streets. I want him where I can get to him.)

The woman sits alone, smoking at a table, drinking from a pint glass. From the half-filled pint opposite her I judge she's not alone.

I go to the bar and wait patiently to be served, trying to look as if I'm meeting someone here. I surreptitiously watch the woman.

A moment later a man in his late thirties emerges from the toilet. Despite myself I hold my breath, but it's not the Oi Man.

Yet this man joins the busty blonde at her table. He slides into the seat across from her and picks up the pint, taking a long drink even as he reaches for her hand.

The Oi Man's woman (or friend, I really don't know yet) looks uncomfortable and her eyes dart around the room. She allows the man to hold her hand for a second, then she pulls away and I can see the flash of a wedding ring on her finger. They're too far away for me to overhear, but I can tell she's nervous, unhappy, even, and her eyes keep flicking to the door.

Is this man not her husband? Could she possibly be the Oi Man's wife?

Does she fear the Oi Man will find her here?

I hope that she is the wife of the Oi Man and that she is having an affair. It would be the absolute perfect vengeance against him. He'd be so humiliated. He threw the broken glass at a man he accused of merely looking at his wife (even if it hit me instead) so finding out she's having an affair would destroy him. I could live with that.

It's easy for me to hang back and let others be served before me. I pretend I'm meeting someone and keep glancing at my watch and scanning the room.

The Oi Man's female friend, wife or not, stands, and her male companion downs his pint and follows her to the door. They leave.

I wait a moment, forcing myself not to run after them. I glance at my watch and sigh loudly. I shrug my shoulders and head towards the door. No one pays me any attention and it's just how I want it. (My shoulders are slightly slumped and I'm wearing some old Alex clothes. I don't want to stand out, I want to blend into the crowd.)

What if I'm too slow? What if they've already climbed into a car and are driving away? How will I find them? How will I follow them?

I emerge into the sunny evening and breathe a sigh of relief. They're walking, carefully apart and not touching, down the street. It's an innocent picture. Or would have been if they hadn't kept glancing nervously over their shoulders.

I know they see me as I start to head in the same direction they're taking, but they don't seem concerned. Is it only a husband they're worried about?

Please, please, let that husband be the Oi Man.

The Oi Man hurt me, hurt Alex, physically, but not only physically, my anguish was also mental. I felt a failure.

A failure and a coward in front of Amber. In front of Amber and Noreen and Clarence and Diana. Bleeding like a stuck pig, standing there gaping like a fool, covered in spilt alcohol, is not a way to impress one's new flatmates.

They continue to walk and I follow but not like I'm following them exactly, just that we're all heading in the same direction. Thankfully they're headed towards a main road so I'm less suspicious-looking.

I wish I'd thought to bring my camera with me. If this is the Oi Man's wife I'll need photographic evidence to ensure his humiliation. The complete and utter degradation of his pride, of his image in front of his loutish mates.

But I'll worry about that later, for now I just need to know where they're going so I can discover their usual haunts.

What would I, the old I, have done in this situation? Absolutely nothing. Alex wouldn't have been here today. Alex would have stayed away from that pub for the rest of his life, too scarred by the memories to enter it. And Alex would never have sought vengeance. He would have been upset, angry, but it would have ended there. He would have done nothing.

It's better that I'm Alexander now. I can look out for myself, for my interests, as Alex could never have done.

The busty blonde and her lover turn on to a side-street and I slow my steps. To follow or not to follow? I walk slowly but decide it would look suspicious if I just stopped so I follow them and turn on to the street. I'm just in time to see them head down another street. They're standing further apart now and they've stopped looking over their shoulders. It's like they're scared. Like they're getting close. Like they're nearing their destination.

Dare I hope they're headed for a house?

These are residential streets. They must be going to a house.

His house. Or her house. Maybe – please, God – the Oi Man's house.

I speed up, cross the street they turned on to and see the woman unlocking a house in a long, 1930s terraced row.

Bingo.

She holds the keys. Her house, then. Not the man's. It's not their house, that much is obvious.

The house is half-way down the street, opposite a park, and as the woman opens the door I can see that it's painted the bright, deep blue of a cloudless desert sky. Like a beacon. A lighthouse light calling all ships safely home to port.

They enter the house and then I turn on to the street, passing the house and barely glancing at the door. It's the only one with a blue door. I'll have no trouble finding it again.

The park is a small neighbourhood park, rather sparse and forlorn as parks go, but it has a small set of swings and a bit of grass where a pair of small boys half-heartedly kick a football back and forth. It's perfect for my needs.

I aim at the blue door. My camera's got an auto-focus so there's not much else for me to do, but I'm poised and ready, waiting, waiting.

I'm standing in the park, hovering among a group of trees holding a bird book, a pair of binoculars around my neck. (Thank you, Noreen.) If anyone gets close enough to see me they'll think I'm an eccentric and not very effective bird watcher.

I shift slightly, tired of being on my feet.

How long are they going to shag anyway?

I've been standing here for twenty-five minutes. It took me half an hour to rush back to my room, grab my camera and insert a new role of film (thirty-six exposures, just in case) and borrow the binoculars and bird book from Noreen before returning to the park and finding that the football boys had gone.

I told Noreen that I'm an amateur ornithologist and now I'm terrified that she'll corner me as soon as I get home and insist on holding an in-depth discussion concerning the child-rearing regurgitation methods of magpies compared to those of smaller birds such as sparrows and robins. I'll try to convince Amber to join us in the kitchen for a glass of wine. (I can do it, I can just be friends with Amber. It's feasible, I know it's feasible, I'm in control.)

It's possible that the lovebirds have finished their shag, that in the half-hour I was away they had their fun and it's all over. But I don't feel unlucky today. I think they're still inside.

Now, the question comes, is she the wife of the Oi Man?

The front door opens and my finger hovers over the button, itching to press it and take my first picture.

Come on, Alexander. Go, Alexander, go, go, go. You can do it. You're a winner.

The woman, the wife, but not necessarily the Oi Man's wife, appears in her dressing-gown. Silly fool, doesn't she know the whole street can see her? You'd have thought she would have got dressed.

But it's good for me.

I snap a photo of her.

Oh, sweet Lord, I can't believe my luck. The man steps outside and he runs a hand down her cheek. In full view of the neighbours. In full view of my camera.

Snap. Snap.

The only thing I can say for them is that they don't kiss. Their lips don't touch.

Do they want to get caught? Is that what they're hoping for?

(Well, then, today is their lucky day, after all.)

They're chatting. Both look sad, you can tell neither wants to part, but part they must. (Sob, sob, sob, sob.)

And then, oh, my God, I'm one lucky son-of-a-bitch (sorry, Mum, that's just an expression, I don't mean anything by it), he slips his hand inside her dressing-gown.

Snap, snap, snap. I zoom in and the angle's perfect. His hand. Inside her robe. I get six shots in quick succession.

I snap more pictures, suddenly glad I can't hear what they're saying. It must be so pathetic and excruciating.

I love you. I'll miss you. Call me. When will I see you again?

Finally the man leaves, he walks down the street, heading away from the pub. I snap a few more photos of him, getting a couple of good shots of his face.

Little Mrs Wife goes inside and closes her door, shutting out the big bad world.

Poor dearie. Is she sad?

I put my camera away, but I continue to stand among the trees, staring at the house. Is this the right thing to do? Am I being fair? If this woman is Mrs Oi Man she'll be punished too and it's not her fault that I want revenge on her husband.

Maybe I should think of something else.

I've always said I don't want the innocent to suffer.

I feel doubt, I feel uncertain, I feel uneasy. I'm torn, undecided. What should I do? Alex would say I'm being mean, that it's not her fault, that she's done nothing.

But the opportunity is there. It's perfect. If she's the wife of the Oi Man.

Would the wife of the Oi Man be an innocent? Would she be nice? Would she be a member of the society of the gentle prey? I don't know. It doesn't fit. I can't decide. But even if she isn't nice, should she suffer just from her associations? Is that really justice? Is that the kind of vengeance I want?

As I stand there undecided I hear voices approaching. A moment later two men come into view. The Oi Man and another man are walking down the street, nearing the house with the blue door. Will they stop? Will he stop?

They both stop on the pavement. They're chatting.

Icicles up and down my spine. This is it. This is the moment of truth. One of these men will go inside. Who will it be?

A minute later, perhaps two, but it feels more like ten, twenty, a hundred, the Oi Man pulls a set of keys from his pocket and turns towards the house.

Sorry, Mrs Oi Man, it'll all have to come out. It's too perfect a chance to miss. And, besides, I'll be doing you a favour: I'll be giving you grounds for divorce. It's obvious he doesn't make you happy.

The Oi Man heads towards the house with the blue door.

Towards the adulteress wife.

The other man walks away, down the street, following

unknowingly in the steps of the wife's lover. The lover of the Oi Man's wife.

The Oi Man unlocks the blue door.

Vengeance on the Oi Man?

Stage one complete.

THE RESIDUAL AFTER-EFFECTS
OF SUCCESS, OR HOW GIDDINESS
CAN BE GOOD FOR YOU

The first thing that strikes me as I open the front door to my flat is the quiet and I finally allow the grin I've been suppressing for the last thirty minutes to stretch across my face. It's safe now. I no longer need to worry about remaining incognito out on the streets, no longer need to hide the smile of pure, radiant delight that would make me stand out from the crowd, for my mission, or at least the first leg of my mission, is over and I don't have to pretend to be a nobody like Alex for one single second more.

I head straight to my room and shed my disguise, leaving the old clothes in a heap on the floor. They say that clothes don't make a man, and they don't, not on their own. A man needs the right attitude to wear expensive clothing properly, without looking like someone dressing up for a special occasion, all pink and freshly scrubbed and oh-so-obviously uncomfortable. But the right clothes help, because once I've changed into my costlier, well-cut garb I instantly feel better. And more myself.

Opening the door a crack, I listen for signs of life, signs of habitation. Silence. No TVs, no radio, no talking, nothing. Seizing my chance, praying Noreen is taking a nap in her room or that she's gone out for the evening and that I'll be spared a lecture about birds, cleverly disguised in Noreen's mind as a discussion, I grab the binoculars and bird guide and make a dash for the kitchen. Trying to move both silently and as quickly as the wind is not easy, but I do my best for I don't want to be seen. I reach the kitchen, fling open the door and rush inside.

Amber is sitting at the kitchen table writing a letter and she jumps as I enter and gives a little scream of fright. I'm startled, too, but I manage to hide it and act like I knew she was there, that I was trying to sneak up on her. The truth is I got carried away. I'm feeling so slap-happy and flushed with success after my photography session with the lovebirds that I was half reliving the stalking and hiding games my brother and I played as children. We spent weeks of the school holidays engaged in our own private wars, being soldiers, spies, assassins, whatever our missions required. The fact that it's been nearly fifteen years since my last participation in such a game didn't seem to matter: I reverted to old form without a flicker of thought and it would have been downright embarrassing if someone had surprised me and seen me in hunter-stalker mode. But it hadn't happened. My image remains intact. And anyway, tonight is my night for victory, I can celebrate any way I want to, even if it makes me look stupid. (Though, obviously, looking foolish is only allowed inside the flat and preferably when no one else is home.)

I smile at Amber and join in her laughter when she says, 'You scared me.'

'Then I'll make it up to you,' I say. I set the binoculars and bird guide on the counter, leaving them where Noreen is sure to find them, then cross the kitchen and lean against the table next to Amber. I'm close, very close, and it could be considered an invasion of personal space, but I don't think she'll mind. And she doesn't, she just smiles up at me. 'What are you writing?' I ask, and peer at her letter as if I'm about to start reading it.

Amber colours, a flattering pink that sweeps up her neck and covers her face in seconds, and gathers up the pages, folding them and slipping them inside their envelope. 'Just a letter to a friend,' she says.

I quirk an eyebrow. 'A boyfriend?' I ask, half teasing, half serious, wanting to know the answer.

'No.' She shakes her head. 'A friend from school.'

'Good,' I say. And I just smile.

'She's working with the Red Cross in South America,' says Amber, quickly filling the pause I let hang deliberately in the air. 'She's the only person I write letters to.'

My smile widens. Do I make her nervous? 'Is Noreen home?'

'No. She popped out to get some more vegetables for dinner. She should be back soon.'

'You mean we're here all alone? Just the two of us?'

Amber's flush deepens. 'Yes.'

I grab her hands and pull her to her feet. 'Then we're running away.'

She laughs. 'What?'

I slip an arm around her waist and propel her out of the kitchen and towards the front door. 'We're going out, I'm taking you out.'

'Now?' She glances at her clothes so I use the excuse and glance down at her too. She's wearing jeans belted over a snug shirt. She looks sensational. 'But I'm not dressed for dinner.'

Dinner? I pause. I shouldn't be taking her to dinner, I shouldn't let her think I'm taking her to dinner. What am I doing?

'Then we'll go for ice cream,' I say, using the clothing as an excuse, dinner would be too much, dinner would send the wrong message. 'We'll go to Leicester Square and we can eat ice cream and guess the tourists' nationalities at the same time.' I give her my best smile as I continue to usher her to the front door. 'Come on, say yes, it'll be fun.'

'Okay, okay, you've convinced me.'

I grab her coat from the coat rack, slip it over her shoulders, and we're through the door and out on the street in moments. I take her hand and we set off running, fleeing the possible arrival of Noreen, heading for the main road.

Escape. Freedom. I hail a cab and it stops. We climb inside, it drives away and we're safe. No Noreen lectures tonight. I grin and flirt with Amber and the journey seems to take no time at all and then we're getting out and I insist on buying Amber a triple-scoop sundae despite her protests that she won't be able to eat it all.

And as she takes her first bite and rolls her eyes heavenward in ecstasy over the taste of all that chocolate, I have this irresistible urge to kiss her. I want to kiss her. I want to do nothing but kiss her. Instead I start talking, blurting out the first thing that comes to mind and it's only after the words have been spoken, after they're out there, in the air, forever irretractable, that I realise what I've said. What I've asked.

'Really?' asks Amber. 'You want me to come to your father's birthday party?' Her cheeks are glowing and her spoon hovers half-way to her mouth.

Did I really invite her? I know I spoke, I know that, but was I insane? Was it a moment of temporary insanity? I can't do this to Amber. I'm sending her all the wrong signals. Well, not the wrong signals, they're the right ones, I do like her, I am attracted to her, but I'm not going to do anything about it. We're friends and that's the way it's going to stay.

I realise suddenly that she's waiting for my response. What else can I do? I say, 'I'd love you to, please say yes.' My soul is frozen with horror – what have I done? – but the words still pour out, flowing naturally, with that flirtatious tone in my voice that seems to curse me whenever Amber is near and I'm trying to be good.

'Yes, I'll come.' She's smiling, she's happy, she's jumping to the wrong conclusions.

'Good.' I take a bit of my sundae. It's done now, I can't take it back. I'll have to guard my tongue more cautiously in the future, but I'll be careful, I'll make it work. We'll just go as friends, it's not like this is a date, it's not like we've been on a proper date, we're just flatmates, that's what it is. Amber can help protect me from my mother; she can shield me from all those questions and disappointed glances my mother will direct my way over my split with Sarah. All those demands to know exactly what happened and what I did wrong to make Sarah feel neglected and have an affair. 'Sarah's a slut, everyone, she's a nymphomaniac,' that's what I'd have to say and my mother wouldn't like that, not at all. But with Amber there, none of that will happen, my family won't quiz me in front of her.

I nearly blurt this out to Amber, nearly tell her she can protect me, but I glance into her shining eyes and I regain control of my senses in time. I can't tell a girl that she'll come in handy so I won't have to answer questions about my ex-girlfriend: that's not something you say to a woman, particularly not to someone as fetching as Amber. That would be unkind and I will not be unkind to Amber.

I watch Amber take another mouthful of ice cream and I snap out of it, for tonight is a night for joy and celebration. What am I worrying about? It'll be fun. I'll have fun. She'll have fun. And that's all there'll be to it.

Today the office is officially mine. I know that Camilla wanted to be present for the grand opening, but it was something I wanted to do on my own. So here I am, keys in my hand, unlocking the door to my office at eight a.m.

It's empty. There are no desks, no computers, no telephones, nothing. But it's mine.

Less than two weeks ago Jed thought he'd permanently stymied my career and now this. Wilmington-Wilkes won't know what's hit them. Have they realised they've lost clients yet? Even if they have it doesn't matter, they won't have strung it all together, not yet, and on Saturday, at the gracious home of Charles St John, good old Kenneth will discover the awful truth that I'm in competition with him. It may not mean much to him on the night, but it will when he realises that I'm the one who's stolen his clients. Then he'll be afraid. He'll be very afraid.

I spend an hour walking from room to room, visualising how it will look when it's full of equipment and staff. My staff. Working for me.

On the way to the day's meeting I stop at Boots and leave my precious Oi Man film at their one-hour processing. I leave a false name and number, and order double prints.

LUNCH WITH JED'S WOMAN

A few hours later, with a new client and a packet of photos (so clear and deliciously incriminating) in my pocket, I catch a cab to Sarah's office.

The stupid woman is waiting on the pavement, looking guilty and shifty as she tries to keep out of view of the office windows.

She doesn't want anyone to see her with me. Has she kept our appointment secret? Has she hidden it from Jed?

Does anyone at work know her sordid tale? Has she confided in her girlfriends? Would they think less of her, knowing she's chosen Jed but is still meeting me?

Does Sarah feel guilty? Does she feel like she's cheating on Jed?

Is this how it all begins? With an innocent luncheon?

I'd like to ask how her affair with Jed started – I'm curious, I'd really like to know – but I can't. It would make me seem jealous and upset and that's the last impression I want to give.

But when did it move from an attraction to a kiss then a cuddle and then finally a full-blown affair? Was it a matter of weeks or days from the first illicit meeting to the nudity?

I'll never know the truth.

And that saddens me.

It would hurt Alex, but I feel that he needs to know, that I need to know, that it would make that little bit inside me that occasionally responds with Alex's conscience a little harder and more steady. That it would make Alex more like me, that all of me would think as Alexander.

But give it time. I'm getting better at being Alexander with every day that passes.

We make small-talk as we walk to a little café around the corner and as we're eating our sandwiches I realise that she's wearing the blue silk blouse I gave her for Christmas.

Is she trying to remind me of how much I cared for her? Does she think I'll go easy on her if I recall how much I loved her?

It won't work, Sarah. Alex would have fallen for your ploy. But I'm not Alex. And I will never be him again.

I think she's surprised at how good I look, that she's a bit shocked that I'm so happy and positive, so put together and confident. Poor Sarah. Have I hurt her feelings? Did she expect me to commit suicide over the loss of her love? Is that what she wanted? Would she have felt flattered then? Would she have had a tale to tell at parties for the rest of her life? Would it have given her comfort in her old age to know how much she was once loved?

I smile at her across the table and I know that she's going to be mine again. Mine to do with what I will. And I'll have her, but it won't be for long. It's not like she'd fit into my new life and I hardly want to reward her for what she did to me. But I can be civil, I can keep up the front, I will be a gentleman. For now. I plan to do this properly. And it won't be with vicious words. Those wounds can heal too easily.

As we chat about this and that, Sarah flirts with me. I was with her for two years. I know the signals. The coy laugh, the smiles, the blushes, the rapt attention to my words.

What's the matter, Sarah? Are you missing having two men to fuck you? Is skinny Jed not enough to satisfy your baser urges?

'So where are you working now?' asks Sarah, fluttering her eyelashes.

I'm spending every second of every day working towards the moment when I crush Kenneth and Jed beneath the heel of my boot. And then I'll see Jed cast out into the street in rags. Will you love him then?

'Sorry,' I say, thinking, That's a good touch, it'll throw her off the scent, Alex used to say sorry all the time, 'it's a secret.' I smile to take the sting out of my words. 'I had to sign a contract saying I wouldn't talk about it.'

Liar, liar, pants on fire. Alex was never a liar. The worst lie of my life as Alex was telling my father that the hairpiece he bought for himself when he reached sixty looked completely natural. (He was just so happy and pleased with himself, he thought it made him look dashing and young, and it put a spring back into his step so who was I to tell him it wouldn't fool a seven-year-old?)

'Come on,' she says, batting her eyelashes, her lips soft and curving into a smile, 'you can tell me. I won't tell anyone.'

Not even Jed. She doesn't say the words but we both think them. They hover in the air like a bad smell in a closed room.

The wench. As if I'd believe anything she has to say. Has she been trying to lull me into a false sense of security so that I'll tell her? Has this all been a ploy? Has she been flirting merely to ferret out my secret? Does it drive her crazy that I'm suddenly doing well for myself? That she no longer has any say over the smallest details of my life?

'Sorry,' I say, 'I can't.'

She rolls her eyes. 'You work in advertising, Alex. It's not top secret. You're hardly in MI6.'

I almost order her to call me Alexander, but I stop myself in time. Let her think I'm still the same old me, that I'm merely trying to change. Let her think I've finally discovered that backbone she was always nagging me about. Let her think I'm trying to change so that I can win her back.

Oh, Sarah, Sarah, Sarah, how much should you be punished?

The scales of justice will have to be weighted.

Should Sarah suffer equal to what I suffered? Or do the laws of vengeance demand that my revenge is twofold, threefold or even higher?

What punishment is enough for what she did to me?

Suckers. That's all I can say about those poor working stiffs out there. I should know: I used to be one of them. Now that my generation is expected to support this vast bubble of the population that will soon reach retirement age they tell us that we need to look out for ourselves, that by the time we want to retire there won't be any state money left.

Well, I can tell you what will happen: everyone my age will work for the next thirty-five years, they'll reach sixty-four and then the bloody retirement age will be moved. It'll be upped to seventy-five. And then, get this, when we reach seventy-four, it'll be moved to eighty or eighty-five.

Sure, sure, they tell us that we'll be living longer. But will we be any healthier? Will a ninety-year-old fresh retiree have all the spry energy of the sixty-five-year-old who could have retired a few years before?

No. Of course not.

Too right I want to live as long as possible. But I want to have quality of life, not just quantity. (And having a long retirement is part of that quality.)

And I know that what I'm about to say is going to offend ninety-nine per cent, maybe ninety-eight per cent if I'm lucky, of the female population, but it's got to be said. Yes, I agree that women have a harder time succeeding at careers. Yes, they are paid less. Yes, they generally don't get promoted as much. But so what? You're the lucky ones. You should bless your lucky stars that you're women. For you have a choice. You can give up your careers. You can stop working in your twenties or thirties and raise children. Yes, I know that's hard work and I sure as hell wouldn't want to do it myself, but you can escape the drudgery of spending three hours a day as a sardine on the Tube. And then when the babies become children and start going to school you can still stay at home.

You have a choice.

Most men don't. It's nine-to-five, or eight-to-seven – let's be fair, those were my normal hours at Wilmington-Wilkes – five days a week for the rest of your bloody life.

That's the sort of thinking that even the old Alex would have found depressing, would have decided it was best not to consider at all.

Thirty-five, forty, forty-five, fifty more years of work.

But I am Alexander. It won't be like that for me. I won't let it be like that for me.

REVENGE IS IN THE AIR
(AND I'VE A SPRING IN MY STEP)

I hum the tune to 'Love Is In The Air' singing, '*Revenge is in the air,*' to myself as I sort through Mrs Oi Man's photos. It's rather a cheery melody and if I hadn't already been happy it would have put me in a good mood.

I've changed into some of my old Alex clothes so that I won't draw attention to myself and I'm wearing gloves (no finger-prints for me, no, sir). It won't do me any harm to take precautions.

I flip through the photos, choosing the best three for home delivery. I didn't get thirty-six good shots, but there are fifteen that I'm rather proud of. It's a shame the Oi Man and his wife aren't famous or I could have made a bob or two from the tabloids. I shrug. *Que sera sera*.

Fifteen pictures developed as double prints leaves me thirty photographs. It doesn't matter that there are doubles, not for what I have in mind.

From my pile of boxes I dig out an old typewriter my mother gave me when I first went to university and which I've been intending to dump at a charity shop ever since. I type the Oi Man's address on the envelope, but I don't know his real name and I can hardly type Mr Oi Man, so I just label it 'To the Male Head of Household'. I'm hoping that he's a tyrant and that he insists on his wife putting all the post into a pile so that he can open it when he gets home.

But it doesn't really matter if the envelope never reaches him: I've got other ways and means. My revenge against him will be as public as possible while keeping my identity a secret.

For a second I feel bad for Mrs Oi Man. She's going to be humiliated too. It's a shame she'll be stuck in the crossfire, but really there's nothing I can do. This is simply too good an opportunity to miss.

Once I'm finished with the typewriter I put it back among my boxes, slide the three best photos into the envelope and seal it shut with a moist sponge. No spittle and DNA for me. I attach the stamp in a similar manner, slide the envelope, photos, and a role of tape into the pockets of my jacket and I'm ready.

Revenge is in the air.

I stop whistling as I leave the flat, I don't want anyone to notice me, but I keep singing the words over and over in my head, having to fight an urge to skip and dance and run and laugh and leap into the air from sheer delight. *Revenge is in the air.*

Keeping my gloves on, I pop the envelope into a post-box near the pub where I spotted Mrs Oi Man. Was it only yesterday?

Revenge is in the air.

I'm left with twenty-seven photographs and I work my way around the area, visiting twenty-seven pubs, having drinks where I can't avoid them, keeping to myself, using the lavatory at each establishment and leaving behind a nice little shot of Mrs Oi Man and her lover taped to the wall above the urinals (I wear gloves, of course).

Revenge is in the air.

As the hours pass and I trudge between pubs, I think back over my lunch with Sarah. Only once, when she mentioned the play she'd seen last night, the play I'd told her I wanted to see only the day before I came home early and found my big surprise, was I tempted to throw the contents of my glass in her face and reveal her for the trollop she is. But I kept control, and when we said goodbye I drew her into my arms and I kissed her. I really kissed her, with tongues and everything, and I could taste the spices of the chicken tikka she'd had in her sandwich. And as we were kissing I let one hand stray to her breast and I felt the nipple harden beneath her silk blouse.

Then I released her and merely said goodbye.

I left the ball in her court. I wanted to make her ask me out. I didn't want to make it too easy for her.

And the whore didn't let me down.

We're meeting for lunch on Friday.

Will she spend the next two days in heated anticipation or in frenzied guilt?

Revenge is in the air.

Finally my pub crawl is over and I head home and collapse on my bed. Despite my best intentions I've had too much to drink and I need a nap before I can go out for the evening. I set my alarm for an hour and fall into a deep sleep.

I thrash in bed, fighting off images of a forked-tongued demon loading me down with chains and I wake shouting, 'No.' The bedclothes are tangled about my legs and I'm drenched in sweat.

I take a shaky breath.

I've been dreaming about the levels of Dante's Inferno. Hell is not a pretty place.

I sit up and rub my eyes. Is this supposed to be some kind of prophetic dream? A warning that I'd better change my ways before it's too late?

I snort. I know that it's a message from myself, from the part of me that is still Alex, that he's stronger while my consciousness sleeps.

The Oi Man deserves everything he gets. And Mrs Oi Man, well, the whole street saw her. It's not like she was trying to hide anything. It's not my fault she conducts her affairs at her front door for anyone to see. The Oi Man was bound to find out sooner or later. I'm only helping things along. And making certain everyone knows he's a cuckold.

I try whistling my little song. *Revenge is in the air.*

It seems a little flat so I stop in mid-flow.

I feel like a trendy out-of-season snowman as I set off on foot for Camilla's wearing my my trusty gloves from the pub crawl. I'm in my Alexander garb now (showered and clean, the smell of pub cigarettes washed away) and the gloves are definitely Alex-wear, but I'm not overly concerned. I'm better dressed than anyone else on the street.

As I walk I sporadically throw away tiny pieces of chopped-up, snipped apart Oi Man negatives and unused photos, spreading minute portions of superfluous revenge into the bins across London. I've left no traces at home.

I keep walking, calling it a trudge because I like the word but not considering it a chore. Ten minutes after my pockets are emptied – I turned them both inside out to make certain – I slip off my gloves and at the seventh bin I toss them in. And when the gloves are gone I feel lighter, happier, and I start to hum my little tune. *Revenge is in the air*. It's a jolly little song, but I only sing it briefly. My vendetta against the Oi Man is over. Whatever happens, I've done my bit. I am free of him. My only regret is that I cannot be a fly on the wall and see his face the first time he spots one of photos and realises it's his wife. Maybe he'll go to the pub tonight and he'll be pissing side by side with one of his mates into the urinals and they'll see one of the photographs, perhaps the one with the lover's hand inside Mrs Oi Man's dressing-gown, and they'll recognise her at the same instant.

Revenge is in the air. I hum it one last time and then I stop. That part of my day is over. I'm nearing Camilla now and she's done me no wrong. She didn't contribute to Alex's downfall.

I'm an hour late when I ring Camilla's bell.

It rings. And rings. And finally the door is thrown open and Camilla says, 'Come in,' and stalks across the room to her sofa.

Ah. Call me clever. I sense trouble.

'Sorry I'm late,' I say. I should have stopped and bought her a present. I should have phoned. If I want to keep Camilla on my side, if I want to use her connections, I need to think about these things.

'Yeah, whatever.' Camilla throws herself on to the sofa and picks up the remote control, turning up the volume, watching an episode of *The Simpsons* I've seen three or four times.

(Name a show. Name any television show, excluding soaps, and I can guarantee that if I've only seen one single episode of that series from all its years of broadcast, I'll have seen that one episode two, three or even four times. Years apart, but it's true. I seem to exist in some weird sort of *Twilight Zone*, that whenever I fancy a repeat showing of *Seinfeld* or *Frasier* or *Friends*, *Home Improvement* or, indeed, *The Simpsons*, the only episode I have ever seen of that particular show will be on. Is this some kind of sod's law that has yet to be discovered?)

I join Camilla on the sofa, sitting close but not so close that she'll pull away.

'I'm sorry,' I say, trying for a note of sincerity.

She shrugs, eyes focused on Homer and Bart.

I take her hand. 'It was thoughtless of me. I should have rung.'

She doesn't look at me, but she lets me hold her hand. I give it a little squeeze and start to stroke her fingers.

'I was working on some new ideas at the office,' I tell her, 'and I got carried away. I was going to phone, but my mobile needs charging.'

Lying, telling her what she wants to hear, is so much better than the truth.

I scoot closer to her on the sofa, my thigh just brushing hers. 'I'm sorry,' I whisper, trying to sound guilty.

(I don't feel guilty.)

I think I've succeeded, for she turns and looks at me. She's still frowning and her expression is tense, but at least she's acknowledging my existence now. Her reaction, the drama she forces into every scene, reminds me of why I didn't want another girlfriend right away, but these are extenuating circumstances. (I wonder if Camilla sees herself as my girlfriend or if, like me, she thinks we're just trying things out, going for a test run, so to speak.) I need a woman like Camilla. I need Camilla. And she is so very, very good in bed.

'Did you make any plans for this evening?' I ask.

'I'm hungry,' she says. Grudgingly, with no warmth, wanting me to suffer a little longer. 'I'd like to eat.'

'Why don't we head over to my offices and look through the decorating and furniture catalogues I've collected? We could pick up a take-away and eat it there.'

She shudders. 'I don't eat take-away.'

'Then we'll go out to dinner first.' I stroke her thigh. 'Come on, it'll be fun.'

And then she bursts into tears and I pull her into my arms. 'Hey,' I say, 'what's wrong?'

'I thought you were dead. I thought something horrible had happened to you. And I was so angry when you turned up all smiling and cheerful when I'd been so worried.'

I stroke her hair. 'Hush. Hush. It's all right. I won't let it happen again.'

She pulls away, wiping her eyes. 'You promise?'

'I do.' I cross my fingers behind her back where she can't see them.

Why do we do this? Why would such a childish gesture give me permission to voice a lie without making me into a liar? What's the logic behind it? It must be descended from some mystical spell from olden times, but we do it without knowing why we do it.

And why did I even bother? I've got nothing against lying. Not when I'm the one doing the lying.

ANOTHER DAY, ANOTHER CLIENT

I'm like an unstoppable steamroller. No, a vacuum cleaner, a Hoover, sucking clients away from the carpet that is Wilmington-Wilkes. I am bloody invincible.

It's now Thursday afternoon and I have yet another client. Seven presentations, seven clients. I know in my heart of hearts that this cannot continue, that at some point I may run out of ideas, that at some time in the near future I'll be – gasp – turned down, but it's inevitable and I decide grandly, with a wave of my hand, that I won't mind, that I'll forgive whoever it is, that I won't hold it against them personally.

I'm back at the office and I'm sitting on the floor, enjoying the novelty of it, knowing that the furniture is arriving tomorrow and that this won't be a long-term thing. The design Camilla and I decided on (she has expensive tastes, I'll give her that) is sold by a friend of her father's and she's managed to furnish my entire office at cost. (And ensured I jump to the front of the queue. The desk I want for myself isn't kept in stock, but they're giving me one that someone else ordered so I'll have everything all at once.)

That's the secret of wealth. The more wealth you have the less you have to pay for things. Sort of like a reverse taxation where the poor people, the middle classes with all their striving for the trappings of success, pay full price and subsidise the discounts of the rich.

Camilla's opening my eyes to a whole new world and I am amazed at how much fun it is. I thought I'd enjoy it, I've known all along that I'd like being one of those at the apex of the pyramid rather than at the base, but it's good, it's damn good, and it's where I want to stay. And Camilla seems to want to be with me. With me. I stare at the spot in the reception room where we had sex last night and where I think the receptionist's desk should go when it arrives and I snap out of it.

Of course she wants to be with me. I am successful and charming and popular. Everyone loves me.

Love?

Do I want her to love me?

Maybe I do. It would make things a hell of a lot easier if she doted on my every word and command.

The idea has possibilities. I don't love her, I don't know if I'll ever love anyone again, it seems foolish to let yourself be ruled by so capricious an emotion as love, but I would like it if she loves me. I need a woman like her. I've found Camilla so I may as well try and keep her. She's easy on the eyes and she seems a reasonable sort of companion, and I certainly can't complain about the physical side of our relationship, if relationship it is.

I doodle on a pad, brainstorming for ideas for Charles St John's charity. Ethics in genetic engineering. I want something futuristic. There's e-mail and v-mail for electronic mail and video mail. I need something suitably catchy. I know Wilmington-Wilkes, I worked there long enough so I should know them. Kenneth will come along on Saturday and present some clever acronym like EDGE, Ethical Decisions in Genetic Engineering. Or, if they're more desperate just EG, Ethical Genetics, or EEG, Ethically Engineered Genetics. Don't think they'll go with GOD, Geneticists Opposed to Debate or Geneticists Opposed to Discussion.

My bet goes on EDGE or something similar. Kenneth would like it. Kenneth may even come up with it himself. He thinks he's good at catchy little phrases. And sometimes he is. We all get lucky.

I need to think about who these men are. They're all likely to be wealthy and successful, and I imagine most see the business possibilities inherent in genetic engineering. So generally they'd support it, with perhaps a few qualms and a few more worries, which is why they want to promote ethics. And it's always good for the punters. Calm a few of society's uneasy speculations. It's better to support a company that signs up to ethical charters than companies who don't. Hmm. That's got to influence my choice of names.

There's e-trade, e-mail. How about e-dig? Ethics – decisions in genetics? Nope. Too boring. Not enough punch.

What about e-genes? E-genes. Yep. That's the one.

If the charity gets in there quickly they can claim this name. It can stand for Ethical Genes, Ethical Genetics, even Engineered Genes. It's perfect. It's a word describing a thing but can come to represent the ethics of it all. Just think of it: one day, maybe ten, twenty, thirty years down the road, expectant parents are going to talk about how many e-genes their child is going to have. Or maybe not. Maybe E-genes the charity will stop such activities; maybe they'll only promote the growing of replacement organs from our own DNA and the less controversial uses of Gen Eng. (Gen Eng, another name Kenneth would like, if it's not already in use.)

I ring my mother and apologise for being short with her when she rang the other day. (She's my mother, I don't need to be Alexander tough with her. She's not one of the ones who deserves to suffer. She doesn't need to pay for anything.) Her instant forgiveness makes me smile. I know that she's mentally reapplying the halo over my head even as we speak. I've always been her golden boy.

'No, it's my fault,' she says. 'I shouldn't have been asking you about Sarah.'

'That's okay. I know you meant well.' Control, control, it's all about control. She doesn't need to know my true thoughts about that woman.

There's a pause and I know my mother wants me to elaborate, that she genuinely thinks it would be a good thing for me to tell her all about my split with Sarah, but I don't. I'm protecting my mother, she wouldn't want to know all the sordid details, it would upset her. I sit back in my chair and relax. I can deal with this conversation. I can deal with my mother. She loves me. She loves me no matter who I am or what I do. It's up to me to shield her from the truth.

After a moment my mother speaks again, her tone different now, my previous testiness forgiven and dismissed.

'Our new neighbours, the ones who moved into the old vicarage, are having a party on Saturday night and it just struck me that you might like to come. They have two gorgeous daughters just a few years younger than you, identical twins, and I know you'd get along smashingly.'

The thought of a pair of gorgeous twins is tempting. I've not known any identical twins, but I doubt my mother's rating of gorgeous would match my own and, besides, I'm busy. 'Sorry,' I say, 'I already have plans for the weekend.'

'But you're still coming to your father's dinner?'

'Yes, Mum.' I smile. That's reminder number eleven, even if it's camouflaged as a genuine question. 'And I've invited some-one. I hope you don't mind.'

'You've invited someone?' she asks. 'A date?'

I can hear the smile in her voice. And just like that she's hoping that I have a new girlfriend, that there'll be a new woman in the picture, that she'll be able to hope for wedding bells, after all.

'A friend,' I say. 'One of my flatmates.'

'A female friend?'

'Yes, Mum, a female friend. You should know that she's a vegetarian.'

'You know all about her eating habits, do you?'

'We share a kitchen. It's come up in conversation.'

'I'll fix her my special nut roast, but check with her and let me know if she doesn't eat nuts. I'll have to make certain your father doesn't wear that orange paisley tie of his. We wouldn't want to frighten her off.'

'She'll survive,' I say.

And then she's off, she's rambling about this and that, but she hasn't fooled me: I know she's dying to meet Amber. I let my mother talk, for it makes her happy. She's a firm believer in communication.

DETAILS AND DISAPPOINTMENT
(BUT DON'T FORGET THE OPPORTUNITY)

The good news is that my beloved Jaguar XKR will be ready for collection by lunchtime tomorrow as promised and Camilla won't be forced to soil herself in a mere hire car. The bad news? I don't have any.

I wonder if Camilla has some kind of cut-off point. Is it the value of the car she objects to? Does it have to cost over forty thousand, or even fifty thousand, to be acceptable for her to ride in? Or is it the brand name that matters? And what about lower end BMWs? I'm sure she likes the name, but you can pick up a decent three series for around twenty. Would that be expensive enough? Or is it the look of the car? Does it have to be sleek and fast or classical and elegant? And what about 4 × 4s? Are they trendy enough for her? Or too trendy?

I'll never understand her.

I spend the last hour of my workday on endless details and it's boring but necessary.

(The temp starts tomorrow. Hurrah.)

My mobile rings and I wonder for a second if it's a client, if I'm needed, if someone wants my expertise, but it's Camilla and I taste the sour tang of disappointment.

'Darling,' she says, purring in a way to make that word seem special, reserved for me, when, in fact, I know she calls everyone darling. 'I'm afraid I have to cancel tonight.'

Cancel? She's cancelling on me? How dare she? Doesn't she know that I don't respond kindly to being taken for granted?

'Della's having a crisis,' says Camilla. 'I've got to go to her.'

Della? Camilla says her name like I should know who she is.

I frown and then it hits me. Della. The blonde from the club. That Della.

'What's happened?' I try to modulate my voice and make it sound sympathetic.

'Man trouble,' says Camilla, and I can picture her waving her hands in the air as she talks. She's very good with her hands. 'Simon's dumped her.'

'Simon?'

'He was at Seb's last week. Della's been lusting after him for absolutely ages and they finally got together at the party, but now he's dumped her. She's devastated. Absolutely devastated.'

Devastated? After a week? Embarrassed, humiliated, that I'll accept, but devastated? Please. Devastation has got to be reserved for the engaged, the cohabiting or the married. Distraught, disappointed, even desolate I'll accept but a week is not long enough for complete and utter destruction.

'You don't mind, do you?' says Camilla. 'I know we were planning on dinner, but we'll be together all weekend.'

'No, of course I don't mind. You go ahead.' I bloody well do mind. I was looking forward to the sex. How dare she leave me in the lurch like this?

I catch a cab home and as I sit in the back stuck in a traffic jam midway between my office and the flat (sheer weight of traffic or an accident), I decide there's no reason I have to suffer this enforced solitude. Camilla may be otherwise occupied but that doesn't mean I have to sit on my own in my room counting daisy petals. I was expecting female companionship and there's no reason why I shouldn't have female companionship. I'm not a man who copes well with celibacy.

Oh, Alex, he was okay with it, he once went eleven months between shags, but now, as Alexander, I don't like to let it build up for more than a day. It's not healthy.

I give Kate a ring, foresight having caused me to program her number into my mobile, but there's no answer. Where the hell is she? Why isn't she waiting by the phone for my calls? Ungrateful woman. It's only been a few days since Sunday. I told her I was going out of town. Her answering-machine clicks in and I leave a message, telling her I'm in the city tonight. (Thursday, I say, to avoid confusion.)

The traffic clears and the cab starts to move. My mood lifts as suddenly as the jam disperses.

Why am I being all grouchy and out of sorts?

This is a free evening. I've been let off Camilla's hook for a night. I am young and rich and free and single (no commitments, Camilla, remember that). I can do anything I want to do.

First things first. The Oi Man's not stupid. He's not about to sit around and ponder the identity of the man – the insane man – who sent him the photos. No, that's not the Oi Man's style. He'll be after revenge, just like I was. He'll talk, he'll listen to the word on the street, and when that fails (I was pretending to be Alex, I was pretending to be him, no one will remember me, Alex is not memorable, Alex could wear a badge with his name and address and national insurance number on it and still no one would remember him), he'll go to the police. The Oi Man will carefully destroy the more scandalous of the Mrs Oi Man photos (I wonder how many pubs he'll visit before he's satisfied he's found them all, his friends are bound to find at least one or two and that will set the Oi Man's reptilian brain to wondering, his blood to boiling, his fists clenching, and leave him with an overwhelming urge to beat some sorry fool into a great bloody pulp).

But will he find all the photos? Each and every one? Or will one or two lurk in the deep and the dark and jump out at him in a week or two or even three?

He'll go to the police claiming harassment. (He'll enjoy complaining to them and giving them a piece of his mind, blaming them for not keeping his family safe. He's a taxpayer, after all, he'll think it's about bloody time the police did something for him rather than persecuting him like they normally do whenever his lawful business just happens to take him too near the scene of a crime.) The Oi Man will tell the police that his wife is being stalked and he'll toss the photos of Mrs Oi Man in her dressing-gown on to the counter like a gauntlet. (But only the photos where she is alone.)

The lover will be airbrushed out of the story. The Oi Man will never admit that he's a cuckold.

If the police take him seriously, and I know they'll at least look into it, they'll search for the Oi Man's enemies and eventually, eventually, they might find out about the night the Oi Man glassed me. I could even be a routine enquiry as the incident – my incident – took place at one of the photo gallery pubs. (They'll find me easily enough, all my details are in police records.)

Poor little Alex with a broken glass in his face.

And what if the police think there's something fishy going on? What if I act too cool and self-assured? If I play it too forgiving or too angry? Would they begin to suspect me?

Would they want to do a search? Would they rifle through my room of boxes?

Would they want to prosecute me? Me?

(It would be so unjust. Alex was the victim and I am he so it would be unsporting to punish me for my justifiable actions of vengeance.)

And that is why I remove all traces of incriminating evidence. The negatives and spare photos are already gone, I got rid of those last night. It takes me under an hour to dump the typewriter, wiped of prints, at the door of a charity shop across London and discard the various pieces of clothing I wore on the night of the twenty-seven pubs. (I pop the shirt, trousers and jacket into separate carrier bags, tie them up and drop them into bins a minimum of three streets apart.) They're only Alex-wear so it's no sacrifice.

When I am done, when it is all finished and there's not a shred of physical proof left to tie me to the Mrs Oi Man photos, I head for the gym.

My intent was to spend a good hour lifting weights, but when I see Kate pedalling away on a stationary bike I change my mind.

Doesn't she have a life? Is she some kind of exercise addict who has to get her daily fix of endorphins?

She sees me. I know that Kate sees me as soon as I enter the room – is she looking out for me? – but she pretends that she hasn't. I nearly leave her to it and head to the weights, Let her come to me and beg, I think, but then I change my mind. The sooner I say hello the sooner we'll be shagging.

'Hi, Kate,' I say, and climb on to the bike beside her.

She barely glances at me. 'I didn't know you were back in town.'

That's nearly it. I almost stop pedalling and walk away. I don't want to deal with her emotional insecurities. It's only because Camilla is busy and I want to feel a woman's body beneath mine that I stay.

And what right has she to castigate me? I could have returned an hour ago from spending four days and nights locked away in a boardroom and be desperate for some physical exertion. She's not my keeper. I don't owe her anything.

I waste five minutes of the night in making tedious small-talk, starting by telling her, after a pause, that I telephoned and left a message on her machine earlier today. Let her feel guilty. Let her want to make it up to me later.

Ten more minutes pass. Yawn, yawn, yawn. Why do I have to pretend to be interested in her opinion on the location of the next Olympic games? We have sex with one another. That's what we do. That's it. Why does she want to maintain the farce that there's anything more?

At last we head back to her place.

She lets us inside and before I can take her into my arms, she dashes across the room and presses play on her answering-machine. 'I just need to check my messages,' she says.

Enough talking.

I grab one of the large candlesticks from the table by the door and smash her over the head.

I don't, of course, I'm in control, but it's tempting all the same.

She doesn't trust me. She's checking up on me. She's making sure that I did phone before she sleeps with me. What a slap in the face. She should believe me, she shouldn't need confirmation.

Am I losing my touch? Is Alex, the old Alex, the old me, seeping through? Are there holes in my persona like the gaps in the ozone layer? Must I be on constant lookout for contamination?

Mine is the only message, and as my voice plays out over the crackly tape Kate relaxes. She slips off her shoes.

'Make yourself at home,' she says, talking over my words, wanting me to stay now that she's satisfied herself I'm not a liar.

Send her to the guillotine. Off with her head.

I return her smile as she slips her T-shirt over her head, her grey sports bra flattening her lovely breasts.

'Would you like something to drink? Or anything to eat? I've got some food in the fridge, I can whip us up something for dinner.'

That's it, I've had enough, I stride across the room and take her in my arms. As I suckle her neck I inhale the distinctive musk and vanilla scent of the perfume – Camilla's favourite – that I gave to her on Sunday.

After the second shag I've had enough. I have a free evening, all to myself, and I can do whatever I want to do and for now I want to go home. I don't want dinner and I don't want to talk.

I smile as I kiss her nose. 'Thanks for that, Kate.' I roll off her and start to dress.

'You're going?'

I nod. 'I've got to catch a flight to Singapore at four.' (Safe subject this, if she insists on grilling me. I was there on a business trip only six months ago.)

'Oh.' She blinks rapidly and I can see the moisture in her eyes. Her lip is trembling.

What the hell is she playing at? Is she some sort of delusional psycho woman? Has she been telling herself that we're having a relationship? There's never been anything but sex between us. I've never pretended otherwise.

'When will I see you again?' she asks.

I shrug, deliberately casual. 'I'll be away two or three weeks.'

'Call me.' Her eyes aren't merely moist, they're wet: I can see tears trembling on her lashes.

She has no right to cry. She has no right to try and guilt me into promising I'll phone or forcing me to feel sorry enough for her that I'll arrange a date. She made her bed the day we met and now she has to lie in it. She can't give me one thing and then demand another. That's not how the world works. If she'd insisted on acting like a virgin I would have taken her out to dinner, but she didn't and this, Katie girl, is what happens when you play with the grown-ups. I am not Alex, I will not be forced into anything. I feel no guilt.

I give her a perfunctory kiss on the lips. See, I'm not a complete bastard. And I said thank you. My mother taught me always to say thank you.

'See you around, Kate,' I say.

And then I leave.

I slam the door behind me.

Why did she have to make it so complicated? We've never had a relationship. We're never going to have a relationship.

It was just sex.

I never came to Kate for the conversation and there were never any emotions beyond the physical. Never. She's an idiot if she thinks otherwise.

I pound down the stairs and kick the ground-floor banister.

Goodbye, Kate. Have a nice life.

THANK YOU, I LIKE THE THINGS YOU'VE DUMPED IN THAT OPEN FIELD, THEY REALLY ADD SOMETHING TO THE POSTCARD QUALITY OF THE SCENE

Maybe it's something that happens as you get older that you become more aware of the world around you, but it seems that this country has become littered with abandoned cars in the past few years. (I know. Cars. There might be lots of refuse and debris strewn across the land, but it's the cars I notice.) On city streets, in town centres, dumped into rivers and left at the edge of forests. What is the point? Sure, some have been smashed and dumped by gangs of joyriding youths, spotty or not as the case may be. But not all.

I know of a man who buys very old, clapped-out cars. He strips them of all their usable parts and then, at dead of night, he loads the shells on to the back of his tow truck. He's an independent man and makes his own decisions. He doesn't want to pay for the rubbish tip. Why should he waste his hard-earned money?

Aren't we glad we've got him to decide that a rusty hunk of metal left among the trees is as pretty as a giant Christmas bauble?

I just love people.

I'm not supposed to be a nice man. I'm Alexander, not Alex. Women might think they like nice men, they might think they want a nice man, but they don't, not really. Nice men are boring. Sarah proved that. There's no point in being nice.

I reach the flat, wanting nothing more than a hot shower to scrub away the residue of my time with Kate, but laughter, genuine, honest, delighted laughter, rolls from the kitchen and my feet move as if under their own volition and then I'm pushing open the kitchen door and I'm in.

It's like one of those scenes on television where the hero has been away from home for years and when he returns the family is all grouped around a fireplace or a kitchen table and everything looks incredibly cosy and welcoming, and you think, Why did he stay away so long, how could he bear it?

Amber and Noreen are playing a complicated form of double solitaire called nerts. Amber showed me the other day or I wouldn't have had a clue what it is. It's like solitaire only for two people (each with their own deck) and you have to compete, using the same central piles to count from ace to king and the winner is whoever finishes his or her cards first.

There's an open bottle of wine at the far end of the table and, next to it, an empty bottle.

They're playing fast and furious, ignoring the wine at the moment, but both girls take the time to flash me a grin and say, 'Hi, Alexander,' in unison before turning back to the game.

Amber adds a seven to the pile of hearts and speaks to me without looking up again. 'Help yourself to the wine, there's another glass in the cupboard.'

I no longer feel like being on my own so I pour myself some wine and slide into the chair beside Amber to watch their game.

They're not bathed in golden light, there's no symphony announcing that this is a special moment, but I feel privileged to sit here in this kitchen with these people. I, Alexander Fairfax, am happy to be here. It's not what I would have expected this morning, or even yesterday, but it's true. I feel happy. Content.

Everyone's allowed a little downtime from the battle for supremacy and spending a little time enjoying the company of friends qualifies. Friends. Yes, I admit it, I consider both Amber and Noreen friends, in a bizarre way that wouldn't include introducing them to Charles St John or Camilla or even inviting them out for my birthday meal next year. But I do like them. And I really like Amber. (I'd take Amber out for a private meal, just the two of us so she'd never know that she wasn't invited to my proper birthday celebration. It's nothing personal against her, she just wouldn't fit in with my new crowd. She wouldn't have fun, she wouldn't feel comfortable and I wouldn't want her to feel out of place.)

Their game finishes a few minutes later, with Noreen storming ahead at the last moment in a whirl of cards and motion. When it's over both girls turn to me with gratifying smiles, their pleasure at seeing me both obvious and genuine. (They'd invite me to their birthday parties.)

'Been working on those muscles again?' asks Noreen. Her eyes dart to Amber's and both women start giggling.

'I do what I can to keep fit,' I say. And a shag a day keeps the doctor away.

I smile as I recall a few choice details of the night's workout and take a sip of my wine. It's cheap supermarket plonk and not very nice, but it doesn't taste like the cat's piss I feared it would.

We all laugh and flirt and tell one another outrageous jokes for over an hour. I can see that they're both attracted to me, that they like me, and I wonder for an instant if I can persuade Amber into my bed tonight.

I've got spare time now that I'm finished with Kate.

Then Amber bursts out laughing at one of Noreen's impersonations of the Teletubbies and I give myself a rueful smile. Who am I kidding? I can't sleep with her. I'd feel like I was killing Bambi every time she turned to me with disappointed eyes. That would be cruel and I don't want to be cruel. It's not a daily requirement, there's nothing that says I have to be malicious to two people a day, it's not like it's a doctor's prescription. There's no formula for being Alexander. I'm in control and I make my own rules.

Oh, but I do want Amber. I've wanted her from the very first moment I saw her.

It's like Noreen is telepathic, that she somehow picks up on my thoughts and feelings, for she suddenly yawns this great big yawn and says she's off to bed. 'You coming?' she asks Amber.

Amber blushes and looks down at the table. 'I'm not tired,' she says, 'I think I'll stay.'

'Goodnight, Noreen,' I say.

She stares at us both for a moment. And then she grins. 'Night, night. Have fun.'

I hesitate. I shouldn't do this. I can't succumb to my desires, I'm stronger than that, it wouldn't be fair on Amber. I like Amber. I respect her. I don't want to hurt her.

And as I'm telling myself I can't sleep with Amber, that I mustn't touch Amber, she leans forward and kisses me softly on the lips.

Oh, God, she tastes so good.

And then we're kissing, properly kissing, and I pull her on to my lap.

I've been so good, I've tried to be so good, but she kissed me and I can't help myself. Surely I'm being rewarded for being so good. She's so cute and I really like her. How can I help myself? I'll be careful, I'll look out for her, I'll make sure she doesn't get hurt. She doesn't need to know about Camilla. If she doesn't know about Camilla she'll be happy. I'll make her happy. I want to make her happy.

I can't resist her. I want Amber.

We keep kissing.

A minute later I pull away and run my hand down Amber's cheek. She looks up and meets my eyes. Her face is shining. She's happy. I said I'd make her happy.

'I need a bath,' I say. I have to have a bath. I have to wash away the Kate smells, I can't go to bed with Amber stinking of Kate, even if Amber thinks I've only been to the gym. 'Care to join me?'

Her face flushes. 'A bath?'

'Uh-huh.' I kiss her gently on the lips. 'It'll be fun.'

'Okay,' she whispers.

OH, WHAT A NIGHT
(OR, AMBER, WHAT LOVELY TOES YOU HAVE)

I wake to sunlight streaming through the windows of Amber's room and Amber curled around me as if she's always slept this way. I stroke her hair and then her arms, moving on gradually to her hips, her waist, her breasts. She opens her eyes and we make love. Make love. I can call it that. And it does feel special, it's more than just a shag because I like her. To call it anything else would be too coarse. Too coarse for Amber.

I hold her for a few minutes in my arms. 'I have to go to work.'

'I know. So do I.' She shows no inclination of disentangling her limbs from mine.

I kiss her mouth. 'I really have to go. I'm sorry. My temp is starting today. I have to show her the ropes.'

Amber sighs. 'Will I see you tonight?'

The question doesn't annoy me as it would have done if Kate had asked the same thing. I want Amber to want to see me. She should want to see me.

'I'm sorry,' I say, 'I can't. I'm taking some clients away for the weekend.'

'Oh.'

I shower her face with kisses. 'Will you miss me?' I want her to miss me.

'Maybe.'

'I'll see you Sunday night,' I say. 'I'll get back as quickly as I can.' And I'm not lying. After a weekend with Camilla I'll be rushing back to Amber's arms: I'll be looking forward to her openness and lack of pouting.

'I'll be home,' she says. 'I'll be waiting.'

YOU'RE A GOOD SPORT, SARAH.
OR AM I LYING?

Once I've directed the furniture delivery, settled the temp into the office and explained her duties for the day (all stuff I don't want to do, but things that need to be done), I collect my car.

My beloved Jaguar XKR. Will it ever be the same?

It's all shiny and clean, the new leather seats soft and supple, tyres and windows replaced, and I'm careful as I drive it through London. It seems as good as new, but there's something different and it takes me a moment to pinpoint it. I'm tense as I drive it: I no longer think my Jag is invincible.

Bad things do happen.

My stomach churns and I'm queasy as I turn into the NCP car park around the corner from my office (ready for an early-afternoon departure). I find an empty space and I sit there, inside my car with the ignition off, pulling myself together.

What's happening here? Alexander doesn't have nerves.

I take a few deep breaths, counting to ten.

Breathe in. Breathe out. Everything will be fine. Everything is fine.

I am Alexander. It's only the thought of seeing Sarah that's upsetting my equilibrium. But I'm aware of it now, I won't let her upset me again.

I leave the car park and catch a cab to Sarah's office.

The trollop is wearing a short skirt and four-inch heels. Not appropriate for an office but more than adequate for an assignation.

'I found one of your ties,' she says, once I've kissed her cheek in greeting. 'I meant to bring it along and give it to you today, but I left it behind. Maybe we should stop by the flat and pick it up before lunch. So we don't forget.'

What's Sarah's asking is if I want to go back to her flat and fuck but in language not so crude.

She makes me sick. She's like a bitch in heat. She's got no patience, she doesn't want to wait, she doesn't want all the pleasures of anticipation for the hour or so it would take to eat.

Was this what she was like with Jed?

Did the little whore take him to our bed on the first date? Did she even get him to buy her a sandwich first?

I hail a cab with Alexander style and we have to wait less than a minute. We're holding ourselves apart, not touching, but our faces are flushed and we lean towards one another. We're fooling no one. It's obvious we're about to have sex. Our cabbie knows that we're dashing home for a lunchtime quickie.

When we arrive Sarah unlocks the door and it doesn't seem strange to enter the flat – her flat, Jed's flat, the place Alex used to call home – and find it filled with Jed's things. I've already seen it, of course, but it's more than that. I'm glad he's moved in. I want his possessions to witness Sarah's betrayal. I want them to witness the whore at work. I want them to know I've fucked their owner's girl.

'The tie's in the bedroom,' says Sarah.

Is she feeling nervous? Guilty? Does she want to pretend that this is an innocent situation? Is she hoping that later she'll be able to excuse her behaviour to herself and pretend she didn't know what was going to happen, that we merely got carried away by our lustful memories of the past?

As we enter the bedroom I imagine I can smell vomit in the doorway and it makes me feel nauseous, but I know it's only in my imagination.

The last time I was in this bedroom with Sarah she was naked. In bed with Jed.

I imagine the sight of Jed coming home early from work, a

headache pounding in his ears, and his shock at entering the bedroom and seeing me in the bed with Sarah.

It's time for a little revenge.

Sarah withdraws a tie from her lingerie drawer and hands it to me. It's an Alex tie: I'll never wear it again. Even if I liked it I'd never wear it again, forced, as it was, to spend hours in a drawer with that whore's knickers. I'd never be able to get rid of the smell.

I nearly run my hand down her cheek, but I catch myself in time. I like touching a woman's face, but this is Sarah. I don't want to touch her face. I don't want to look at her face. So I pull her to me and kiss her hungrily, making her want me, making her miss me.

We're tearing one another's clothes off and it's like I haven't had sex in weeks I'm so eager. It's not that Sarah's brilliant in bed, she's fine, I'd rate her alongside Kate, but she comes nowhere near Camilla's expertise.

(I won't even compare the harlot in my arms to Amber. Amber deserves better. I shouldn't even be sullying Amber's good name by thinking of Sarah in the same breath.)

It's the consequences of this act that are so exciting.

I push Sarah on to the bed and flip her over on to her stomach. I don't want to look at her face. I want to keep my eyes open, I want to savour the moment, but I don't want to have to look at her and I don't want her to look at me.

I take out a condom (I brought my own along, always prepared like a good Boy Scout) and slide it on. I haven't used condoms with Sarah in nearly two years, but we're no longer together and neither of us is exactly monogamous. I don't believe in unsafe sex. It's not like I know where she's been.

Sarah is ready, waiting in the doggie position she likes so well.

Said she was in heat.

I pound into her. With each thrust I curse her for what she did to me. Bitch, bitch, bitch, bitch, bitch, I chant to myself.

Traitorous whore.

When we've both come I withdraw immediately and discard the condom. Let her worry about hiding it properly. It's not up to me. I don't care if Jed finds out she's been screwing around.

I'm not satiated. I could do with more, but once is enough with Sarah. I never want to fuck her again. Not ever.

I'm glad my bags for the weekend are already at the office. I wouldn't want to head home and bump into Amber. I'd have to make up some excuse to explain why I didn't want her to touch me until I'd had a shower.

And what of Camilla? I shrug. I'll think of it as her just reward for blowing me out last night. I won't be able to have a shower, but I'll have a wash in the toilets at work. She'll never know.

I start to dress. Sarah lies in bed, naked and wanton.

'When will I see you again?' she asks.

'Soon,' I say, and smile. I should win an Oscar for this performance.

'Alex?'

That's not my name, you slut.

'Yes?'

'I'm sorry, Alex. I'm sorry about Jed.'

It's Alexander, whore. Didn't you hear me?

'Don't worry about it,' I say. 'I'm glad we've been able to put it behind us. I'm glad we can still be friends.'

I manage to get that out without bursting into hysterical laughter. I feel like I've just been forced to swallow ten peeled, juicy lemons; it's an effort to keep my face straight.

'Maybe I made a mistake,' she says.

No? Really?

Sarah continues when I don't respond. 'We were good together.'

I'd better say something. 'We were,' I say, and that much is true. We were good together. Alex and Sarah were good together. But Alexander and Sarah have no future.

'I'd like to see you again,' she says.

'Let's take things slowly,' I say. I don't want her to break up with Jed, not yet. I'm not ready. Not all of my plans are in place.

'Okay.' She smiles at me and I wonder suddenly if I would have been content to spend my life with her if she hadn't messed everything up.

I think I would have. I think Alex would have been happy. Alex would have liked to grow old with Sarah.

Am I wrong to be punishing her?

Hold on. Wait a minute. What am I thinking? Am I starting to feel sorry for her because I loved her once?

Screw Sarah. She doesn't deserve my sympathy.

But I don't let her see I feel that way.

Not yet.

The time isn't right.

Camilla took the day off so she'd be packed and ready to leave mid-afternoon.

She took a day's holiday to pack for a weekend away. Not a long weekend. A weekend. When she told me I decided not to comment.

After the foodless lunch with Sarah I return to the office and chat to the temp. I send her home early, then drive to Camilla's, arriving exactly on time at three.

'Thank God you're here,' says Camilla, and drags me into the apartment.

Clothes, more clothes than I would have thought it possible for a single person to own in a lifetime let alone all at once, are strewn left and right, in piles and bundles, tumbling this way and that.

'I don't know what to wear,' she says.

In the future I'll encourage her to start packing a week before any trip, and if we go away for an entire fortnight she'll need at least three weeks to prepare.

I run a hand down her back. 'You need to relax,' I say, pulling her close for a kiss, planning to rub her shoulders.

Camilla breaks away from me, she stalks across the room, and I let my hands drop.

'All you ever think about is sex,' she says. 'I don't have time. I'm not interested. Can't you see that I'm busy? Can't I ever have a little time on my own? It's always sex, sex, sex with you.'

She runs into the bathroom and slams the door behind her.

I leave. I walk out and leave. I don't say goodbye. I say

nothing. I don't care if she's a family friend of Charles St John, I don't care if she's his precious goddaughter. I won't put up with this shit. Not from her. Not from anyone. I didn't become Alexander so I could be a punch-bag. Alex would have taken it, but I won't be treated like that. I bloody well won't allow it. I don't *need* her: she would have made things easier, my progress would have been faster with the support of her family and friends, but tough luck. I'll survive on my own.

I reach the street and head towards the meter where I left my car.

'Alexander.'

It's Camilla. She's run out on to the pavement without any shoes. Maybe she'll step on some glass. I take out my keys, press the unlock button and open the driver's door.

'Alexander. Wait. Please. Wait.' She runs up and throws her arms around me. Tears stream down her face. 'I'm sorry,' she says. 'I'm so sorry.'

I don't return her hug, but I don't shake her off. She would come in useful. And she's awfully good in bed.

'Oh, God, I'm such a bitch,' she says.

I don't argue. Even Amber wouldn't argue and Amber's like Alex, she likes everybody.

'You must hate me.'

I sigh. I don't like seeing a woman in tears. 'I don't hate you,' I say.

'You do.'

She's pushing her luck. She'd better not ask again or I might be tempted to remain silent out of spite.

'No,' I say, 'I don't hate you, Camilla.'

'I'm sorry. I know I shouldn't have yelled at you,' she says. 'It's no excuse, I know, but I just get so stressed when I have to decide what to wear. Everyone always expects me to look my best.'

Here comes reassurance time. I know. I've seen it all before. Why are women so insecure?

Noreen would say it's because society judges women by their looks alone and that we're constantly bombarded with pictures of perfection and that no real woman can compare. That even the supermodels must submit to five hours of makeup and hair before they can represent the ideal.

'But you're beautiful,' I say. 'You'd look good in sackcloth.'

She sniffs and wipes her eyes. 'You're not going to leave me, are you?'

Is it me she really wants? Or doesn't she want to turn up without a boyfriend?

I allow Camilla to drag me back inside her apartment and she says that there isn't time for sex, that she's sorry, that she's ever so much to do before we can leave. But to make it up to me, to soothe me, to make me forget her fishwife impersonation, she gives me the best blow-job of my life.

Has she had lessons? Is this what she was taught instead of physics? Is it a required subject at finishing school? Are there practical lessons?

Eventually, hitting the tail end of rush-hour by the time Camilla has finished packing, we arrive. (Camilla has been charming, entertaining and even-tempered throughout the drive.)

The house is a Georgian mansion with twenty bedrooms. Camilla informs me that they retain seventy-five of the original acres of land. There's pride in her voice. Her family built the house two hundred years ago and has lived there ever since.

Camilla is an only child.

We're looking at her inheritance. (Or at least part of it.)

I like this house. I want this house.

I'm glad she ran after me. I'm glad I let her persuade me to forgive her for her outburst.

Camilla's parents turn out to be disappointingly normal. I'd have passed them on the streets of London without a second glance. No fierce whiskers, no shotguns over the arm to turn me away, no visible eccentricities at all.

Both Rupert and Celeste hug their daughter.

What? Not even unfeeling-family problems to keep me entertained?

I'm not quizzed overtly about Platypus-fox, Charles will have kept them informed, but the rest of my life is poked, prodded and analysed, leaving me feeling like the inside of a runny egg after it's been bounced in the back of a van for seven hundred and fifty-five miles.

'Where are you from?' they ask.

Translation: which swamp have you crawled out of?

'Surrey.'

Ah. Good county. That much is fine.

'What do your parents do?' You're not exactly wealthy, now, are you? they wonder. Otherwise we'd already have heard of your family.

'Dad's a retired doctor.' He was a GP, but I don't tell them that. Let them ask if they want to know. 'My mother's never worked.'

'Is she involved with any charities?' asks Celeste.

Camilla's mother wants to know if she's a benefactor, if she would have heard of her.

'Oh, lots,' I say, 'she's always helping out with one cause or another.' Mostly for the WI and the Oxfam shop. No posh fundraisers for her.

'What school did you attend?'

'The local grammar school.'

Ah. That's a wrong answer, I can tell, but I could hardly pretend I went to Eton. It's obvious I don't come from the same background.

Alex would have hated this. Alex would have broken down, crying, and apologised for dirtying their house with his presence. But I don't care. I know that one day soon they're going to be begging me to be their friend.

Money is the greatest equaliser of all. If Platypus-fox does well I'll have no trouble passing muster.

I'm sound asleep in the blue guest room when the door creaks open and Camilla tiptoes in.

'I'm awfully sorry about my parents,' she whispers, climbing into bed with me. 'They can be such bores. Getting permission to date me is like a job interview.'

'So did I pass?'

'They never say, in case I fall in love with a man they don't think is suitable. Daddy's mother hated Mummy in the beginning – because one of Mummy's ancestors supported Cromwell in the Civil War – and it caused a huge family row when they married. My parents are determined not to put me through the same thing.'

I decide to read nothing into her remarks. She has a long night ahead to compensate me for my understanding of her earlier grumpiness and I don't want to waste any more time talking.

Saturday is filled with country-landowner activities: riding with Camilla's parents, patrolling the estate on foot, sex alfresco.

Alex would never have survived. The chasm that exists between the lives of people like Camilla and people like the old me is enormous. And it's not just the money, it's the centuries of breeding, not the breeding of the genes themselves, but the breeding of attitude. Camilla's father knows – he *knows* – he's superior to the vast majority of mankind and nothing anyone says to him will change that. Ever.

I want to fit into this world. And the quickest way in is to marry someone like Camilla. I want to fit in, I need to fit in, I'll have to marry someone like Camilla.

Rupert and Celeste accompany us to Charles St John's house in Rupert's chauffeur-driven Rolls-Royce. Rupert is on the committee of the genetic-engineering charity so I can hardly accuse them of being interfering in-laws.

It's my first time in a Rolls and it takes a real effort for me not to pat the bonnet as I pass it. I'll always be a car man.

The house of Charles St John, a sixteenth-century manor house, is more than a match for Rupert's, and I wonder whether they would have formed some feudalistic marital alliance to join their estates together if either of them had had a son rather than only a daughter apiece.

Charles and Grace stand just inside the Great Hall, greeting their guests as they arrive. And as Charles is shaking my hand, who should arrive but Mr and Mrs Kenneth Wilmington-Wilkes. The Fates are smiling on me still.

With a twinkle in his eye, Charles greets them and then indicates me. 'You remember Alexander Fairfax,' he says

He's enjoying this. He's looking forward to the showdown.

'Ah, yes, Alexander,' says Kenneth, shaking my hand.

I knee him in the groin and kick him while he writhes upon the floor.

Or do I squeeze his hand a little harder than I should?

I certainly do one of the two.

As we shake hands I can see that he doesn't know who I am. Kenneth is wearing a blank but friendly expression on his face, he doesn't associate Alexander with the Alex he left quivering in the office on the day of the sacking.

Elizabeth Wilmington-Wilkes clearly finds me familiar for

she studies me closely and then she gives a gasp of outrage. (She remembers me now.)

Some people have no manners these days.

Charles is smiling faintly as he claps me on the back and I know, at that moment, that he's aware of the story of my ignoble departure from Wilmington-Wilkes. And he doesn't seem to care. If anything, he's using me to get at Kenneth. Charles must really hate that smug bastard.

But does he hate him as much as I do?

'Alexander's your competition, Kenneth,' says Charles.

'Competition?' He looks confused.

Elizabeth looks like she's about to pee her pants she's so desperate to have a quiet word with her husband.

Poor woman. Does she think I'm soiling the air she's breathing? If her glares are anything to go by she clearly disapproves of a person such as me being at this gathering. Or who she thinks me to be. For Elizabeth and Kenneth don't know the new me. The real me.

But they're about to.

Charles smiles broadly. 'I thought we'd better hear two proposals. Wouldn't want to let the charity down. Wouldn't be fair. Even if you are on the committee.'

So Kenneth is on the committee for this new charity along with Charles and Rupert and most of the other people here tonight. But if Charles is leading the show, why did he invite Kenneth to participate if he despises him so? Could it be that Kenneth doesn't know Charles dislikes him? Is Charles planning some kind of mass public humiliation for my old managing director?

As these thoughts are whirling through my head I exchange small-talk with Grace and Elizabeth. A moment later Harriet enters the room, accompanied by a very tall, very thin young man. His skin is riddled with acne and he has that awkward look about him that shouts adolescence. Harriet's three or four years older than Camilla, probably my age or thereabouts, which makes this man, this boy, about ten or eleven years her junior. Suddenly I feel sorry for Harriet if this is her date. She's a bit loud and brash and horsy, but she seemed decent enough when I met her.

With the money her family has I'd expect a number of hot young bloods to be after her.

Harriet greets Camilla with a glad cry and a hug, and even hugs Rupert and Celeste. She's polite to me and flashes Camilla a little grin, as if to say, Ha, you lucky devil, you've still got him. (It's not conceit. I simply know that look.) As Harriet turns to Elizabeth and Kenneth her eyes lose their sparkle and her smile is fixed and frozen. 'Elizabeth. Kenneth. So good of you to come.'

Elizabeth murmurs a polite reply but her face flushes a deep red. You'd think it would add colour to her pale complexion and make her more attractive, but it merely draws attention to the heavy layer of makeup she's spread over her face in an attempt to disguise the years.

Charles looks like a man bent on vengeance and I have to repress my smile. It's all beginning to make sense. No wonder Kenneth suspects nothing. It was Elizabeth all along, Elizabeth who insulted the St John pride and joy. Poor Harriet. The wicked witch of Wilmington-Wilkes can be very fierce.

The young man is introduced to us all as the Honourable Alastair Archibald, Harriet's second cousin on her mother's side. An escort then, not a date, even if he is the son of a baron.

I'm watching Charles and see him throwing concerned glances at Harriet. A moment later he hastens everyone off to the dining room. It's rather abrupt, Charles hasn't left enough time for the initial socialising, but no one is rude enough to comment.

It's a father speaking and his daughter comes first.

Dinner is delightful. I couldn't have asked for better company or better conversation. Or a better seating placement.

Charles St John's table is at one end of the room, raised slightly on a dais as if in medieval times, so all his retainers can have a good view. At the head table sit Charles and Grace, Harriet and Alastair, Rupert and Celeste, Camilla and I. That's it. Eight of us on the dais. Is Charles signalling his favour for me and my proposal? Is that his deeper meaning, even if his unspoken excuse is that I'm accompanying Camilla's family and hence am being welcomed into the inner circle merely for this reason?

And where is that delightful Wilmington-Wilkes couple?

In social Siberia, of course, stuck on the table with the least glamorous people in the room. Dare I conjecture that their delightful dining companions are the token scientists included on the committee?

Are Kenneth and Elizabeth fuming at the seating arrangements? Are their smiles as false as they look? Do they feel dumb and ignorant as the scientists relive the decoding of a particularly interesting gene sequence on chromosome seventeen or sixteen or something equally confusing to the layperson? And the scientists, well, they're probably trying to be polite, but they can't restrain their enthusiasm for the subject and despite their best intentions they're soon talking over Kenneth and Elizabeth. I can see what's happening even if I can't hear the words. I smile all the more broadly as I slide my hand on to Camilla's knee beneath the table and give it a little squeeze. She looks beautiful tonight. I belong here at the head table, with these people. This is my world.

Dinner is delicious, but I'm not here for the food. Finally the last course has been served and cleared away and Charles rises to his feet.

'Thank you all for coming,' he says. 'Science moves at a rapid pace and as frequently as scientists tell us that science is neither good nor bad, that is has no intentions, good or evil, by our presence here tonight we acknowledge that we are all concerned where this pursuit of knowledge can lead. We all agree that it is necessary, that it is vital that ethical decisions are used to influence scientific achievements. Particularly today when genes are being studied and the potentials are staggering. Soon our scientists might be able to clone humans, to make designer babies, to manipulate our DNA down to the lowest levels. Now is the time to think about the implications of all this great science. Now is the time for ethics.'

I glance at Kenneth. He meets my eyes, trying not to glare, but I can read his stare, I can read his mind. I know the nasty thoughts he's thinking. He knows exactly who I am now.

Charles continues speaking: 'I invited you here tonight for two reasons. First of all so that you may meet your fellow committee members and, second, so that we can choose a name for our new charity. I've asked for ideas from two advertising firms. Most of you know Kenneth Wilmington-Wilkes of Wilmington-Wilkes.'

Kenneth smiles and waves, and people turn, glance at him and smile. They know him. But is to know him to like him? Will people choose his idea because they're friends? Because they're acquainted with him?

'Also here tonight is young Alexander Fairfax.' Charles indicates me with a sweep of his arm and a fond smile. 'He's a bright whiz-kid of advertising and he's here representing Platypus-fox.' Charles smiles at me and gives Camilla a wink. 'I think it's safe to say we'll all be seeing a lot more of Alexander. You might even say he's almost family.'

Camilla blushes. The audience laughs and I give them a

sheepish smile that I think they'll take as the smile of a man who's not yet proposed. It's like they're my audience, waiting for me to speak. I sit on the stage, I look official whereas Kenneth is merely one of the crowd. You'd better get used to it, Kenneth. For this is how it's going to be from now on.

'First we'll hear Kenneth's presentation,' says Charles, 'and then Alexander's. Kenneth?' Charles takes his seat.

Kenneth stands. 'Thank you, Charles. Thank you, everyone. I'll be direct and to the point. We all know why we're here so I won't bother with a slogan or a spiel about our cause. We want a name and I've come up with two that I think you'll all adore.'

Adore? Inwardly I smirk. Kenneth must be fuming. Does he know what he's done to infuriate Charles? Does he even realise Charles is out for his blood? Does he know how much Charles despises him?

Kenneth clears his throat loudly and then he speaks. 'EDGE. Ethical Decisions in Genetic Engineering.'

Bingo. That was my first guess. I knew Kenneth would like it. I'd worked there long enough to know the sort of things he favours. I scan the faces of the audience. They like it. As they should. It's fine. It's easy to remember. The name explains what they do. It's adequate.

'Or if we,' Kenneth emphasises that we, shooting a little glare of hatred at me, indicating that I, of course, am the outsider, that I am not on the committee, 'want something a little simpler, I'd suggest two letters. EG.' He says it EEE GEE. 'Ethics in Genetics. Thank you.'

There's polite applause as Kenneth takes his seat. He's smug. The bastard thinks he's so clever. He thinks I won't have thought of anything better. He thinks I'm just a little punk he was forced to sack because I was useless at my job.

If I had a pea-shooter I'd shoot him in the eye.

I smile and stand as the applause dies away. 'Thank you, Kenneth,' I say, as if he'd presented his ideas at my request, 'that was very illuminating.' Illuminating in that he's crap, that is. 'I, too, initially thought you might like an acronym,' I tell the audience, my eyes slowly moving across the crowd, meeting each and every person's gaze, 'but then I thought you deserved something better. Something unique. Something modern, something for the twenty-first century, something indicating the incredible technology at hand.'

I pause, holding the moment for half a second.

'E-genes,' I say.

Heads cock and people look contemplative. Camilla flashes me a brilliant smile, as if to say, You're fantastic, I always knew you'd win.

'E-genes can be the name of the charity and the name of the subject of the charity all in one. E-genes. Ethical Genes. Ethical Genetics. Engineered Genes. A threefold name for a complicated subject. E-genes.'

I am a gracious genius displaying my talent to the crowd.

'Thank you,' I say.

I sit to rapturous applause.

I smile at Charles and Grace, at Camilla and her parents, at my whole table. I accept their congratulations gracefully. I smile at the audience, acknowledging their response. I glance at Kenneth and Elizabeth, seeing their sickly smiles as they join in the clapping. They're not very good losers, are they? What's happened to their stiff upper lips?

The vote is carried out by secret ballot, with every person in the room (bar the staff, they don't count in this world) receiving one vote. I abstain, saying I don't want to sway the decision if it's that close.

(Kenneth, I note, does vote.)

I'm going to win. Alexander is here tonight and I have no doubts. I will win.

Charles sorts the votes into three piles at a side table where no one can peek at the count.

EG gets one vote, EDGE four and E-genes thirty-four.

I watch Kenneth as Charles announces the results. A muscle in his cheek twitches violently.

Charles speaks over the noise. 'Let the charity E-genes begin.'

I'm given a round of applause and I smile graciously and nod, trying to remain modest at the scale of my victory. Amber would be proud of me.

Kenneth, owner and leader of one of the top advertising agencies in the country, has been defeated by a young whippersnapper. How deeply does he feel the humiliation? Will he have nightmares about it tonight? I certainly hope so. I'd be disappointed otherwise that all my hard work had been in vain.

Charles takes a cheque out of his pocket and signs it with a flourish. He walks back to the dais, almost marching. He looks as happy as I feel.

Thrust one against Kenneth has been a success.

Will Charles want more vengeance or will this satisfy his thirst for Kenneth's blood?

Charles reaches the head table and presents me with the cheque. 'Your fee, Alexander.'

'Fee?' I'm confused. The cheque is for two hundred thousand pounds. And it's made out to me.

Charles claps me on the back. 'The winner's fee.' He lowers his voice. 'You don't think Kenneth agreed to do this for free, do you?'

'But it's for charity,' I say. 'I didn't think—'

'It's yours,' says Charles, smoothly interrupting my protests. 'I'd rather you have it than Wilmington-Wilkes.'

I shake my head, amazed at my determination in this. The old Alex wouldn't have accepted the money, he wouldn't have wanted to accept the money, but he might have been persuaded to keep it. He would have been persuaded to keep it. Alex would never have held strong against a personality like Charles. But I'm Alexander now. No one tells me what to do.

I stare at the cheque. Even to the new me it's a lot of money for ten minutes' work, but I know what I have to do.

'Thank you, Charles, I appreciate the gesture, but I can't accept this. Put the money towards E-genes instead.'

I tear the cheque in two. I, Alexander Fairfax, refuse two hundred thousand pounds.

I'm not being nice. I'm not. This is the sort of gesture Alexander can make, and it's not being nice, it's being calculating. It's making me look good. (I hope.)

As I set the torn cheque on the table I become aware that the room is silent. Everyone is watching me.

Charles is taken aback. He seems like a man who prides himself on judging a man's character and I think I've surprised him.

And I've shown myself that Alexander isn't only skin deep. I can stand up for myself. I can do what I want to do. I will do what I want to do. I am me. I am Alexander.

Charles holds up his hands for quiet. 'Thank you, Alexander, for your donation of two hundred thousand pounds.' I hear a gasp from the audience. 'I'm certain I speak for everyone present when I invite you to join our board of directors. E-genes needs a man like you.' Charles claps me on the back again and then he offers me his hand.

And just like that I'm a hero.

And a member of the board alongside men like Charles St John and his ilk. It'll look good when I've got an entry in *Who's Who*.

BASKING IN GLORY
(LOVELY, LOVELY SUNDAY)

Camilla sleeps in the passenger seat and I drive along in the fast lane, drumming my fingers on the steering-wheel in time to the music.

Rupert and Celeste seem to approve of me now.

Bloody followers.

It's okay to like me now that I'm so popular – and when I'm obviously not a fortune hunter, for a true fortune hunter wouldn't have turned down two hundred grand.

Before we left Rupert gave me his card. He told me that he's involved with British Gas and he knows they're looking for some punchy new advertising so why don't I give him a call in a few days and he'll set up a meeting for me?

I drop Camilla off at her apartment. 'I have to work today,' I say. 'I'll call you tomorrow.'

She's not very happy, but my masterful victory and success with E-genes is fresh in her mind so she doesn't argue.

And I know what she must be thinking. If he doesn't work there will be no money, and if there's no money there will be no fun.

I race home, letting the power of the engine roar, surging like the adrenaline inside my body.

Will Amber be home? It's not even five. I didn't think I'd be back so early.

I screech into an empty space on the street. Is it safe to leave my Jag here? It's very vulnerable to hooligans. Pah. It's insured. I'll get a garage next week. Sod the expense and sod the waiting lists. I have connections now, I'll be able to get whatever I want. And I'll buy a new car if it's damaged again.

I tiptoe into the flat and find Amber alone in the living room, chatting on the phone to her sister. She's curled into a ball on the sofa and when she sees me she smiles this gigantic smile and I feel happy.

She's glad to see me.

I run towards her in slow motion, making exaggerated gestures with my arms. When I reach her I throw myself on to the sofa, trapping her where she sits.

I kiss the palm of her hand and then the tip of every finger. And then I start to tickle her. She tries to fight it, she tries to carry on her conversation like nothing is happening, but soon I have her bursting out in laughter. 'I've got to go,' says Amber into the phone, desperately squirming away from my hands. 'Alexander's here. I'll call you later. 'Bye.' She hangs up.

I lift her shirt and press my lips against her belly and blow, making loud noises, like fathers do to their six-year-olds. She wiggles and writhes, and then she starts to tickle me. It feels funny and I laugh and scoot away, out of her reach. Amber leaps from the sofa and I chase her across the room, catching her about the waist and dragging her with me to the floor.

I smile into her eyes. 'I missed you,' I say.

And as I say it I know it's true. I did miss her. She'd have enjoyed staying in a Georgian mansion, I'd have enjoyed staying there with her. It's good to see her again. I don't need to pretend.

'I missed you, too,' she says.

I lower my lips to hers.

Ten minutes later we move to her room and let's just say she never has time to ring her sister back.

Monday, Monday. I love Mondays. Mondays are days to reflect on the glorious successes of the weekend before. And to start work on brilliant new campaigns. I need to come up with some ideas for British Gas so that I'm ready when Rupert gets me a meeting slot.

And, lo and behold, just when I think the day can't get any better, the phone rings and my temp answers it and tells me that Kenneth Wilmington-Wilkes is on the line. That Kenneth is phoning me.

'Kenneth,' I say, taking the call, all hearty chums, 'good to hear from you.'

'Hello, Alexander.' His voice sounds funny and I wonder if he's choking on his own bile, so greatly must he hate me.

'I'm right in the middle of a creative flow,' I say, deciding he must have held his shame in check and rung Charles St John to obtain my number, 'so can we cut right to the point?'

'Of course.' He doesn't want to prolong this conversation any more than I do. 'I, uh, I've been hearing some good things about your firm, Alex.'

'It's Alexander.' My name is not Alex. (I wonder which defections of his old clients he's discovered.)

'Oh, uh, Alexander, then. I was hoping you'd be able to come over for a meeting this afternoon.'

'A meeting? With you? At Wilmington-Wilkes? I didn't think I was welcome at Wilmington-Wilkes.'

'That,' says Kenneth, 'was a silly misunderstanding. I'd like to put things right. Will you come?'

'I don't know. I've got a lot of work I'm hoping to get done today.' Let him think I'm reluctant when in fact I'm dying to get into the Wilmington-Wilkes offices again. My plan, my master plan, won't be complete without a venture into the old place.

'I'll make it worth your while. Please, Alexander. Please come.'

Please?

Is Kenneth begging me to come?

I smile like a Cheshire cat. 'Oh, all right,' I say, in an exasperated tone, as if I'm giving in against my better judgement. 'Say three?'

And the pathetic bastard seems grateful.

Can't he afford to lose so many clients? Hasn't he been gaining new accounts? Was he relying on repeat business? Did he really want that couple of hundred grand from E-genes that I tore up in front of him? Does he need money?

Kenneth Wilmington-Wilkes himself is standing beside the security desk waiting for me. Kenneth is a man who doesn't like to leave the sanctity of his own office unless it's to meet clients or sack an employee. And here he is greeting me. Where's his smugness now?

'Alexander,' says Kenneth, hurrying over to shake my hand.

I grip tightly, using the same trick I used on Saturday night, punishing him with the only physical violence I can get away with. I squeeze until he betrays himself with a wince and then I release him. 'Kenneth.'

Kenneth's smile turns sickly. He's not used to men like me calling him by his Christian name. In this domain he's known as Mr Wilmington-Wilkes, sir, yes, sir, but not by me. Not any longer. I'm a free agent, not an employee. And I'll never be an employee again. Not of him. Not of anyone.

'Come on up to my office,' he says. He leads me towards his private lift. (Kenneth does not like to sully himself through contact with lesser mortals.)

And just as we reach it the doors to one of the main lifts open and disgorge a group of a dozen or so employees. They're carrying laptops and folders and heavy briefcases, and I know that look: they're on their way to a presentation. As I pause and watch them I begin to recognise faces and, more importantly, I see that those faces see me and stare for half a second before their expressions turn guarded. They pretend not to notice, but I can see them watching us. They've seen us. They've seen me. They've seen Kenneth in the lobby escorting me into his private lift. What will the Wilmington-Wilkes gossips make of this?

I take my time, wanting as many of the employees as possible to recognise me, to remember my ignominious departure. It'll be good for morale, I think. Or good for the morale of my staff, the ones I take from this godforsaken place.

Kenneth's office. It might as well have been Valhalla for all Alex saw of it. Not once was I, was he, summoned to this floor.

I stride into the room, letting my eyes wander over the paintings, the walls, the furnishings. Let Kenneth think I'm in an avaricious mood. Let him think my eye is on his job.

Kenneth sits behind his desk (with the window behind him, no doubt wanting the light to illuminate him and make him appear godlike and strong, but I've read the books too, Kenneth, it won't work). 'Have a seat,' he says, indicating the chairs in front of his desk.

'I'll stand, thank you,' I say, and walk over to a side window, peering out at the view of London.

I hear Kenneth's chair sliding back across the carpet, the wheels squeaking ever so slightly. 'I understand you've been poaching my clients,' says Kenneth, the façade of friendliness gone.

I turn to face him. 'Poaching?' I say, one eyebrow raised incredulously. 'Your clients?' I tilt my head and appear to think. 'I didn't know you owned any clients. How curious.'

He flushes. 'You know what I mean. I want them back. They were mine first.'

Bet he was the bully on the playground. Every school has one.

I shrug. 'So sorry, but that's for them to decide. They like my campaign ideas. If you can do better I'm sure they'll go back to you next year.'

'I'll sue you, you smug bastard.'

I laugh. I stand in Kenneth's office, the window now at my back, illuminating me, and I laugh in his face. 'For what? Fair competition?'

His face turns an ugly mottled red. 'For poaching. For breach of contract.'

I sigh. 'Prosecute me if you want. My lawyers will look forward to taking your money.'

'Give me back my clients.'

Wah, wah, wah. Alexander stole my blankie, Mummy. Make him give it back.

'Kenneth, you're getting tedious. You're like a parrot. Now why don't you shut up and listen to me?'

He just gapes at me, stunned.

Does my language shock him? Has no one ever told him to shut up before? I can't imagine why not, he's such a wearisome old windbag.

When he remains quiet – from outrage as much as anything else I should think – I continue: 'Good. That's better. If you'd bothered to do a little homework, Kenneth, you'd know that I'm not in breach of contract. There's nothing in my contract about taking clients with me. And I didn't even take them with me, they came to me afterwards. You can take me to court and try to sue me but you'll lose. Can you really afford to waste all that money, Kenneth? What would dear Elizabeth say?'

He seems to fade a little, almost to deflate, and I know I've hit it right on the button. He's having financial difficulties.

Poor Kenneth. Is he having to worry about making the mortgage payments? (If he even has a mortgage, which I doubt. Maybe it's just Elizabeth's lavish tastes he's finding it difficult to support.)

'You're right.' Kenneth's voice is a croak, and if he weren't such a bastard I'd feel sorry for him.

No, I wouldn't, but Alex might have done. Alex would have done – I was such a sucker. Alex would have felt sorry for Kenneth, and Alex would have given him a bone to tide him over so he'd feel better and then Kenneth would have snatched the whole bloody bag. But I will do no such thing. I know what I have to do to succeed and helping out pitiful little (and I'm not talking short) men like Kenneth isn't part of the programme.

Kenneth sighs. 'I've already looked at the contract.' He runs a hand through his thinning hair and then he straightens, visibly regaining his stature like a balloon being filled with hot air. 'I have a proposition for you, young man,' he says, his voice brisk, businesslike, back to normal.

'A proposition?' I can't believe this. 'First you invite me into your office where you threaten and insult me, and now you want to make me an offer?'

Kenneth nods. 'We're both men of business, Alexander. We know how these things work.'

I want to snort and laugh in his face, but I don't. I'm enthralled. Whatever will he say next?

'How would you like to come back to Wilmington-Wilkes? As one of our directors?'

'You're serious?' I say, keeping my voice neutral.

'Yes, of course. I can see now what a valuable contribution you made to my company. To our company. I'll make it financially worth your while. Salary is not an issue.'

I doubt he can match my current earnings, but I keep silent on that point. It's not important now.

'If I'm such a valuable contributor, why did you sack me?' I ask, no more pussy-footing around.

A muscle twitches in his cheek and I stare at it in fascination. Does he feel his empire crumbling about him?

'Yes, well, I'm sorry for all that, I must say. I was led astray by rather unfortunate advice,' he says.

Lame, I think, lame, lame, lame. 'You didn't bother to check the facts. You wouldn't listen to me. You didn't wait for an investigation. You didn't even wonder if Jed was lying.'

'Why would Jed lie? He's one of our best employees.'

'He was screwing my girlfriend.'

I can see this isn't what Kenneth was expecting.

'Ah,' he says. 'Why didn't you tell me?'

'You didn't give me a chance. You didn't want to hear what I had to say. You'd made your judgement.'

'What can I do to make it up to you?' Kenneth looks earnest now and I wonder how far he'll go.

'Jed will have to be punished,' I say.

'Of course. He lied to me.'

'Yes, he did lie to you, Kenneth, but he also got me sacked and that's what I consider the more important offence. And wrongdoers have to be punished in kind, do they not?' No, I don't believe they do, but for Jed that's what I want.

Kenneth licks his lips. 'What are you saying?'

'Jed will have to be sacked. Immediately. In my presence. He has to be sacked and the papers signed and sealed so that there's no going back. I refuse to work with him.'

No hesitation. 'Done. I'll do it.'

Poor Jed. I know he thinks Kenneth really likes him. That they're buddies in a weird sort of master-and-servant way.

'Now,' I insist. 'Do it now.' I'm relentless, eager. This is the moment I've been waiting for ever since I was reborn as Alexander.

'Now?'

'Yes,' I say. 'Or I'm walking out of this door.'

Kenneth sits, defeated.

I step closer, pointing at his phone. 'Call him,' I say. 'Summon him here.'

Kenneth does as I order, and five minutes later Jed knocks and walks into Kenneth's office. To say that he's shocked to see me there is like saying that Romeo was merely a tiny bit glum to find Juliet dead. Jed's floored. He can't believe his eyes.

'Hello, Jed,' I say. 'How's Sarah?'

(Have you had any clues that she's no longer so keen on you?)

'She's good,' Jed says, looking from me to Kenneth, wondering what's going on.

I indicate Jed with a sweep of my arms. 'Proceed, Kenneth,' I say.

'I'm sorry, Jed,' says Kenneth.

I clear my throat. 'You're sorry?' I ask Kenneth. 'Your employee lied to you and you're sorry?'

'Look, I can explain,' says Jed, obviously knowing I'd spilled the beans. 'I was crazy, I wasn't thinking clearly. I was jealous.'

I laugh. 'So you admit it? Good. Carry on, Kenneth.'

Kenneth sighs. 'You're sacked, Jed.'

'What? But what did I do?' His eyes dart about the room, seeking a way out.

But there is no escape. Not from Alexander.

'For lying to me.' Kenneth's voice is getting stronger and I'd guess it's slowly dawning on him just exactly what Jed did. Is Kenneth starting to feel a little outrage on his own behalf? 'And for causing me to lose my most valuable employee.'

'Valuable employee?' Jed's mouth drops. 'Him?' he says, pointing at me.

Didn't your mother ever tell you it's rude to point?

I'm happy to help clarify the situation for him. 'I've gone into the business,' I say. 'I'm a competitor now.'

'I don't know what he's been telling you,' says Jed, pleading with Kenneth, 'but he's a nobody. Nothing. A loser. He'll never amount to anything.'

Was that how Jed saw me? Saw Alex? He thought I was nothing? That I was less than nothing?

But what does that say for Sarah who spent two years with me?

Jed's right. I'd agree with him. Alex was a loser. And that means that Sarah must also be a loser for losers always stick together, right? Therefore, by association, Jed's labelled himself a loser too. I could go along with that.

Jed's still pleading, but I can see that Kenneth's eyes have glazed over. He's not listening. Kenneth can't afford to listen. 'You don't have to worry about his so-called competition. I'll take care of him,' says Jed. 'Come on, Kenneth, you can trust me. You can rely on me.'

'Obviously not,' says Kenneth, pressing a button on his desk.

'If you were going to use my company to carry out your personal vendettas you should have made damn sure they worked and didn't blow up in your face. I don't appreciate being caught in the backdraught.'

Jed flushes. 'But—'

'You're sacked, Jed.'

'Please, I can—'

The door opens and two beefy security guards step in. Not the two who were present for my sacking, I'm sorry to say, and I wish they were, for it would have made the whole thing that little bit more perfect. It would have been a complete and absolute form of poetic justice, but I don't mind, not really, it's near enough perfect as it is.

'You'll pack your things and leave immediately,' says Kenneth.

Jed swallows. 'What about severance?'

'You'll get the normal package.'

'Uh-uh,' I say, wagging my finger. 'The contract states you aren't required to give severance in the case of misconduct.' Alex sure as hell wasn't given any.

Kenneth closes his eyes for a moment, clutching the edge of his desk. When he reopens his eyes, his words are clipped. 'No severance package,' he says.

Jed stares at me as the security guards escort him out.

Is he wondering how he could have so misjudged me? But that's just it. He didn't misjudge me. Doesn't he realise that he helped to create me? He's like Dr Frankenstein. I am who I am because of what he did to me. He's my creator, not the sole creator but the leader in charge of creating the monster.

It's because of Jed that I have my own company, that I have Camilla and the lifestyle she represents, that I'm on the board of E-genes. Without Jed none of this would have happened. And now Jed is getting his just reward. Let's see what he does with a little adversity. Will it make a new man of him?

Once Jed is gone and the door is closed, Kenneth speaks: 'When can you start?'

'I want to see the paperwork,' I say, 'the papers about Jed.'

'Fine.' Kenneth looks annoyed, but there's nothing he can do. He's made his choice and now he has to live up to it.

Kenneth rings his PA and she enters a few minutes later with a document. Kenneth signs it with a flourish and hands it to me to read. This paper terminates Jed's employment, stating serious misconduct as the cause. I read it and hand it back to the PA who takes it from the room.

'I'd like a copy for myself,' I say.

'Why?'

'To ensure he doesn't return.'

'He's been released, he's betrayed me, he's guilty. He's not coming back,' says Kenneth. 'I won't take him back. I need employees I can trust to tell me the truth.'

So long as you remember that.

'One other thing,' I say.

'What is it?'

'I'd like the expenses of the entertainment of the Shire Horse representatives to be refunded to me. You'll have to take it out of Jed's last pay packet. He is the one to blame.'

'Consider it done. Anything else?'

'Just my copy of Jed's dismissal.' I'm going to frame it and hang it on the wall so I can look at it when I stare at my daisies. (Not that I'm planning on sleeping in my room when Amber's bed is available.)

Kenneth rings his PA. 'Make a copy for Alexander.'

Doesn't he know he's supposed to say please to the ladies?

He folds his hands on his desk. 'Now, enough of this. When are you starting? When are you returning my clients to the fold?'

'Starting?' I ask.

'Working for Wilmington-Wilkes?'

'Oh, that. I'll think about it.'

'You'll think about it?'

'That's what I said,' I say. 'You can fax me your offer. I need details, Kenneth, and then I'll think about it.'

'But I sacked Jed. I liked Jed.'

I shrug. 'It needed to be done. He lied to you, Kenneth. You can't have people like that around you. You said so yourself.'

'But I sacked him. For you. That's what you asked for.'

'Yes. And you did well. Now I'll think about your proposition. You can't expect me to decide without the figures in front of me. Goodbye, Kenneth.'

And I leave his office before he can respond, picking up my photocopy of Jed's dismissal form from the PA on my way out.

Sucker. Kenneth is a fool. I have absolutely no intention of joining Wilmington-Wilkes. Not soon. Not ever. I'm my own man now. Why would I want to subordinate myself to Kenneth? I'm not that gullible. I won't succumb to a little bit of flattery. And there wasn't even much flattery: Kenneth needs more practice at eating humble pie. I'll see what I can do about that in the future.

For the rest of my life I'll treasure the look on Jed's face when he saw me standing in Kenneth's office looking like I owned the place.

And maybe one day I will. If Kenneth's finances are ailing perhaps Wilmington-Wilkes will be susceptible to a take-over bid. Wouldn't that be something if in a few months or next year Platypus-fox buys out Wilmington-Wilkes? Not a merger of equals. A take-over. A hostile take-over. It's worth keeping in mind. And the first thing I'd do is get rid of the Wilmington-Wilkes name. The whole entity could be known as Platypus-fox or Platypus-fox and Fairfax. I'll see when the time comes.

I am the giver of vengeance. Jed has been reduced to dust. My opponent has been vanquished and I am the victor.

I head to the Embankment and sit on a bench near Cleopatra's Needle. It's nearly time for me to collect Amber and head down to Surrey for my father's birthday dinner, but I told Camilla I would ring her so I do.

As we're talking and Camilla is telling me about her day, it suddenly strikes me how glad I am that I invited Amber along tonight. If I'd asked Camilla I'd be spending the evening dreading the moment when my mother discussed the time I peed all over the back seat of my father's brand new car when I was three, or the time I put my pet worms on the pillow beside my head and how they dried out and died overnight and how I was inconsolable with grief for a week. But for some reason I'm not worried about Amber learning these things. I have no need to hide my past from her: she won't care where I've come from or what I've done, she doesn't judge people like that.

And I don't really feel like seeing Camilla tonight, I'm too wired, too full of energy after the day I've had and I might want to shout, to leap, to run and jump, and Camilla would approve of none of those things. It's good I'm seeing Amber instead. She'll jump with me if I want her to.

When Camilla invites me over I say, with a tone of regret, that I have to entertain clients tonight and it's not a social outing so she can't join us.

She's pouting, I know she's pouting: I can hear it in her voice.

'I'm sorry,' I say. 'Why don't you come over to my office after work tomorrow? We can eat and maybe look at property.'

'Property?'

Aha. I bet she's sitting up now.

'I want to buy a house,' I say, 'and I'd appreciate your advice.'

'What are you looking for?'

'Something in London with a minimum of four bedrooms so I won't have to move when I get married and have children.'

Have I stunned her? Is she shocked to hear a man talking about marriage like he really wants to do it?

'What sort of area?' Her voice is warm, it's practically purring, and I know I've got her on my hook.

'I trust you,' I say. 'Think of somewhere you'd like to live. A place we'd be happy to stay in for a number of years.'

I throw in that 'we' deliberately to see if she'll notice, to see if she'll comment.

'Leave it with me,' she says. 'I'll see what I can do. I'll try and make us some appointments for tomorrow night.'

Us, she said. Appointments for both of us and not just for me.

It's like we're speaking in a subtle code, neither of us wanting to come out and say what we're thinking exactly but willing to hint at what we're feeling. (Or pretending to feel.)

I decide to go one step further: I don't have the patience for a long courtship.

'I love you,' I say.

An instant response. 'Oh, Alexander, I love you, too.'

'See you tomorrow,' I say.

'I can't wait.' Her voice is low, sexy, throbbing, promising a great deal.

It takes me a few minutes to end the call, but when I do I'm feeling calmer, more in control. Everything's going to come together exactly as I want it. Success and revenge, revenge and success, life is awfully fine.

To me it's always been just my bedroom. My room with my things. Exactly the way I left everything when I moved away from home at eighteen. My things, my stuff, all of it ready and waiting for my return visits. There to make me feel comfortable and cosy and immediately at home. I may not have slept in this house for more than ten nights a year since I finished university, but it's still the place I think of as home, or my permanent home even if I no longer live there and have no intention of ever living there again.

But Amber gazes around my room and, with a touch of awe in her voice, says, 'It's a shrine to you, their eldest son and heir. My parents boxed up all my belongings and turned my room into a guest room the month after I left.'

She turns slowly in a circle and stares at my things: my athletics medals (fun runs I entered by the dozen when I was a teenager where every contender gets a medal, hence my seeming prowess when I never finished in the top third of any race), posters of Nirvana, Pearl Jam and Metallica, shells collected on family holidays from beaches around the world and, worst of all, a poster of Princess Leia I'd put up at the foot of my bed when I was twelve and never got round to taking down.

But Amber doesn't laugh, rather she seems to take everything in, as if it will allow her to understand me better.

A shiver sweeps up my back, starting at the lowest point of my spine and travelling upwards faster than a thought, and I just have to get her out of there. I feel as if she's staring into my soul and it's scary. She's not supposed to know me, not the real me, she's only supposed to see what I want her to see. I don't mind her learning embarrassing tales from my childhood, but this is different. I thought I didn't mind her knowing things about me, but now that she's here, now that she's in my bedroom, now that she's inside this room filled with my likes, my dreams, my past, myself, I'm uncomfortable.

I should have known this would happen, I should have had an excuse prepared, I should have refused my mother when she practically ordered me to give Amber a guided tour of the house when we arrived a few minutes early and she hadn't finished laying the table and wouldn't let us help. To distract Amber before she can think about the true significance of Princess Leia being in the position she's in, I draw Amber into my arms and kiss her. I kiss her until her eyes close, until her senses are befuddled, until thoughts of me as a teenager are driven away.

The meal goes well. My mother has clearly taken a shine to Amber and all of her disappointed grandmotherly genes have found a new focus. Despair over the loss of Sarah and the delay that that will cause in my fathering children has been forgotten now that she has a new target on which to concentrate. My father likes Amber too, helped by her laughter at his jokes. He always likes a fresh audience. My brother and his wife are practically oozing welcome-to-the-family slogans out of every pore. It's downright embarrassing and from their smirking looks and smug comments about my 'friendship' with Amber you'd think this was the first time I'd brought a woman home to meet my family. If they keep acting like this it might very well be the last.

There's not a single mention of Sarah and I'm doubly grateful for Amber's presence; I didn't want to have to relieve the whole sorry affair – I have no need to open up and share my feelings to make myself feel better. The revenge is doing that quite well on its own.

Dessert is over and we're all having coffee and being quite civilised when my mother starts her offensive. She bides her time carefully, waiting until I'm in a conversation with my brother, telling him about my latest client.

'And what do you think is the best age to start having children?' my mother asks Amber.

Everyone is suddenly very busy drinking coffee, pretending not to listen, hiding their smiles behind their cups. We've been through this before. Many times. This is one of my mother's favourite topics – almost a crusade, you might say. And not, she's insisted in the past, a deliberate attempt to embarrass us.

She carries on before I can stop her: 'Too many of you young women, these days, want to wait until you're in your thirties, but you need all the energy of your twenties. Toddlers are hard work. And how old are you, Amber?'

'Mum,' I say sternly, 'Amber is my guest.'

'Yes, dear,' says my mother, smiling sweetly, pretending to be innocent when we all know she has ulterior motives, 'I'm aware of that. But I don't get to meet enough young women and I'm interested in her opinion on this matter. You know how important it is to me.'

What is my mother doing? I don't want Amber thinking about babies. I don't want Amber thinking about babies and me together. It's not a context with which I'm comfortable. Most women don't need encouragement to start thinking of marriage and children, and I certainly don't want my mother giving Amber dreams of a future together that's not going to happen. It can't happen, I can't let it happen. I won't let it happen. We're not serious, this is just a bit of fun, that's all.

Amber laughs. 'I think you'd better concede defeat,' she tells me, then turns to my mother. 'I'm still in my twenties, you needn't write me off as a lost cause yet.'

My mother smiles. 'You really should promise yourself that you'll have your first child by the time you're thirty. I'll just have a word with my son and see what I can do.'

There's a pause and we're all staring at one another, we can't quite believe our ears, and I find I can't look at Amber. Then my mother bursts out laughing and we all join in.

'And you thought I couldn't tell a joke,' says my mother.

'That wasn't a joke,' I say, finally able to meet Amber's eyes and finding her smiling and laughing along with the rest of us, 'that was cruelty.'

After that things are easier and there's no more talk of babies. Everyone assumes that Amber and I are an item. Well, we're here together, that's true, but we're not, you know, an item. Not really.

At last the grandfather clock chimes eleven and I'm given a reprieve from the delighted look in my mother's eye. We say goodbye and we're able to make our escape.

My parents watch with fond smiles as I help Amber into the car and slide behind the wheel. They wave us off, looking like a busybody sitcom couple as I pull out of the drive in my Jag.

I don't want to think about dinner, I don't want to talk about what happened, I don't want to reassure Amber that my family love her (they do), I just want it to be like it was.

So I chat about this and that, I'm lively, I'm amusing, I'm entertaining as I drive us home, but we don't talk, not about anything real. We're happy and excited and everything's back to normal as I park and we go inside and straight to Amber's bed. Afterwards I wrap strands of her hair around my fingers. She keeps glancing at me and then away. Poor baby has something to say.

'What is it?' I ask gently, tucking the duvet around her shoulders so she won't get cold.

'It's about us.'

Oh dear, here it comes.

'What about us?' I ask.

'I'm sorry, I don't mean to be awkward.'

I kiss her cheek. What a darling. She's such an angel. 'You're not being awkward,' I say. 'Ask away.'

'Are we a couple now?'

'A couple?' I stop fiddling with her hair and look into her eyes. After tonight I should have expected this. My mother's comments were hardly conducive to continuing our casual arrangement without discussion.

'Are we seeing only each other?'

What can I say? I can hardly tell her the truth. I don't want to be cruel to Amber. I didn't want to lie to her, I was hoping to avoid the issue altogether, but it's too late for that now. I'll have to tell her what she wants to hear. What she needs to hear.

She rushes on before I can speak: 'It's just that, well, I'd feel awkward if you wanted to sleep around. I don't think I could do it. I don't want to sleep with anyone else.'

And so you shouldn't.

'But I don't want you to sleep with anyone else either,' she says, 'not if you're sleeping with me. I want to be in a relationship or out of one. I can't handle the limbo world of anything in between. It would destroy me.'

It would destroy me.

Those four words freeze the lie on my lips. I'm silent. I stare into her eyes, stricken.

It would destroy me.

'Say something,' she says.

It would destroy me.

I can't lie to her. But I can't tell her the truth. She'd hate me. And I don't want her to hate me.

'Say something, Alex.'

I'm not Alex. That snivelling coward would never be in this situation. He would never have had the balls to sleep with Amber in the first place – it would have taken him six months to ask her out to dinner.

'Please,' she says, 'say something. You're scaring me.'

I can't speak. I say nothing.

It would destroy me.

I'm going to marry Camilla, or a woman just like her. I need to marry a woman like Camilla. I have to marry a woman like Camilla.

It would destroy me.

I say nothing.

'You're seeing someone else, aren't you?' asks Amber, tears pooling in her eyes. She scoots away from me, holding the duvet above her breasts, shielding herself from view.

I stare at her. It's like I'm mute. I cannot speak.

It would destroy me. It would destroy me. It would destroy me.

A few words, one or two little lies, and all would be well. She'd believe me, I could make her believe me, but I can't.

You pathetic worm, I scream at myself, you want her, you want to keep her, you like her. What the hell are you doing? You're pushing her away.

It would destroy me.

I can't be the one to destroy her.

You fool, you're not nice, you don't have to be nice. You'll destroy her anyway. Can't you hear her crying?

It'd be worse when I marry Camilla. Or Camilla's clone.

I should never have slept with her. I should never have given in to the temptation. I'm supposed to be strong and look out for her kind. I'm supposed to be a defender of the meek and mild, the protector of the nice. What was I thinking? I don't want the innocent to suffer. Especially not this innocent.

It would destroy me.

'I'm sorry,' I whisper.

What have I done?

I flee the room to the sounds of heartrending sobs.

I lock myself in my room and try to count the daisy petals, but my eyes won't focus. Why won't they focus?

I can hear Amber's sobs.

Some time later, it might have been ten minutes, it might have been two hours, Noreen pounds on my door and shouts at me. I know she's there, I can vaguely hear her voice with one small part of my brain, but the only thing that matters is Amber's tears.

I never wanted her to cry.

I wish I could comfort her. But I can't.

I leap from my bed and begin to pace, feeling like a caged lion on his first day in the zoo.

Eventually Noreen goes away and I know this is my chance to escape so I grab a change of clothes for tomorrow and I sneak out of the flat like a thief.

I drive as if the minions of hell are pursuing me and I head to Camilla's. She's asleep when I arrive but she's happy to see me.

I'm frenzied for sex. I let her think it's because I missed her, because I haven't seen her since I declared my love for her. But I need the stimulation, I need the relief. I need it to regain my control.

Camilla's very accommodating tonight. Is it because she's enjoying herself? Or am I being rewarded for saying those three little words?

Camilla sleeps and I stare at the ceiling, hearing Amber's sobs inside my head.

It would destroy me.

SO LONG, SARAH

I must have slept for I wake up with the sun shining on my face. The weather matches my mood. Bright and crisp and ruthlessly cold.

I can no longer recall why I was feeling guilty about Amber. I did the girl a favour. She should thank me. She should never have hung around Alexander if she couldn't handle it. Good thing I cut her loose before she got really burned.

Camilla barely wakes as I shag her, but I don't mind: I'm in a hurry and I want to head right into the office and get to work.

Mid-morning Sarah rings me on my mobile. 'Alex, can we meet?'

My name, you whore, is Alexander.

Sarah's hesitant, she's uncertain, she obviously knows about Jed. 'I'd like to talk.'

Of course we have to meet. It's not finished yet. There's still some revenge to be had.

'Lunch?' I say. 'Sandwiches in the rose garden in Regent's Park?' When we were first dating we used to spend lazy Sundays sunbathing in Regent's Park and Sarah always insisted on smelling at least seven varieties of rose before we were allowed to leave.

'I'd like that.' Her voice is husky now.

Poor dear. Has she misinterpreted my remark? Does she take this invitation as the seeking of a renewed commitment? Well, we shall see. She'll learn the truth soon enough.

'I'll get the sandwiches,' I say. It's the least I can do.

At one o'clock I enter the rose garden, Prêt à Manger bag in hand.

Sarah's already there, waiting, sitting on a blanket in the shade. Did she pop home and retrieve the blanket? Did she have to lie to Jed? Is he sitting at home moping? Is he feeling a little low?

'Alex,' she says, as I sink down on to the blanket beside her.

I don't kiss her cheek. I feel like grinning. I never have to touch her again. I could burst into song it makes me so happy.

'Hi, Sarah,' I say. I open the bag and hand her a sandwich and a bottle of water. It's fizzy water, which I know she doesn't like.

'Thanks.' Sarah takes one bite, chews methodically, then sets aside the food. 'Is it true?'

I unwrap my sandwich and start to eat, savouring the taste of the Brie. I do so love the taste of cheese. I chew and swallow. 'Is what true?'

'Jed.'

I shrug. 'Is it true that he was sacked? Yes.'

She waits, and when I don't say anything else, she sighs. 'He says that you got him sacked. That it was your fault.'

'Not true,' I say. 'It's his fault. All this is his fault. He's the one who started it.'

'I knew he was lying. I knew he was.' She slides across the blanket, throws her arms around me. She tries to kiss me on the lips, but I shift so she kisses my neck instead.

Ugh. Get away. You're touching me.

Sarah pulls away, smiling now, her posture no longer tense. 'I stood up for you when Jed was saying all those horrible things. He was awful, Alex. He was swearing and vowing revenge. That wasn't the Jed I know. I knew. I kicked him out.'

'Did you tell Jed about us?'

'Yes, I told him.'

'You ditched Jed? You dumped him?'

'Yes. He was awful.'

What a bitch. She has absolutely no sense of loyalty. Not to anyone but herself.

I stay silent.

'Say something,' she says.

It's too reminiscent of Amber.

This time I speak. I want to speak, I want Sarah to be wounded. 'What do you want me to say?'

'Aren't you happy?'

'Of course I'm happy.' And I am. My goal has been to shag her and then get her to dump Jed. It's worked. I've succeeded.

'And you'll move back in?' she asks.

'Sorry?'

'Us. You and me. We're getting back together, aren't we? There's nothing to stop us now that Jed's gone. I'm so sorry, Alex. I don't know how you can forgive me. I was awful. I never meant to hurt you. I never meant to leave you for Jed. I got carried away. I'm sorry.'

You never meant to leave Alex for Jed? But you didn't mind having an affair with Jed, is that what you're saying?

'I don't know, Sarah. I don't know if I want to live with you.' That's a lie. I do know and the answer is no. 'I thought we were just spending time together for old times' sake.'

'You thought I fucked you out of habit?'

'Not habit, Sarah. You wanted me. It was a simple interaction between consenting adults. We both knew you had no problem having sex with a man other than your boyfriend. I didn't think you'd have any qualms. I thought you'd enjoyed it.'

'You bastard. How dare you?'

'Jed's right, Sarah. I did get him fired. It was all me. But it's justice, you see, for that's what he did to me. He lied and got me sacked. I merely told the truth to get him sacked.'

Her face drains of colour. 'All this, you and me, this was all about Jed?'

'No, no,' I say. 'It was about you. I loved you, Sarah. More fool me. Look how my love was repaid.'

'We were good together. We were.' She's crying now. 'Why

are you doing this? What's happened to you, Alex? You've changed. I don't know you any more.'

'But I have you to thank. You helped cause me to change. Don't you like the new me?'

Sarah stands, still crying. 'So this is it? You don't love me? We're over?'

I nod, a little sadly. 'I think so. Don't you?'

Tears run down her face. 'Do you hate me so much, then? Because I cheated on you?'

I take another bite of my sandwich, chew and swallow. 'I'm sorry, Sarah, but there are scales of justice and only now are we in the balance. You hurt me and I hurt you and now we're even.'

'I don't like the new you, Alex. You're not nice. You're not nice at all.'

'No,' I agree, 'I'm not nice.' I take a sip of water, stand and walk away.

I leave the rose garden. I leave Regent's Park. I leave Sarah behind me.

TRUTH OR CONSEQUENCES
(AND NOT THE TOWN IN NEW MEXICO)

Camilla arrives promptly for once, spurred on, no doubt, by the thought of property appointments. We're viewing one place in Mayfair and two in Knightsbridge.

She's showing me the particulars when the office door opens and Sarah enters.

'My, my, isn't this a cosy picture?' says Sarah. Her tone is decidedly nasty.

'Hello, Sarah.'

Camilla raises one delicately plucked eyebrow. 'You know this woman?' Her gaze sweeps up and down Sarah, clearly rating her a step or two below swamp algae.

'This is Sarah,' I tell Camilla. 'An old friend.'

I deliberately don't introduce Sarah to Camilla, but Sarah doesn't seem to notice.

'A friend? We were more than friends,' says Sarah. 'And not that long ago.'

'And why exactly are you here?' I ask.

Camilla checks the time, flashing her Rolex at Sarah. 'Is this going to take long?'

'Don't you want to know the sordid details of Alex's past?' Sarah's words are addressed to Camilla, but she's speaking to me. I'm the one she wants to maim.

'The only thing sordid about my past is you,' I tell her.

Camilla sits in the temp's empty chair, her lips curled in disdain as she studies Sarah.

'Don't you want to know how I found you?' asks Sarah.

'You can thank your old buddy Kenneth Wilmington-Wilkes. Guess he still has a soft spot for Jed.'

'Why are you here, Sarah? What do you want? Have you come to beg for mercy?'

She flutters her eyelashes. 'No, merely to tell you that Jed and I are getting married.'

I burst out laughing. The two failures deserve one another. Will they spend their evenings Alex-bashing? Reliving their shame and defeat at my hands? Sharing their hatred of me? 'Is that supposed to make me jealous?' I ask.

Camilla yawns delicately. 'We're going to be late, Alexander.'

Sarah glares at Camilla. 'I won't be long.'

I sigh. 'Go away, Sarah. It's over. We've had our vindictive squabbles, it's time to move on.'

And I genuinely mean it. It is time to move on. We can all have a better future.

Sarah glances between Camilla and me and then she smiles the nastiest smile I've ever seen on the face of a woman. She looks evil.

'Alex and I fucked on Friday,' says Sarah.

Camilla leaps to her feet. 'You did not. He was with me on Friday. He was with me all weekend.'

'That's enough, Sarah,' I say, and take a step towards her.

Sarah opens her eyes wide, feigning innocence. 'Shucks. Are you sure?' she asks Camilla. 'Friday lunchtime? I was sure that's when he left my bed.'

Camilla whirls on me. 'Why, you son-of-a-bitch.'

'We'll discuss this in a moment, Camilla.' I stalk across the room, grab Sarah by the arm, throw her out of my office and lock the door behind her.

I want to kick Sarah down the stairs, throw her in the lift shaft and send the lift to the basement, crushing the life from her traitorous bones. But I have control.

I am in control.

What was I thinking? I should have kicked that slut out the first second I saw her. Why did I wait to hear her news? Why was I talking about moving on? That's Alex-psycho-babble, it's not worthy of consideration – it's certainly not worthy of speaking out loud or even believing for one tiny second.

That crazy-speak isn't me. I'm not like that. I don't believe in letting bygones be bygones. I'd decided we were equal, that I'd achieved a just and fair amount of revenge against Sarah and Jed, but that doesn't mean I want to sit around a campfire and sing jolly songs with them. And if another opportunity to do them down arises I'm going to take it. I'm not going to waste my time searching for it, but I won't turn it down. Vengeance is never really finished. There's always a little more to be had.

Sarah starts pounding on the door. 'How does revenge feel now?' she yells. 'Do you like it?' She laughs and it sounds more like a mad howl.

Drop down dead in the street. I hope she has a stroke and falls to the ground and everyone steps around her, avoiding her like the plague, thinking she's drunk, letting her die. Letting her die alone in the dirt. It's what she deserves.

I say nothing to Sarah. She doesn't matter. The only thing I feel for her is disgust.

Camilla stands with her arms crossed in front of her chest.

'She's lying,' I tell her.

'Is she?'

Sarah's howls fade away and I think she's left. Maybe she'll get run over by a bus while crossing the street if her body isn't ready to slay her with a stroke. Though I honestly don't know why her white blood cells have waited this long to destroy her. She's a virus, isn't she?

'She's lying,' I say. Doesn't Camilla believe me? Aren't we supposed to have a little trust here? And when exactly did we pledge to be monogamous, hmm? 'You're the one I love, Camilla.'

'Do you?'

No. And right at this moment I want to shove you into that lift shaft with Sarah.

'Yes,' I say. 'Of course I do. I said so, didn't I?'

Camilla shrugs. 'How do I know you're telling the truth? Why should I believe you? Why would she lie? Maybe you did fuck her. I don't know why on earth you'd want to, but maybe you did. Maybe you wanted a bit of the gutter for an afternoon snack.'

'I was going to propose to you, Camilla, but there's no point if you don't trust me.'

She uncrosses her arms. 'You want to marry me?'

'I did. Right now I think you'd better leave.'

'Ask me,' she says.

'Ask you what?'

'To marry you.'

Am I suddenly forgiven if I want to marry her?

She crosses the room, stopping six inches away, her face expectant. 'Ask me,' she says. 'Ask me.'

I need a woman like Camilla. She'd make my transition to a permanent place at the side of the élite so much easier.

I speak between gritted teeth. Is this how she wants to remember this moment? 'Will you marry me?' I ask.

'Yes, oh, yes, yes, yes.' A smile of victory, of absolute delight, fills her face and she throws her arms around me. 'Yes, I will marry you.'

Has Sarah been forgotten? Will Camilla pretend our spat of a moment ago never happened? Doesn't she even care if I did sleep with Sarah? Is adultery acceptable as long as it's actual adultery, marital cheating, rather than mere unfaithfulness? Or is it because it occurred before marriage, which means it doesn't count? Does she suddenly believe me or does it no longer matter whether Sarah was lying or not? Doesn't Camilla want to hear my explanation? My excuses? My promises that it'll never happen again?

(It will happen again. Not with Sarah, never again with Sarah, but I have no plans for fidelity to Camilla.)

She presses herself against me, rubbing in all the right places. She's good at this, she knows what she's doing. Physically we've always been perfectly compatible.

It strikes me that I should have a ring to give her, that a woman like Camilla will want a ring. A very big ring. But let's face it, this wasn't exactly a traditional proposal. No lovey-dovey theatrics for us.

'Oh, Alexander, I've been dreaming of this moment for years.'

I bet you have. You and your friends compete with one another for status and a husband is like a gold medal at the Olympics. Especially a rich husband. Alexander is a good catch. I know I am.

'I don't have a ring,' I say. 'I thought you'd prefer to choose it yourself.' I'm lying, of course, I didn't think anything of the kind. A ring never occurred to me.

She tilts her head back and looks up at me, her eyes sparkling. 'That's perfect. I'd love to choose my own ring. The number of horror stories I could tell you about men proposing with hideous engagement rings.'

She gives a little shudder and I know then that if I'd actually gone out and chosen a ring for her, if I'd bought her a ring and presented it to her on bended knee, she would have smiled and said yes, but she couldn't possibly wear the ring as it wasn't big enough or bright enough or it was the wrong shape or the wrong carat or the wrong stone or just too last year.

Amber wouldn't return the ring. Amber would treasure the engagement ring that had been chosen for her, she'd love it because he had loved it and bought it with her in mind. But I didn't propose to Amber: Amber isn't my future, Amber isn't my fiancée, Camilla is my fiancée.

Camilla is my fiancée.

Maybe I won't throw her down the lift shaft after all. I need a woman like Camilla. It'd be a shame to have to woo another and let all this hard work go to waste.

Camilla's still smiling. 'Can we look tonight?'

I don't want to look tonight, I don't want to think about rings or flowers or colours or hymns or any of that. Right now I just want Camilla naked in my arms. I like her when she's naked.

'What about our property appointments?' I say, and start to unbutton her blouse.

If anything her smile grows wider. 'We'll look for the ring tomorrow,' she says. 'But I can't wait to tell everyone. I can't wait to tell Mummy. She'll be so proud of me.'

I undo her last button and slide the shirt down her arms. And as I lower my mouth to hers I think of my family. What will they make of Camilla? They don't know the new me, the real me. They're expecting a girl like Sarah. No, not like Sarah, like Amber, maybe even Amber herself. But I'm Alexander, I don't marry girls like Amber. I'm one of the rich and powerful and I marry one of my own. Men like me marry women like Camilla.

She meets my kisses hungrily and I realise I was right. Camilla hasn't mentioned Sarah since the proposal. It's like Sarah was never here, like Sarah doesn't exist. And then Camilla sinks down on to her knees and soon I'm not thinking anything at all.

I'M SO HAPPY I'M ON TOP OF THE WORLD, OR MAKE THAT IN THE PENTHOUSE APARTMENT OF A FIVE-FLOOR BUILDING

We're late for our first property viewing, but for once I'm not blaming Camilla. The sex with her has always been incredible but tonight was unbelievable. It was the best ever. I like to think of it as my victory shag. Everything's going to plan and Alexander is on the ascendant.

The flat is like something out of a television show covering all the things necessary for a desirable residence. It reeks sophistication and money, everything is just so, but I feel like it's gone through some sort of checklist before being put up for sale: everything is too perfect. Where's the clutter? Doesn't anybody live here? Even the bookshelf is filled with leather-bound editions. No messy modern covers for these people, no way.

As we're being shown through the blue drawing room, the yellow drawing room, the green drawing room, with the estate agent droning on and on about wooden floors, gas fireplaces, reinforced beams to take the weight of chandeliers, Camilla is yapping away on her mobile phone.

'I know, Mummy,' says Camilla, 'I'm so excited. We have to get Eduardo for the flowers.' Camilla frowns and speaks to me. 'You don't have any colours in mind, do you, Alexander?'

'No,' I say. I don't care about colours, I don't care about the wedding ceremony. Let it be Camilla's day, it's obviously important to her. What's important to me is the end result. A society wife.

Camilla flashes me one of her brilliant smiles and returns to her conversation. 'No, not lilac. I know I liked lilac when I was ten, Mummy, but it's simply not me now. No, it has to be white. All white. If you use a colour like lilac or pink or green or even black, everything is dated so quickly. Show me a wedding photo, any wedding photo from the last ten years, and I could tell you the year and probably the month of the wedding. These things follow fads, Mummy. I want to be above the trend, beyond it. I want my wedding to be timeless. It has to be perfect. The photographs have to look perfect for years to come.'

The estate agent leads us to the kitchen. It's very modern and fully equipped, and the overwhelming impression is of chrome. It's not a cosy kitchen. It doesn't make you want to bake a loaf of bread or make an apple pie. Ready-made trays of sushi and platters of the latest find from Italy spring to mind. Though it has to be said that it's larger than the living room in Sarah's flat. See what you're missing, Sarah. I smile at the thought of how sick Sarah will feel in the pit of her stomach when she hears of my wedding, when she sees pictures in those glossy magazines she loves so well, when she first learns about the size of my house and guesses at the extent of my bank balance. Maybe the jealousy will drive her insane. My smile widens, I can't help myself. It's just too delicious.

The poor estate agent misconstrues my smile and returns it when he'll never share in the moment. It's private. My pleasure in this is very personal and very private.

'This is a state-of-the-art kitchen,' says the estate agent. 'Everything is top quality. It's—'

'I hate it,' says Camilla. 'This is a man's kitchen. It's disgusting. I'm almost expecting to turn round and see black leather bar stools or barbed-wire frames surrounding photos of concentration-camp victims on the walls. I could never pour myself my morning glass of orange juice in a room like this. It's such a stereotype. It'll have to be torn out.'

I peer around. She has a point. It's too modern. It's trying too hard. The estate agent looks crushed. Did he expect this kitchen to add fifty grand to the price?

Camilla speaks into the phone. 'What, Mummy? No, just some nauseating interior design. Don't worry, it'd never stay.'

We move on to the main bedroom suite. The dressing room alone is twice the size of my daisy-painted room.

'No, Mummy, no adult bridesmaids, not if I'm having white. I thought we could use Annabelle. She's only ten so she'll look cute in white and no one could ever mistake her for the bride.' Camilla listens a moment. 'Yes, yes, all white flowers. Only white.' She glances at the four-poster bed and then her eyes sweep the room searching for faults, looking for flaws, however minor. 'That's a window-seat,' says Camilla, staring at a charming bay area.

'Yes,' says the estate agent, smiling, not realising that the flat tone in Camilla's voice isn't one of surprised pleasure.

'Window-seats aren't for bedrooms,' she says. Camilla can be very patronising when she wants to be. 'They're for drawing rooms or the ends of corridors. Not for bedrooms. I don't want to lounge around in my nightie next to an open window. I don't want a window-seat in my bedroom.'

I like the window-seat. You could curl up with a book or bundle yourself in a thick blanket and sit there and watch the snow fall in winter. Or at least hope for a few flakes every year. I like it. Amber would like it.

But Amber isn't here, Alexander. Amber will never be here. This isn't her world. It's Camilla's. And mine. Amber could only enter it as a mistress and I could never do that to Amber. She deserves better.

'But it has lovely views over the communal gardens at the back,' says the estate agent.

'Communal gardens?' says Camilla. 'Communal gardens?'

She's so stunned, so stricken with horror, that her mouth moves but no more words come out. I watch her for a moment, forcing myself not to laugh, wanting to store this memory in my mind for later reflection. She's not quite so perfect when she's gaping like a goldfish. I decide to take pity on her, as for once we're in complete agreement.

'No, we couldn't possibly live somewhere with a communal area,' I tell the estate agent.

'But there's also a small private garden at the—'

'No,' I say. 'It's not for us.'

And it's not. I want my privacy. I want no communal areas. I demand a private entrance, a private lift and most certainly private gardens. I don't want to share my life, my space with just anyone. I deserve only the best. And that includes people.

Too small, too dark, too modern, too old-fashioned, view not quite right, needless to say we didn't find the perfect property tonight. Oh, they were all fine, but none of them will do for Alexander and his bride. We need something grander, larger, stunning. Camilla wants her friends to die of envy. And I want the same. My home should reflect my position of supremacy. Nothing less will do.

We're back at Camilla's now and I'm flipping through the latest Hampton's catalogue, hoping to spot the brick and mortar equivalent of paradise. And Camilla? Camilla is on the phone.

'Harriet, you'll never guess what's happened,' she says, into the telephone receiver, 'Alexander asked me to marry him. We're getting married.' She listens for a moment, grinning widely, accepting the congratulations as her due. 'Oh, I wish I could have taped the proposal so you could hear it. It was the most romantic thing.'

Romantic? Has she forgotten exactly how it happened? Has she rewritten history in her mind? By tomorrow will the scene have been transformed into me down on one knee in front of her, begging her to be my beloved wife? Will she think I pledged my undying love? That I said I couldn't live without her?

'Alexander's so wonderful and he loves me so much,' says Camilla.

In her dreams. I switch some of my attention back to the catalogue, half listening to her, half interested in the property, but I turn the page again, not wanting a seven-bedroom house near Guildford. Too close to my parents and old friends who used to know Alex. That's the past. My future's in London. And Gloucestershire, a twenty-bedroom Georgian mansion to be precise.

'I can't talk long,' says Camilla. 'There are so many people I want to tell. I just wanted to let you know that Mummy is throwing a small luncheon for us tomorrow, a sort of pre-engagement-party gathering. I know it's mid-week and a lot of people are in town so it'll just be a few close friends and neighbours. Do say you'll come.'

By the time I'm finished with the property magazine Camilla has told three other people and now she's phoning another. Henrietta, she told me, as if I cared. Henrietta is an old schoolfriend of Camilla's, temporarily indulging in a career at Asprey & Garrard, jewellers to the Queen. Camilla wants her to open early so we can buy an engagement ring, so that Camilla will have one to wear at the luncheon tomorrow.

'Hen?' says Camilla. 'I have a huge favour to ask. And you'll never guess what's happened. I'm getting married.'

WHAT SURPRISING
TASTE YOU HAVE, CAMILLA

At eight o'clock in the morning – well, four minutes to eight to be exact – Camilla and I arrive at the doors of Asprey & Garrard. Camilla is early and I think that this would do her street cred a lot of damage but for the fact that the infamous Henrietta is ready and waiting, grinning, simpering, including me in her joy, assuming I fully appreciate my luck in gaining Camilla's hand, allowing that this is one occasion a girl can't be too eager for.

My smile of euphoria, of the happy groom-to-be is perfect. I practised in the mirror for a good ten minutes before breakfast. A man has to be prepared for these things. It's all about image. And image is all about appearance. Appearances are normally accepted at face value. Oh, look at him, look at her, look at them, they look so happy, they must be so happy. To look happy is to be happy. Isn't it?

Last night I fell asleep to the sound of her voice relating the joyous news over and over, and when I woke this morning Camilla was applying the last finishing touches to her makeup. I don't think she slept (too many people to tell, too much gloating to do), but you couldn't tell by looking at her. She looks radiant. A perfect picture of health and happiness.

I stare at Camilla while Henrietta leads us to the engagement-ring area. This won't be such a hardship. I can't complain. A beautiful, wealthy, classy wife. What more could a man want?

There are trays and trays of rings. Diamonds, sapphires, rubies, emeralds. Yellow gold and platinum bands. Brilliant cut, pear, emerald cut, heart shapes, oval, marquise, blah blah blah blah blah. I don't know what the hell they're talking about and I soon lose interest. The displays look beautiful, the rings look beautiful, they're shining and glittering and there's something in the lighting or the air or just the atmosphere that screams money and privilege and cries out, 'I've made it,' to the world. She'll find something appropriate.

Camilla and Henrietta throw terminology back and forth at one another like a tennis ball. Is this one of those subjects women instinctively know everything about? Would my mother, daughterless and married for over thirty years, be able to join in this conversation? Would she be able to hold her own when discussing carats and clarity and brilliance?

Camilla tries on dozens of rings, mostly focusing her attention on the image of her hands in the mirrors or discussing the various options with Henrietta. Occasionally a 'What do you think of this one, Alexander?' is thrown my way.

Whatever you want, dear. I don't say it, but I think it. Is this what it's like for most men? Do we just not care or is it something in me? Let her have what she wants. I don't care. I don't care what it looks like, I don't care what it costs, I just don't care. It's her ring, she's the one who'll have to wear the thing.

I should have cared.

Camilla turns to me, her eyes as bright as the diamonds in the display. 'This one,' she says, lifting her hand, flashing a ring at me. 'I want this one. Do you like it, Alexander? Can I have this one? Let's get this one.'

I can do no more than smile my smile of euphoria, earning my second Academy Award of the day, as I stare at the ring on her finger.

I make some sort of noise in my throat, a noise Camilla takes as one of assent, for she turns to Henrietta and says, 'We'll take it.'

Camilla gazes down at the ring, at her ring, a tone of love in her voice. 'I've always wanted a platinum and diamond engagement ring.'

Are you sure it's platinum? Looks more like stainless steel to me. (Shiny like the set of saucepans I bought for Sarah two months ago for no other reason than that she wanted them.)

How has Camilla managed to choose the only ugly ring in the whole place? I thought her taste was supposed to be impeccable. Is this a signal that the thought of a big, white wedding with hundreds and hundreds of guests has turned her mind to mush? Will she walk down the aisle in some hideous concoction of tulle, lace and crinoline? What's happening to the world? It's all topsy-turvy and Camilla has gone mad. Any other ring would do. Why did she have to choose this one?

How to describe it in one word? Hideous. Tacky. Gaudy. It's like the most disgusting piece of jewellery my grandmother ever owned. It's too much. Garish. Is this what all the girls are wearing? Is this a fashion trend so new I've yet to hear of it? Where has minimalism gone? I want it back right now.

There's one huge solitaire diamond, about three carats give or take, and it's so shining, so sparkling, there's so much fire inside this diamond that I feel like it's alive, that it's the eye of some creature, that's it's looking out and winking at the world. If we're in the countryside and we go out at night we'll no longer need a torch: her diamond will reflect the starlight back a thousandfold, it'll light up the night.

The stone itself is pretty, I admit that, I like diamonds, but it's so big on her dainty finger it looks silly. And as for the rest of it, well, the band is thick and chunky and it's encrusted with diamond chips so that there's diamonds twinkling at you from every direction. It's not a feminine ring – even with all those glittering diamonds. It's like some sort of futuristic bauble. I thought she didn't want her wedding to be dated. To be datable.

It costs so much and has so many diamonds that only the wealthy will truly appreciate the beauty of this ring. No middle-class woman would ever wear such a thing. Sarah wouldn't. Amber certainly wouldn't. They wouldn't dare be so ostentatious.

I'm going to make certain that everyone knows Camilla chose the ring. That it's what she wanted. Either people will like it and think Camilla has excellent taste and congratulate me on having such a woman, or they'll think that I must really love Camilla to have bought her such a grotesque ring because it's what she wanted.

It's a win-win situation. So long as I try not to look at the ring too often. Wonder if I'll get used to it over time. Maybe as the years go by it will seem to shrink. Or eventually my eyesight will fade and dim and then I'll be glad it's so big and bright, glad that there's one thing I can still see without my trifocals.

When Henrietta has finished measuring Camilla's finger and has ascertained her ring size, she takes the platinum monstrosity away to get it resized. As we sit there waiting for her, Camilla turns to me and kisses me passionately, her hands, her lips, her limbs promising more, much more.

'I can't wait until we're home,' she says.

Neither can I.

We kiss again and then she pulls away, smiling.

'I've got a surprise for you,' she says.

So long as she doesn't expect me to wear an engagement ring or change my surname upon marriage.

Camilla takes out her mobile. 'Just let me make one call and then you'll see.'

I feel like this proposal thing has taken on a life of its own, that it's following some preordained path that is confusing to the uninitiated male, but to the female of the species is as clear as a glass of mineral water.

'Hi,' says Camilla, into her phone, 'let me speak to Janey.'

Janey, whom I haven't met, is Camilla's boss.

'Janey, it's me. I quit.' Camilla laughs.

She quits? Surprise. I knew this would happen, I just wasn't expecting it to happen today. It's not like I mind – I mean I don't expect her to work, her job is to be my wife and make me look good – but surely we should have talked about this. She could have mentioned it to me beforehand. We'll have a discussion about these hasty decisions of hers after the wedding. Then she'll remember to consult me in the future. And if she does anything like this again I'll throw her from the top of an office building in the City and watch her body fall on to the spiked railings below.

'Yes,' says Camilla, 'I am getting married. To Alexander. He's simply gorgeous. Yes, and loaded. And Mummy and Daddy approve.' She slips off her shoe and rubs her foot up and down my ankle. 'I'll stop by tomorrow or the day after and collect my things and show you all my ring. Uh-huh.' She smiles at me. 'Uh-huh. Thanks.' She ends the call.

'I hope you don't mind,' she says to me.

It's a bit late for that, isn't it, sweetheart?

'It's just that planning a wedding is such a huge undertaking. It'll be a full-time job for me. And for Mummy too.'

Aren't I lucky to have such a dedicated mother-in-law-to-be?

Camilla pouts sexily. 'I couldn't let myself be distracted by all those boring little PR things now, could I?' She kisses me. 'You don't mind, do you, darling?'

'No, it's fine,' I say. 'But next time let's discuss things first.'

And it is fine. I require the best wedding possible. Everyone will be there. It has to be perfect. And if it takes all of her time to plan it then it takes up all of her time.

'But I wanted it to be a surprise. I wanted to give you something priceless, to show you how much I love you. I was thinking only of you,' she says, still trying to convince me that it was the right thing to do when convincing isn't necessary. 'You deserve my full support and attention. I did it all for you.'

Yeah, right, Camilla, sure, Camilla, I believe you. Of course I believe you when you say you don't mind getting up early, that you don't think promoting someone else is tedious when the time could be spent so much better by talking about yourself, I believe you, I do. You've had your stint in the real world, or as near to it as you'll ever get, you've realised that working isn't as glamorous as it seems on the big screen and now you've had enough.

And wanting a spectacular wedding to best all of your friends has nothing to do with it, does it?

But that's as it should be. Success is no fun if no one else knows about it.

A few hours later we're in Gloucestershire and our small, cosy luncheon has turned into a celebration for fifty. Mostly wives and daughters, it is true, but a handful of men such as Rupert (of course the father of the bride is here), Charles, and a few others who obviously don't bother to work are also present.

Camilla stays glued to my side, showing me off as she drags me around to accept congratulations and flash her ring at everyone. The women all ooh and aahh over the sparkle of the diamonds and the men, well, the men catch my eye for a brief second and I wonder if we're having some kind of male solidarity here – do they hate it too? – but everyone says complimentary things. You do, don't you?

And as I'm making small-talk it suddenly strikes me that I've made it.

These people want to be with me. These people like me, or like me as much as they like anybody. They're flattering me. They consider me one of them. They recognise that I am one of them. I'm being welcomed into Camilla's family with open arms.

I'm a success. I'm at the top. I've made it.

I've had my revenge against Sarah and Jed and Kenneth. I've got everything I wanted when I had my first moment of clarity upon becoming Alexander.

And I can never go back to being Alex. I don't even want to be Alex. I don't like Alex. (He was pathetic. I was pathetic.) And Alex, well, Alex wouldn't like me either. We wouldn't be friends.

I know I was Alex, but I can no longer just look inside my

mind and know instinctively what he would do in every situation. I can only guess – *guess* – at his most obvious actions and reactions, like I'd do with my brother. It's like Alex is a different person. Like I'm a different person now. I'm the pure Alexander Fairfax undiluted by Alex.

I can never be Alex again even if I wanted to go back. I don't know how to be him. I can't remember what it feels like to be Alex. I wanted to kill him, to rid myself of his annoying little ways, and now I have. Alex is dead.

Alex is dead. Long live Alexander.

It's good to be Alexander.

I'm in control of my own fate, my own destiny. I've got my life in my hands. I can do anything I want to do because I am me.

A handful of servants (the females all presentable, average, but none even approaching pretty, Camilla and her mother obviously want no competition) circulate with champagne.

As soon as everyone has a glass Rupert clears his throat and says, 'I'd like to say a few words.'

They accept me. I am one of them. It's all about success and I am successful.

Rupert continues speaking. 'My darling daughter has always made me proud, but today, the day she arrived on the arm of her future husband, I realised that she is a woman. She's a woman embarking on her own life and I couldn't be more proud of her choice. Welcome to the family, Alexander.'

He accepts me. He wants me to marry his daughter.

I've made it. I'm standing on the top of the world. I am the king of the mountain.

Life is not about love. It's not about friendship. It's certainly not about honour or virtue or living up to some imaginary morality. It's not about kindness or caring or giving. Or even sex. It's about success. And, above all, it's about money.

I have plenty of money. I'm a success.

I see Rupert's mouth moving, I know he's still speaking, that words are coming out, but I can no longer hear him. My world narrows to the sounds of my own heartbeat.

I am a success.

But I wanted to marry Camilla so that I could be a complete success, so that she could help me in my rise to the top. If I'm already there – and I must be there, the proof's in my acceptance here today – I don't need Camilla. I don't need to marry a woman like Camilla. I don't need to marry Camilla.

The world speeds up and suddenly it all comes back into focus and I can hear Rupert. 'Please raise your glasses,' he says. 'I'd like to propose a toast.'

I don't need to marry Camilla. I don't need her kind. I don't need her.

I don't even like the bitch.

Rupert, Celeste, Charles, Grace, Harriet, they all raise their glasses, smiling at Camilla and me.

I don't even like the bitch. I don't want to live with her, I don't want to put up with her pouting and whining and tantrums, I certainly don't want to spend my life with her. I don't want to marry her.

But I hurt Amber. I hurt sweet, dear, innocent Amber because of Camilla. Because I thought I needed Camilla. Oh, God, I did. I hurt Amber. I should never have done that to her, I could have lied. I should have lied. I should have told Amber what she needed to hear. I could have let us drift apart naturally. I could have made it seem mutual. I could have saved her all those tears. And it was all for nothing, I didn't even need to hurt her. I didn't need to leave her, not when it's over with Camilla.

If this horrible feeling in the pit of my stomach is guilt then I don't like it. I'm not supposed to feel guilt, Alexander was never supposed to feel guilt. I'm not supposed to hurt the prey, I was never supposed to hurt the prey. What have I done?

I was wrong. I was very wrong, and I can't take it back. But I can try. I will try. I'll apologise. I'll apologise and try to make it up to her. It may take days or weeks or even months, but I'll keep apologising until she forgives me. I can be patient, I can be persistent, I can do this for Amber.

'To Camilla and Alexander,' says Rupert.

I'd forgotten about the toast. Don't they know? How can they not know I've changed my mind?

'To Camilla and Alexander,' repeats everyone.

I don't want to marry Camilla. I can't marry Camilla.

I am Alexander and no one is going to make me do anything I don't want to do.

They all take a sip of champagne.

'No,' I say, whispering, the word inaudible, my throat dry. I don't want to marry Camilla, I'm not going to marry Camilla, but I can't do this now. I can't break off the engagement here, in front of all these people, I can't do that to her. Even Camilla deserves better than that.

I take a gulp of champagne and plaster a smile on my face when Camilla slips her arm through mine and gives me a kiss on the cheek. No, this isn't the time and it certainly isn't the place. Camilla may be spoilt and selfish and she is one of life's predators, but that alone doesn't give me an excuse to be cruel to her. She's never been vicious to me, she hasn't destroyed my career or my social life. She's helped me, from the very day I met her she's been good to me. I can't dump her now. She does not deserve mass public humiliation. I may not want to spend my life with her, I may not want to marry her, but I can wish her luck in her own life. I can even be generous and wish her happiness.

We circulate and socialise and I have to say I'm witty and entertaining and I make people smile and laugh when inside my soul is turning over and over in torment. What about Amber? She's had two whole days to cry and feel used and dirty and wretched. I have to make it up to her, I have to make it all better. I have to do it now, today, there's no more time to waste, I can't wait four more hours for everyone to leave, I can't wait until tomorrow – Amber needs me now. I have to end her suffering. She needs me. I have to go to Amber.

I steer Camilla towards the door and I smile at her tenderly and whisper in her ear, knowing it'll appear as if I'm whispering endearments, and say, 'We have to talk. In private.'

I can feel her body go rigid at my tone, but by looking at her face you can't tell anything is amiss. She gives me a brilliant smile, takes my hand and we slip out of the room. Slip, I think, but I'm not fooled, I know everyone is watching us as we walk down the hall until we're out of sight. We are, after all, the entertainment and Camilla is the undeniable star of the ball.

We don't speak until Camilla leads us into the library at the other side of the house and shuts the door. She steps away from me, crosses her arms and says, 'What is it?'

I feel a moment's regret for the loss of this house, for the loss of Camilla's inheritance, for the loss of her world, for the loss of her skills in bed when she's trying to get her own way, but then I look into her eyes and I know I don't want to spend my life with her. I have no doubts about my decision. This is something I have to do.

Life is not about love, I'll accept that. I know it's true. Life is about success, but isn't a part of success about being happy? I'd never be happy with Camilla. We're just not suited. And I don't love Camilla. I don't love anyone at this moment, but I think I could love Amber. I haven't allowed myself the luxury of feelings, but I like Amber, I've always liked Amber, we have fun together, it'd be easy to love Amber. I want Amber. I want to be with Amber. I don't want Camilla.

Even if I take Amber out of the equation I don't want to spend my life with Camilla.

I am me. I am an Advertising God. Marrying a woman like Camilla will do nothing for me, being with a woman like Amber will not change me, I'll still be Alexander. And to Amber I can be sweet and kind, to her I can be Alex. Alex is dead inside me, but I can practise, I will practise, she'll make it easy. I want to be Alex for her. I want to be kind and gentle to Amber. I want to make her happy. I'll save Alexander for people like Jed and Sarah and Kenneth. And Camilla. I could never show her my sweet side.

'I don't think this is going to work,' I say, filling the silence, realising I've been thinking too long, that Camilla has been standing there, tensely waiting for my words.

'What?'

'I don't want to marry you.' Six little words. Too harsh, maybe, but they get my point across. There's no sense in prolonging this discussion. I want to get on my way. I want to get out of here.

'But you asked me to marry you, Alexander,' says Camilla. 'You proposed.' Her face is white, her eyes are huge, wounded, like a fawn's, and I feel a flicker of sympathy.

'I'm sorry,' I say. 'I really am.' I decide to lie, it'll make her feel better. I can be magnanimous in my victory, she's never been on my list of revenge, she's never done me any personal harm. 'It's me, not you. I thought I was ready to settle down, but hearing all these people congratulate us today and call us engaged was too much for me. I'm too young for marriage, I want to enjoy life a little more.'

'But—'

'I'm truly sorry, Camilla. You don't have to tell everyone today. We'll think of something. You can blame me, I don't mind.' I nearly snort, but I catch myself in time. She can blame me? Of course she's bloody well going to blame me. It is my fault, after all, and she'll make me out into some black-hearted villain, but I don't care. It's not like I'm leaving her at the altar, my reputation will survive this lovers' spat.

Will it make the papers? Will some vindictive gossip columnist who hates Camilla print this juicy tale? I don't care if it does – it doesn't bother me. It's not like I left her during the wedding ceremony, I only proposed one day and called it off the next, and anyone who's seen beyond Camilla's perfect face will understand. It won't harm my career. It won't harm my standing in society. No one will be foolhardy enough to think to shun me, for I'm too important. I'm invincible.

Camilla stares at me, her lips curling with disdain. She uncrosses her arms and slaps me across the cheek with the flat of her palm. Her beautiful face is contorted with rage.

But there are no tears. Camilla sheds no tears.

'You bastard,' she says.

Yes, I'll accept that. I am a bastard.

I feel my smile of euphoria stretching across my face, but this time it's for real. I am euphoric. The world suddenly looks like a better place. It has sunshine and flowers and birdsong and joy. I will be happy. I can be happy. I am happy.

'You fucking bastard. How dare you?' says Camilla. 'I'm pregnant.'

The smile is wiped from my face. Each and every last trace of joy is gone, removed in an instant, vanished in less time than a puff of smoke. Gone. Obliterated. Utterly and totally destroyed.

'What?' My voice is hoarse. 'Pregnant?' Oh, God. I feel sick. All my plans have come crashing down upon me.

'You heard me. I,' she says slowly, 'am carrying a fucking child inside me.'

'How can you be certain?'

'I went to the doctor, Alexander. There's a thing called modern science, these days. Maybe you've heard of it? There's tests and everything.'

A baby. I never thought there'd be a baby. But then I frown as something dawns on me. 'But isn't it too soon? How can you know already?'

'I'm three months pregnant.' And then she smiles, a vicious, evil, wounding smile.

'Three months?' I feel like I'm some sort of automaton, doomed for ever to repeat the last thing I heard. 'Three months?'

She pats her belly. It's as flat as ever. 'Three months.'

'But I haven't known you for three months,' I say.

'No, you haven't, have you?' Her smile grows wider.

I feel a jolt of white hot rage pass through me. It's not my baby. 'You were going to pass it off as mine?'

'You've got it in one. What amazing intelligence you have, Alexander. You don't think I actually wanted to marry you, do you?'

'Who's the father?'

She shrugs. 'You'll never know.'

'You don't even know, do you?' I feel sick inside. She either doesn't know the guilty party or she doesn't like him or she'd have her father hounding the poor man, bribing or blackmailing him with whatever it would take for him to marry Camilla. No wonder she was so keen on me so quickly. I must have seemed like a heavenly angel sent to save her. 'Three months gone is a long time. The baby won't exactly appear premature, will it?'

'My doctor fancies me. He would have sworn it was three months early, you'd never have known.' Camilla smiles at me and then studies the ring on her finger. The engagement ring I had just spent a fortune on. 'Such a pretty diamond,' she says. Then she looks up at me. 'If you leave me I'm going to tell everyone you abandoned your pregnant fiancée, that you abandoned your child.'

'It's not my child.'

'Do you think anyone will believe you? And then when I have a miscarriage from the stress and grief of your leaving it'll be even worse for you.'

'You'd kill your baby to spite me?' She's unbelievable. I don't know how I thought I ever came close to understanding her.

Camilla laughs. 'You're a fucking gullible moron, Alexander. I'm not pregnant. I never was pregnant. You should have seen your face. Like I'd keep a baby at this stage in my life. I don't want a baby. I don't want babies. I want a husband, not a family. You think I'd destroy this body just like that?'

'You still want to get married?'

'No longer to you.' She studies the engagement ring. 'Such a pity. You would have done wonderfully, you'd have felt eternally grateful to me for helping you climb out of the pit of social nothingness. You'd have treated me like a princess.'

I ignore her insult and concentrate on what I want to hear. She doesn't want to marry me. 'So you'll let me go? We'll call it off?'

Camilla looks up from her studying of the diamond and smiles. 'You go ahead and call it off, Alexander.' Her smile falls and she puts on a worried face. 'Oh, no, oh dear, I feel a pain in my stomach. You don't think I'll lose the baby, do you?'

'You're not even pregnant.'

'Aren't I?'

If I weren't so angry I'd concentrate on studying her manipulations. She's a master: she's had her entire life to practise getting her own way. She is the ultimate in selfishness and be damned to everyone else.

'No,' I say, 'you're not. And if you are you'll have to produce either a baby or a foetus and then we'll do DNA tests and prove it's not mine.'

'Such a shame the poor little miscarried thing will be cremated immediately, isn't it?'

'Then I will fight you in the courts, I'll smear your name across the papers, I'll fight dirty, I'll hire someone and dig up all your disgraceful past experiences, I'll make your father ashamed to call you his daughter. I'll deny that the child is mine, I'll accuse you of anything I can, and I'll air your mistakes and indiscretions in public and tell them all how you fuck strangers hours after meeting them.'

She gasps. 'I'll sue you for defamation.'

I'm the one who's smiling now. 'And even if you win and I have to pay you a million pounds there'll always be those who wonder. Mud sticks, doesn't it, Camilla? Isn't that what you were hoping would sway me?'

'You're a bastard.'

'You've already said that, Camilla. Let's both accept a little truth here. I'm a bastard and you're a bitch and you'd think that would make us deserve one another, but let's not put ourselves through the misery. Let's just pretend this is a mutual split. I'm sorry you're upset about this, but come, now, we really would get on one another's nerves after a few months. No doubt you can rustle up some lord or other who'd be delighted to marry you.'

Her eyes are wet now and I could almost feel sorry for her. 'But I quit my job,' she whispers. 'I've told all my friends. Everyone will laugh at me. They already hate me for being beautiful when it's not my fault, I was born like this, they've always hated me for being prettier than they are. Now they'll talk about me behind my back. They'll be happy I'm humiliated.'

Even after all that's happened here, even after I've seen into the shallowness of her soul, I feel a stirring of pity for her. I decide to be kind. I decide to ignore her threats, even if half of me wants to throttle her where she stands, passing off her ghost baby as mine. I shudder to think of Camilla and I playing happy families together. How could I ever have thought it would work?

'You pretend that our engagement was merely a ruse to make your true love jealous,' I say.

'I do?'

I nearly take her hands, but I don't want to touch her, not now, not ever again. 'Yes, you do, then you marry someone as rich as you are and you get your big wedding and a country estate of your own.'

Camilla stares at me for a long time, then she nods. 'Good idea.' She slaps me again, taking me by surprise, and I wonder if I imagined her despair. 'But I'm keeping the ring.' She smiles.

'And I'm not telling anyone today. I'll say you've had to head back to London on business. Our engagement will last as long as I need it to.'

'Fine,' I say. And just like that I walk from the room. I leave the house and go to my car and I drive away.

I've had a narrow escape. I'm glad I'm not marrying her. She's hard and rather annoying and horrid when it comes down to it. I can feel no real sympathy for her. She'll survive. It's Amber who needs my concern. Soft, gentle, adorable Amber.

And as I drive through the gates and leave Camilla's family behind I feel not even a second's regret. I've made the right decision. My future is not here.

Have a nice life, Camilla.

That's becoming a favourite of mine. Have a nice life. It has a good, honest, Alexander ring to it. An appropriate air of finality.

FLYING HIGH, OR WHOEVER NEEDS DRUGS FOR THIS FEELING SHOULD GET A LIFE, IT WORKED FOR ME

I smile my smile of euphoria all the way back to London. I can't help myself, I'm sitting here behind the wheel grinning like a lunatic. I haven't been this happy since the night of my transformation when the world suddenly had all these great and exciting possibilities.

This is how life should be. It's meant to be fun. I'm supposed to enjoy my success.

I meet the beginning of the rush-hour crowds but traffic's moving enough so I don't have to come to a standstill. I've worked it all out in my head. I know Amber's not going to leap back into my arms, but if I'm really contrite, which I am, and we take things slowly, I know she'll give me a second chance. I won't tell her the whole sorry tale, not about Sarah or Kate or Camilla or any of that, but I'll tell her I was confused. That much is true. I was scared of feeling anything. I knew I'd be safe inside my shell with Camilla, but I'm willing to risk it with Amber. I want to feel something. I want to feel alive. I want to feel excitement and joy and happiness. I want to feel all that with Amber. I want to give it a try. We deserve that chance.

It may take a lot longer than I want it to, but I will succeed. I'll win her back. I'm good at achieving the seemingly impossible. I'll make it up to Amber. It'll take time but I will make it all better. We can start over, we can have a relationship, just like she wanted. We can be a couple. We can have fun.

I could kick myself for causing her these two days of sorrow, but I needed this experience, I needed to realise the truth for myself. I'm the only one who can keep me on top, it's up to me – not some woman and her father and her family connections, it's about me. It's always been about me.

Oh, sure, it's too bad about the loss of Camilla's contacts. I don't fool myself: even if Camilla uses my plan to catch herself a new husband – a brilliant plan worthy of an American soap opera if I do say so myself – she'll find some way to make me look bad. In the final tale I doubt I'll be her bosom pal helping her to win her true love, she'll probably claim I was in love with her, poor sod, and that she broke my heart, but it took our engagement to make her realise how much she loved so-and-so (insert name of new man here). But if anyone hears the tale then sees me, they'll guess the truth about my emotions soon enough. Camilla never had a chance to dent my heart. My pocketbook, yes, but never me. I've got to assume that British Gas and E-genes are both write-offs, but it doesn't matter: it'll be easy to get other clients and there are lots of charities wetting their pants to get me on board. My entry in *Who's Who* will still look good. No, it'll look better, it won't mention Camilla. There'll be no question that I made myself into who I am.

And if, by some miracle worthy of mention by every town crier in the land, Camilla's tale doesn't destroy my E-genes and British Gas opportunities, then I'll stay involved. Business is business. It'll be easy to schmooze with Rupert and Charles in public and pretend that everything's all right. I don't think it will happen and I don't particularly care one way or the other, but I could do it. I would do it. I'm a professional.

I turn up the volume of the car stereo and allow the sounds of Jimi Hendrix (always a favourite) to pour over me as I wait at a set of traffic lights. I think I should feel a bit angrier, a bit more insulted at Camilla's manipulations, but I'm too happy at the moment to want to seek any form of petty vengeance against her. If she'd succeeded in her plan of passing off her imaginary miscarried child as mine, then I would have had cause for revenge, but she didn't and she won't and I'm just delighted to have escaped.

And I do have a great office at a great rate. I always knew I'd need that lease in the end. At least I gained something from my time with Camilla. (In addition to the furniture. And the sex, I can't fault her for that. Though I do suspect she's one of those women that as soon as the wedding night has passed will start doling out the sex like it's sweets to a child, as a reward to be used for good behaviour.)

As I'm nearing the flat, by some quirk of fate or luck or something I pass a florist. Feeling like James Bond, I nip my nifty Jaguar into a space on the side of the road (the sign says one-hour parking only, but that's long enough for me) and go into the shop.

What would Amber like? I want to give her flowers so she can see that I am sorry, so that she knows I've been thinking about her, that my apology is planned. (I'll even get down on my knees and beg her to forgive me: I can do that for her.)

I want to get her roses, but not red, it's too soon for that. There, those pink roses, I'll take two dozen of those. Two dozen roses for my lovely lady. Once she's forgiven me I'll find out what her favourite flower is and give her three dozen a day every day for a month so she'll know how very sorry I am.

The florist smiles at me knowingly, knowing this is a special day, but not guessing the real reason, oh, no, no one would ever guess that this smiling man has just walked out on his overnight fiancée. Camilla my fiancée. Who was I kidding? The woman's a predator, she doesn't deserve to be rewarded with my bounty. I don't like predators who prey on the prey, I certainly don't want to marry one. I must have been insane. What was I thinking?

Glad I've finally come to my senses, I pay for the flowers, gather them up into my arms, anticipating Amber finally, one day, though I know it won't be today, succumbing to my charms and forgiving me, and leave the shop.

I sniff the roses. They smell divine, not like they've been grown in a greenhouse. I'm glad: I want the scent to fill Amber's room, I want her to sleep in a haze of perfume, I want her to live in a rose-smelling world, I want everything to be perfect for her.

I notice a newsagent's as I head towards my car and I glance at the *Evening Standard* on display in the window, trying to draw in the crowds with the latest headlines.

I see the photograph on the front page and I stop.

My smile wobbles and falls, crumbling like a building under the expert hands of a demolition team, and I go inside the shop and buy my own copy.

NEVER FORGET THAT
REVENGE IS A UNIVERSAL GOAL

The Oi Man has a name, a real name. His name is Henry Johnson. His name is Henry Johnson and he's thirty-six years old.

A huge, full-colour photograph of the Oi Man appears on the front of the *Evening Standard*. It's a flattering photo. He looks normal. He could be anyone. He could be your neighbour.

According to the leading article the Oi Man (Henry Johnson, say the printed words) tried to murder his wife with a garden spade at his home earlier today.

Allegedly. Although there are eyewitness accounts, so things are looking pretty cut and dried. And he's been carted away and charged with attempted murder

Stupid man involving witnesses. Revenge isn't just about impulse, it has to be thought through, revenge has to be focused. Planned.

Is he a moron? A half-wit? An imbecile? What was he thinking? I mean, in the back garden? Was he not thinking at all?

There's a photograph of Mrs Oi Man beside the photo of her husband, but it wasn't her picture that caught my eye as I was walking by. No, I didn't even recognise her, didn't even know it was Mrs Oi Man until I began to read the article and looked more closely. It's one of those glamour photos where your wife or girlfriend is supposed to be transformed into someone else, and for Mrs Oi Man it worked. She looks different. Her skin is still coated in heavy layers of makeup and her hair is all big and puffy, a far cry from Hollywood glamour, but she looks better, not so cheap. She doesn't look classy, she could never look classy, but I bet she likes it. I bet the Oi Man likes it too. Or liked it. Something tells me he's not so keen on her now.

Henry Johnson, Oi Man *extraordinaire* and professional lorry driver, returned today from a trip to France.

I'd ceased thinking about the Oi Man: I'd assumed he'd received his dose of humiliation last week, but all this time it was just lingering, dark, black revenge hiding, hovering there, waiting to strike like a cobra from the shadows.

How did he find out? Did his friends stumble across the photos in the pubs and save them for him? Did Mrs Oi Man – Mrs Johnson – set aside the envelope in a pile for husband Henry and did he open it as soon as he returned from his work abroad?

Henry Johnson has a history of violence.

This should come as no surprise to me – he nearly cut off my ear with his makeshift missile – but it does. I didn't expect him to try to kill her. I didn't expect him to try to kill anyone. I knew he was a thug, but not all thugs are murderers.

I never predicted this. It wasn't my plan. I didn't intend this to happen. It's my fault. I caused this. I. Me.

I saw a means for vengeance on the Oi Man and I got swept away, not caring that she might suffer too, not thinking beyond my own desires.

Mrs Oi Man – Clare, her name is Clare – was brutally attacked. Clare was assaulted in her back garden with a spade.

According to the newspaper, Mrs Oi Man was planting a new rosebush. A Princess Diana rose. She was using the spade to plant it. Does she like gardening? Or does Mrs Oi Man simply love Princess Diana? Is Clare one of the People's Princess's people?

I can just picture the scene. Mrs Oi Man gardening in the back in a skimpy top with her breasts straining to pop out, the net curtains of the overlooking windows twitching, the elderly gent next door desperate for a peek, wanting to enjoy a spot of harmless ogling, when the Oi Man storms into the back garden shouting and yelling, swearing and cursing. The Oi Man grabbed the spade from her hands.

Did Mrs Oi Man suffer? No, her name is Clare. I have to call her that even if I wish I didn't know her name. I owe her that much. Did Clare suffer as she was beaten to unconsciousness? I think she did.

Henry Johnson tore the garden spade from her hands and beat her nearly to death. He beat her to the ground. He beat her again and again. He beat her when she'd stopped moving.

The neighbour, neighbours, one, two, maybe more, I don't know, phoned the police.

The Oi Man beat his wife nearly to death with a garden spade.

I don't know how she's still alive. Did some small measure of mercy move him? Did the Oi Man remember his love for her when they'd first met? Did he pull himself back so that he didn't split open her head like a watermelon?

Did it take her a long time to sink into oblivion? One minute? Two minutes of agony?

She was nearly dead when the police finally subdued the Oi Man. Fortunately for her, fortunately for me, the paramedics were there and they saved her life, they prevented her slipping away. They whisked her off to hospital, but the newspaper says her chances of survival are slim. Clare's in a critical condition.

They don't expect her to make it. If she dies the Oi Man will be charged with murder.

If she dies it'll be my fault. It's my fault anyway.

Will she die? Please don't die. I don't want you to die.

Even the glamour-photo people could do nothing for her now. Her body will be a mass of bruises, swelling and cuts, and she'll be multi-coloured and puffy, something to haunt a child's nightmares.

Oh, God, please let her live. Please let Clare live. Not for me,

I'm not asking for me, I'm not so stupid that I'm asking anything for me, but for her. Please, God, let her live. She doesn't deserve to die.

And what about the rose? Was Clare able to plant it? Or does it lie on its side, forlorn and abandoned and covered in blood, part of the crime scene? Will it wither and die, slowly suffering the torments of thirst as it's hidden behind police lines for weeks on end?

Clare might die because of me.

It wasn't supposed to be like this. My revenge was against the Oi Man, not Clare, never Clare, I didn't want her to suffer. Sure I knew it'd make things awkward for her, but I didn't want her to experience physical harm. I certainly don't want her to die.

Maybe it would have happened without me. Maybe the Oi Man would have returned a day early from one of his trips and walked in on his wife and her lover and maybe he would have beaten them both to death. Is that my consolation, then? Do I tell myself that maybe, just maybe, I saved the life of the lover by letting the Oi Man find out my way? Yeah, right, some consolation prize.

What if. What if.

Well, what if Jed and Sarah had never betrayed me? If that hadn't happened none of this would be happening now. But it did happen and this has happened. There's no turning back the clock.

Clare might die. Clare might die because of me. I told myself that she'd want a divorce, that she'd want to be free of him. But not like this. This was never my plan.

And will the police learn about the photos? Will they try to find out who took them? Who sent them? Will they discover the twenty-seven pubs?

But they won't find me. I was careful. I didn't break any laws, legally I did nothing wrong. I wasn't trying to blackmail the Oi Man. No, I wasn't interested in blackmail. I wanted my revenge. It was as simple as that. Revenge.

Does this count? Do I now sit back and smile all happy and content that I can remove the Oi Man from my list?

Clare's in a critical condition. She's nearly dead because of me.

I'm one of the élite, but I'm not supposed to prey on the weak. I don't want to be like the Oi Man, I don't want to cause anguish and suffering, not to the blameless. I'm not like that. I don't want to be like that. Clare isn't as white as snow, she probably isn't even nice, but she didn't deserve this.

It's like I'm the murderer – oh, okay, attempted murderer for the moment – and the Oi Man was merely the implement. My puppet. My weapon. All I had to do was tug gently on his strings and he kicked out. The fact that I didn't forecast the forcefulness of his response doesn't exonerate me.

I pointed the Oi Man in the right direction and off he went. I practically sentenced Clare to death.

What have I done?

Was she crying as he struck her? Did she plead for her life? Was she screaming in terror?

She might die. She might die because of me.

And I'll have to live with it for the rest of my life.

Will it get easier? Will this horrible guilt ease? Will I gradually gloss over the true extent of my responsibility as the years pass?

Maybe, but I don't think so.

Even if she lives (please, God, let her live) I'll know what I've done.

I'll have to live with it.

How will I live with it?

I wish I could vomit. I want to vomit. I want to stand here and vomit all over the newspaper. I want specks of food and stomach bile to cover the words, to eat them up, to obliterate them so I won't have to read any more. But I can't. I can't even taste it. My stomach has a funny feeling inside but there is no sick: I don't have it in me to be sick. I wouldn't even mind if some got on my shoes, if spots stained my trousers, it'd wash away, nothing's permanent. But it's not in me to be sick. Not any more.

I CAN THINK OF
ANOTHER NAME FOR ME NOW

I've been standing on the pavement for twenty minutes, reading and re-reading the Oi Man article over and over and over again.

Where's my euphoria now? Was that really me? Am I really the same man who was grinning and smiling and happy such a short time ago?

Is Clare still alive? I have to know.

A cab passes and I hail it. I can't drive, I can't think how to drive, I can't think how to get there. The only thing I know is that I have to get to the hospital and find out if she's still alive.

I must have spoken, I must have told the cabbie where I want to go, but I can't remember speaking, I can't remember opening my mouth and speaking, but he's driving and he's driving and then we're there, we're pulling up out front. I hand him twenty pounds, telling him to keep the change, not feeling generous and philanthropic, merely not wanting to bother about the money. It's only money. Clutching my newspaper and my two dozen roses, I climb from the car.

A crowd has gathered outside the hospital. Photographers, journalists, maybe a neighbour or two. Waiting, all waiting.

I approach with hesitant steps, trying to school my face into an expression of normality, but I haven't practised this look. I can hardly do my smile of euphoria and I doubt I'd manage that convincingly even if I tried.

Maybe I'll pass for a grief-stricken relative distracted by the crowds. I'll pretend that I'm here visiting my mother, and on my way in to see her I can spot all the people and wonder what's going on. I roll up the newspaper, hiding the front page, keeping it tight in my hand, concealing the fact that I already know.

'What's happening?' I ask a man at the edge of the crowd.

He holds a camera with a massive telephoto lens attached and his attention is focused on the hospital. He doesn't even look at me. Not a bloodhound of a journalist then, or he'd sniff out my guilt instantly and start snapping pictures of me.

'Woman was nearly murdered by her husband,' he says.

Yes, I know that. And?

'Is she okay?' I ask. My palms are damp and I can feel sweat break out on my forehead. I'm an innocent gawker, I tell myself. This has nothing to do with me. Act unconcerned. General horror is acceptable but nothing specific.

He shrugs, watching the entrance, still not looking at me or he'd know, he'd be able to tell that I'm involved. 'Doctor said she's slipped into a coma.'

I curl my hands into fists and dig my fingernails into the flesh of my palms. 'Is she going to make it?' I ask.

I hold my breath, waiting for the answer.

'Doesn't look good,' he says.

Clare's in a coma. She's dying. She's going to die.

I turn and walk away.

THE AWFUL TRUTH
(I'VE TURNED INTO WHAT I MOST DESPISE)

All I want to do is go home to my room and stare at the sky of daisies. I don't care if Amber and Noreen and the others are there, I'm numb and I just want to go home.

I walk away from the hospital, away from Clare, away from the seeds of my destruction. I want to take the Tube, I want to feel a mass of warm, hot, alive humanity pressing against me, but I'm not entitled to this comfort. I'm alone and I deserve to stay alone.

I pass a bin and toss in the flowers. They were for Amber. They were for Amber from Alexander, but I'm not good enough for her. Why did I think I could just waltz in there with a pathetic bunch of flowers – as if twenty-four roses was enough to make it up to her – and she'd instantly smile and kiss me and open her arms to take me back?

I've been such a fool.

A minute later, two, three, four, I don't know, time is passing in some strange *Twilight Zone* world and it could have been two hours for all I know, I reach another bin and throw in the paper.

If only my memories – my selected memories – were so easily discarded.

I'd purge myself if I could. Purge myself of being Alexander.

If this is what it's like being me, being the Alexander in me, then I don't want to be him any longer.

How can I live with what I've done? How could I have let this happen? What if Clare dies? I didn't want anyone to die.

I can't flush the impurities from my memory.

If Alex weren't already dead this would be enough to kill him. Alex could never live with what I've done. How he would respond to my actions is not a secret: it's clear what he'd do. He would break down and confess his sins to the newspapers. He would become a pariah and for ever more be blamed for the Oi Man's crimes, blamed for the attack on Clare Johnson, apple of her mother's eye.

But he is dead. I realised that earlier today and it's still true. Alex is dead.

And what of Alexander?

I'm not Alexander either. I don't know who I am.

I'm some crazy man. A ruthless, selfish, crazy man.

I've gone beyond my initial Alexander-brief. I'm out of control.

What the hell was I thinking?

What about my vows to stand up for the weak? I was only supposed to be a predator to other predators, I was supposed to look out for the prey, I was supposed to protect them. They needed me.

And I let them down.

I wasn't thinking of them. I was thinking only of me.

Alexander as I wanted him to be would never have slept with Amber. He should never have slept with Amber. I should never have slept with Amber. Not if I was going to hurt her like I did.

Sarah, Jed, Kenneth, they all deserved what they got. But not Amber. How could I have hurt her? Sure I felt guilty, I didn't mean to hurt her, but I did it anyway. I did it even though I knew it was wrong. No one made me do it.

And what about Kate? I kept telling myself she was a predator, but why did I think that? Because she looked like she was on a manhunt? Just because she wanted a man doesn't make her a predator. I was wrong: Kate wasn't strong, she was just like anyone else, wanting to find her partner, her true love, The One for her. She might not have gone about it in the way I think she should have, but that doesn't make her a predator.

She didn't harm anyone. She didn't harm me. I shouldn't have dealt with her the way I did. She deserved better.

I treated her like she was my own private whore and I didn't even pay her or take her out to dinner. All I gave her was one lousy bottle of perfume that was another woman's favourite. I didn't bother to find out what scent Kate preferred, what scent she'd have liked to receive.

I just walked out of her flat after shagging her and never saw her or called her again. She wasn't mean to me, she wasn't vicious or cruel. I had no excuse to treat her like dirt. I could have talked to her, I could have taken her out for a meal, I could have at least allowed her to cook for me when she wanted to. I could have found a kinder way to break things off. I didn't have to do it that way. I wasn't thinking of her, I was only thinking of me, of what I wanted.

And Clare?

My revenge was supposed to be against the Oi Man. I can't just decide I hate a particular person and determine to get hold of a bomb and blow up the building where that particular person works merely so I can get rid of him or her. Revenge has to be focused. It has to be earned. It's like a retaliatory strike. How a retaliatory strike should be. Civilian casualties are unacceptable.

I've become one of them. I've turned into what I most despise.

I've become a predator who preys on the prey.

God, help me, I'm one of them. I've preyed on the prey.

The flat is blissfully silent, empty when I arrive. I head straight to my room, needing to see the daisies.

I open the door. And stop.

It's not so empty after all. Amber and Noreen are in my room. Amber and Noreen are in my room, holding my things.

My boxes have all been torn apart and the contents smashed and scattered around the room. My clothes are slashed into dozens of tiny pieces. My records have been broken in half. My comics – I catch a glimpse of them beneath my shredded Savile Row suits – are ripped and crumpled. My Armani jacket looks like it's been hacked apart with a knife.

The bed is heaped with piles of cassettes, the tape spilling out in long ribbons, CDs snapped in two, book covers separated from their text.

Amber flushes and tears gather in her eyes. 'Alex,' she says, in a whisper.

I cannot speak, I just stare at them, stare at Amber.

'Alex,' she says again, and her voice is a little stronger, 'it's not what you think. I—'

'I did it,' says Noreen.

I glance at Noreen. I still can't speak. Do they think I care about material possessions?

My things, my ruined things, are mere trinkets. Knick-knacks. Clutter from someone else's life. Belongings of another man. They don't matter. They were Alex's things. Not mine. Alexander only had some clothing, but I don't care. None of it feels like mine. None of it feels like me. If I have the urge I can go on a shopping spree tomorrow and buy whatever I want. The comics, the old clothes, the books and CDs, I inherited it all from Alex. And now it's gone. Soon there'll be nothing left of him at all. Nothing left but for a few memories in my mother's head.

Aren't I glad I'm me? Aren't I pleased I'm such a winner? I have more money now than I ever dreamt I'd have. I must be ecstatic. Is that what these feelings are?

'Amber wasn't even here, she went to her sister's, she didn't know what I was doing. She was so sad, she was crying so hard when she left that I just had to do something. I'm sorry,' says Noreen.

I realise she's been speaking, explaining why she did what she did, but I don't care. It doesn't matter. Nothing matters.

'It's okay,' I say.

Noreen looks guilty. 'But—'

'I just want to be alone.'

Noreen nods. 'I'm sorry,' she says.

She walks to the door, turns and waits for Amber, but Amber shakes her head and motions for Noreen to go.

Noreen does.

At last I'm alone with Amber. I've wanted to be alone with Amber for hours, but not like this. Never like this.

'I'm really sorry, Alex,' she says. 'We were trying to clean it up before you came home.'

Doesn't she know that I'm not Alex? Can't she tell the difference?

'I'll replace everything,' says Amber. 'We can do an inventory and work it out and I'll buy you new things. I'll replace it all.'

That's really sweet, but I could never take her money. It'd take her years to pay me back. She could never afford it.

She stares at me and I stare at her. I love the sound of her voice, I love the sight of her cute face. I don't care what's happened here. It means nothing to me.

At last she speaks. 'Please say something. Say you forgive me, that you'll forgive me.'

'There's nothing to forgive. You did nothing wrong.'

Amber blinks away tears. 'I'm sorry, I'll leave now.'

She passes near to me, unable to avoid me as I stand by the door and as she passes she places her hand on my arm and says, 'I'm so sorry.'

I catch her hand. I hold her hand and I stare down at her slender, artistic fingers for a moment before I meet her eyes. 'No, I'm the one who's sorry. I never meant to hurt you.'

'I know.' She smiles at me through her tears. 'Oh, don't mind me,' she says. 'I cry about everything.'

My eyes drift to the daisies, I need to see the daisies, I need to count the daisies.

'I'll leave now,' says Amber. And then she's gone.

I close the door behind her.

I'm alone in my room.

I stand there for a moment, head pounding, clammy and hot all at once, and then I go to my bed, sweeping the ruins of my life on to the floor, not caring if I'm doing more damage, knowing there's nothing left to save.

I lie on my back and count the daisies.

I AM NOT WORTHY

Can I forgive those who've wronged me? Even those I've yet to repay in full? Those who may wound me in the future?

I don't see myself as a forgiving man. I don't believe in forgiveness. Not for them. And not for me.

Certainly not for me.

I stay in bed and stare at the daisies. I toss and turn, I twist from side to side, I kick off the duvet, I pull it up again, I shiver, I sweat, my head hurts, my body aches, I see spots of light, my forward vision is obscured by the start of a migraine and I have to turn my head to the side so I can see the daisies out of the corners of my eyes, I blink and I blink and hours pass and finally the lights are gone and I can see normally. I lie on my back, I lie on my right side, my left side, but never on my stomach, for that would mean I couldn't see the daisies and I have to see the daisies.

I spend the next two days in bed, thinking, trying not to think, lying there, staring at my sky of daisies.

I don't eat, I don't bathe, I don't shave, I don't go to work, I don't unlock the office so the temp can get in, I don't go and retrieve my car, I don't leave my bed. I lie there. I'm hot and sticky, I'm dripping with sweat, I'm weak but I feel no hunger.

Once or twice I hear voices outside my door, they may be calling to me, they may be talking about me, but I don't know and I don't care. I'm in my own world now.

If I stay here long enough will my muscles atrophy? Will I slowly fade away and die, sinking down into the mattress, my dead cells sloughing off and merging with the bed so that a part of me will be here, staring up at the daisies for years to come?

It'd be a nice way to spend eternity.

Nice. I don't deserve nice.

Friday night, I think it's Friday night from the number of times the sun has come and gone, but I couldn't say for sure, I wouldn't bet money on it, there's a gentle rap on my door and then it opens.

'Alex?' says a soft voice.

It's Amber.

I turn my head. I can look away from the daisies for a moment, I know they're there, I know they're close, I know they're waiting. I'll have to remember to tell someone I want daisies planted on my grave. Or my ashes to be strewn in a field of daisies.

Amber enters my room, carrying a tray with a bowl of soup on it.

Should I tell Amber about the daisies?

I can see her shock at the continued mess of my room, at the state of me.

'I was worried about you,' she says.

I cannot speak. I don't know what to say.

'I've brought you some chicken soup,' she says, smiling, indicating the tray. 'I thought you might be hungry. Noreen said you didn't leave your room all day.'

I stare at her. She is like a Disney heroine. So lovely, so perfect. Like Sleeping Beauty. Do woodland creatures flock to her side when she sings?

Amber hesitates, I can tell she's unnerved by my silence, but I can do nothing to help her. I don't have it in me to speak. I don't want to speak. What would I say?

She isn't turned away by my lack of words, she walks forward, then she sits on the edge of the bed. 'Come on, Alex, please eat something. Eat something for me.'

For Amber? Amber wants me to do something for her?

I blink. Amber doesn't hate me? Does Amber care?

Amber looks at me, her eyes full of concern and then she

touches my forehead, smoothing my brow. 'You're burning up. You have to eat something, you need your strength.' She fiddles with the soup, scooping up a mouthful with the spoon. She holds it in front of me like I'm a child. 'Eat,' she says.

And I do. I open my mouth and swallow. I let Amber feed me the entire bowl of soup.

When she's done, when I've finished, she sets the tray and the empty bowl on the floor and then she takes my hand and looks deep into my eyes. 'Talk to me,' she says. 'Talk to me. I want to help.'

Amber.

I open my mouth, try to speak, but no words emerge.

'Please,' says Amber, 'talk to me.'

And then it all comes gushing out. It's like a dam has been blown in my mind and I cannot stop the torrent of words. I tell her about my last week as Alex, I tell her the story in all its Technicolor horror and gory details, I tell her about walking in on Sarah and Jed, about Jed sabotaging my career, I tell her about the night in the cinema, I tell her about my point of breaking and punching that man on the nose, about the next moment of perfect clarity. And then I'm ashamed. I start to tell her about my revenge. I tell her about my revenge against Jed and Kenneth. I don't want to tell her about Sarah and Kate, I don't want to see a look of revulsion in her eyes, I don't want her to hate me, but I have to tell her, I have to tell her everything. And as I utter the ugly words I can see her withdraw, I can see her recoil away from me, but I clutch her hands and don't let go. I have to tell her, she has to hear, she has to know everything.

I tell her about me, about Alexander, I tell her how I was determined to reach the top and be a success, about how I thought I needed a woman like Camilla, about how I was going to marry Camilla when I don't even like her, when in actuality I can't stand the woman.

And then I tell Amber about how wrong I was to sleep with

her, about how much I liked her, about how much I like her still, about how it was never my intention to hurt her, about how I was coming home to apologise. I tell her about the roses. And then, finally, I tell her about the Oi Man. She was there the night the glass was thrown in my face, but she doesn't know what I did, what I've done. I tell her the truth. I tell her about the photos. I tell her about Clare Johnson. I tell her that Clare is in a coma, that Clare might die because of me.

It all spills out. I try to explain how I was fed up with horrible people, how I became a horrible person myself. I tell her about the predators and the prey, I try to explain and I can see that she's listening. She's nodding and she's listening to me. She hasn't pulled away, she hasn't stormed from my room in disgust even after what she's heard, she's holding my hands and listening.

I talk and talk and talk and then I'm crying and she's crying and she's holding me in her arms and I'm sobbing against her chest like I'm a little boy and I've found the only safe place in the world.

Eventually she falls asleep and I wrap my arms around her. It's innocent, we could be children, we're both fully clothed, there are no inappropriate touches, I merely give her one chaste kiss on the lips before I close my eyes and join her in the Land of Nod.

I wake to the sensation of Amber in my arms and I realise that I'm no longer hot and sweaty and that my fever, if fever it was, body fever, mind fever, whatever it was, has broken. I'm weak, I need food, I have a horrible taste in my mouth and I'm in desperate need of a shower, but Amber's still asleep and I don't want to wake her. I want this moment to last for ever. I want to stay here, right now, holding Amber in my arms for the rest of my life. I press my nose into her hair and I inhale. I breathe in the fresh, clean smell of her.

Amber opens her eyes.

I smile at her, a soft, gentle smile filled with tenderness. She starts to smile back, but then her expression freezes, her smile slips and she frowns and pulls away. I want to do nothing more than to hold tight, to cling to her, not let her go, but I open my arms and let her roll away from me and stand, leaving my bed. Leaving me.

'How are you feeling?' she asks. Briskly, as if she'd rather not remember last night's tears, last night's confessions.

'Better,' I say, sitting up. I study her face, but her expression is not the friendly Amber face I know: she's stern, hard, even, and that's not a word I ever thought I'd use to describe her. 'Thank you. For everything.' I needed to tell someone, I needed someone to understand, or if not to understand then to know. I needed her. I don't think my mind could have coped with all the knowledge on it's own, I needed to share. Amber saved me. She's my salvation. But I don't tell her that. I don't think that's something she wants to hear.

'Yes, well, I didn't like to think of you in here all on your own.' Amber studies the daisies on the ceiling, her eyes scan my ruined belongings still scattered across the room. She looks anywhere but at me.

'That's what friends are for,' I say, half joking, half serious, knowing that there's nothing more in the world I want at this moment than Amber. How could I have been so blind? How could I have been such a fool?

'Friends?' Amber's eyes swivel to mine and we stare at one another. 'I don't know if we can be friends. I don't know if I want to be your friend. I can't just forget what you did to me, what you've done to others. You're not the man I thought you were.'

'I know. But I'm sorry. You can't even begin to imagine how sorry I am. Can't we start over? Give it another try? It'll be different this time, I swear it.' And I mean it, I really do. I'll never be cruel to Amber again. I'll never take her for granted. I want her to be with me. We'd be wonderful together – we *were* wonderful together: I was just too blind to see it before.

'I don't know,' says Amber. 'I look at you and all I can think of is what you've done. And it's not even all the other women, though that alone makes me feel sick to my stomach, it's everything. Even if I could forgive you I don't want to be with you. I want to be treasured for who I am. I don't want someone who's embarrassed by me, who's ashamed of my background or my dress sense, who thinks he's settling for me when he knows in his soul he could have done better. I want to be my man's dream woman. However corny that sounds, that's what I want.'

She makes me sound so petty, she makes it all sound so simple. I think I should say something, that I should protest, but she's in full flow and I don't have the heart to stop her. I want her to speak the truth of what she's feeling, I want her to get it out of her system so the hurt and sorrow don't fester inside of her and grow worse over time. I let her words sink into me, knowing I deserve them, wishing I hadn't done anything to be ashamed of, wishing that I didn't feel like the world's vilest scum with her looking at me like that.

'I don't want to be the woman you'll hate in a year or two when you read about Camilla's father and his latest business venture and think that you could have been involved if only it weren't for me, if only you'd stayed with Camilla,' says Amber. 'I want someone who wants me for myself. I deserve that.'

'I do want you for yourself,' I say. I do want her. I know I want her.

Amber's lips are trembling and I wonder if she's about to cry. Please don't cry, Amber.

'For how long?' she asks. 'What makes you think you won't change your mind again?'

'I won't. I know what I want now. And it's you. Please give me another chance.'

'I don't know, Alex.'

'Please. I'll make it up to you. Oh, Amber, I'm so sorry.'

'I know you're sorry,' she says. 'I know you didn't mean to hurt me. Not really. I know you didn't mean to hurt Kate or that poor woman in hospital, but you did. You hurt us. You, no one else. You.'

'Don't you think I know that? Don't you think I'd take everything back if I could? I've made mistakes. I know that. I've made terrible mistakes, but I've learned my lesson. I've changed.'

'Have you? What about Clare Johnson? She's in a coma because of some stupid bar fight when you just happened to be in the wrong place at the wrong time. It didn't even involve you. You getting that glass in your face was an accident. An accident.'

Is that how it seems to Amber? Does she see me as some kind of insane seeker of retribution? It wasn't like that, I want to shout. It wasn't. At the time I felt the world was conspiring against me. I didn't want a bastard like the Oi Man to have such an easy ride in life. He deserved to suffer as I was suffering. He's an animal. But, then, so am I. I, in all my pride and glory, am no better than the Oi Man. I can't even plead ignorance, for I thought it through. I knew Mrs Oi Man, Clare, would suffer when the photos came to light. I just didn't care. I made some sorry excuse to myself about her having good grounds for divorce and I didn't let the tattered shreds of my conscience bother me again.

But I'm not like that now. I'm not. I'll change. I have changed. It's different now. I'm different. I've learnt my lesson.

But then I think of Clare. I think of her in her hospital bed surrounded by tubes and wires, hooked up to countless machines, keeping track of heart-rate, blood pressure and temperature.

How could I have been trying to woo Amber? How could I think everything would just go back to the way it was? I have to face this, I have to face reality, I have to face what I've done. 'She might die,' I whisper. 'She might be dead.'

Amber, her face full of sympathy, sits beside me on the bed. She takes my hand and squeezes.

Does this mean she still cares for me? Does she not hate me, then? Does she know she's giving me hope when I don't deserve it? That she's letting me know there's still a chance for me?

I turn to her, my eyes wet. 'I didn't mean it. I didn't mean it.'

Even to my ears I know I sound like a child who's broken his sister's favourite toy, that the words I'm using cannot even begin to describe the guilt I feel. The guilt I deserve to feel.

'I know you didn't.' She touches my cheek briefly, so briefly I might have imagined it were it not for the warm imprint left behind on my face. Amber stands then and clears her throat. 'Well, I'll leave you to it.'

'Don't go.' The words are out before I can stop them. 'Please. Stay for a few minutes. I'm going to phone the hospital and find out how she is. I want you here. I need you. If Clare's dead then I'm a murderer and I don't think I can face that alone.'

'I'll stay, but just for that.'

Before Amber can change her mind, I dig out my mobile, dial Directory Enquiries, then phone the hospital. I claim to be a nephew and ask about Clare's condition.

Clare regained consciousness last night. She's no longer in a critical condition. She's going to recover.

She's alive. Clare is alive. I didn't kill her.

I didn't kill her.

IS TO KNOW ONE'S SELF TO
LOVE ONE'S SELF? THAT IS THE QUESTION

My body feels like it's run a marathon, I'm stiff, I ache, I feel like a feeble old man who hasn't risen from his sickbed in two decades. Amber leaves – I let her use the bathroom first while I sort through my room, searching for some undamaged clothes.

It's funny because I don't feel on top of the world and I don't feel suicidal, I'm in a kind of limbo where I'm trying not to think. I just want to shower, shave, get dressed and go outside. I won't look to the future, I won't think beyond lunch.

At last I find a pair of jeans that Noreen missed. They're Alex jeans, but I don't care. And as I hunt for a shirt I realise that I'm not putting Noreen on my list: I require no vengeance against Noreen. She's like a cornered animal that reacts to oppressors. I can't blame her and I know she feels bad. She was only trying to lash out against the man who hurt her friend.

And she's not a predator, she's just a follower. As much as she might fight against it, as much as she might protest and demonstrate and join in the anti-capitalist riots, she's still soft and gentle on the inside. She's prey. I could make mincemeat of her, but I won't.

(She was only looking out for Amber. I certainly can't fault her for that.)

Showered, shaven, clean and properly fed for the first time in days, I leave the flat, and walk and walk. I head south, walking into central London, walking, walking, walking down to the Embankment, walking to Hungerford Bridge.

I stand on the bridge and let the tourists, the locals, everyone walk past me as I stare down into the water. If I'd had the energy to get out of bed yesterday, would I have hurled myself from the bridge? Would I have wanted to kill myself? I'll never know.

I'll never know if I would have had the courage, the cowardice to kill myself. And if I had succeeded it would have proved that I was Alexander through and through and maybe I wouldn't have deserved to live. For suicide would have been my most selfish action. It would have been cruel: it would have shattered my family, left my mother trembling and crying and wondering why, why, why for the rest of her life.

I'm glad I had my sky of daisies. I'm glad they kept me safe and warm so I didn't want to leave, so I couldn't leave, for I don't know what I would have done if I'd had a quick option like throwing myself from a bridge. Willing yourself to die takes a lot longer and Amber saved me from that. She halted my decline and brought me back to life.

And as I stand there staring down into the water, staring down the river, it's suddenly clear to me.

There's nothing in a name. A name can't change who I am. A name can't change who I've become. A name can't change who I am.

Call me Alexander, call me Alex, call me Ishmael. Call me the man formerly known as Alexander.

There's nothing in a name. I can only be me.

I am not Alex. I am not Alexander. I am not one or the other. I am both. I'm not the good Alexander, I'm not the bad Alexander, I'm all of the above. I am me: it doesn't matter what I call myself.

I am me.

And I'm a success. Platypus-fox, the advertising ideas, the skill in attracting clients, that was all me. It hasn't suddenly ended. I did that. It was me.

I may not be nice, but I can choose to act nice. I'm going back to my moment of catharsis on the night of the cinema fight, when I stopped being a spineless wimp, a doormat, and stood up for everyone in that theatre. That's who I want to be, that's who I am.

And I'm going to be a success, no, I am a success, I want to be king of the mountain, I want to stay on top of the world, I will stay on top of the world, but I'm not going to be just like everyone else. I refuse to be a cold-blooded predator.

I refuse.

I am me. I will be a predator to the predators, but I'll be good to the prey. I'll be their friend, they can rely on me, I'll stand up for them. I'll never take advantage of their kind again.

And if in the future I start to stray once more I'll only have to think of Amber, of what I did to her, of how much I hurt her. The thought of her will keep me in line. I want her to be proud of me. I want her to love me. I want to make it up to her. I will find a way to make it up to her.

I will be what I intended to be. I am strong and powerful but I am in control and I will never be lost to the truth again.

I am Alexander to the predators and Alex to the prey. That is who I am.

Before I can go back to my life, the life I want to have, the life I already have, the life I will have, I have to try and make reparations to Clare Johnson. I'm willing to put on a hair-shirt, smear myself with ashes and do penance, but I don't know if that will do much good. I'd like to make it up to her, but I don't know how I can even begin to do that.

I decide to retrieve my car while I'm working out what to do, how to start. I'm expecting the worst. It has been almost three days and my Jag is a pretty distinctive car (so beautiful, so clean, so smooth, so sexy) and I just left it parked on the street near the florist's.

It might not even be there.

But as the cab I hailed near Charing Cross pulls up and drops me off in front of the newsagent's – the newsagent's where my life fell apart sixty-seven hours ago – I see my car.

It's in one piece. There are no scratches, no dents, no broken windows, no slashed tyres, the stereo panel I neglected to remove remains in place, there is no ticket even though it's in a one-hour zone, has been in a one-hour zone all this time, the wheels aren't clamped. Nothing has happened. It's perfect.

And I know then that if there is a God, if there is a divine figure sitting in judgement, looking out for the world, that this is a sign that I've been forgiven, that I will be forgiven, that I get another chance. I'm being given the opportunity to correct my mistakes.

For God, for He or She or Whoever, knows how much I love

my car. If I was going to be punished it would have been easy to hurt me. And I wouldn't have complained, I would have thought I deserved it.

But there's no mark, no scratch, no ding, no dent, not even a splash of mud. It's clean and shining and it's waiting for me.

The weight on my shoulders lessens and I climb into the car. I'm sitting behind the wheel, my hands are sliding around it and I take a deep breath.

The luck of Alexander has held. My luck. I'm a lucky man. And everything is going to work out the way I want it to because I will make it happen.

I will find a way to make it up to Clare. I will find a way if it takes me the rest of my life. I'll be her silent and secret guardian angel for the next four decades, if that's what is required. I'll pay for her physical therapy, I'll be an anonymous donor giving her money to start a new life in Australia if that's what she wants. I'll do whatever it takes to try to cancel out the harm I caused her, the wrong I did her. I'll help her start again, though she'll never know who I am.

And once I've started on my path to redemption I will court Amber, slowly and hesitantly, so carefully that she won't know what's happening until it's too late and she's forgiven me and is willing to start again at the beginning.

I glance up at the sky, for once so clear and blue and I can't see a single cloud, then I start the car and watch the people pass as I wait for an opening in the traffic. I wonder who is prey and who are the predators. I, of all people, know that appearances can be deceptive but actions speak for themselves.

I smile a little half-smile, not joyful, not happy, but ready to face the world once more. I have to be ready. I am, after all, an Action Hero. Oh, yes, I'm back in business.

I'm back and I'm here to stay this time.